Immortal Longing

Jax Garren

Copyright

IMMORTAL LONGING

Originally released as Stripped with the Vampire, First edition. March 11, 2015.

Copyright © 2015 Jennifer Hinson.

ISBN: 978-0-9911641-6-5

Written by Jax Garren.

Editor: Rhonda Merwarth and Heather Long

Copy Editor: Abby Webber

Cover by Daqri Bernardo (Covers by Combs)

To Scott:
I could not have done this without you.

To Chris:
You are missed.

Also to Dakota K.:
I promised I'd write an M/M. Here you go.

Vampire Lineage

Queen Modron - muh-DRONE
- Silures (modern Wales); turned in 32CE at age 16

The queen's fledglings are numbered by their turning order. For example, Modron turned three vampires between Winnie (2) and Cash (6), but since they aren't mentioned in the book, they're not on the list.

I) **Alaric (1)** - ALL-uh-rick
- Visigoth (modern Spain); 445CE at age 29
- Unknown number of fledglings
- four generations later...

A) **Joseph Crackin** – JOE-seff CRACK-in
- Mexico (modern-day Texas), 1834CE at age 37
- fledglings include...

1. **Emmaline** Granger - EM-uh-line GRAIN-jer
   - Republic of Texas, 1837CE at age 22
   - 1 fledgling:

   a. **Javier Reyes** – HAH-vee-air RAY-ez
      - Austin, Texas, about a week ago, at age 28

II) **Galswinth "Winnie" (2)** - GAL-swinth
- Visigoth (Spain); 447CE at age 18
- married to Nikolai Vyhovsky
- fledglings include...

A) **Nikolai "Kolyan" Vyhovsky** – NICK-oh-lie COAL-yun vee-HOV-skee
- Cossack (Ukraine); 1659CE at age 30
- Nikolai is claimed as a fledgling of Modron, though he was turned by Winnie... against Modron's wishes. That's a story for another day, though.

III) **Cassius "Cash" Geirson (6)** - CASH-us GARE-sun
  ♦ Norseman (Norway); 863CE at age 26 (uncertain)
  ♦ no fledglings
IV) **Demetrios Tzykandyles (11)** (not seen in the book)
  ♦ Greece, 1347CE at age 39
  ♦ fledglings include…
  A) **Ramón Triquell** – rah-MOAN TREE-kill
    ♦Republic of Florence (Italy), 1490CE at age 32
    ♦Not a member of CoVIn
    ♦fledglings include…
    1. **Charles Travert** – CHAR-lee TRA-vert or
       shar-luh tra-vair
       ♦ France, 1732CE at age 35
       ♦ no fledglings

Chapter 1

"Tooth and Nail looks as ominous as it sounds." Vince Pagano tried to keep his voice light as he eyed the deep purple door of the Victorian house turned goth club. Private parties were always a better haul than dancing at LongHorns with the other guys. But the ramshackle steps leading up to a porch full of ostentatious gingerbread and the sultry bass grinding through the night from inside the club gave him a prickly feeling on the back of his neck.

Rhiannon, his best friend, came around his Miata to take the driver's seat. She was supposed to go back to the club to run the technical side of tonight's show and was going to be late if she didn't get moving. Instead of getting in the car, though, she leaned against the door next to him and contemplated the place. "You don't have to go in."

"They already paid."

"Yeah, but if you don't feel safe, Kurt won't bitch about refunding them. You've done that, what, twice in six years? He trusts your judgment." She pulled the rubber band from her hair, letting her freshly dyed apple-green hair fall around her shoulders before gathering it up again in a tighter ponytail. "I'll be honest. Since Javi organized the gig, I didn't even check into it. I just assumed..."

Vince snorted at the mention of her straitlaced older brother. "That it would be completely lame?"

Rhi's hazel-brown eyes angled to him, then back to Tooth and Nail as half her mouth curled up. "I was going to say 'safe.'

But… yeah, that too."

The June night was warm, and a breeze blew the scents of cigarettes and fresh-cut grass. East Austin was a haphazard mix of genteel decay, Mexican culture, artists' studios, hip nightlife, and DINK invaders sprucing it up. The energy was creative, intense, and a little dangerous. His kind of vibe. Vince shrugged his shoulders to loosen them. Tooth and Nail was just another club, and Javier was in it. It was perfectly safe. Vince leaned away from the car. "Who's the party for, again? Ceci?"

"Tzitzi. Like the 'tsie' in Tootsie said twice." Rhi leaned forward, too. "I'm going in with you. Brother dear doesn't call in two days, despite my nine million messages about Mom's newest debacle, and then he finally does to ask for a stripper? I have words."

"Your mom has a new debacle? Shock!" Rhiannon and Javier's mom required saving from her own crap decisions often enough Vince couldn't blame Javi for avoiding her latest mess— but it was out of character.

Rhi punched him on the shoulder.

Vince rubbed his arm, feigning pain as they headed past the wrought iron gate and down the cracked sidewalk, then got distracted by the fencing. It was old—real smithing, not factory pressed—and appeared in good repair. If somebody was interested enough in quality metalwork to keep it in this good of condition, maybe he could pitch them a job.

In his dream world, where he made a living from metal craft, they'd take him up on it. But this was reality, where people would rather pay a couple hundred dollars to see him mostly naked for half an hour than a hundred dollars for a piece that took weeks to create. He puffed his cheeks out, blew a hard breath, and caught up with Rhi.

She stopped at the top of the porch steps and completely

switched subjects. "Tzitzimime are demons in Aztec mythology."

Vince chuckled and patted her on the head. "Pagan Nerd Girl strikes again. One day we'll find something about ancient culture that you don't know."

She didn't drop the concern. "They're ragingly freaky. They wear necklaces decorated with human hearts and shell skirts that rattle right before they kill you. They're always pictured with blood from their victims pouring down the front of their mouths and bloodying their clothes. At the end of the world they'll come down from the night sky and kill everybody. One reason Aztecs did so many human sacrifices was to stop them."

"Uh-huh." Rhi knew more mythology than anyone he'd ever met. Usually he found it interesting. Less so tonight, when it was about human-heart necklaces and he was already on edge.

On the other side of the door the music changed to a more pounding beat. A couple smoking cigarettes gave them a hard look and straightened up, threateningly.

Vince peeled an inch of Velcro off the side of his pants. "It's a costume." He smiled, smoothing things over as he stuck the waistband back together. "She asked for a conquistador. I told her the closest I could do was a cop."

One of the men snorted a laugh, and they both went back to smoking.

Rhiannon bit her lip. "She asked for a conquistador? See, this is what I'm saying."

Vince leaned against the porch railing and crossed his arms. "You're saying she's an Aztec demon who, instead of ending the world, is hiring strippers?"

Rhiannon leaned in and lowered her voice. "Well, if vampires are real, why not tzitzimime? You think only European mythology is legit?"

Vince deflated inside from an old memory, that unexpected

kick to the gut still too fresh for the five years that had passed.

She groaned. "No, don't think about your ex. This isn't about him. I'm just saying, if he was a real, living myth, then maybe she's a real one too."

He tried not to growl at her. It wasn't Rhi's fault he was still bitter. "One, Charlie had a name. He didn't go by 'Vampie.' Don't you think she'd have an actual name if she was one of these tzitzi-me-muh things? And two, on the odd chance she is, so what? Vampires, according to mythology, are also bloodthirsty monsters. You met Charlie. He was a woodworker, for fuck's sake." A damn fine one, with calloused hands that could coax maple into exquisite forms. Or tempt a body into ecstasy. Vince shoved the memories of that year away, back into the locked box where he kept them. "Besides, if supernatural whatevers were running around all over the place, everyone would know about them. That's what cellphone cameras are for. Have you ever encountered a supernatural creature, other than Charlie?"

She shrugged. "Maybe I have and didn't know it."

The door opened, and Javier stepped out, his smile bright and a little tipsy. "There you are!" He jerked forward toward Rhi, arms open in an oddly possessive motion. "Sister!"

She leaned in for the hug. "You are in so much trouble. Are you sniffing me?"

A petite blonde in bright, rumpled club attire—not at all goth—came out behind Javi and wrapped her arms around his waist, pulling him off Rhi. "Let's get 'em inside, sugar." Her accent was decidedly east Texas—the one the rest of the state thought sounded hick, making an odd counterpoint to Javier's determined urbanity.

Rhi's eyebrows raised. "You're still with *her*?" Then she blushed at the outburst. "Uh, Emma, right? Good to see you again."

"Party's downstairs," Javier announced, his voice full of excitement. He wasn't tipsy; he was hammered. And his date was rubbing her hands on him like they'd be finding a dark corner of that room immediately on entry.

Suddenly everything made sense, and Vince squelched a laugh as he relaxed. Javier had met someone who was helping the tightly wound, mid-fellowship neuropathologist blow off some steam. *About fucking time.* Tzitzi must be a friend of hers. Vince turned to Rhiannon and squeezed her hand. "Go to work before Kurt fucks up the light board trying to turn it on without you. I got it from here. I'll grab a rideshare and be back for the final number, okay?"

Emma's laughter was as loud as her hot pink sequined shirt. "Unless he decides to stay here and party!" She got a firm grip on Vince's shoulder and dragged him forward. "I got me two hot-as-shit men here! It's a good night."

Rhi scowled at her brother, but Vince knew her well enough to see her train of thought. Chewing Javi out in front of his date when he was drunk would do as much good as chewing out a puppy. Besides, Mr. Goody-Two-Shoes deserved a break. She rolled her eyes and turned to Vince. The fear was gone, replaced by irritation. "Sounds good." She squeezed his hand back. "You have your wristband on and your emergency supplies?"

He shook his wrist, showing off the medical bracelet he'd made for himself, and tamped down his irritation. He'd been diabetic since he was eleven, but Rhi couldn't help mothering. "Mints are in my pocket and my injector pen's in my boot, not that I'm going to need either. Go to work, little mama."

Rhi genially flipped him off and headed back to the car as Emma and her fierce grip pulled him into the club.

Despite Tooth and Nail's old-fashioned exterior, the inside was sleek modern. Interior walls and most of the upstairs floor had been removed, making a large, two-story space painted light gray and maintained somewhere between clean and immaculate. The main room was fitted out in the decadence of a Hollywood movie set with chain benches and walls decorated with modern reinterpretations of old weapons, like maces and spiked chains.

Maybe he *would* approach them about a commission. Weaponsmithing was fun.

The AC was on full blast, but the packed club smelled of leather and sweat from the patrons wearing catsuits with dog collars, velvet dresses, and silk cloaks, all way too warm for Texas in June. The energy was high, people having good fun playing bad. Vince chuckled. How many of them were CEOs and schoolteachers catching a break? He smiled at the thought.

Javier and Emma kept going, guiding him past the central bar with one hand on each of his arms, like sentries. "So y'all met the other day?"

"Yep," Emma said lightly. "Javi's my boy."

"Your boy?" Vince couldn't help asking. Javi was a stick in the mud, but Rhi and her brother had bounced from foster home to foster home, back to their bio-mom, then back into the system for another round whenever their mom inevitably collapsed into methamphetamines again. He wasn't a boy; he was a damn impressive man.

A damn impressive man who was studying Vince with a covetous fascination that looked a helluva lot like sexual interest. How drunk was he? Rhi would kill both of them if Vince helped Javi experiment. Not that Rhi cared about gender when it came to love, but she would care if Vince, the commitment averse, had a one-nighter with her brother, the good-boyfriend material.

Besides, hot as Javi might be on the outside, his cold drive, impressive at it was, turned Vince off. He didn't have any art to him. Not like Charlie, the most brilliant artisan Vince had ever met.

Dammit, he was thinking about his ex again.

Vince pulled his arm away. To his surprise, Javi resisted.

Emma cleared her throat. "Why don't you run on down and tell Tzitzi who's here?"

Javi let him go and jogged away.

"Slowly," Emma admonished, and sure enough Javier slowed down to a quick walk.

Vince slowed down his own pace, weirded out by the way she ordered him around. "What's going on with you two?"

Emma turned a brilliant smile on him. It didn't reach her chilly blue eyes. "Whatcha mean?"

"You and Javi..."

They reached a curving staircase going downward, and some of Vince's earlier hesitation came forward. To his right, the wall of weapons had given way to a twisted mural—if you could call it that—which made the wall appear to fester and bleed. Disgusting. And still Emma hadn't answered him. He stopped and studied her.

Her thick hair nearly fell to her waist with no layers or any particular cut. It reminded him of a Rossetti painting of an old-fashioned damsel with unbound hair. She was petite and her figure spare in the same way Charlie's had been—lean, with ropey muscle instead of the gym-cut precision Vince had to keep for work. Her skin was as tanned and freckled as Charlie's too, like someone who'd grown up in a time before SPF, with the same tan that faded up the forearms instead of on the biceps, where modern clothes ended.

His stomach turned. Vampires' physical bodies froze at the point they'd died, scars and freckles, haircuts and tan lines, and everything else. Charlie had been thirty-five when he'd turned. She looked like she'd been younger, more like Vince's twenty-four.

It seemed an absurd question, but he had to ask. "Are you a vampire?" What were the odds that Javier would be dating one? Charlie had said they were rare—so rare he'd never introduced Vince to another one.

Emma tilted her head like the question was unexpected, but not like it shocked her. *Holy fuck.* He was right.

Vince's heart rate picked up as he looked around the room, but everyone else, decked out in their child-of-darkness best, seemed like poseurs next to an authenticity that didn't need leather or a spiked collar.

"You ask strange questions," she finally said in that twanging voice of hers. "Ain't they supposed to be all formal and whatnot from Transylvania and fancy places? I grew up in the ass end of nowhere."

He took a deep breath as a weight settled in his stomach. "I knew one who was a carpenter from rural France." Holy hell, he was standing in the presence of another vampire. "Do you know him? Charlie Travert. He lives in Austin." He shouldn't care how Charlie was doing, but they'd been friends before they were lovers. He'd always carry around this curiosity, tinged as it was with anger and regret.

She narrowed her eyes, thinking. "That name sounds familiar."

"He makes gorgeous furniture. Functional works of art." Hope stirred in him, but he didn't know what it was for. He wanted to hear news. Maybe to make contact. See if he'd ever finished that chest of drawers they'd designed together as a showpiece.

No, he didn't want to reconnect. Charlie hadn't responded to any of the nine million attempts to reconcile Vince had made that first year after the breakup.

A breakup that was entirely Vince's fault. He'd fucked up a wee bit by lying about his job for, oh, their entire relationship. Nineteen-year-olds in love did seriously stupid-ass shit.

He'd never gotten a chance to apologize. Charlie had kicked him out with a note and never looked back. Vince's jaw set in an old anger that had mellowed to frustration. A fucking note. The man he still thought of as the love of his life had ripped his heart out with three sentences scrawled on the back of a poster.

"What's taking so long?" Javier was back, his smile eager. "Tzitzi's waiting."

Oh, damn, he was here for a job. The strangest job ever. Vince tried to settle his zinging nerves with a breath and a quick stretch of his arms. He leaned in and asked quietly, "Is Tzitzi a vampire?"

Javier's eyes widened. "He knows about—"

"No," Emma interrupted, ignoring him. "She ain't."

Vince had to ask. "Is she a tzitzimime?"

"A what? I don't even know what that is. She's human. I know that for a fact 'cause I can smell it. I'll ask around about your Charlie and see what I can tell you before you go. Redhead with freckles? Voice like a bass drum?"

"Yeah." That was Charlie. His voice was the most soothing sound, like rumbling thunder at night.

"Shall we?" She pointed to the stairs.

Vince nodded. That would be really cool to know something, anything, about his ex. He caught Javier's gaze as they headed down the stairs. "We have a lot to talk about. My vampire was bossy too." He bumped Emma with his elbow. "Javi's a full-grown man, you know. He may not be however many hundreds of years old you are, but he doesn't need you ordering him around like a kid."

They reached the bottom of the stairs and entered an

underground private room where a birthday party was in full swing. The space felt small because curtained alcoves lined the walls on two sides, cutting into the usable square footage. A well-stocked bar took up the third wall. A door on the final one led to a well-lit hallway he glimpsed as people came in and out of it.

"Javier may be a full-grown man, but he's a baby bat. They can get out of hand without a little guidance." Emma handed Vince a green glass of milky-white liquid. "Pulque—it's made from agave, like tequila. It's Tzitzi's favorite."

Vince looked from the strange drink to Emma. "Bat?" Did she mean Javier was a vampire? Had she made him one? His throat went dry, and he looked at Javier again, trying to tell—but he couldn't, not just by looking. Rhi was going to freak the fuck out.

"Stripper!" a woman yelled as she came rocketing across the room. "Welcome to my party. You are gorgeous." She ruffled his hair with slim fingers, and he managed a distracted smile. "What do you think of pulque?" She raised her own glass to her lips and drank a quarter in one drain.

That's right. He had a job to do. They'd paid for him.

No, fuck it, he needed to call Rhi and tell her about this. "Tzitzi?" he guessed.

She nodded. How old was she? It was hard to tell. Colorful tattoos of Santa Muerte decorated her pale shoulders. Thick bangs skimmed her eyes in front, and thin, brown dreadlocks ran down her back. Piercings in her nostrils and septum and gauges in her ears must've involved more pain than Vince would ever willingly submit to, but she was lovely in her radical self-decoration. He'd guess she was younger than him. Normally he'd be happy to dance for her. But not tonight. He hoped she would be cool about it. "Is Javier a vampire?" he asked point blank.

Her thickly lined eyes widened. "A vampire? Does everyone

know about them now?"

"Just tell me. Please."

"Javier," she said with a perfect Mexican Spanish accent. Javi joined their group. "He wants to know if you're a vampire."

Rhiannon's brother closed his eyes, taking a big whiff of the air. When he opened them, his lips parted.

Vince felt sick.

His friend's skin smoothed, his eyes gleamed like moonlit water, and his teeth elongated, the canines coming to needlelike points and the incisors to smaller, more jagged ones.

Vince had only seen Charlie vamped out like that a couple of times, but he couldn't forget the unearthly aura Charlie had possessed. You couldn't look at him and not know what he was, not feel the otherworldliness in your gut.

And now Rhi's brother was one. She was going to panic. "How... why?"

"How do you know about vampires?" Tzitzi asked. "I wouldn't think a stripper would let anyone scar him."

"Scars? No. Charlie never bit me." Vince had offered, but Charlie said it hurt too much and bottled blood was fine with him to drink. "Look, I'm really sorry, but I need to get back to the club. I will send somebody else." So unprofessional, but this was...

His thoughts drifted off as he looked around. Unlike upstairs, this room was not full of poseurs. Eager faces watched him from alcoves and swayed to the driving music with eyes riveted his way. He was used to all eyes on him, but the eagerness took on a new light. They weren't aroused. They were hungry.

Fear fisted in his stomach. Why the hell had Charlie told him vampires were rare? There were over a dozen in this room. He'd stumbled into a club full of them.

He took a step back toward the staircase. He wasn't sending anyone here. He was getting the hell out and sticking this place on the blacklist.

But what about Javier? Should he get him out too? That earlier interest in his eyes, that hadn't been sex. Javier was interested in his neck.

Shit.

The door deeper into the interior banged open. A man in, of all things, a cowboy getup, complete with a ten-gallon hat, burst into the room. "Death to tyrants!" he screamed for no apparent reason and lunged across the floor at a blurring speed.

Vince yanked Tzitzi behind him to hide the only other human in the room, but the cowboy knocked him out of the way with ease. He grabbed Tzitzi by the neck, hauling her up in a choke hold as Vince backed away in fear, butt sliding across the warm tile. Tzitzi coughed and spit, gasping for air. What was she even doing with a party full of vampires?

The same door opened again, and the hall light backlit a man in a leather ski mask and trench coat. Though thin and average height, he carried himself with the distinguished presence of a king. "My apologies," he announced in a clipped accent Vince couldn't place.

"Stay back!" the cowboy yelled as he turned to face the newcomer, dangling Tzitzi in front of him like a shield. "Can't control me. No one can!"

"That so?" The masked man raised a crossbow and shot with a twang. An arrow threaded a narrow gap between Tzitzi's arm and chest to thump into the cowboy's sternum. With cool efficiency, the masked man reloaded. "I suppose we don't need you, then."

The cowboy grunted. And exploded into dust.

Tzitzi dropped to the ground in a crouch and rubbed her

neck.

Emma stumbled backward, sucking in air like she'd held her breath for too long, as her hand clutched at the railing and her back hit the stairs.

Tzitzi stood slowly, her once friendly gaze growing lustful as she glanced at Emma, then stared at the masked man. "I told you we needed another heart. The spell is failing."

Javier, too, then stumbled backward to crumple at Emma's feet as his chest rose and fell in heaving gasps.

Confused as fuck and pulse racing with adrenaline, Vince crawled toward them on the staircase, trying to avoid notice. Maybe he and Javier could sneak out?

Emma sat up, confusion in her gaze, like she'd hit her head. "Who're you?" she asked Vince like she honestly didn't know.

Javier sat up, too, the same lost fog in his expression. "Vince? Where are we?" he asked, looking around the room.

Tzitzi tapped her thigh with a gold-painted nail and stared at them. "Well. Fuck."

Emma's weary gaze took in the rest of the room and her eyes went wide. "Out," she urged, hauling Javier up with one hand and Vince with another and shoving them both behind her up the stairs.

Vince didn't need urging from her inexplicable change of heart. He lunged toward the light at the top of the curving stairs.

A billy club cracked Emma across the skull, sending her sprawling. The masked man was already behind them, from mid-room to here at an unreal speed.

"Go, go!" she still yelled as she slid downward on her side.

But Javier stopped and shoved at the masked man, trying to get to Emma.

The masked man picked him up over his head like he

weighed nothing and threw him toward the middle of the room.

Javier landed and flipped himself to standing with unnatural grace. A crowd of vampires circled him, blocking his access to the stairs.

Stay or go? How could Vince leave without Javi?

Then again, how could Vince get Javi away from that circle of fucking vampires?

Emma kicked upward at the masked man, aiming for a groin shot. The man dodged, putting his head in Vince's range.

Vince punched with all his strength.

The masked man swayed, righted himself, and smiled with the cunning grin of a predator. "Run," he whispered. "I'll catch you."

Terrified, Vince charged up, still looking behind him to see what was happening. The masked man dodged another blow from Emma and grabbed her head. Three snaps led to a horrifying crack, and Emma lay still, her neck at an unnatural angle.

Vince faced forward and sprinted, horror giving him speed. He'd bring help—somehow—but there was absolutely nothing he could do by himself.

His right ankle was caught in an iron hold, tripping him. He slammed face first onto the stairs.

Twisting onto his back, he kicked out. The masked man was somehow already on the staircase, moving too fast to follow. He ignored the blows and gripped Vince's ankle firmly, dragging him down toward the jeering crowd.

Emma's body blocked the path, and Vince knocked into her soft form, sending her corpse thumping down the stairs with him. Bile rose in his throat at her inert body gliding with the bonelessness of a snake. Nobody alive moved like that.

"Don't hurt him," Tzitzi ordered. "I still want him to dance."

Dance? Was she kidding?

No. She was shit-brained crazy.

His ass hit the ground, and the masked man yanked him to standing. On the other side of the room, Javier was carried out, screaming for Vince and for Emma as he fought to get away.

Legs shaking, Vince jerked from the masked man's grasp. His fear fed his fury with each scream down the dark hallway. "Like hell I'll dance for you."

Tzitzi strode forward, all confidence and no grace. "You're not dancing for me. You're dancing for the gods. You will dance, my army will drink, and you will offer yourself in sacrifice."

Mask shoved him forward, making Vince stumble and then right himself. "I suggest we skip the formalities and go straight to the sacrifice," Mask said. "We can feed ourselves elsewhere."

Tzitzi placed her hand on Vince's chest, right over his thudding heartbeat. Oh, God, they'd mentioned something about needing another heart. As in Aztec human sacrifice? The room closed in on him as fear made him dizzy.

"I feel your heart racing," she said, her voice full of awe. "He has to be willing. Our Lord won't look kindly on an unwilling sacrifice."

"Fine," Mask grumbled. He snapped his fingers, and someone shoved another pulque into Vince's hand.

Vine shoved it back. "I'm never going to be willing." Not that it would do him any good. Dozens of hungry faces surrounded him, their excitement infecting the room with manic power.

"Drink," Mask insisted, sounding far too reasonable. "It's going to be a long night."

Vince licked his lips. "And if I don't?"

Mask shrugged, his voice chillingly calm. "She said she can't cut out your heart until you agree. She didn't say I can't break all your fingers to garner that compliance. I suggest instead that you drink and dance and have a pleasant last night."

Beside them a vampire dragged Emma's body out the same door they'd carried Javier, hauling her by her ankles with her face scraping the floor. It shouldn't matter how they carried the dead. It wasn't like Emma could feel it. Still, the casual disdain was inhuman.

He wasn't going to make it out of here alive. Tears came unbidden to his face as he thought of Rhiannon and his friends.

Of Charlie. What had that vampiric fucker not told him?

Chapter 2

In the night-dark woodshop, Charles Travert dragged his fingers along the newly made edge he'd created on a poplar board. Each fault in the craftsmanship felt like a reprimand. He was off his game tonight. Maybe he should pack it up early and go home before he made a mistake he couldn't fix. Carpentry was an unforgiving craft, taking months of labor and destroying it in an instant's false move—and he'd destroyed his fair share of pieces in three hundred years at the labor he loved.

It was just past one in the morning. Usually he liked this time when he could stretch himself, use his full strength, and create without boundaries instead of limiting himself to something reasonable for a human of his pretended age. But tonight the air breathed wrong, setting him on a tighter edge than the one he'd just constructed.

A psychic had once told him he had a touch of the sight. Not enough to predict anything concrete, just enough to feel the pulse of a situation. Just enough to know when things were about to go to the devil. He said a quick prayer to the Virgin.

It didn't make him feel better.

His gaze settled on a half-finished chest of drawers, the custom metal knobs and brackets lined up across the top like trophies—or gravestones. Five years of shop dust coated it in maple shavings and grime, but even a glance brought aching memories of a mischievous smile, puckish brown eyes, and thick curls that had felt soft wound between his knuckles. Vince had happily kept absurd hours with him, rolling open the door between here and the forge as soon as everyone else cleared out for the night so they could work in the companionable noise of hammer, flame, and saw.

Or not work. The devil looked like an angel when he was naked except for sawdust snowing across his olive skin.

Charlie should break down the chest. An unfinished project was a poor substitute for a man. He focused back on the poplar in his hands.

A crash outside set his skin shivering with goosebumps. Logic said feral cats. His gut said something else. He grabbed a hammer as he headed for the exit.

Something slammed against the sliding door, like a weight had fallen into the old metal. He drew back as the stink of sour vomit and the salted copper smell of blood overcame the wood and oil in the shop. Scratching grated upward, as if nails scrambled for the handle. Two banging knocks. A panicked cry of, "Please, God…"

Another whiff of that sweet, pungent blood and Charlie had a sick feeling he knew who was on the other side.

He wrenched the door open, unease chilling the sweat on his arms. A half-naked bundle of muscle and dark hair fell onto his feet. Hands he'd once known intimately clutched his ankles in supplication. Bloodshot eyes darted from one thing to the next, never lighting on anything for long. "Help me. Please, god, Charlie. I don't know what they are."

Charlie's heart squeezed and stomach revolted at the sight of his ex in pain, and he knelt next to him. Nothing moved in the streetlights outside, but that didn't mean nothing was out there, haunting the night. He jerked Vince inside and bolted the door behind him.

Vince wobbled to sitting, a chain between his hands scraping on the cement floor. Tears tracked down his beautiful face as his unsteady voice barely whispered into the room, "I'm sorry. I'm so sorry to come here. I didn't know where else…"

Using a supernatural speed he rarely employed, Charlie dashed for bolt cutters and back, unwilling to leave Vince for long in this state. "Shh, it's okay. You did right. It's okay." Charlie took Vince's wrist to break the cuffs. The man hissed in pain. His forearms were purple with bruises and gouged where the restraints had cut into him.

He'd been dragged with them. Fury made Charlie's sluggish heart beat fast. What the devil had happened?

The blood from Vince's wrists, arms, and torso tracked in twos. Deuces—the double puncture of canines—showed angry and red just below the crook of his elbow, on his collar, on his stomach…

Merde. Children of the blood plague—soulless vampires, *real* vampires—had gotten to him. Charlie's own dark instincts roared to jealous life, urging him to reclaim his former boyfriend with a bite of his own. But the soul he still possessed saw a loved one pain and just wanted to cradle Vince in his arms until the horrible world became a better place—a safe, kind, beautiful world for kind and beautiful people like Vince.

Through force of will, Charlie kept his voice steady, hiding his dual longings behind clipped words. "Vincent Caesar Pagano, you smell worse than I ever imagined. Hold still." He got the bolt cutters around the cuff, careful to avoid Vince's damaged skin.

"Nice to see you too." Sarcasm. It hurt, but it was healthier for Vince than panic. Charlie would take it. The first manacle fell, and Vince released a sobbing laugh. "Motherfucker."

Charlie wasn't sure if that meant him or the night in general. Didn't matter. A scraping noise outside arrested his attention. With more speed than care, he cut off the second manacle and dropped the bolt cutter to pick up his hammer. It made a better weapon. "You were followed? By a vampire?" Charlie was nearing three hundred, making him older than average, but not a truly old vampire. And a fighter he was not and had never been. Vampires grew stronger with age. This could go poorly.

Vince's breath came out ragged as Charlie turned for the door. "Not vampires, not at the end. I don't know what followed me, but there are two of them. They looked like rats, but huge." His voice turned hollow. "Vampires are crazy. Why aren't you crazy like them?"

Vampires in the plural, and something else with them? *Merde*, that didn't happen. Not with chaos-happy Plague vampires anyway. You needed a soul to play well with others. "I told you normal vampires are psychotic and to stay away from them."

"But you're not."

"I'm not normal." He opened the door. Nothing immediately caught his attention, so he strained his eyes for a sign of whatever danger had followed Vince. A shine to his left—eyes reflected in the streetlamp. Were-rats. They lived near vampires and scavenged the corpses. Apparently these considered Vince close enough.

Not while Charlie was around.

He'd tried to shield Vince from this insanity. Failure clamped hard into him, and he gripped his hammer tighter.

A rat leaped, growing from rodent to human in mid-air. The elongated claws of a beast, though, still reached for him.

Charlie stepped back into the shop and swung his hammer with all the frustrated anger seeing Vince had brought back. His wrist jerked in recoil as he connected with the skull. A squeal, and the rat-man collapsed to the stoop—not that he'd killed it.

Another one leaped. Charlie ducked and flipped the hammer around. The words of his Viking friend rang in his head: *Get the kill. Truly dead things don't attack.*

He wished Cash were here now. The ancient warrior would gleefully behead them, then ask for something else to kill.

At least Charlie knew how to use a hammer. He ignored the new guy and swung underhand at the first rat. His attack came from an odd angle, but the flat still connected with jawbone. The rat-man's head whipped to the side as teeth went flying. He landed in heap outside the doorway, unmoving.

Some disconnected part of Charlie's brain realized that should appall him. His hammer was bloody—bone was crunchy, skin fragile and easily ripped—but whatever used to connect him to that human empathy was missing. He cared about violence before it happened—feared it or loathed it, depending on who it was aimed toward. Afterward? Bodies looked like meat. He wasn't sure if that was the vampire in him or the man who'd seen too much.

"Watch him," Charlie ordered Vince. "Yell if he moves." He pivoted and backed up so he could see both the door and the standing rat. Adrenaline made his fangs drop. The details of the room focused and grew richer as the motion of the world slowed. Wood chips and shop grease popped in pristine clarity, as did the scents of sweat and alley trash from the rats and Vince's soap under the lingering, enraging odor of multiple attackers. Ten individual scents. Vince had faced a mob. How was he alive? Anger made him unsteady. He had to keep it in check. To think.

Three heartbeats pattered aside from his own. The first rat wasn't dead.

The other rat-man shrank back, pupils wide, arms loose and out as he visibly debated fight or flight. In a rat versus vampire contest, the vampire had the edge in speed and the ability to take a lot of damage and keep fighting. On the other hand, Charlie didn't have any silver readily available—the best way to dispatch a were-creature—and getting teeth on something was a lot harder than getting claws into it.

Not that he wanted his mouth anywhere near these vile beasts. But they didn't know that. They could smell a vampire, but they couldn't smell whether or not he had a soul.

"You know *what* I am. Do you know *who* I am?" Charlie intoned, giving his cadence all the color and depth he could. Without his vampiric aura, he didn't look like much—five foot seven and wiry—but he'd been told his voice had the power of a Russian weightlifter on steroids. Fangs out and eyes shining with the monster inside, he knew his voice would make an impression.

The rat shook his head, expression cautious. "I don't know you. Should I?"

No, not really. Charlie lived a pretty unassuming life. But in this case, that worked to his advantage. For all the rat knew, Charlie was a deranged monster capable of anything, not a genial artisan with an unfortunate soft spot—and still-too-frequent hard-on—for the man huddled on the floor. He shot the rat the cruelest smile he had and strode forward with heavy steps. "You come into my workshop. Leave your trash at my feet." He jerked his hand toward Vince. "Attack me on my grounds. Who do you think *you* are?"

Vince hissed in a sharp breath. Charlie wanted to reach out and reassure him, but that would blow the whole act.

The rat sashayed sideways, angling toward the door. "My apologies. We'll take our trash and be gone." Another sidestep, this time toward Vince.

Charlie narrowed his eyes. "Leave the blood doll in payment. Beneath the stink, he smells like a treat." Only Plague would use the slur "blood doll." Charlie managed to say it with casual disdain, hoping the rat would buy his act. *I'm a bad vampire. This will all be simpler if you believe that.*

The rat hesitated, eyes flashing between Vince and Charlie as if calculating odds. Vince had curled in on himself, staring at Charlie like the world had turned sideways.

Trust me. You know me. "I guarantee he won't bother you again." Charlie kept his voice slow and steady, feigning he had control of this situation.

Vince's gaze met his, scared and unsure. It hurt to see him like this—not just the physical damage, but the terror. Vince was the king of swagger, brashly walking anywhere as if he owned the universe. Loving Vince had been cliff diving into the ocean with no clue what waited below. To see him again, regardless of the circumstances, was heartbreaking. The good kind, the kind that meant something.

The lines around Vince's eyes eased. He was going to trust. Charlie felt light from the bit of faith.

The rat-man backed off, heading ass-first for the door. This might be over easier than Charlie had hoped.

Then the rat-man grinned. Charlie focused on him, watching for his next movement.

He jumped, feet leaving the ground with the grace and height of an animal.

Charlie raised his hammer—

But the attack came from below. The impact on his knees sent him sprawling backward. Hot blood spattered across his chest as the injured rat crawled over him. Fear curled in his stomach. Rats won when they got you on your back and swarmed. He had no idea how many were out there waiting to join the hateful surge...

But it didn't attack. It screamed and flattened against him, dead from another impact. Beside Charlie, Vince dropped to the ground, clutching a bloody chisel.

He'd stabbed the damn thing himself.

Righteous anger filled Charlie's blood, making him even

stronger. He shoved the dead rat, sending it flying toward the other, then sprang up. "Take your dead and go." He reached down and grabbed a handful of Vince's soft curls. This had to be convincing. He yanked up, bringing Vince face to face with him. He had to convince the rat that he was evil. "You just bought yourself more time, pretty boy. You might be sorry you did that."

The remaining rat struggled under the awkward weight of his companion.

"Why are you not gone?" Charlie yelled, channeling his anger into his voice. Three charging steps, dragging poor Vince behind, and the rat scrambled out, his dead in tow.

Charlie slammed the door. Shaking from adrenaline, he carried Vince to the floor as gently as he could. "This is going to hurt," he whispered in warning. "Do us a favor and scream."

Feeling every bit the monster he was, he bit down into the soft bend of Vince's elbow, leaving him one more cursed deuce to heal. Vince screamed loud enough to wake the neighborhood. Blood trickled into Charlie's mouth, warm and so comforting— so *Vince*—that Charlie didn't want it. He turned away, letting it drain in wasted rivulets down Vince's arm to mix with blood and whatever else was dried onto his skin.

The scent of fresh blood would reach the remaining rat, and he'd believe Charlie was torturing Vince now, not cradling him in his lap, running fingers through his curls in a gentle circle as Vince cried.

"It's over. I'm sorry," he whispered. He didn't know which of so many things he was apologizing for. The pain of the small bit of blood he'd drawn was nothing compared to the pain of what Vince had just been through.

Most of all, Charlie regretted—as he'd regretted every day— the way he'd ended things five years ago, kicking Vince out with a note. Vince and the time they'd shared deserved better than that, but Charlie had felt so betrayed, so devastated, that he hadn't possessed the strength of character to do anything else.

Vince's arms went around him, tentative and weak. Charlie held him closer, and Vince's hold grew tight and needy.

Shallow scratches ran over Vince's arms and back like a torturous claim. Bruises had formed on his torso and one nasty one across his face. Nothing was life threatening and nothing that wouldn't heal with rest and time. It was awful, but still Charlie breathed in relief. "Are you all right?" Stupid question. Of course he wasn't all right. Vince the ever-chipper was curled into a sobbing ball and clutching Charlie's shirt with desperate fingers.

A stupid question got a stupid answer. Between gulps of air, Vince managed several sounds that each approximated, "Yes."

"Yes. Okay." Charlie held him tighter. The past was still there, a wall between them that wouldn't break down, but for the moment it didn't matter. Vince needed him. He would do his best to make it right for the man in his arms, then let him go to lead his own life again. "You're safe. How's your glucose?"

Vince made a sound that was almost a laugh. "Fine. Insulin's in my boot. Seriously, I know how to take care of myself. Why does everyone think I'm weak?"

Charlie stroked his hair. "I never thought that. Not ever."

"We have to go back. Javier and Emma—she's not dead, they broke her neck and she's not dead..." Vince babbled and then stirred like he had some notion he could get up and go face a pack of crazed monsters in his condition.

"Stop. You're not going back anywhere. You need food and a safe place to sleep."

"But they're still there. They got me out, and Emma said to get cash—like money?"

"No, Cash—Cassius Geirson—is a mutual friend who can help." Charlie picked him up, startling him into submission. "I'll call him. You, though, are not going anywhere but to food, a bath, and a bed."

Vince stilled. "I forgot how strong you are."

Charlie looked away as he carried Vince toward the exit. "I don't show it off. But you're…in bad shape." It was telling that Vince allowed himself to be carried. Charlie had never left the shop this messy, but everyone would have to forgive him. Vince needed care, and he needed it now. "You were smart to get out and get help. Can you reach my phone? Left pocket."

Vince reached his long arm down to Charlie's back pocket. He tried to remain unmoved as Vince's hand dug in and slid out his phone, but he couldn't stop the tingle of awareness that made his skin feel thin. He ignored it. Vince didn't need complications or old attachments rearing up. He needed a friend. They'd been friends long before they were lovers; they could be just friends again. At least for a few nights. "And the lights."

Vince flipped them off, leaving the shop in the dark. His breath hitched lightly as he squirmed, like he feared the dark.

It wrenched Charlie's heart to see his strong man so broken. He smelled the air and took a good look around as they exited. Sensing no one, he headed for his car at a moderately quick pace. "I'm going to get you h—to my place." Home. He didn't think he'd ever quit thinking of his little place as Vince's home too. It had never felt like a home more than when they'd shared it. "Then I need you to tell me what happened so we can fix it."

"We?" Vince asked, voice quiet with surprise.

No, that wasn't what he'd meant. "Me and other vampires. *We'll* fix it. You stay safe."

"We. You and I and other vampires," Vince insisted. "I need to understand what happened to me."

Charlie winced, his heart heavy with worry. But he couldn't stop Vince from jumping into this world now. The best Charlie could do was arm him with all the answers he'd denied him in the past. It was going to be a strange car ride. "Fine. Together."

Vince typed something on the phone, then blew out a familiar, disapproving breath that made Charlie smile. "You haven't changed your passcode."

"You're surprised? Look up Cash Geirson and give him a call."

Chapter 3

Vince huddled in the passenger seat of the bright yellow '55 Thunderbird Charlie had bought new and never stopped driving. The top was down, and the wind sent his hair blowing as wild as his thoughts. It was weird to be in the passenger seat—he liked to drive more than Charlie did—but he alternated between too numb and too shaky to do much of anything besides stew over whether it was possible the man Charlie'd had him call looked as much like a Scandinavian model in real life as he did in the photo on Charlie's phone.

It was pretty much the only thought that distracted him from the need to vomit in terror as he told the guy's voicemail the story of what'd happened, from getting the gig to Emma's neck breaking to dancing with sadistic monsters to Javier and Emma— not dead—somehow getting back into the party and hauling his ass out. He hadn't had a chance to ask how they'd done that.

They'd stayed behind defending his exit. If they were dead, it was for him. Hopefully Mr. Norway would check his damn messages soon.

What the fuck was Vince going to tell Rhi? Did he even try before he knew if Javier was alive?

"Got that, Cash? Call me," Charlie said before hanging up.

"I don't know what one guy's going to do against that," Vince said.

Charlie patted his leg, and the contact felt so good—so necessary—Vince almost started to cry. "Cash is resourceful," was all his ex said.

Vince forced the tears back and stared at Charlie and his solemn mouth and strong jaw. His hand went back to the stick shift as he kept his calm gaze out the window, his shoulders pulled back stiffly and his brilliant mind whirring away. He always managed to stay calm; if people were yelling, if chaos was flying, Charlie was a rock—the rock that had sheltered Vince when he needed it most, keeping him safe from a chaotic family who wouldn't accept him. Vince couldn't think of anything sexier than a man you could rely on. Even after everything that'd gone down, he'd asked for help and Charlie had once again answered.

A shudder of longing ran through him, and he pressed his temple against the leather seat. When Vince had been sixteen and first realized how broad Charlie's shoulders were and how nicely his ass curved under his jeans, Charlie had rebuffed him time and again with gentle words and a bemused smile.

The rejection would not be so kind if he reached out now. He had to think about something else.

"They're going to look for you." Charlie sounded dangerously calm.

Vince shrunk in on himself. "Why?"

"Because they'll want to finish the hunt. Do you still work at that place?"

The derision in his tone regarding LongHorns should've raised Vince's hackles, but he couldn't muster the effort. "Yes, I do. Javi called me in for the gig."

Charlie's calm blew off. "You took a gig for Liberi? Have you lost your ever-lovin' mind?"

"Liberi?" He swallowed, memories from the last few hours rising up, and he tried to shove them back down. Emma—god, he hoped she and Javier weren't dead—had used that word. "Liberi Pestorum Cruenta. What does that mean?"

"Children of the—"

Vince interrupted, "Blood Plague. I went to Catholic school for ten years. I can translate the Latin. What is that?"

Charlie glanced at him, a little of the anger replaced with interest. "I didn't know you spoke Latin."

"Dead languages don't come up much in conversation." Vince pushed up on the seat, trying to sit more and hunch less. He still hurt, but the crunched position made him feel like a victim. He wanted to be strong, even if he felt anything but.

Charlie pretended not to watch him struggle, giving him his dignity, and answered the question. "Liberi—Plague vampires— are real vampires. The kind with no conscience or empathy or soul or whatever it is you want to call the difference between a man and a monster." He tapped the steering wheel. "Our queen says it's *awen*, an old Welsh concept of inspiration. It's the part of your soul that makes art."

"How did you keep your...awen? Who's the queen? Are you saying the difference between a normal person and a crazed sadist is the ability to make art?" Why hadn't he told him any of this before?

"That is her contention, yes. In third-century Wales a nest of Liberi was harassing a tribe. To save themselves, they sacrificed the tribal chieftain's eldest daughter—Modron, a warrior-bard— by transforming her into a vampire with her bardic abilities still intact, meaning she kept her awen. Modron became the protector of their tribe, and any vampire descended from her also keeps his or her awen."

"Whoa." Fascinating. And yet anger shot Vince up straight. That wasn't some gut-wrenching tale. It was an explanation so simple it could be fully elucidated in three sentences. "Are you fucking kidding me? That would've been nice to have known." Before tonight.

Charlie pursed his lips. "I told you not to trust other

vampires if you met any."

"You were always full of wiser-than-thou shit. How was I supposed to know which statements were your opinions and which had science behind them?"

Charlie raised an eyebrow. "You consider third-century shamanism science?"

And just like that, Vince's temper diffused. Charlie could always do that, crack a dry joke in the midst of everything and make him want to smile. Even if the feeling didn't reach his lips. "Whatever. It's a reason. Not some 'I'm nearly three hundred years old; you should listen to me' fatherly crap." His father would tell him he'd brought this on himself with his immorality.

Vince looked down at the shredded mess of his clothes. He needed to get out of them and into a shower. He was disgusting, coated in filth, and his shoulders tightened with shame. He wrapped his arms around his midsection, cold despite the warm night.

More silence, then Charlie's voice softly rumbled, "The memory never goes away, but you learn to live with it."

Vince studied Charlie's stoic profile. Something had happened around the time he'd been turned that haunted him far more than growing fangs. Vince had a guess, based on the few things Charlie had admitted, that his ex knew what it felt like to be dragged out of town by a lynch mob—but not because he was a vampire. Because he was gay. "I can't imagine all the memories you haul around." He shook his head. "I don't know why anyone wants to live forever."

"Most of my memories are good." Charlie put a tentative hand on Vince's knee and squeezed lightly. "Some better than others."

Vince shuddered at the small touch he badly needed. He wanted to beg Charlie to hold him again. That little squeeze was like choking on scraps when he was starving.

Oblivious, Charlie stared at the road as they headed into the old neighborhood. The quiet streets, lined with Craftsman-style homes and families tucked away in their beds, seemed a lifetime away from Vince's apartment downtown. Nobody who knew him now would guess how happy he'd been here. But Vince loved them both—the excitement of crowded bars at midnight and the serenity of a safe neighborhood at two in the afternoon. Why choose one or the other?

"My home is yours now. Do you understand?"

Joy overtook the pain in a wash of stupid-ass hope. Then, like hope was wont to do, it crashed just as quickly into bitterness. "Looking for a new house ward?"

Charlie wouldn't look at him, and that was all he needed to know. One of the few things Charlie had let slip before was that as a human, wherever Vince considered his home was "warded from evil." He wasn't sure what that meant, but it sounded like a good thing about now.

However, it meant Charlie didn't want him; he wanted the protection Vince provided. "You know what, just stop the car. Thanks for the rescue. I'll take it from here."

"As if I'd let you wander the streets like that."

"How long before you kick me out again? A night? Two?"

Charlie sighed, but his voice was small. At least he felt bad about the deception. "I'm not human, I don't ward the house, and I almost died facing two rats. I don't care if wasn't fair to say that. If a party of Liberi get in, we're both dead."

"Whatever." The sad part was, no place had ever felt like home the way Charlie's had. Not the house he'd grown up in— and gotten kicked out of when he'd finally come out to his dad. Not the apartment he'd gotten for himself after they'd broken up. Charlie's house stood in his mind like a haven. Not because of the place itself. It was a fine little building with astonishingly nice cabinetry, courtesy of the owner. But the way Charlie had made him feel wanted, like he had a family who appreciated him, that was a home. "You could still have your precious ward. I was willing to stay and make it work."

Charlie snorted. "Yeah. As long as I was okay with you being a stripper."

"I was trying to contribute to the household, and my previous job wouldn't cut it financially."

"A, I have enough money. You didn't *have* to pay rent. B, you couldn't have found a different line of work, one where you kept your clothes on?"

"A," Vince mimicked, "I already had that job before we were dating. B, it's just skin—not that big a deal. C, you didn't even have a conversation about it, just bolted."

"I didn't want to get in the way of you infuriating your father."

"Ooh, a biting insult. How long did it take you to come up with that one? Five years?" Vince set his jaw. One thing he'd been dying to say finally came out. "It's not like I ever would've cheated on you. I even quit taking gigs for guys while we were together. Just women. And men pay better."

"I don't care if it's women. Other people putting their hands all over you *is* cheating. You knew it was wrong or you wouldn't have lied about it." Charlie pulled into the garage of his small but tidy home, his voice dry and matter-of-fact. Which meant he was pissed and straining to contain it. Good.

"I didn't lie because I thought it was wrong. I was afraid we'd have a fight."

Charlie threw up his hand, putting an obstacle between them. "We clearly aren't right for each other. You need more excitement than I can give you." He turned to him with a disgusted expression. "God, how long after you moved out were you in somebody else's bed, huh? Don't answer that. I don't want to know."

"It's like you don't know me at all." Charlie said it like he expected the answer to be hours. Wrong. Nearly a year. And Vince had cried the first time like a regretful virgin. Not that he'd tell Charlie either of those facts. "Dude, you broke up with me. What I did to get over you has nothing to do with what I would've done with you." He propelled himself out of the car and limped toward the old house—the one that, to his shame, did still look like home.

Pausing at the door between garage and kitchen, he wondered if the inside was still sage green with maple cabinetry containing dishes no one used. Longing and grief filled his chest, dulling the pain of today. He hoped nothing had changed.

It probably hadn't. Charlie needed constancy like Vince craved motion and change. Well, except for one thing. Vince had never wanted anything more than to wake up every day next to Charlie's unchanging face.

He turned back. Charlie hadn't moved from the car, his hands still settled at ten and two on the wheel. Charlie had been thirty-five when he died, but his sandy-red hair and light freckles made him look younger, like a grown-up Huckleberry Finn. Charlie didn't think of himself as good looking, but he absolutely was, in a boy-next-door sort of way. After spending the last six years with dancers—all bodybuilding, romance-novel-cover hunks—the contrast was even more apparent.

Charlie didn't look like a fantasy. He looked like comfort, like constancy. Like home. And right now there was nothing Vince wanted more than comfort, however it came.

He leaned back against the door for support. He could barely stand, but there was something he still needed to say. "I know I'm a small dot in your long life. I can't imagine all the people you've met and things you've done with them. But I've known you since I was nine. That's most of my life. For me, you're not a dot and you never will be. I get that we'll always be unequal that way." He blew out a hard breath. He was getting dizzy. "I was okay with that."

Finally Charlie tipped his head to look at him. "It's not weird to you? The age difference?"

Vince laughed, but he was starting to see spots. "You're two hundred and seventy-nine. Unless you're waiting for another gay immortal who's nearly three centuries old, you're going to be older than everyone you date. When we dated, I was eighteen, had graduated, and had been trying to get you into bed for two years—young, sure, but old enough to make my own decisions. One of these days you're going to realize I grew up."

Charlie's gaze flicked over him with a covetousness that sent his insides trembling. He remembered that look well. Dreamed of it at night even after all this time.

"I know you're an adult." The deep rumble of Charlie's voice made Vince feel weak-kneed and yet a force to be reckoned with. But his next words put an icy knife through that hope. "That doesn't change any of the reasons we broke up."

"We didn't *break up*. You kicked me out and ran away to Las Vegas while I packed. I'm going inside and taking a bath. I don't think I could stay standing through a shower." He reached for the door handle, and the world went black.

Chapter 4

Charlie launched out of the car and caught Vince's head just before it smacked against the concrete. If he'd been human and slower, Vince would have one more bruise—or worse—to add to his collection. Anger gone into worry, he checked for breath and pulse, but everything seemed fine. His ex's body was shutting down for repair, not giving up. In relief, he held Vince against him. "What have you done, babe?"

Charlie pressed his face against Vince's hair, smelling under the night's refuse, the rain-and-musk scents Vince favored. The situation be damned, a rush of endorphins lit his system, making him want to hold the man and take care of him. To keep him.

Carefully as he could, Charlie scooped him up and carried him inside. Vince still felt good, if awkwardly bulky, in Charlie's arms. Vince was bigger, not just taller but more muscled, than he'd been when he left. Charlie swallowed against the lust all those new muscles caused. Cleaned up, Vince would look even better than he had before, and with his cut features and killer grin, he'd already fulfilled "tall, dark, and handsome" before the added workouts and a few years to beautifully roughen his features.

As they went through the kitchen, then living room, Charlie tried not to think about old times. But every corner seemed full of Vince's boisterous laughter and his flirtatious smile. A sad comparison to the broken man and the quiet house.

He crossed to the guest bathroom, the one that had become Vince's when he'd been seventeen and his awful father had kicked him out, and carefully laid Vince on the floor to prepare the bath.

The room hadn't changed. Same white walls and cherrywood floor Charlie had installed in the rest of the house, protected by a handmade, colorful rag rug he'd traded a side table for. A white-painted tub he'd plumbed in the twenties when he'd built the house took up most of the space.

He wanted his home to be comfortable for guests, nothing too ostentatious. Normal. Would Vince like that it was familiar or wonder what was wrong with Charlie that he still had the same powder-blue towels hanging up five years later?

Vince's opinions shouldn't matter. But they did.

"Are you going to wake up?" Charlie needed to feed him something, but there wasn't a thing in the house. Not for humans anyway. But he could at least get a glass of water, which he did while the tub filled. He'd order food. Vince said his blood glucose was all right, but had he had a chance to check? He needed to eat every few hours or risk health problems, and the alcohol his breath indicated he'd consumed wouldn't help.

Fury at what nearly happened made Charlie's movements jerky as he pulled out his phone and ordered takeout from Vince's old favorite, hoping that would still work.

Charlie had known there were a few Liberi in town, but for them to have the wherewithal to hire a stripper? That was...unusual. While a vampire's IQ didn't change at death, Liberi were so id-driven they didn't usually have the patience for dinner plans more complicated than "dress up and hit the streets." Sure, hiring a stripper might seem like Meals on Wheels, but it wasn't a hunt, and they did like to hunt.

Which meant somebody—the woman who'd hired Vince?—might be organizing them, and that was a terrifying thought. Charlie rubbed his forehead. Right when the queen was moving to Austin, too. Terrible timing for the Liberi to evolve.

Or, back to the idea of organizing, was the timing on

purpose?

A groan overtook the sound of the filling tub.

Charlie rushed back in with the glass of water and helped Vince to sit. "Wake up, babe." He winced at the slip, but Vince didn't seem to notice. "I've got water to drink and a bath running." He cleared his throat. "Do you need help getting out of these?" He tapped Vince's boots to clarify he didn't mean out of his pants. Although he might need help with that too. Charlie's cheeks burned, and he looked away.

Vince reached for the glass, but his fingers slipped and he couldn't seem to hold on.

"Here." Charlie lifted the glass to his lips and tipped it until just a trickle came out.

Vince drank greedily, so Charlie poured more until Vince waved the cup away. As Charlie set it on the counter, Vince panted for air, his body shaking from the adrenaline purge. God, he was so frail. Vince had almost died, and the thought terrified and enraged him. But he kept his voice neutral. Jealous anger had gotten the better of him in the car. He needed to stay calm and keep his head on straight. "Better?"

Vince nodded, his own voice careful and polite. Impersonal. "Thank you."

Charlie tried to copy that distance. "Would you like more?"

"No. Thank you. After the way things ended, I didn't expect you to take me home—to *your* home—and draw a bath." He pulled his knees up and rested his head on them. "I wasn't thinking, just saw somewhere I knew and ran for it."

"You can always come to me if you need something. That hasn't changed."

"I can take care of myself." Vince sounded almost irritated as he reached for the laces of his boots. Then he winced. His jaw set in anger as he ground out, "Usually."

Emotion made Charlie's chest feel tight as he knelt to untie Vince's shoes. Vince averted his gaze, his expression looking like he'd rather eat nails than be here. But when Charlie's hand plucked at the first bow, releasing it from its tight double knot, Vince's hard shell cracked, and in a voice soft and gruff with honest emotion, he offered a second, "Thank you."

Charlie's skin heated as he concentrated on the laces, trying not to feel embarrassed. It was a foot, not anything all that interesting, but still he felt the old fascination with this man and all of his beautiful parts, inside and out.

Vince surprised him with a question. "Can you lose and regain your awen? Because I can't explain how *not Javier* Javi was at first. I thought maybe he was drunk, but it was more than that. And then suddenly he was himself again—a vampire, but focused and smart."

"No. You either have it or you don't." Charlie finished the laces and tugged on the first boot, pulling it off as smoothly as he could.

"Any ideas about the masked vampire? He seemed saner than the others, like he thought things through, but he was evil as shit."

"PBC," Charlie muttered.

"Huh?"

"PBC, Plague by choice. Humans have their awens, but that doesn't stop some men from mayhem." He took the boots and stood them up to make a little wall between them as Vince seemed to get enough second wind to remove his own socks. "They're more frightening than Liberi because they have patience and make plans."

"Hell. Have you heard back from Cash? Who is he to you, anyway?"

"Not yet. Cash is… Ramón, my sire, left after he made me."

Bailed before Charlie had woken up undead, confused, and terribly hungry. "I didn't know what had happened to me— *Dracula* hadn't been written yet; I knew of loup-garou, but not vampires—until Cash happened to find me and brought me into CoVIn."

A touch of sympathy entered Vince's face, embarrassing Charlie, as his tone softened a bit. "Coven? Like witches?"

"No. The Confederation of Vampires International—the governing body for Modron's descendants, at least for those who opt-in." An organization he was supposed to have registered Vince with as soon as the human realized vampires were real. But in an attempt to keep Vince from the dangerous crazy that was vampire society, Charlie hadn't.

"You have a government? That's so... organized. Why do you have a government?"

"To have a justice system. To run banks with accounts for immortals, and to create paperwork so we can live among people. To protect us from Liberi. To teach four-hundred-year-olds to use a computer. CoVIn, though only a few thousand strong, is the best organized supernatural society in the world—it's how we stay alive." And the government made literal billions helping other supernaturals adapt to and infiltrate human society.

"Cash is one of the founding members. And a good friend." He couldn't stop himself from adding, "He dragged me to Las Vegas when I was having a rough time a few years back."

Vince's eyes narrowed as he dropped his socks into a heap. "So the Scandinavian model is the one you ran off with?"

That sounded jealous. Charlie hadn't thought it possible to make Vince jealous. "Cash isn't a model." Or gay. "He's a soldier."

Vince shot him a narrow-lidded glare. "Oh. Just a gorgeous, badass guy you've known for a couple centuries and partied in

Vegas with right after you broke up with me. Okay." Jaw set, he casually split the Velcro down one side of his pants, starting at the hip.

As Vince had likely intended, Charlie couldn't help his gaze riveting that way as the black fabric parted, revealing black underwear and olive skin. His heart rate picked up, and he found himself breathing with necessity instead of muscle memory. Excitement did that to vampires, forced hearts to beat and blood to flow, making them more human.

"You know, you've had several years to come to a show. You could've gotten an eyeful." Vince's voice was drier than a Texas summer as he started slowly working on the other side.

Charlie crossed his arms defensively and forced his gaze away. Once again, what was a big deal to him was no deal at all to Vince. He did this every night for a crowd. Anger wasn't helpful, and yet Charlie wanted to choke everyone who'd stuffed a dollar down Vince's unmentionables. "I've seen one of your shows."

Vince stopped, blinking in surprise. "Oh, yeah? When?"

Old disappointment swirled, and Charlie stood, trying to dissipate it with movement. "I had to see for myself if it was true before I made a decision about us."

The pants came off with an angry rip of Velcro, and Charlie tried to look anywhere else. "A decision like flying off to Vegas with Cash and leaving me a Dear John?"

"Watching a room full of people paw you was a good motivator." Centuries could pass, and Charlie would remember that moment with humiliated rage. All those people thinking they had a right. Vince lapping up the attention. Loving it.

Charlie in the back, heart shattering as he realized how little he meant to the man he loved.

Vince started working down his underwear, some little scrap of fabric that barely contained him. Charlie's body stiffened, half with embarrassment, half desire. He crossed the bathroom, turning the water off on the way to the door. The tub was full enough. Vince could take it from here.

"I'm sorry you found out like that. That wasn't right of me. I screwed up."

"Screwed up?" Charlie turned in the threshold to shoot him a glare. "'Sorry, honey, I bought you the wrong size shirt,' is a screw up. You lied to me for a year."

Vince was naked and trying to hoist himself into the tub, his ass in the air as he struggled to get over the lip. "I screwed up big." His voice was rough with straining. "But I was nineteen years old. People do idiot things when they're that age. I thought if you knew about my job you'd react badly." Giving up, he leaned back against the side of the tub, apparently weary from his attempts at maneuvering a foot and a half off the ground. "Boy, was I right."

"I'm helping you in. This is pathetic." Averting his eyes as best he could from all the good parts, Charlie scooped up his ex-lover and dumped him into the tub as efficiently as he could. Thoughts he shouldn't be thinking when Vince had just been tortured swirled through his head and made his body stiff with need.

The warm water hit Vince, and he vocalized something with as much pleasure as pain in the sound. Blood rehydrated, turning the water pink. Vince shuddered, face pinched in misery as tears squeezed from the corners of his eyes. "Fuck." Another struggle, this time to stop himself from crying. "Fuck, fuck."

Charlie froze. Stay and help? Leave and give him space? All of Charlie's anger drained away in the need to soothe Vince's pain.

Vince dunked his head under the water and came back up, running his shaking fingers through his near shoulder-length hair.

It had just curled over his ears when he'd left. Silent tears mingled with the bathwater on his face as he tried to lather up a washcloth. The soap slipped from his hands, and he reached for it with jerky motions.

The sight broke Charlie's heart. He knelt by the tub and placed his hands on Vince's. "I got this."

Vince maintained a death grip on the cloth as his eyes glazed over.

Charlie let him keep it and cupped Vince's jaw. "Come on, Vince. It's okay now. You're with me. We're going to take care of each other until this gets solved. You watch over me during the day. I'll watch over you at night. Just like we used to."

"They thought I was disposable because I'm a stripper. Do you agree with that?" He turned to Charlie, venom in his tone. "Nobody is disposable."

"They thought you were disposable because you're human. They thought they could get away with it because you're a stripper. Because they often kill their donors, Liberi tend to hunt where they won't get caught."

"By donors you mean human meals?"

Shoulders bunching, Charlie reached for the shampoo. "The Liberi would call them blood dolls. We prefer a more grateful term."

Vince snorted like he would argue or say something sarcastic. Charlie stuck his hands in Vince's hair and began lathering. Whatever snark Vince was going to utter died in a relieved hum.

At first all Charlie felt was resistance from dirt, blood, and other dried things he didn't want to think about, but soon his fingers slipped through Vince's hair with ease. "As for your career choice, I didn't want other people watching you take your clothes off or touching you like that. Please don't confuse my jealousy with your father's version of morality. Rinse."

Vince dunked his head under water so Charlie could make the shampoo dissipate. He came back up a few seconds later, shoulders down and defeated. "How do you prosecute vampires?"

Charlie pulled the stopper to drain the filthy water and refresh it. "If they're Liberi, you don't. You just kill them."

Vince blanched. "You? Like you personally?"

"More likely Cash. He's the soldier. I'm a woodworker."

Vince nodded slowly. "Where does he live? In Austin?"

"Currently he oscillates between New York City and Bergen, Norway. Now that CoVIn is opening our official headquarters here and Modron is bringing her entourage, he's added an Austin residence." Charlie's lip curled. "Which is the only good part of her moving here."

Vince's face stiffened, that strange jealousy once again apparent. What on Earth the man who dry humped strangers four nights a week thought he had to be jealous about was beyond Charlie's comprehension. All Vince said, though, was, "I think this conversation is more information than I got living at your house for over a year. Why didn't you share this world—*your* world—with me?"

"I keep my head down and avoid politics. We have a bureaucratic monarchy run by someone over a millennium old. It's the worst of all worlds." The water from the showerhead was warm, so he used it to finish rinsing Vince's hair. The bubbles sluiced down Vince's shoulders, down to the sinking water level around his midsection.

Vince had put the soap back on the tray, and the washcloth now floated freely on the dwindling water surface. Charlie grabbed them both and lathered up the cloth. Then he hesitated. How much did Vince want to be taken care of? Unsure, he swallowed heavily and stuck out the foamy washcloth. "Here's this. Or shall I?"

Vince's head rolled to the side. "Aw, you're blushing." He gave what might be the weakest smile the planet had ever seen, and then looked away, struggling with his decision. Charlie knew that look. Vince wanted help and didn't want to ask for it. Not from him, anyway.

Charlie squeezed the washcloth a little harder than necessary. "Never mind. I got it. Close your eyes. Let me get this off your face." Despite all efforts to remain calm, his voice was as rough as his woodworker's hands.

With a breath of relief, Vince obeyed, closing his eyes so that long lashes fanned over his exquisite cheekbones. He tipped his face up, inviting Charlie's touch.

Vince had always loved to be touched. They'd sit together, and Vince would lean against him or move Charlie's hand onto his knee. They'd pass each other in the hall, and Vince would pat him on the backside or squeeze his shoulder. It had been odd and yet welcome after living alone for so long.

But then he'd wanted to do it in public, and that was a type of exposure Charlie couldn't handle. Sure, things were a lot better than they'd ever been in Charlie's long life, but Vince was fooling himself if he thought there were no consequences for men holding hands in public.

Here in the house, though, they could touch and no one would know or stare or give a damn. So right now, as he hesitated with the stupid blue washcloth in his hand, an inch from Vince's skin, it wasn't public fear holding him back. It was the weight of everything he wanted and couldn't have. It hurt to touch Vince again.

He accepted that, put a steady hand on Vince's chin, and gently wiped the first streak of dried blood from his forehead. "Tell me more about Cash," Vince asked with a swallow.

"He's a Viking."

Vince opened one eye, looking interested against his will. "Like a real Viking?"

"He grew up sailing dragon boats and raiding villages along the coasts of what is now France and the UK." Charlie kept his tone light, but he couldn't stop the trembling in his fingers. Wiping the gore from Vince's face was like dusting the grime from a Michelangelo. Vince's cheekbones had become even more pronounced, his jaw firmer. He probably made a bundle as a stripper. Charlie's shoulders clenched at the thought.

They never should've been lovers. Still, their nine months as a couple were quite possibly the most magnificent error Charlie had ever made.

And here Vince was in his life again, sighing as Charlie stroked the washcloth over his supple skin, down that strong chin to his throat, then used a gentle setting on the sprayer to rinse him off.

"What's he like now?"

"Cash is a walking cannon. Point him at a problem, and it will die. Just, you know, make sure you're pointing him in the right direction. He's not unintelligent, but thinking first is not his preferred order." Kind of like Vince could be.

Vince was quiet as Charlie soaped between each long finger. Some men who loved men were openly wearing wedding rings now. It was amazing. Charlie was immortal; he couldn't get married. But maybe one day Vince would.

Ouch.

Charlie shoved the thought away and leaned Vince forward to clean his back. The lower he went, the harder it was getting to keep his thoughts ordered. He ran the washcloth over the firm muscles of Vince's lower back. He used to put his hands right there as... *Don't think about it.* "You've been working out."

He did not just say that. Yes. Yes, he did. He stuck the washcloth out, realizing this had left help and entered the territory of longing and all the stupidity that came with it.

Vince laughed, but the sound had no joy. "Don't want to wash my dick for me?"

A flush heated Charlie's face. "I don't think this is a good idea."

Vince shot him a come-hither smile as he started working the washcloth down his chest to his abdomen.

The action brought Charlie's attention to Vince's legs, his hips, his cock. From the moment Vince had moved in, halfway through his senior year of high school, he'd hit on Charlie with a single-minded determination that had thrown him off balance. The fact that Charlie had held out giving in to him until the summer after graduation, the modern interpretation of an adult, shouldn't have to be a point of pride—and absolutely was.

"The problem, I guess," Vince continued softly, his motions excruciatingly slow, "is that you've never needed me."

Charlie's mouth went dry as he watched the washcloth caress his ex's inner thighs. "Define 'need.'" The words slipped from him before he could stop them.

Vince's eyebrows raised in a glance both accusing and tempting.

Charlie pushed away from the tub until his back slammed against the toilet, out of temptation's view. "I'm sorry. I can—I should leave you in peace."

"Don't bother. I'm going to require some help getting out of the tub in a minute." His voice was so dry. His humor so much rougher than Charlie remembered.

"Clothes." Charlie stood up. Good views again. He forced his eyes to Vince's face. "There were some of your things in the laundry. I meant to get them back to you, but I, er…" *kept them on purpose.* "I'll get them now. They may be a little tight." *Because you've got muscles on your muscles now.* "Be right back to help you out. I called for food."

He made it to the door of the bathroom before Vince stopped him. "Can I use your phone? I need to call Rhi, tell her I'm okay, and mine's gone."

"Oh. Yes." Charlie dug his phone out and handed it over. "Don't tell her about us. About vampires, I mean."

Vince was already punching buttons, texting with a speed that looked practically vampiric. "Why not?"

"Because we don't randomly let people know."

"You let me know."

Charlie grimaced. "You sneaked into my room while I was sunsleeping."

"Where you had a nice note warning me not to call an ambulance because you'd be fine at sunrise. Yes, I distinctly remember that afternoon. The Day I Found Out I'm Living with a Vampire is a notable life event."

Charlie remembered that afternoon too, but for different reasons entirely. Vince had still been in high school, just turned eighteen, and they weren't dating yet. Charlie had woken up with Vince spooning him, the note clutched in his hand and dried tear tracks down his face.

Charlie had turned over to face him in a movement that would later become rote for them. Vince had woken up confused, then flirty, then panicked. His arms had tightened around Charlie as Charlie had whispered, "It's okay."

Then Vince had kissed him.

It had been the first taste of what was to come and had left Charlie panting for more. Not that he'd never noticed Vince that way. How could he not with the little flirt running around the house shirtless, spouting innuendo on a regular basis? But that kiss had changed things. It wasn't friendship with a side of ignorable lust he felt anymore. The two had intertwined into longing, the first nudge of love.

But he'd done the right thing that day. He'd gotten up out of the bed, put the younger man aside, and offered a basic explanation while swigging a jar of cold blood from the mini-fridge he kept upstairs.

The cold meal had done nothing to cool the want waking up next to Vince had inspired.

"She already knows. I told her the day after I found out."

The revelation threw cold water on the memory. "What?" There were two people he should've registered at CoVIn? Uh-oh. "How many other people did you tell?"

"Just her. Rhi may not be blood, but she's family." At least Vince looked a little chagrined. "Although, I'd give it a nine out of ten chance she told Javi, that's her brother, despite swearing to her namesake goddess that she wouldn't. Shit, I guess that doesn't matter now."

A swirl of worry churned in Charlie's stomach. That wouldn't go over well if it got out, and his relations with other vampires—other than Cash, anyway—were already chilly at best.

Vince's fingers hovered over the screen, suddenly still. "How am I going to tell her?"

Charlie would worry about all of this later. "Just say what you must in order to pacify her for now and invite her over tomorrow. Tonight you will eat and go to bed."

He groaned. "I don't have a monitor. I have to go to the drugstore. I probably don't want to know how off I am right now. This is annoying." In the past Vince had always been good-natured about the disease. It made Charlie sad to see his frustration.

"Walgreens is right around the corner. I'll be back in five

minutes. You get dressed, and there's an extra toothbrush in the cabinet. Let me take care of you tonight."

Vince set his phone on the floor and looked up with wide eyes and a pinched mouth. "How did you turn out so kind? I know you haven't had an easy life."

"Some of the cruelest people I've ever met have had the easiest lives. I don't think those things are related." Charlie took a step back toward the tub, trying to figure out the best way to warn Vince what CoVIn was really like. "You're about to get involved in a new world where I'm not the most popular figure. It's not going to be easy. When you're born in a different era, you think differently about *things*. Be careful, okay?"

Vince pulled the plug out of the tub and on wobbling legs managed to push himself onto the tub edge. "I got this. Thanks for finally letting me in."

Chapter 5

Heart heavy with bittersweet memories, Charlie poked his nose into the doorway to the guest room to check on Vince. He slept restlessly, clutching a pillow tight against his chest. Charlie couldn't help thinking of the way Vince used to sleep, with his arm around Charlie, his nose pressed against Charlie's head as they lay curled together.

A car door slammed outside, and footsteps jogged up his sidewalk. Somebody was coming in a hurry. One person probably didn't mean an attack.

Charlie dashed to the living room and opened the door before the person could ring the bell or do something loud. Before him was a hunger-thin woman with green hair and a determined expression. He looked at her closer and realized he'd met her before. "Rhiannon?" Vince's best friend had never seemed at peace with Vince and Charlie's relationship. Charlie hadn't thought twice about it, as that was par for his life. But if she knew what he was, that gave her a different reason for concern.

"Charlie," she said, her voice cold. "Vince is here?"

He nodded, not sure exactly what Vince had texted her. "He's sleeping."

She lifted an eyebrow in jaded accusation.

"In the guest room." He'd mumbled a vague offer to let Vince sleep wherever he wanted. His own room was in the attic, more secure and better outfitted than the guest room. It was also the only place Charlie could sunsleep with no chance of getting burned by stray sunbeams as the yellow ball of fiery vampire death made its way across the sky. He'd be in his own room out of necessity come dawn and insensate until his body finished its daily regeneration. He hadn't been surprised when Vince had marched into the guest room. "He's exhausted and needs the sleep. I'll have him call you when he wakes up."

"Exhausted? It's only two. We're normally winding down around now. Not passed-out exhausted." Her eyes narrowed at him. "He came here and then he started lying to me. The kind of bald-faced lying he hasn't done since, oh, he was dating you. Let me see him."

She tried to push her way in, but Charlie held the door firm. Without knowing exactly what Vince had said, he feared her panicking when she saw her friend's wounds. "I'll have him call you as soon as he's awake. As I said, he's sleeping. He needs it. I told him to invite you over tomorrow. Would two-thirty work for you?"

Her index finger pounded into his chest. "Don't you dare play the 'caring for him' card. You've had five years to play it while I've been the one actually taking care of him. I'm not leaving without at least seeing that he's okay."

Her words stung. Charlie would've provided everything for Vince—a home, clothes, a car, anything he'd wanted—if the man had let him. "Vince is quite self-sufficient. He takes care of himself, even if it means pandering to people's baser tastes."

"Judgmental much?"

Anger roared through him as she echoed Vince's censure. "I'm not the villain here. It isn't judgmental to break up with someone for lying. He needed his freedom to live some other life, and I gave it to him. I've had enough of this discussion with you. I understand Vince told you what I am. Then you have some sense of what I'm capable of. Get off my property and return tomorrow at two-thirty." Not that he'd hurt her, but the threat usually worked.

Her eyes widened in fear as she vibrated with energy. "Fine," she spat. But she didn't leave. From the back of her jeans she pulled a silver cross and brandished it at him. "Pater noster, qui es in caelis…"

He flinched at the brightness of the holy symbol and took a step back as the Lord's prayer scraped through his ears. "Espèce de con," he cursed in his native French.

She got louder and darted past him. "Sanctificetur nomen tuum."

He grabbed the back of her shirt with one hand and a pillow off the settee with the other.

She screeched when he pulled her backward and pushed away the cross with the pillow. "Good try. I still attend mass. I have some practice withstanding these."

"What's going on?" Vince stood in the arched entry to the living room, rubbing his eyes. He looked so beautiful, all shirtless and sleepy eyed, that Charlie stared, swallowing back a lump.

"Vince!" Rhiannon yelled.

A line of fire seared into Charlie's arm. "Hey!" He jumped back. The crazy woman had shoved the cross against him. He rubbed his arm. "Would you calm down? Vince, go back to bed. You're injured."

"Holy shit, what happened to you?" Rhiannon ran to Vince and started examining him with prodding fingers, cross dangling from her left hand with subdued brightness. "Where's Javi? You're a terrible liar, you asshole."

Charlie flinched. "I don't know. In my experience, he lies pretty well."

Vince glared at him. Okay, so that was uncalled for. But Charlie was bitter and his arm stung and Rhiannon knowing about him—for six years—had the potential to bring him a whole new forest of trouble.

More footsteps outside brought, thank the Virgin, Cash Geirson into the open door.

"Ooh, a party?" his old friend asked.

Rhiannon spun, cross up again. "Adveniat regnum tuum!"

Cash dropped to a crouch. "Whoa! Put the damned cross down, woman!"

Charlie faced the glare, eyes half closed in strain, and forced himself to move forward. Just a cross was one thing, but someone brandishing it with intent to harm while chanting holy writ was like walking into a bonfire.

Before he could get to her, Vince had the cross out of her hand and tossed into a corner. "Rhi, it's cool. Chill."

Rhiannon panted, eyes dilated in fear as she turned her gaze from Charlie to Cash and back. Breath slowing, she blushed. "Sorry. I'm a little on edge. I didn't know if that would work. And you were keeping me from Vince. And *nobody will tell me where my brother is.*"

Cash shook like he was throwing off water. "That's all right. I like a woman who attacks first and asks questions later. Sign of a decisive character." He raised an eyebrow at Charlie, no doubt asking if he knew where her brother was.

"Congress Bridge." Where Austin's bat colony congregated. Cash would know he meant Javi was a vampire.

"Team?"

"Ours. I think. I don't know how to explain to—"

Cash turned to Rhiannon. "Congratulations, your brother's a vampire." He nodded at the direction Vince had thrown the cross. "Clearly you have some concept of what that means."

❦

Well, that's one way to break life-altering news, Vince thought. "A little tact, maybe?" he ground out. The gorgeous guy off Charlie's phone—the one who'd taken him to Vegas after the breakup—had entered the room, looking every bit as perfect as he had in pixels, with ice-blue eyes and wheat-blond hair that just brushed his shoulders. Dude was handsome as hell. And an asshole.

"What?" Rhi screamed. She shoved Vince, a puny push that wouldn't have hurt if her palm hadn't landed square on a bite mark, and he grunted in protest. "Did you know that and not tell me?"

"Sorry, but it's been a rough night. I wasn't going to keep it from you for long."

Rhiannon groaned. "Sorry I hit you. You lied to me on the phone. Don't do that." She pressed against him, glaring at the other two men in the room like they had something to do with this. "Where's Javi? Why's he a vampire?"

"He's still at the club." Vince turned to Cash and tried not to care that his gray suit was cut to perfection, the fabric falling with the grace only pricey materials achieved. Cash was handsome, wore bespoke suits, and was on Charlie's speed dial for being a resourceful warrior. A vampire James Bond. Jealousy twinged Vince's insides. It irked him to need the help of the man Charlie had turned to after ditching him, but he'd worry about that after Javier and Emma were safe. "You're supposed to rescue him. Emma told me to get you. She needs rescuing, too. They seemed to know each other but didn't really get along."

"Why does my brother need rescuing?"

Cash rolled back on his heels, shocked. "Emmaline Granger? Blonde little thing with a sassy mouth and godawful accent?"

Vince nodded. If Cash knew her, he should be more likely to help. Vince turned to Rhi. "I'll explain."

"She has a baby bat?" Cash's voice was full of awe, like he'd just found out an old friend was pregnant. He punched Charlie on the shoulder. "That was not in the message!"

"And they need rescuing," Vince prompted again, as Cash seemed to have forgotten already. He was getting nervous that their great hope was a pretty boy who couldn't focus.

"From who?" Rhiannon asked.

Cash turned his wandering attention to her. "Correct me, stripper-boy, if I'm missing something." Before Vince could voice his frustration at that appellation, Cash was already going. "Your brother and Emma are in a Liberi stronghold where a masked vampire, possibly CoVIn, is helping a human with an Aztec fetish hold a coalition at a goth club. Vampires are switching sides willy-nilly, and for some reason the priestess—"

"Tzitzi—I told you there was a weird Aztec connection!" Rhiannon interjected.

"Thanks. For some reason Priestess Tzitzi thinks she needs a human heart—hence the kidnapping of Vince. That implies hardcore blood magic is involved. Or she's a psychopath who likes playing Operation: Live Edition! But I'm betting the former. So, we rescue them, a bigger danger is revealed, CoVIn is threatened at a crucial moment in our history, and blah blah blah. The important thing is, my good friend has a baby bat."

Okay, he had actually listened to the message and seemed to have put Vince's rambling into a surprisingly coherent narrative. "So, shouldn't somebody get them now?"

"No. We'll go at dawn when the Liberi are asleep. If they're going to kill Em and her fledgling, they're already dead and we can't do anything about it. But my guess is, we've got time. When Liberi have organized in the past—it's rare but it's happened—they've had some fun with old-fashioned brainwashing. Emma and… Javier you said?… may be full of new holes, but they'll survive. We may not if we go in there when everyone's awake."

"How are *you* going to be awake?" Vince asked. Charlie fell into a deathlike sleep at exactly sunrise every morning.

"I have ways." He waved his hands like a bad magician.

Charlie groaned. "We're taking caffeine pills, aren't we?"

"Yup."

Rhiannon clutched Vince's hand. "The blond girl was a vampire? Why did she turn my brother into one?"

Cash smiled and kissed her hand like an old-school courtier. Which maybe he'd been at some point. "I don't know the story, but congratulations. Drinks on me after we bring him back, and they can tell us."

"Cash," Charlie said, "we're not taking Vince back there."

Vince paled. "Me?" Going back? To the drums and the crowd of bloodthirsty monsters? Without thinking, he took a step closer to Charlie and his comforting presence.

Cash shot them a look of disapproval. "Hiding behind his skirts? Charlie may be a little twisty, but he's not your mama."

The words washed over Vince like freezing water. "Was that a slur?" He stepped even closer to Charlie in solidarity.

Charlie immediately walked away from him, shaking his hands like he'd touched something unclean. After all the closeness they'd shared tonight, the rejection was a surprising kick to the gut. Cash wasn't his lover—no way he'd say shit like that. He was a straight friend who wasn't a very good friend, and Charlie was hurting because of it.

"Apologize to him." Vince reached for Charlie, but he should've known better. Charlie dodged his touch. "Charlie, don't listen to him. He's being an asshole."

"Vince doesn't know what he's getting into. We can't take him," Charlie said, pretending nothing had happened. He wouldn't look at Vince.

With a thoughtful, "Huh," Cash looked from one of them to the other. Then he turned to Charlie, his voice carefully neutral. "The human knows better than anybody what we're getting into because he's been there."

"Vince can draw us a map. He's not going."

Charlie's insistence suddenly didn't feel like help. It felt like hiding the gay ex when they'd agreed to solve this together. And Cash's sudden thoughtfulness made Vince wonder if he was more glib than malicious. Maybe he was an idiot who hadn't meant to hurt Charlie with that remark.

Regardless, Vince was not about to give Cash the satisfaction of thinking him weak or cowardly. "I'll go." His voice came out rough, but at least he said it.

Another considered look from Cash turned into an amused smile. "Are you enlisting? I hear that's allowed now." He lifted one shoulder in a tiny motion. "Not that it hasn't always happened anyway."

He seemed to be speaking in some code Vince didn't follow, and Charlie's words from earlier came back to him. *When you're born in a different era, you think differently.* "I'm not in your army. I'm just going to save Javi and Emma. They saved me."

Cash nodded. "It's settled then. You"—he pointed at Vince—"go back to bed. I need you rested. "You"—he pointed at Rhiannon—"I've got time for twenty questions, while you"—finally at Charlie—"download and fill out some fucking paperwork on two humans who aren't registered. Yes, it's stupider than a vampire touring Alaska in June, but you're going to get your ass handed to you by somebody with a hard-on for bureaucracy and too much time on their hands, and I don't have time to bail your ass out right now."

"You can't order me around," Vince told him.

Cash turned to Rhiannon. "Green, I'll start answering your

questions as soon as he's horizontal."

Rhiannon turned to Vince, a fiery determination in her eyes. He sighed. "Fine. I'm tired anyway."

Chapter 6

"Look, thousand-year-old macho asshole, I'm not staying in the van. That's my brother!" Rhiannon exclaimed.

Vince, in the backseat of the windowless van, wanted to sympathize. But the entirety of his emotion was fixated on the four steps leading up to the alley entrance of Tooth and Nail, shadowy and black in the predawn light.

Charlie sat quietly next to him, but Vince didn't dare reach out. Instead, he rubbed his fingers over the gray Dolce & Gabbana T-shirt with a medieval knight on the front that had shown up along with Marc Jacobs jeans and Tod's driving shoes. He'd never felt cotton quite this soft or slick before.

Hell, he'd never even tried on anything this expensive before. Charlie didn't give a crap about clothes and wasn't stinking rich. But based on the perfectly tailored suit Cash had shown up in and the casual finery he'd changed into for the raid—with an ax strapped to his back—he did and was. But why Cash would give a shit about Vince's sartorial needs was beyond his comprehension. The vampire certainly didn't act like he cared much about anyone but himself.

"I'm not asking you to stay in the van because of your anatomy," the man said, voice even. "If I had a choice between Emma and Charlie, I'd take Emma. It's a question of, if one of us is knocked out or if the caffeine wears off, who's got the strength to carry someone and not slow down? Indecent Exposure back there is my best bet."

Vince frowned. Like *that* sort of shit. Men who were that

obnoxious didn't spend a grand on clothes that wouldn't fit them and loan them out. Or give them out. Or whatever this was.

He wanted to keep the shirt.

And the shoes and pants.

Charlie leaned forward, voice respectful. "Cash, this does beg the question of why *we're* here with you instead of Alaric and Nikolai."

Cash thrust his chin toward Vince. "He said there was a masked man who didn't belong. If someone from CoVIn is involved, we're better off keeping this to ourselves until we can talk to Emma." His fingers gripped the wheel a little tighter in irritation. "Any more questions from the peanut gallery before we move? Dawn's coming."

"It's not fair!" Rhiannon was still pissed. "And I change my hair color all the time. Green is a bad nickname!"

"Charlie, take him out of the car and get to work on the lock."

Charlie opened the car door and motioned for Vince to do the same, like Cash's word was law.

The automatic compliance frustrated Vince, but not knowing what else to do, he followed, growing more nauseated with each step. He didn't want Rhiannon in the club either, though. She and Javi had survived ten years in and out of the foster system by watching each other's backs, and now, given a choice, Rhi would condemn the world to save her brother. She and Javi weren't rational when it came to each other. Rhi needed to be a part of this team less than he needed to go back inside this hellhole.

Alleyway rubble scratched under his feet as he moved toward the back door, and he shivered despite the warm morning. He needed to think of something else. "Why does he act like everyone should obey him?"

"Cash? Because everyone does. Queen Modron sired him."

"Oh. Shit." *Prince* Cash. Of course. Vince had a lot of things to learn about vampires. "How do you say her name again?"

"Modron. Rhymes with cologne. It's Welsh." Charlie pulled something from his pocket and unrolled it, studying Vince more than whatever he was playing with. With a frown he kneeled before the lock and started working on it.

"You can pick locks?" Charlie had a lockpicking kit and appeared comfortable using it; the answer to Vince's question was obvious. "I didn't know that."

"I work for the Axes occasionally, when they need to make a quiet entrance. Usually I do this, then get back in the car to drive."

"The Axes?"

"The Three Axes—Cash, Alaric, and Nikolai. They're like the Musketeers, but with, you know, axes. Queen Modron's eldest fledgling is Alaric. He's a Visigothic warrior priest. Her next eldest is Galswinth, a Visigothic princess who, about four hundred years ago, turned and married Nikolai Vyhovsky, a Cossack warrior and psychic. You'll hear Cash refer to Nikolai as Kolyan, but don't do that. The nickname is only for friends. You'll also hear Cash call the queen Mo, just not in front of her. Don't think you can do that even in the quiet of your room, alone with no one around for miles. She will somehow know and kill you.

"To sum up, Cash, Alaric, and Nikolai are CoVIn's greatest warriors. They are tight as family and brutal with problems. They're the Axes."

The names came too fast and too foreign for Vince to follow, but at least his confusion eased the tension as he tried to focus on something other than where he was and what he was doing. "You just threw, like, nine million things at me. And I'm glad. Except I won't remember any of it. Do I need to?"

The lock *snicked* open. "Eventually. Right now, just know to stay out of the Axes' way. They're the queen's favorites, they're absolutely loyal to each other, and together they can stop armies. Also, stay out of Galswinth's way. She seems unassuming, but she comes from a time when clever women ruled from behind the scenes, and she does it well. Any of the Axes would murder for her without asking why."

"And one of these extremely powerful vampires, a son—er, *fledgling*—of Queen Modron, is your friend and one of ten people whose number you have in your phone."

Charlie looked toward the van, a little smile on his face like that pleased him. "Yes. He is."

"But the others are not."

"No." The smile disappeared. "Don't get caught alone with Alaric, and don't associate too closely with me in front of him. Any of them, really. Alaric puts on a good face for the court, but if he thinks you're bent, he's going to make your life hell. Nikolai is all right. Cold, but not vicious. I have no idea what goes through Galswinth's mind. Ever."

Vince crossed his arms, an old frustration rising. "I'm not bent. *We're* not bent. We're gay. I won't listen to anyone use terms like that. Even you. And I'm not going to deny who I am or avoid people over it." Vince turned to watch Rhiannon and Cash, who was finally exiting the car with a come-hither smile on his face. Had he been flirting with Rhi?

Charlie stood, holding the club's door slightly ajar as he leaned in, voice serious. "This isn't modern Austin, Vince. These are ancient warriors creating a society that looks a lot like feudalism with less mud and more paperwork. Any one of the Axes can kill you without remorse and, given who they are, will likely get away with it. Set your expectations accordingly."

Could it possibly be that bad? Or was Charlie being his

overly cautious self?

Rhi smiled from the car as Cash marched toward them. How had he done that? When he got to the door, Cash slapped Charlie on the back. "Feudalism? You say that like it's a bad thing. The paperwork's a bitch, though. I prefer mud. Are we in?" Charlie nodded, and Cash set a timer on his watch. "Time to go." He pulled a bottle of caffeine pills from his pocket and downed half of them.

Charlie took it, downing the other half with a grimace.

Good lord. "Is that safe?" Vince asked. He'd been aware they'd take caffeine to trick their bodies into staying up a short time longer. He hadn't realized it would be half a bottle of NoDoz.

"Have to keep the heart going," Cash answered. "They make me jittery, though, so you two might want to stop questioning everything I do for a while. Or for the rest of your lives. That would be good. We have about twenty minutes. Allons-y."

*

Cash crossed the tiny kitchen in three strides. No food prep here, just an industrial fridge and plenty of booze. And a tank against one wall that looked almost like a keg, but had three brown drops stained onto the concrete below.

Vince froze. "What's in there?"

Charlie looked where he was pointing and huffed a laugh. "Cash, did you know they're buying from CoVIn?"

Cash grinned. "I don't see the downside to that."

"What's in there?" Vince insisted, though he already knew.

"Blood," Cash and Charlie answered in unison.

"Humane harvest," Charlie added.

"How do you humanely harvest blood?"

Cash held up a finger. "Twenty. Minutes. Discuss food ethics later. Now, let's get Emma and her baby bat." Without waiting for an answer, he slunk into the next room.

"Are you going to be okay?" Charlie asked again.

"Quit asking me that." Vince brushed past him into the main club.

And stilled. The mural was the most grotesque art he'd ever seen, a bubbling, crimson, and putrescent wound that made the wall look like it bled infection, and the reality of where he was sunk in with nauseous fervor.

"Cash can stop anything. We'll be safe with him," Charlie reassured, patting his shoulder.

Vince flinched. "Don't touch me." His voice was harsh because it was such a lie. He wanted Charlie to wrap him in his arms and squeeze him until the fear was all gone.

No. He would handle this alone. They weren't together, and he couldn't depend on Charlie. He strode forward, determined to beat his fear on his own.

Only skylights lit the club. A central bar gave three-hundred-sixty-degree access to alcohol. Toward the front was an empty dance floor painted black. Around the edges, couches made of metal and chains showcased a sadistic aesthetic. At the back was the door leading down.

"What do we have here?" Someone entered from a side door.

Vince jumped, heart pounding. The androgynous figure wore shapeless black pants and a once-white shirt that was spattered to saturation with rust-colored stains. His or her face had been dusted black and hair tied back in a white scarf. Scarlet ribbons ran vertical next to gauged ears. Though dirty and utilitarian, the outfit still looked ceremonial.

The kind of ceremony where people's hearts were removed? He looked back at the stains and wanted to gag. Old blood.

And one bright, wet splash of crimson across the chest.

Female chest. Vince's gaze shot to the room she'd come from. Was there a body back there? Possibly one missing a heart?

His gaze found hers, and she smiled. His knees buckled. It was Tzitzi. But nobody would recognize her from his earlier description.

Cash's voice was soft but had a ring of authority to it. "Go to sleep, little human."

Vince felt drowsy at the sound of the words. "What is that?"

"Command. Some of the old ones can do it," Charlie said. "We're fine."

"But that's *her*."

Tzitzi's eyes widened. Instead of obeying, she stomped forward, chanting with a lot of consonants.

"Fuck me," Cash muttered. His body flew backward into a wall, impaling itself mid-abdomen on one of the decorative spikes. His head slammed into the drywall, creating a spider web of cracks and a cloud of dust. Blood soaked his black shirt from the hole in his center, and he flopped forward like a puppet.

"Cash didn't stop her." Vince whispered as he backed toward the kitchen. They'd barely started and their fighter was out—maybe dead. He forced his escalated breathing to slow. Hyperventilating was not going to help.

Tzitzi's eyes lit back on him, and she grinned. "You came back. I think that qualifies as consent."

Vince shrunk inside.

"Have a drink, Vincent, while I deal with the other one." She placed a bottle of Scotch and a tumbler on the bar and patted a seat next to her. "Sorry there's no pulque up here. But this one's on me for coming back. And with offerings." She cocked her head at Charlie. "I've got two prizes. You can go if you like. Or I can have you killed. Or tortured. I think a quick death is more efficient, but my minions are less interested in efficiency."

Charlie lightly squeezed Vince's arm, though his eyes never left Tzitzi. "Get a drink. Witches are *humans* with magic." He emphasized humans, like he was trying to tell Vince something. Charlie had a plan? Whatever it was involved walking away from him, and each step away made Vince want to sink further into the ground. It was a bad plan. But he took small steps to the bar and sat, bile on his tongue at the proximity to Tzitzi. She smelled like sour pulque, burnt ash, and blood. He breathed into his shirt to filter out the foul smell.

Was Cash dead? No. He was twitching. Death twitching? Or revival twitching? Hope helped him climb through the fear and think.

Charlie circled the witch. "What are you doing with vampires?"

She turned as he went, wary though not afraid of his movements. "Ruling the world."

He snorted. "A witch with delusions of grandeur. Of course."

Human. Why was it important that she was human? Vince looked at the heavy bottle she'd set out for him and then at the back of her head, in easy reach. It was important because humans were easy to hurt. And she thought he was too cowed to do anything.

He uncapped the bottle and poured a shot with shaking hands. Hair of the dog. He downed it. Liquid courage burned its way through his system, giving him false hope. He'd take it.

Tzitzi now faced directly away from him, following the movements of Charlie, the perceived greatest threat. "So you're going to stay. Got a plan for getting out, or just want to see a real ceremony?" She tapped a sheathed dagger, hidden in the folds of her coat. Somebody was dead because of her. Anger gave him strength.

"Duh," Charlie answered.

Cash twitched again, fingers scraping at the wall by his side. He was waking up. They could still get out of this.

"Duh?" Tzitzi asked. "You have an obvious plan?"

Vince tilted his head one way then the other, trying to loosen his stiff-as-steel muscles. He'd never knocked a person unconscious before, but it was now or never. He swung the scotch at Tzitzi's head. She turned, eyes wide, just before it connected with her temple.

His wrist rebounded from impact. She made a sound somewhere between a grunt and a shriek and crumpled.

Vince loomed over her, the cold bottleneck clutched tightly in his hands. He'd knocked her out? She wasn't moving.

"DUH. Don't Underestimate Humans," Cash said, his voice strained. "It'll get you killed." He shoved himself off the spike and staggered toward the bar. "Kilt chaser." The words came out like a command.

"What? What is that?" Vince's eyes never left the crazy girl at his feet. Charlie was down next to her, feeling her pulse. "Did I kill her? I didn't mean to kill her." Not that he'd lose too much sleep over it.

But he didn't want to kill anybody. That would make him… He glanced up at Charlie and Cash. That would make him a lot more like the two of them.

"She's alive, but she'll be out for a while. Good hit." Charlie put one hand on the bar and hopped over it like the chest-high structure was a low wall. It was freaky how high he could jump. He'd never done that so casually in the past. Or, at least, he hadn't in front of Vince. "Cash will need blood and a few moments for his internals to reconstitute. Watch for anyone else coming in."

Vince swallowed heavily as he scanned the doors—the locked front, the office Tzitzi had come from, the kitchen, and the one downstairs. No signs of life or unlife.

"Congrats on getting taken down by a ninety-pound girl," Charlie teased as Cash stumbled to the bar like a drunk.

"Girls were different in your pansy-assed era. If you met a Viking woman, you'd be proud to be her bitch. But if the Axes hear about this, I'll kill you both." Cash put both hands on the bar and leaned heavily on it, like he'd just gotten punched and not gutted. "Why doesn't your ex know how to make a kilt chaser? Didn't you two live together?"

"He didn't mix my cocktails."

"Why not?"

Vince pointed to Tzitzi's wet shirt, trying to keep his finger steady. "Should we check for a hurt person? She has blood." Although the amount looked more like "dead person" than "hurt."

Cash eyed Charlie and nodded at the room she'd come from. "Go. I'll teach Bartending 101 until I'm useful."

Charlie wrinkled his nose, back stiff like he didn't want to see whatever was in there. Vince didn't blame him. But Charlie's voice came out a forced calm as if looking for desecrated bodies was a normal thing. "Or you could just drink red like a normal vampire in need of a quick heal." He tapped one of the sprayers and motioned to Vince without looking at him. "Here's the one you need."

Vince thought of the blood keg in the back and recoiled. They had a blood *sprayer*.

"Vikings thrive on alcohol. You French fell too far from the tree. I blame the Romans."

Shaking his head, Charlie headed for the back room. "Says the Viking with a Roman name. Are you seriously suggesting the French don't drink?"

"Cassius was my grandfather's name, and wine is wuss

alcohol."

Vince stared at them in appalled awe. There was an unconscious witch on the floor. There was possibly a heartless body in the next room. God knew what was downstairs. And they were telling jokes.

But Vince had volunteered, insisting he wanted in. That meant he had to act more like them. "I can check the room." The thought made tears spring to his eyes.

"No," they both answered at once.

He exhaled in relief as Charlie opened the door to Tzitzi's leavings and went inside.

"Are we going to take Tzitzi with us? Like as a captive?"

"No," Cash grunted as he grabbed a glass. "Mix while we talk."

Vince tried not to think about what he was spraying as he filled a glass halfway with red liquid. Charlie used to drink a bottle every morning. This was no different. Right? But it felt different.

"CoVIn's not currently set up to contain a witch. They're a bitch to jail. Each one has a different spell library, but opening locks is pretty universal. You can probably guess how well it goes to have a murderous spellcaster loose in your headquarters." Cash pushed the bottle of Scotch at him. "One shot. Tell Charlie it was three."

As Vince poured, Charlie appeared, white faced, and his gaze riveted to Vince with haunted fury. Vince shoved the finished drink at Cash and headed for him, wanting to comfort him. Then he stopped short. Charlie didn't want him close, not around his friends. The thought stung.

"Were-jag," Charlie announced. "I guess she's going tribal."

Were-rats and now were-jags? Vince assumed that meant jaguar. How many different animal-human combos were there?

Cash's drink was already finished. "Is he dead? They can look pretty damn dead and not be."

"That's why I went into the room, to check. His heart's on the table with a silver knife through it, and we interrupted her in the midst of flaying him." His furious gaze flicked back to Vince. "He's dead."

"Flaying him?" Vince sank onto a barstool. He'd been here last night with an utter psychopath. She'd seemed so normal at first. Somebody he wouldn't think twice about smiling at on the street. "I'm sorry you had to see that disgusting—horrifying—scene," he muttered. Gratitude filled him that they hadn't let him go in. He was pretty sure he would've fainted.

Charlie maintained several feet in distance, yet still managed to feel like he was hovering.

Cash shoved up to standing but had to brace himself on the bar as he wavered. "He doesn't care about the jag. Charlie's seen worse. He's pissed because he's imagining you there instead."

"Me?" Vince turned to Charlie. The man looked away as his jaw twitched in anger, but a moment later his gaze was back, watching Vince like he couldn't help it. Cash was right. "It wasn't me. I'm okay."

Charlie turned away again, and this time didn't look back. He felt protective, sure, but it didn't mean any more than that. Still, it was better than nothing.

Cash yanked out his phone. "Siri, call Marcos." As he staggered forward, he kicked Tzitzi none too gently in the ribs. "You are one sick bitch."

"Should we kill her?" Vince asked, surprised he was the one suggesting it. Although killing an unconscious person, even one as evil as she was, didn't sit right with him.

"She's not on the DB," Cash called over his shoulder. "Yet."

After Cash's back was turned, Charlie helped Vince stand.

His hands were cold and shaking, and his voice held a forced calm. "She's human. By CoVIn law, she gets a trial before she's on the death blood list. Once on the DB, though, she can be killed without consequences." To Vince's surprise, he took Vince's arm protectively, like a concerned parent in a crowd, and they headed for the staircase together.

"But you said he could get away with anything, queen's fledgling and all."

"Not *anything*. We don't know enough about what's going on here—or who she is behind the makeup—to make that call."

As they passed Tzitzi, Charlie's look of loathing worried Vince. Suddenly he found himself pulling Charlie away, afraid the man was debating those consequences he'd spoken of.

Charlie wanted to kill for him. The thought was disconcerting. Was that because he cared enough to? Or because he was a vampire and a life didn't mean as much?

Ahead of them, Cash spoke Spanish on the phone.

"Who's he talking to?" Vince asked, trying to get Charlie's mind off of murder.

"He's calling someone from Familia de Tejas—the jaguars. They'll want to know what happened." His eyes glittered a bit in anticipation. "Their laws on violence aren't as... strict. It's entirely possible they'll take care of the problem"—his gaze flicked back to Tzitzi—"for us."

At the bottom of the stairs they entered the twenty-by-thirty space that would feature in every nightmare for the rest of Vince's life. He stopped as scenes from a few hours ago ran through his mind like the trailer to a horror movie. "I can't..."

Charlie caught him. "You can. Let's finish this."

No, he was going to pass out. What had possessed him to think he could do this? Charlie's arms tightened around him. He wanted to sink back into them and let Charlie protect him. Once again, Vince the dependent. He jerked up, straightening his back. He would stand on his own feet, for fuck's sake.

The door on the fourth wall opened, and three men came out. Their eyes had the same jittery instability as Cash's and Charlie's. Drugged vampires.

"G-G-Geirson? But you're in Rio," one of them announced in wide-eyed recognition. The other two drew swords and held them out protectively, as if Cash worried them.

"Maybe this time he won't get immediately impaled," Vince murmured.

Cash tossed his phone over his shoulder. "Catch."

Vince bumbled then recovered the phone. Somebody was still speaking on the other end. "Uh… no hablo español. Cash is fighting now." He recited the address and hung up.

With a practiced motion, Cash drew the ax strapped to his back. In the car he'd stated that immortals weren't affected much by "weapons of efficient destruction, like guns." Melee and its severed-limb violence still reigned in the immortal world.

The weapon looked impressive. Or it did until a broken handle—probably from the impaling—caused the axe head to fall off the shaft. The metal landed on the ground with an impotent *thunk*. "*Motherfucker*," Cash huffed. "Not my day."

The sword-wielding immortals smiled, suddenly liking their odds better.

"I'm going to die here," Vince said. He'd thought that a few hours ago. He'd just delayed fate. At least he'd gotten to see Charlie again. Except now Charlie was going to die, too.

The first vampire leaped at Cash. Cash ducked and scooped up the axe head.

Without stopping, he rotated and swung the blade. The first vampire's head rolled.

As the body started to crumble, Cash didn't stop to enjoy the kill. The axe head changed hands, and he tossed it like a discus. Another head rolled.

The last vamp dropped his sword and turned to run. Cash pulled a fancy, metal-and-wood stake from his pocket as he ran after him. A sweep-kick and the last vampire went down.

Cash staked him through the heart and had the weapon wiped off and back in his pocket before Vince could blink. "Holy fuck."

Charlie patted him on the back. "That's what I meant. He's like a cannon. Point and shoot."

Vince stared at the third body, now a decaying skeleton on the floor. "Why didn't it dust like the others?"

With his left hand, Cash grabbed Vince's arm and yanked him onto his own feet away from Charlie. His right hand pressed on his still-open gut wound. Cash's grip was almost painfully firm. "Are you with us? We're going farther in. I need you with us." He shook him hard enough to knock Vince's teeth together.

The force of it shocked the growing wooziness from him, sending adrenaline to replace the fear. "I'm with you. I'm good."

"Good. Skeletor's a baby. I almost feel bad for killing him, except… nah." He let go and headed toward the door. "We don't technically *dust*. We decompose very quickly to the state we should be in. It takes a canivet to kiss ash right."

He was already through the door. Vince followed, feeling better now that he'd seen Cash in successful action. "What's a canivet?"

"Don't use that word unless you are one," Charlie said. "It's *anivet* based on the Latin anima vetus."

Vince focused on translating as his swinging emotions centered again. "Old soul. Then canivet is…" He ventured a guess. "Canis vetus? Old dog?"

Cash's voice projected down the hall like they weren't in an enemy stronghold. "Which I am. Hup two. Daylight's wasting, caffeine's spending."

They picked up the pace, following Cash as Vince's frustration grew. "You have this whole world. There's lingo. And drinks. And enemies with strongholds. You have a fucking queen. And you never told me any of this. Did I mean that little to you?"

Charlie's eyes snapped in anger. "Little? I let you move into my house. I didn't want you to freak out at how dangerously convoluted all of this is."

"What part of our entire relationship makes you think I freak out easily? When I found out you were a vampire, did I panic? No. I started cutting your hair for you every afternoon when you woke up with it all shaggy again. I handled it pretty damn well."

"Is he consistent?" Cash asked. Vince looked up to find him jogging backward, a sly grin on his face as he listened to their fight.

Charlie blushed and scowled. "He's very consistent, but he's not cutting your hair."

Once again, Charlie was dictating what he could or couldn't do. "Why not? That's not your call."

"He offered to kill you when we broke up. You want to go to his house every day?"

"He can't kill me. I'm not on your death blood list."

"And," Cash added, "I'll want to kill him less if he's my hairdresser."

"I'm not a hairdresser. If anything, I'm a barber."

Cash raised an eyebrow. "Hairdresser too gay for you?"

Vince shot him the finger. "My father is a barber. Everything I know about hair, I learned from helping him. I never went to school for it."

The damn vampire smiled as he turned to Charlie. "He's less of a simpering douchebag than I pictured." Back to Vince. "I wake around eleven, not-a-douche. I'll see you then."

"Do all vampires order everyone around, or are you two special?"

"Charlie's bossy? I know I am. But I make listening to me worth your while." He patted Vince on the shoulder, his hand heavy but not unfriendly, as if he didn't realize his own strength. "And I think you're idiot enough to stand up to me if you need to. What's in here?" The door to his left opened on silent hinges. Cash's focus narrowed as all humor left his face. "Emma."

Chapter 7

Charlie grimaced as Vince, who should be shrieking in a corner right now, marched into the room shoulder to shoulder with Cash, the most in-your-face vampire Charlie knew. Maybe he *had* sheltered Vince too much.

But Vince had been so young, so bright eyed, and so very fragile. When Charlie had seen the body of that jaguar hanging by its heels, skin peeled from the chest cavity and down one arm, it hadn't disgusted him. It had incensed him. That would've been Vince.

Charlie would see Tzitzi dead, even if it meant showing his face at CoVIn to do it.

And Cash, manipulative ass that he was, had known that would happen if he sent Charlie in there. He'd always wanted Charlie to get more involved in society. Charlie set his jaw. At least for the time being, Cash had his wish. To keep Vince safe, Charlie would endure the judgmental hostility that always came with CoVIn.

The room they entered had six cells, two of which were sun cells—cells where sunlight came in at certain times of day. A Latino male Charlie thought maybe he'd met before was collapsed in the shadowed corner of one. That must be Javier, Rhiannon's brother.

Next to him in a dark cell was Emma Granger, a petite blonde and one of Cash's on-and-off-again lovers. Spikes through each forearm pinned her to the wall as she leaned forward in sunsleep. Blood had dried down her arms and dripped into a still-sticky pool on the floor. Her clothes were ripped and likewise stained with blood.

Vince went right to Javier's cage to study the metal design. Within a few moments he'd be able to ascertain all there was to know about the construction of the cage—including the best place to kick it in.

Across the aisle from Emma one more man was locked up. Charlie headed for that cage, a bad feeling slinking through his veins. One man was in it, flopped on the ground like a dead fish. Auburn curls matted his forehead and clung to his cheeks. His mouth was open, like he'd fallen screaming. A shudder passed through Charlie. He hated that he wished the man *had* died screaming. But Ramón was alive, sunsleeping too peacefully.

Cash, who'd appeared next to him, muttered something in a different language—probably Old Norse, which meant he was pissed.

"You're telling me," Charlie said.

Vince didn't stop assessing as he asked, "Who is it?"

Cash's gaze turned hostile. "Charlie's sire."

It had been a hundred years since Charlie had seen him, in a hotel in New York. Ramón had been creating yet another vampire and dumping the unsuspecting man in a room with no clue what was happening.

"I suppose we have to take him." Charlie jiggled the door, hoping it had a lock he couldn't pick and was made of something Cash couldn't break.

Vince shook the bars of Javier's cage in a few places, and the creak and rattle echoed around the room. "The one who left you to get lynched?" he asked Charlie.

"That's the one," Cash answered. "We don't have to take him. He's not CoVIn."

"I thought all children of Queen Modron—" Vince started,

but got interrupted.

"Keep their awen," Cash answered. "But joining CoVIn is a choice that means you have to abide by our rules. This *nifling* is a fucking sociopath—no rules, no membership, and not my problem." He put a hand on Charlie's shoulder as his voice turned cheerful. "Charlie, I will break your fingers if you try to get that dickwad out."

Relief flooded Charlie. His sire was locked in a Liberi prison. He should help Ramón, but seeing him here felt like justice.

Cash, not one to let moral dilemmas slow him down, had already turned his attention back to Vince and Emma. "What are you, a cagemaster? What are you looking at?"

"Kick here." Vince pointed to a spot on Javier's cell.

Cash shot him a disbelieving look, then kicked. The metal broke at a weak joint, and the door sprang open from the hinge side. Cash's eyebrows shot up. "Okay then. Next?"

Vince studied Emma's door. "Would you really break his fingers?"

"Yes."

"You're kind of an asshole." Vince pointed again. "Can you reach this high?"

Rolling his eyes, Cash grabbed a handhold on the bars to launch up and slammed a heel into a spot just above his own head. This time the door hinged from the bottom, dropping forward into the cage.

Cash could be an asshole, but he meant well. Usually.

"I declare you useful," Cash said.

"What, knocking out the bad witch didn't seal that?" Vince's voice wasn't steady yet, but he was regaining a sense of humor. Charlie marveled at how quickly he'd managed to do that. The man was resilient.

Cash grinned. "Eh, maybe. Now go be useful a third time and walk through that sunshine to Emma's baby bat. Try to keep him from crisping too much when you carry his ass back."

Vince obeyed with a huff. "Emma's baby bat has a name. Javier Reyes."

As Cash entered Emma's cell, his smile left. Metal plates stopped Emma from pulling her arms off the pins. Cash studied them, lip curled in disgust. "Sorry, Em..." A fierce yank pulled the first out of the wall. Emma dropped until she hung by one arm. Bones popped in her wrist, snapping under her jerking weight.

At the sound, Vince's equanimity left in a hunch of shoulders.

"She's a vampire," Charlie assured him. "She'll heal up in no time. I'll carry Javier when you bring him out." It wasn't the first time he'd heard bones popping, but he didn't think it was possible to get used to the sound.

Cash caught Emma's weight and yanked the other pin out. "Doubly sorry..." She dropped to the ground as he pulled his modified stun gun out of his pocket. Placing the device over her heart, Cash shocked her, then did it again...and again, counting a second between each one, like heartbeats. Charlie had never been shocked awake, but he'd heard it was hell. She wouldn't get any sleep today, either, to heal up from those nasty wounds. Emma was in for a miserable twenty-four hours... which was still better than whatever they had planned for her here.

But there was another problem that worried him more. "Are you sure that's wise? What if she's back to being one of them? Tzitzi got a new heart."

Vince froze, Javier in his arms, eyeing the sunlight like he'd jump into it.

"If she's crazy, do it," Charlie told him. "You'll be safe there until Cash takes care of her."

"Fuck me…" Emma announced in her thick east Texas accent. "Get that fucking thing off me. I'm awake." She sat up, looking dazedly about.

Cash tensed for her reaction, hand in his coat for his stake. It would kill him to dust her, but he'd do what he had to in order to keep everyone alive.

"Cash?" Emma asked, blue eyes confused. Then wide. "Damn, I knew you'd show. You are a sight for morning eyes." She threw herself on him, kissing him with a full-body attack that bordered on wrestling. After a tense moment, Charlie realized Cash was kissing her back.

Regardless of what had happened a few hours ago, everything was fine now. Cash scrubbed his fingers affectionately through her hair as they split apart with a smack of lips. "Of course I showed. You look like shit. What happened?"

She growled. "That is a long story, and I need a drink. Where's—uh, shit! What time is it?" In a sudden panic, she spun to the cell where Vince still held Javier. Seeing that, she leaned back in relief. "He's okay. Cash, I got me a baby bat, and I don't recollect his name. I'm a shitty sire." She may not know his name, but she clearly cared what happened to him. That was as it should be, unlike Charlie's espèce de chien of a sire behind them. Just thinking about Ramón's callousness tensed his shoulders and neck.

Like Cash, Charlie had never sired anyone. Rumor was that Emma had tried once with a man she'd deeply loved, but the turn hadn't taken and at midnight, the time when new vampires woke, instead of greeting him she'd had to bury him.

Charlie glanced at Vince, an old chill making him shiver. Vampires had known for centuries that turning was not a way to save someone from a terminal disease. He didn't know for sure if

Vince's counted or not, since modern medicine had made what was once terminal completely livable. But Charlie had studied the issue, and it wasn't a good bet. The treatment for diabetics didn't fix the malfunctioning part of Vince's body; it artificially provided the insulin his body couldn't make. Without his injections, Vince would die. The likelihood of him surviving a turn was tiny.

Going through what Emma had, holding Vince while he died his mortal death and then holding him long past the time he should've woken up, Charlie knew he wouldn't recover from that. He'd take Vince to a field with no shade for miles and keep holding him until the sunshine immolated them. More importantly, Vince deserved a long life, not one cut short on a selfish risk that was too high to take.

"Hot, hot, hot!" Vince ran through the band of sunshine, Javier smoking with each beam that hit him.

Charlie opened his arms and collected the burning vampire as soon as Vince was back in shadow. "Are you all right?"

"Is *he* all right? You guys catch fire fast." Vince rubbed his own forearms where minor burns were already forming from the contact.

Emma hopped up, pulled Cash to standing, and hustled to check on her fledgling. Charlie softened at her concern. It was heartwarming to see her exuberant care.

Cash followed at a slower pace, shaking his head at her officiousness. "Eh, we can toast to sticky ash and still survive."

A memory made Charlie chuckle. "You can, anyway." He and Cash had gone from acquaintances to friends during the Revolution—the French, not the American—after Cash had fried himself crispy trying to rescue a pretty aristo from guillotining. Charlie had cared for him in a wine cellar outside Nantes for two weeks while Cash recovered enough to hunt for himself. Luckily blood was in easy supply during the Terror.

After the war Cash had asked him to move to America to help with a nascent organization for Modron's descendants. Though CoVIn hadn't exactly welcomed him with open arms, Charlie had fallen in love with the New World and never looked back.

Cash poked his head out the door and motioned everyone forward. "I had a particularly adept nurse who never once hit on me. It started to change my mind about some things."

Charlie lost his footing in surprise. True, Cash never harassed Charlie about whom he dated, but he rarely acknowledged it either and had spent most of their friendship circumventing the topic. Well, except five years ago when Cash had gotten him rip-roaring drunk on the terrace of their suite at the MGM. For the first time ever, he'd encouraged Charlie to talk, and Charlie was quite sure he didn't want to remember what all he'd admitted or explained.

"I got him," Emma whispered, trying to pull her baby bat from him as they entered the hallway.

Cash shook his head. "Em, you're my fighter. Let Charlie keep him."

She frowned but obeyed and pointed in a different direction than they'd come. Vince had said he'd left via an easier route than the club, but between being sick-drunk and carried, he couldn't remember the directions.

"Charlie can fight," Vince said. He sounded belligerent, like he took the assessment of Charlie's fighting as an insult to his masculinity.

Charlie shifted the weight of Javier in his arms, getting a better hold of him. "He's not making a political statement. If Cash says she's a better fighter, she's a better fighter."

A decade ago he would've made the same assumption as Vince. If it had been anybody but Cash now, he would know it was meant as an insult. But on that same Vegas trip, after passing out from inebriation, Charlie had woken from sunsleep tucked into the master bed next to a pillow that smelled like Cash. Crashing next to each other wasn't sexual for vampires like it was for humans, seeing as they were technically dead during sunsleep and there couldn't be any "funny business." Men sunslept next to each other all the time. But it had been made abundantly clear that none of the other men Charlie knew would crash anywhere near him.

That Cash would was better than a handwritten note declaring his acceptance. He still wasn't going to stick his neck out for him. But he mostly treated Charlie like he did everyone else, which after nearly three hundred years of being "other" was a pretty damn big deal.

Emma pulled his mind back to the present, saying, "I don't remember much of the last few days. It's a nightmare of a jumble. But I think Joe's dead." Sorrow laced her voice. Joseph Crackin was her sire, a friendly rambler of a vampire, and he and his fledgling had remained friends. Joe would be missed.

"The cowboy?" Vince asked. "He screamed, 'Death to tyrants,' and charged after Tzitzi. The masked man shot him with a crossbow."

Emma hissed a breath somewhere between a laugh and a sigh. "Well, least ways he died true to form. I think his mind'd been tampered with too, though. I have a vague memory of eating with him, and it ain't a pretty one."

Vince pointed to a bruise on his jaw. "He gave me this on his way to Tzitzi. When he died, you two got your senses back." He frowned in thought. "Tzitzi seemed surprised by that."

She shook her head. "Got that bitch on the DB yet? I'd like to kill her myself."

They rounded the corner and found a ladderlike stair going

up to a metal door.

"Not yet. But she will be." Cash pointed to Vince. "Check for sunlight."

Vince, surprisingly obedient, headed up and into the warehouse above.

Cash turned to Emma. "Do you have any idea who the masked man is?"

She shook her head. "The time is all blurred. I remember him being there. He was tall and narrow. Well, tall for me. Not tall like..." She motioned up at Vince. "He had the shape of an anivet, strong and gaunt, and walked like he'd been tall in his own time."

Vince crouched down, and Charlie relaxed to have him in his sight again. "There's a path to a loading dock that doesn't have light until the end. I texted Rhi. She's meeting us there with the van."

Charlie headed up the ladder, anxious to be able to watch his back again.

Below him Emma said, "I got one more question. Cassius, darling, how'd you get impaled? Did a squadron of ninjas drop from the rafters? 'Cause I figure we could all use a funny right about now, and you versus ninjas would be hilarious."

Cash's feet pounded hard against the ladder. "Time to go."

✠✦✠

Rhi stopped the van in front of a gated house in one of Austin's most exclusive neighborhoods, her mouth open wide enough that a small bird could get in. Vince understood the feeling. Past the wrought iron gates, a circular drive led up to a three-story, Mediterranean-style mansion sprawling along the cliffside. The lawns were done in immaculate xeriscaping, full of blooming lavender and tall grasses. All in all, it was not the hidey-hole he'd expected to retreat to.

"This can't possibly be the right address," she said.

Vince held up his phone to show the navigation. "I had him double check it before he passed out."

They both shifted uncomfortably. "It's a really rich house," he added. As in *lord of the manor* rich. *I live here when I'm not on my private island* rich. Or *my rug costs more than your life* rich. "I'm guessing it's Cash's home."

Rhiannon took a deep breath, apparently steeling herself. "He's pretty old. He's had time to invest, right?" She laughed without much humor. "He's a Viking. Maybe he bought it with gold he stole from Lindisfarne."

"What's Lindisfarne?"

"The Viking Age is counted from the sacking of Lindisfarne, the first major raid on a church."

"Oh."

She cleared her throat. "Pagan nerd joke."

Vince snorted. "Maybe he decorates with stolen reliquaries. Want to find out?" Some buttons were attached to the visor, and he hit what he'd initially thought was a garage door opener. The gate opened in front of them, the two sides parting in elegant slowness. He looked to Rhi as the reality of Cash's position sunk in. "He's one of their queen's fledglings. I guess that makes him like a prince. Charlie is good friends with a prince." He frowned, resentment growing. "And he never introduced me to him. That takes 'hiding the gay boyfriend' to a new level."

"Maybe he didn't mean it that way." She didn't sound convinced, though.

"Yeah, yeah. Protecting me. Whatever." Maybe it was both.

"Does Charlie have this sort of bank too?" Rhiannon asked as they passed through the gate. "Isn't, like, everyone over a hundred capable of being a multimillionaire?"

Vince laughed. "No. I mean, he's not worried about money or anything, which is rare for someone in his line of work. But he lives in a small house he built himself in the twenties and drives a fifty-year-old car—he's not sporting a Piaget and driving a Lambo."

"What're a Piaget and a Lambo?"

"A watch that costs more than my annual income and a Lamborghini. The car."

"Oh."

He smiled faintly as they came up to the four-car garage, and he hit the second button. "Sorry. Fashion nerd joke."

As Rhi pulled into a spot, Emma spoke up for the first time from the back of the van. "Charlie's rich as fuck. Not quite like this, but after a certain point, I figure it don't make much difference."

Rhi hit the brakes too hard, sending herself and Vince lurching into the seat belts. Behind them, Cash's body dropped off the bench seat with a thump. "Excuse me? While Vince worked at a strip club to make ends meet?"

"I like my job," Vince parroted yet again. To be fair, he added, "Besides, Charlie told me I didn't have to work." Still, the idea of Charlie being effortlessly rich didn't sit well with him. Vince had thought his contributions were at least helpful, if not strictly necessary. But if Charlie had millions stashed away, he must've thought the comparative pittance Vince provided in rent was cute.

And the rationale that Vince had taken his job for money? That would've meant less than nothing to him.

Vince grimaced and tried to keep cool, but Rhi was fired up. Money was a tough subject for her, seeing as she'd always been without it. Charlie holding out on him—from her perspective, at least—would be a mortal sin.

"Tell me you would be taking your clothes off for strangers if you knew Charlie was loaded. You wouldn't. You would've finished high school without the burden of a job outside the smithy and would've been serious about your art when you got out."

He shifted uncomfortably. "Not like I'll ever make ends meet with it."

"You don't know that because you've never tried—and it wouldn't freaking matter if you had a multi-millionaire boyfriend supporting you and your work."

What was so ironically stupid was that Charlie would've been happier and financially no worse off if Vince had treated him like a free ride. Or, no, like an old-fashioned patron, the wealthy aristocrats who used to support artists in the old days.

He looked back at Charlie, crumpled in a sunsleeping heap on the floor of the blacked-out van. His eyes were closed, and in the dim light Vince could just make out the freckles he loved and Charlie hated. It was too easy to lay blame and too simple to say *if only*. The truth was always more complicated than a single statement or accusation.

There were even days Vince wondered if breaking up had been good for him. Not because he and Charlie weren't amazing together. Nobody made him feel as capable or at ease in his own skin as Charlie did. But despite all his protests about being an adult at eighteen, he'd grown up a lot in the time he'd been on his own.

He ducked his head, frustrated. "I would've taken the job anyway. I wanted to work, I wanted to thumb my nose at my father, and it sounded like a fun way to do it." It *had* been fun. The guys were great, the audience was hilarious, he kept in good shape, and it was good money for the work. If he had the same decision to make for his life right now? He'd spend more time at the anvil doing what he really loved.

Vince looked from Charlie to Emma, who was listening with interest, and tried not to bristle. "Yes, I'm a stripper."

That got a shrug. "I ain't one to judge. I was a whore." She gathered Javier in a careless bundle under one arm and Cash under the other. "Mind pulling up a smidge and shutting the garage door so we sunlight-averse can head into the house? I ain't seen it yet."

After a black look at Charlie, Rhiannon complied. "How rich is he?"

"I don't know, but CoVIn's been investing for its members since the early 1800s. When you gain full membership at your hundredth year, you're guaranteed at least a million. Or you were back in 1937, when I gained full membership. I don't know what it is now." She opened the sliding door and hopped out like she was carrying pillows and not two full-grown men. Javi's and Cash's hands dangled to the floor and dragged along behind her. She didn't notice or didn't care as her voice turned serious. "Guess I need to learn that, seeing as I'm a sire now. Shit. I got a fledgling." She headed for the door to the inside, chattering nervously. "At least Cash picked a looker of a place this time. Not like that crazy house in Cali. I like this one."

Vince undid his seat belt and slowly got out. Rhiannon, though, hustled out and followed her brother, trying to scoop up any body parts that dragged the ground.

Emma kept talking. "Cash has this house in California designed by some fancy-pants architect, Franklin Right or something."

"Frank Lloyd Wright?" Vince asked, trying to get Charlie off the floor of the van without dragging his face across it. "Cash owns a Frank Lloyd Wright home?"

"Yeah, that's him. It's ugly. Charlie convinced him to get it while we were all drunk in Monte Carlo a few years back. Went on and on about revolutionary stylistic influences of yada yada. But I don't get it."

Charlie, the one percenter, picked locks and went on rescue missions. He also toured the world's finest gambling halls, got drunk, and helped idiots buy national treasures. It was like Vince had never met the man.

Emma grinned at him as he caught up with her, carrying his ex like a child. "You know, you can drag him by the ankles and he won't know the difference. He's dead to the world and will heal up any damage afore he wakes."

Vince was exhausted, beaten, ready to sleep for a week, and his arms, normally strong, were barely holding up under the weight. But he held Charlie closer, unable to treat him so callously.

Emma snickered. "You're so cute with him."

As worried as Charlie was about everyone hating on gays, Cash didn't seem bothered, and Emma was taking it in stride. "You don't care, do you?" It came out half a question and half a statement. He hated that he had to even ask—the world should be past caring. But as Charlie continued to point out, he was dealing with people who grew up a long time ago.

They headed through an empty cavern of a workshop—a damn cool space with plenty of room for two and a rolling door for air circulation that he thought might look out over the lake. Next came a kitchen that could cook for a party.

Emma looked around it with interest but didn't stop. "I did mention being a whore, right? If you're down with me being a hooker, I ain't got no cause to complain about you being a Nancy."

"What did you say?" Rhiannon exclaimed, dropping her

brother's head to bounce off the Saltillo tile. "Ooh! Sorry, Javi!"

Vince shook his head. He was too exhausted to be offended. "I think I'm going to start a vampire awareness campaign for appropriate terminology for LGBTQ people."

Emma's face lit up in a smile. "Good luck with that." She sounded surprisingly earnest. "Hey, I'm getting a drink and making cookies after we drop these loads off. What's your favorite kind? I'll pour you a human drink if you ain't too tired. I owe you one for rescuing my ass. And Javi's. Damn, I have a baby bat. You can join us too, uh, Rhi, right? You're his sister, huh?"

"Yeah," Rhiannon said, expression so confused and worried as she stared at her inert brother.

They reached a central staircase that rose up in true mansion fashion to wings leading right and left. Vince thought that later he'd be impressed. Right now it looked like a lot of stairs to carry Charlie up. "I'm diabetic. I don't usually eat cookies. And at the moment, I'm going to sleep on the nearest horizontal surface."

Rhiannon had her brother's head again. "I'm crashing too."

Vince adjusted Charlie's weight and turned to Emma, serious. "Thank *you* for rescuing *my* ass. You could've gotten out if you hadn't stopped to get me."

She winked. "I guess we're even then." Together they started up the stairs. "Diabetes…that's the sugar pee disease, right? You don't die from that no more?"

"Insulin shots."

"Hoo-ey, the times they have a'changed. I like the twenty-first century."

Vince looked down at the man in his arms and thought of the possibilities they could have that hadn't existed even fifty years ago—much less in the 1700s, when Charlie had been human. Trick was, Charlie couldn't see them.

Vince still didn't know if Charlie even wanted to, at least with him. But now that they were talking again, he'd get a chance to find out if the ashes of what they'd burned five years ago held cinders or a phoenix.

Chapter 8

The downstairs of Cash's mansion smelled like chocolate chip cookies, and suddenly Vince was ravenous. He'd slept restlessly in a room the size of his apartment. Too much space for one person. He was tired, but it was past lunchtime and he needed food more than sleep. Something other than cookies, though, good as they smelled.

He stretched and did a brief once over in the mirror. The bites on his arms itched and bruises around his torso had darkened, but nothing stood out as particularly torturous. His wrists were the worst—bitten and cut into from the manacles.

A wave of fear made him lightheaded, and he shot out of the room, ready to be with people—even if they weren't people.

After glancing in on Charlie—still out—he jogged downstairs to the kitchen. It was a comfortable room, airy with stainless steel appliances and butcher-block countertops. A large, rustic table took up one side near a bank of heavily curtained windows. Eight could sit with room to spare.

The counters were full of cookies, jars of sauce, chopped vegetables, and... was that pâté? Cash sat on one of the only empty countertops with a black mug full of steam. His chin-length hair was down and sleep rumpled, and his vintage T-shirt read, "Gee, I wish I were a man. I'd join the Navy!"

He used the mug as a shield as Emma tried to hand him a plate. "No. I don't eat mini-quiches. I drink blood. Vampire. Grr argh." He motioned toward Vince with his mug. "Feed it to the human."

Emma popped the concoction into her mouth. "Grumpy-pants." Apparently vampires could eat mini-quiches. "Mornin'!" She set the plate down and pointed toward another on the table. One of his backpacks was on the floor beneath. "There's a bag of your stuff. Rhi told us what to get, and Cash sent someone. Oh, and Javier ended up with your phone last night. It's charging." She picked up his phone—hallelujah—and set it back on the counter. He'd check his messages later, after he'd figured out what the hell to say. He breathed better at the sight of his stuff, of the kitchen full of normalcy—even if he was among vampires—and the faith that they could keep him safe here.

Emma kept going, pointing at a plate of lumpy, cookie-ish things. "On the table are experimental Vince-safe cookies. They're made from pumpkin and peanut butter and dark chocolate and dates."

He lifted his eyebrows. "That's experimental, all right." But it was sweet. She'd made something special for him. He unzipped his bag and sorted through clothes, toiletries… and, bingo, his monitor, lancets, strips, and bottles of insulin. Relief unclenched every muscle in his body as he unzipped the clear bag of safety. Sure, Charlie had picked him up stopgaps last night, and he appreciated it, but these were his. "Thank you, for the bag and the cookies. I'll try them after I inject."

"Brave fool," Cash said. "Want some coffee to go with that debacle? I've got a coffeepot somewhere in this kitchen explosion."

Vince tipped his head at Cash's coffee mug, then realized it probably wasn't full of coffee. Weird. But he could deal with that. "I think I'm going back to sleep. I just need food." He pricked a finger and put the drop in his meter.

"Oh, I got plenty of that." Emma motioned at the counters. "Cooking keeps me calm. It'll be nice to have someone round here who'll appreciate it." She shot a friendly glare at Cash, who grinned back, showing off dimples.

It was weird being back around vampires. And unlike Charlie, they weren't trying to hide it. Cash talked about blood. Emma pulled items from the oven without gloves and stirred her batter with the speed of an electric mixer.

It was odd but refreshing, like they felt they had nothing to hide.

His glucometer beeped.

"What are you doing?" Cash asked.

The results weren't bad, considering what a whacked-out twelve hours he'd had. He liked to keep a tight rein on his blood sugar. It was a pain in the ass to do so many readings and injections a day, but there were fewer chances for complications later in life. "Testing blood glucose levels."

"That means nothing to me."

"He's got the honey piss disease," Emma explained. "People don't die from that no more. Ain't modern medicine cool?"

Vince snorted. "You'll still die from it if you don't treat it. I need an insulin injection. Anyone care if I do it in here?"

Cash looked at him like he'd lost his mind. "Are you dropping your trousers? Or do you think vampires are afraid of needles?"

Vince laughed. "Good point. No pun intended. It's in my stomach, not my ass." He readied a syringe and started to lift his shirt. Then realized the room was absolutely silent as both vampires watched him intently, like this was fascinating. "I'm not going to draw blood." He lifted his shirt for people four nights a week; it made no sense to get shy now. Even if he did feel strangely self-conscious. Shaking his head to clear the feeling, he ignored them, finished the injection, and picked up a cookie. It would be better if he waited awhile to eat, but whatever. He was hungry.

"And now you don't die?" Emma asked, voice full of awe.

"Not for a few decades, anyway. Provided I do this several times a day for the rest of my life."

"Shit." Her word came out like it had at least three syllables. "Modern medicine's amazing."

She whistled something cheerful as she turned back to her cooking. Cash, though, looked like he'd been struck by the lightning of epiphany. And didn't like it.

Vince narrowed his eyes in silent question, but Cash looked back at his table, unwilling to answer, leaving Vince no clue what that was about. Had Charlie said something to him?

Whatever. His life didn't revolve around Charlie anymore. Vince leaned back against the table. The scene was oddly homey, with Emma baking and Cash sipping a coffee mug that wasn't full of coffee while he tapped and swiped on his tablet. The two of them were absolutely comfortable around each other, and that ease carried over to him, like he was part of the group.

He shouldn't trust the feeling. It wasn't like he was finding family with a group of vampires living in a cliffside mansion on the lake. Still, it was nice, a sense of household community he hadn't experienced since he'd lived with Charlie, and even that had been tinged with the mania of love. This was just calm.

He bit into the cookie. The texture was off, like a crumbling brownie. But otherwise, it wasn't as bad as it should be. Which wasn't to say it was *good*.

Cash tipped his head, expression amused, and Vince followed the direction to a trashcan. Another bite of the cookie, just in case. No, definitely trash. Not worth the carb spike. Emma had her back turned.

"Thanks for the cookies," he said, edging toward the metal can.

"Damn. You threw it away, didn't you?"

"I, uh, no." Not yet. It was still in his hand.

"Just toss it. I didn't like 'em neither. I'm going to keep trying, though. You're gonna have good cookies from me one of these years."

"Thanks. I like mini-quiches," he added hopefully. He didn't usually eat crusts, but he could pull the centers out for eggy goodness. "And pâté." A rare treat.

"On the island. The quiches on the right—your right—are gluten-free if you want. I read about that on the internet. Apparently it's the in thing and a great way to move product. I've been doing some market research. These flours, though, they just don't work so well. But I'll figure it out." She turned back, hands empty and clothes covered in flour that would contaminate everything else in the kitchen, making it all very much not gluten-free.

It was funny how she was trying but didn't quite get it—like she was from a different culture. Which, he guessed, she was. He grabbed a couple mini-quiches and scooped some pâté with the provided carrots. One mini-quiche down the hatch, and he gawked, still chewing. "These are amazing." Maybe she *could* figure out a diabetic cookie that tasted good.

"Thanks, sweet pea. All right, civilities out of the way. We ready for business?"

Cash set his mug down and gave Vince a serious look. "CoVIn, the Confederation of Vampires International. How in with us do you want to be?"

"In?"

"You should've been registered whenever you first found out about vampires. Charlie didn't do it."

Vince's jaw clenched. Of course Charlie hadn't. Charlie had never considered him family. But Cash wanted to include him?

"I'm alerting CoVIn to your presence whether or not you agree. We need to keep tabs on who knows about us. But you can choose to join as a human affiliate and gain some benefits from it."

No, his inclusion wasn't personal; Cash was just following the law. Business it was. Vince could be all business, too. "Benefits like?"

Cash smiled. "The right to claim our protection from the Liberi, for one. The right to sue a CoVIn vampire in our courts. The right to attend some official functions. We're dedicating the new building next week, if you're interested in seeing what a vampire ceremony looks like. Of course, that part is boring as Helheim. The after-party, though, that's worth attending. Joining also allows you into our hiring pool. We're only allowed to hire nonregistered humans under very limited circumstances." Cash took another drink, his voice turning wry. "Strippers are as popular with us as with everyone else. Though you'll get paid significantly better if you're willing to get bitten."

"Nobody's drinking off of me." Except Charlie, maybe, if he were dying and really needed it. Or asked really nicely. *Damn, you are pathetic.* "I have skills other than stripping."

"Like?" Cash drank from his mug, going back to his tablet like he didn't give a shit.

If anyone appreciated his real work, though, it would be a Viking. Excitement chased any remaining tiredness away. This had potential. "Like blacksmithing."

The look in Cash's eyes said he didn't believe him. "Aw, that's cute. Got a hobby?"

"I've been studying since I was nine, thank you very much, and Charlie started buying handles and hinges from me when I was sixteen." Everyone else was super casual, so Vince sat on the table to drop his best bomb. "Few years back I was in a funk"—

IMMORTAL LONGING • 99

because the love of his life had dumped him—"so I took a six-month sabbatical to study with a master swordsmith. I can make an edge that'll cleanly slice a three-inch rope that's hanging free and then split paper. Strong and sharp."

Somewhere in there Cash had put the tablet down. He didn't blink as he slowly shook his head. "I don't believe you." But the lusty gleam in his eyes said he wanted to.

Vince shrugged. "Look me up. I'm a member of ABANA and ABS. That's Artist-Blacksmith's Association of North America and American Bladesmith Society. Vincent Pagano. ABS was featuring one of my knives last I checked." He laughed. "I do four shows a week at the club, plus practices." And made more in a week of doing that than he did in a good three months of smithing. "What do you think I do with the rest of my time? Netflix?"

The warrior vampire tried to look cool, stroking his chin all casually, but he practically had a boner at the thought of custom-made sharp things. "I'd be interested in seeing your work."

Vince tried to play it just as cool when he was dancing inside. A whole society of ungodly rich vampires from all eras of history? This had real potential. "I'll get you some samples. And yes. I'm very into CoVIn. Sign me up. I'll go to your parties. Even the boring ones."

Cash made a thoughtful noise and nodded, a light in his eyes.

After a rocky start, Vince found himself liking Cash quite a bit.

"Em. Your turn. What the fuck happened to you, and why do you have a baby bat? Congrats, by the way." He grinned at her.

She blushed and waved a hand at him like it wasn't a big deal, then shoved a tray of crudités at Vince. "Eat whatever you want, sugar."

"He can, but you might want to warn him what's in three-quarters of it," Cash said smoothly.

Emma rocked back on her heels, then forward into motion, putting several trays on the island. "You might want to stick with these things here."

She was baking blood into food? Human blood?

"Story," Cash prompted. "You had a dinner date. Then?"

Emma dusted her hands off, dumped butter and sugar into a bowl, and beat it with renewed mania. "I've been trying to remember what all happened. I thought I'd only been gone one night. Floored me when I found out I missed three days. I met Javier, and we went back to his place. We were attacked there, but I think they were after me—they already had Joe." Eggs and vanilla in next, she stirred the batter too fast and steady for a human baker. And she'd been doing it all morning. "I turned Javi because he got injured real bad and they threatened to turn him. I figured better me than them. We were taken to the tunnels separate from Joe. I don't know what happened to Joe next, but he came back to us totally on his own, no guard. I thought we were escaping, but instead Joe bit me, and that's when things got fuzzy. Three fricking days of fuzzy." From the refrigerator she pulled a canary-yellow carton branded with cheerful fonts and poured an unmeasured cup of red liquid into the batter.

Vince paled. Blood cookies? Emma was back to beating like it was the most normal ingredient in the world. Cash shook his head at her, but Vince got the impression his disgust had to do with the batter, not the blood.

What had Cash and Charlie said about humane harvest blood? It was one thing to bite Javier during a one-night stand. Whatever got your kink on. But cartoned blood? Charlie had drunk bottled every afternoon after waking, and Vince had never asked, just pretended everything was normal. He couldn't do that anymore. Not if he was getting involved. "Where did that come from?"

Emma's hand never stilled as she blinked out of her story and focused on Vince. "What? The blood?"

"Yeah." Vince stared at the carton.

"This being Cash's house—and him letting me use it without fussing, so it ain't select source—I'm supposing it's paid donor. I get mixed bank, but he's fancy." She picked up the carton to read the label. "Yup. Paid donor."

"You pay people to donate blood?" That wasn't bad. He knew a few people who made pretty good money that way.

Were vampires drinking their blood?

"Yup. Well, I don't personally. Fred's Red does." She turned the label toward him. "So do Elixir and Hemo-Pack."

"What are mixed bank and select source?"

"Mixed bank is blood bank rejects. Cheapest way to get blood sans fillers. Some companies'll add animal blood to their cheapest lines, but my system don't do so well with that." She shrugged. "I can't eat meat no more. Ain't that funny? Some folks can. I ain't so lucky. But I can eat cake all day and not gain a pound! Anywho. Select source means it's specific in some way, like all type O or it comes from witches—that's Cash's favorite, and it ain't cheap at all. Select source almost always comes from paid donors."

Cash went to the sink and rinsed his mug. "When the packaged market came out, there were some problems with the supply chain. But CoVIn came down on offenders. We have a certification board now that inspects all facilities and rates them. Even one failing grade gets you shut down. Charlie, actually, was instrumental in creating the humane harvest process. Not that most vampires know it. He writes reports, and I present them."

Charlie the activist? That was pretty cool. "Why doesn't he give them himself?"

"You have met him, right?" Cash glanced over the food as he made his way back to his seat. "Will I like the fudge?"

"You'll like all of the food."

Cash's look said he wouldn't.

"You'll like the fudge."

"No nuts?"

"No. No nuts. I heard you in 1842 when you told me you don't eat chocolate with nuts. I heard you in 1860 and 1925 and last year and last week and every other time in our long acquaintance you've fucking told me you don't eat chocolate with nuts."

He took a piece and nibbled as he jumped back onto the counter, undaunted by her diatribe. "Charlie pointed out that I have more sway in CoVIn, so if we really wanted this to happen, I should be the poster boy. Much as I'd rather he get the credit, he's not wrong and this is important, so I agreed." He took a bigger bite, then reached across the counter to swipe a second one. "The fudge is okay."

"Eat as much as you want of anything, sweet cheeks."

"I don't eat human food."

"Says the man with a mouth full of fudge."

"Chocolate, coffee, and alcohol transcend barriers." He popped the remainder of the first piece into his mouth and talked around it. "Assuming our human is satisfied with CoVIn's food rights policies, I'd appreciate if you'd finish your story." The words were almost polite, but the tone was more *get your ass back on topic.* "You were on the fuzzy part."

She snorted. "I woke up in the middle of some party. Vince was there. Javier was too. I tried to get them out, but there was this guy there, this man in a mask. He was bad news. Broke my neck. I woke up in a cell with Javi. He'd straightened me out—or my neck, anyway. I think my fledgling might be a doctor? We got

Vince out but got ourselves caught, and that's how you found me attached to a wall."

Emma formed cookies, rolling and flattening the dough with precision, the delicacy of her movements at odds with the painful weight of her next words. "They killed Joe. I think I was in the room when he dusted in front of me, and I don't think I cared. Which is wrong because I love that crazy son of a gun. It's like three days living in a bad dream. Honestly, I'm glad I don't remember more."

"You think you were drugged?" Cash asked.

She shoved the pans into the oven. "I ain't been on many drugs to compare by. But I don't think so. It was nothing like being drunk. Drunk is like… it's like you're more like yourself. You don't give a shit what other people think so caution goes out the window. This wasn't like that. It was like something was missing and I couldn't fill the hole, so I just consumed." She turned back, eyes red and sad. "If I had to guess, I'd say they made me one of them for three days—that I know what it is to have no soul. And my god, it's awful."

Vince stopped with a mini-quiche halfway to his mouth, a bad feeling curdling inside. "You said they got your sire first, and the change happened when he bit you?"

"Yeah."

Vince turned to Cash. "She changed back right after he died. It's connected. What if the disease or whatever can be passed down the line like you guys initially passed down your souls?" His shoulders tensed in worry. "They have Charlie's sire."

Cash glared at the tile floor. "And we left him there."

Vince shook his head, the worry growing. "A spell, involving cutting out people's hearts, was cast on Joe—or maybe Joe's sire? They kidnapped Joe's fledgling so he could pass it to her, and she passed it to her fledgling in turn. But when they staked Joe, everything went back to normal. So they have—what's his name, Ramón? So they're going to go after Charlie. If we stake Ramón—"

Cash waved a hand at him. "Whoa. That's a lot of supposition on very little information." He swiped another piece of fudge. "Unfortunately it's better than anything I can come up with at the moment. If they've found a way to disconnect awen, we've got a problem." He hopped off the counter. "Em, you okay for a few?"

"Yup. I'm using all your ingredients. Which I assume is fine as you don't eat them."

He waved a hand. "They stocked before I moved in. Knock yourself out. Pagano, take a walk with me."

Vince slid off the table and retrieved his phone from the charger. "Ooh. He calls me by my actual name. Am I in trouble?"

Cash held the kitchen door open but wasn't looking at him. "Who stocks a vampire's pantry with human food?"

Okay, Cash was giving no clues. "We need to protect Charlie," Vince insisted as he passed through the door. Cash followed.

"We need to protect *you*. You have about a week before the Liberi forget your scent. Stay here until then where we can watch out for you. Consider it a vacation. I'll invite Charlie to stay too, at least until we disprove your theory. This place is too big for one person."

A week in this place? "Sure. I'd love to." It was a fantasy house. He hadn't gone exploring yet, but based on what he'd seen so far, poking around here would make a stellar afternoon. "Why'd you buy it if it's too big?"

"Have you seen the pool?" Cash laughed. "I didn't say it was too big. I said it was too big for one person. When I grew up, everyone slept in the longhouse together. Or in the boat together or the field. I know people live alone now, but that's just weird. I need a house I can fill with folk who don't annoy me too much." The door shut behind them and stuck with a thump as Cash continued at a leisurely pace toward the stairs. "Emma said you were surprised by Charlie's net worth."

That was not at all the conversational direction Vince had expected. "She seems to have an inflated opinion of Charlie's finances. What does this have to do with anything?" He knew exactly what it had to do with everything. Cash thought the stripper had dated Charlie for his money. Maybe he still thought that was where his interest lay.

But regardless of whether or not Vince still wanted his ex, as Charlie had pointed out, nothing that kept them apart had changed. Vince was going to grow old and die. Meanwhile he worked at a strip club. Charlie couldn't publicly acknowledge their relationship. He looked at himself as Vince's protector and provider…kind of like that other nasty "p" word, *parent*.

They could want each other with a fiery passion. Didn't make them right for each other.

On the other hand, they could be as wrong for each other as possible. Didn't change how much Vince wanted to head upstairs and lie down next to him.

"When did you get diagnosed?"

Another non sequitur. "When I was eleven. You are a font of random questions." But maybe he was about to find out why Cash had shot him such an electrified look earlier.

Instead of heading up, Cash leaned against the railing of the stair. "He can't turn you. Did he tell you that?"

A shudder went through Vince, and he crossed his arms to hide it. "Yeah. Both of you seem to assume I want to be immortal. I don't. I'd like a long life. But I'm at peace with it ending. No offense, but you guys are not the natural order of things." Besides, he had memories he'd rather not hang on to for eternity. More now than he'd had yesterday.

One thing, though, that kept him up at night was wondering if his inability to turn was really why Charlie had broken it off. He couldn't be a vampire, so Charlie could never look at them as permanent. If that was it, Vince wished Charlie would tell him. Maybe he'd finally be able to give up on them if he knew the breakup wasn't all the fault of his stupid lie.

Or maybe he'd just be that much angrier.

"Vampires don't live forever."

Vince shook his head. "Yeah. You die fighting witches and Liberi and were-rats, and I don't even know what else is out there."

"No. That's just soldiers like me. Everyone else… have you ever heard of a bell?"

"They ring?"

"Traditionally when someone dies."

Vince leveled a serious look at him. "The cryptic act is getting old, prince of the vampires. I'm tired and worried about Charlie, and yesterday sucked. Can we get to the point?"

Cash smirked, seeming pleased with Vince's insolence. "Vampires, because we don't die naturally, get to decide when our bell tolls. For example, I knew somebody who wanted to fly. He always said that was his bell. Sure enough, after four hundred years of living he got on an airplane for the first time in 1914, flew from St. Petersburg, Florida, to Tampa, and his angel was there to take his life. The airplane was his bell. He got to fly, and he was done."

That was nuts. "He said, 'Kill me when I get off the plane,' and somebody did? Why?"

"Suicide is challenging for a vampire. *You* try beheading yourself. We can greet sunrise—we call it kissing dawn—but burning to death is more glamorous in poetry than practice. Once you catch fire, you don't sleep as survival instincts kick in, and it takes more willpower than most have to do anything other than run for cover while your flesh and muscle burns. It's tradition to designate a death angel, somebody who'll do the deed cleanly and quickly."

The whole idea was so foreign to someone raised Catholic, where taking your own life was a grave sin. Vince tried to wrap his brain around it. "Assisted suicide."

Cash watched him for a moment, letting it sink in before adding, "To quote an awesome movie, 'Do you want to live forever?'"

"I already said no," Vince said slowly. Would it still be a sin if your life had been unnaturally extended? It wasn't like four hundred years was cutting God's gift short. And did he even believe in sin anymore? Not really. Charlie did, though. "But an airplane flight?"

Cash just shrugged like he didn't get it, but it didn't matter. "It was his thing. Everybody's got a thing. Sometimes it's a city that falls or an event that passes. So much changed in the twentieth century a lot of immortals—not just vampires, but all kinds—decided it was time. The millennium change was a mass bell. There were death parties. It was weird." Cash shook his head like mass suicide was irritating. "The most common reason to decide it's time, though, is a particular human has died." Another pause.

Vince fidgeted, not liking where this was going.

"Around Ostara five years ago, Charlie asked if I'd consider being his angel one day."

In March five years ago, Charlie and Vince had still been boyfriends. Cash's implication wasn't correct, and yet tears pricked at Vince's eyes. "It wasn't because of me. I don't know why he asked you that, but it had nothing to do with me." He shoved away from the railing and started up before he freaked out in the hallway. Four stairs in, though, he couldn't help turning back. "What was your answer?"

"I told him to give me a couple of months to think about it. He didn't bring it up again, so neither did I. Not something I really wanted to talk about with my friend."

A couple of months later they'd broken up. Agitated, Vince backed upward a few steps. "I'm glad you were going to tell him no."

Cash made slow progress toward him. "I didn't want to talk about it because my answer is yes. I don't want to be the way my friend meets his maker, but I'll do it right. He won't hurt or have time to be afraid. There are worse ways to go than me." Suddenly they were toe to toe.

He'd seen Cash fight. He believed him. The image of Cash shoving that fancy stake of his through Charlie's heart and watching Charlie turn to dust made him shake in anger. How could anyone do that to a friend?

He looked at the floor as his mind dredged up another image, one he'd conjured too many times when contemplating the future. He was old and in a hospital bed, waiting for the candle to blow out. Charlie, if he were even present, where would he be? Would he come pay his respects while his new, young lover waited respectfully outside? Or would Charlie still be his boyfriend, sitting by the bedside holding Vince's hand, still looking thirty-five with centuries ahead of him? Either way held all of death's bleakness without the reunification.

A new version of the scene crystallized with a clarity that made Vince want to weep. Instead of the hospital, they were home. Charlie held him in the bed they'd shared. When the time came, they left together, as connected in death as they had been in life.

No, that wasn't how it was. They weren't in love like that. But his voice cracked with the emotion of what couldn't be. "If Charlie loved me enough to tie his death to mine, why didn't he tell me any of this himself? Why did he kick me out without a fight? Why did I never meet you or any of his friends? Charlie and I weren't real. I didn't understand that at the time, but I see it now. I never realized how much he didn't tell me."

"You failed to mention something pretty big yourself."

"My job? Yeah, I know. I knew he'd disapprove, and I was young and stupid." It was weird talking about this with someone he'd just met, but after last night and this morning, Cash didn't feel like a stranger. He knew it all anyway, being one of Charlie's best friends. "But this whole life of his isn't a part-time job. It's everything. And none of his secrets offend me. There was no reason to keep them."

Cash frowned thoughtfully. "You lied because you were worried he'd disapprove of your choices. But you like being a stripper."

Vince felt his back straighten. "Yeah, it's fun. And there's nothing wrong with it. And it pays damn well."

"Dude, I don't give a fuck what you do. Just consider this, and then I'm done talking about it. Charlie avoids Modron and everybody other than me as much as possible, which he did centuries before he met you and continued doing after you two broke up. I thought he was going to vomit when I told him we were moving HQ to Austin. None of that is about you. He's one of the most humanlike vampires I've ever met."

Vince took another step up, trying to wrap his brain around that as Cash kept pace. "But he's not human."

"Right. But while you were hiding who you want to be from him, he worked hard to show you exactly who he wants to be.

Sounds like both of you were trying to impress each other instead of being yourselves." They reached the top of the stairs, and Cash turned toward the master suite, then stopped in front of the door. "Thanks for not being a nineteen-year-old gigolo fucking my friend for his money, like I thought you were."

Vince stood rooted to the top of the stairs as Cash disappeared into his room. If Cash was right—and that was a big if, but if he was—Vince had been thinking about his relationship with Charlie all kinds of wrong. Problem was, he didn't know what to do about that.

He dragged his feet past the room where he'd put Charlie on the way to his own lonely space. He was tired, but he didn't want to go back. He hadn't slept well. Too many nightmares.

Now he had a new one. What if Charlie had meant for them to be forever, and he'd fucked it up?

He slid backward on his bare feet until Charlie's door was on his left. He shouldn't go in there.

He pushed open the door. Charlie was out completely on the bed, tucked in as Vince had left him, instead of tossing him on top of the covers like Emma had with Cash and Javier.

Clearly Cash hadn't minded.

Still, it felt better to see Charlie reclining in a comfortable position. Vince moved closer to the bed. Charlie wouldn't know the difference if he was huddled in a mass or sleeping like a human. He also wouldn't know if Vince lay on top of the covers next to him.

He had no business being here, but Cash had opened an old wound that ached afresh. Looking at Charlie's ginger lashes and angular jawline and thinking of all the maybes and might-have-beens made walking away an impossibility. He felt safe here, only here with Charlie.

Fuck it. His ex woke up at two fifteen like clockwork. Vince set his alarm for two. He'd be out before Charlie knew anything. And maybe lying next to him, Vince could get some sleep.

He stretched out on the bed and breathed in the woodsy scent he missed so much. Charlie's sandy-red hair was wild, his freckles stark in the light leaking around the drapes. But none directly hit him, so it was okay. When he was sunsleeping, Charlie completely relaxed, probably for the only time in his life. Vince used to love watching him wake up, going from stillness to life in the space of a breath. It was like a miracle every afternoon.

Charlie's slack face looked younger without a single line on it or smirk twisting his lips. He'd still look like this in fifty years when Vince looked like an old man. If they were together, that would be okay with him. Maybe not completely okay. But worth it.

One work-rough hand was curled into a loose fist beside Charlie's chin. Vince slid his fingers between Charlie's, relishing the scrape of calluses and knotty muscles that came from a life of hard work. His fingers had cooled in the frosty temperature the Viking kept his house. The coolness was strange but okay. They would warm up in the afternoon when he awoke.

A yawn overtook Vince as peace filled his chest. He could sleep now.

Chapter 9

They used to sleep naked, Vince curled around him in an embrace that kept him warm all day. Instead of alone and cold, Charlie would wake up with feeling in his limbs and a slow breath at his neck. He would turn in Vince's arms to watch the last few minutes of his sleep, rejoicing in the perfect companionship he'd never thought he would find. He'd wanted it to last forever.

Once again, Vince's breath was the first thing Charlie heard as he awoke. He inhaled, senses alert and eyes open. Musk and soap, blood that was a little sweet. The room smelled like Vince.

He turned over and there the man was, not holding him this time, but curled up on top of the comforter facing him, one hand clutching the sheets.

Vince had been amazing last night, battling his fear and that damn witch with the same fortitude. And then he'd gotten Charlie safely here, to Cash's—unless something had gone wrong.

Charlie took a brief glance around at the high ceilings, velvet drapes, and... a bed he was pretty sure he'd made in the early 1800s during an Oriental phase. Definitely Cash's new place.

Vince couldn't possibly be comfortable. Not only was it cold in here, but Vince liked the weight of a blanket on him, even in August. They were on the wrong sides, too. Vince was supposed to be on the left. It felt off.

He removed the phone from Vince's grip. A timer was set to go off in five minutes.

Five minutes? It took him a moment to figure it out. Vince

thought he still woke up at two fifteen and was planning to leave before that. He should be mad, but he'd woken up with Vince. Every night was better that started with Vince. After carefully using Vince's thumb to bypass his lockscreen, Charlie turned off the alarm.

Carefully as he could, he pulled the covers back, slid Vince onto his own side, and covered him in blankets. That was better.

He'd be even more comfortable without his jeans on.

Charlie's gaze traveled down the sleeping man's body, and he swallowed heavily. No. He went to the other side, out of temptation's reach. It was one thing to move Vince from above the covers to beneath them. It was another to take his pants off.

And despite his heavy slumber, it would probably wake him up.

He shouldn't be doing this at Cash's house anyway. And yet here he was, sliding under the sheets. Vince's heat and proximity made his skin burn. He settled into a comfortable position with his back to his ex, enjoying the quiet nearness.

Vince rolled onto his side, like he had every night they'd been together, as Charlie slid sideways. The pattern was so natural, the movement of their bodies in this ritual as practiced as a dance. Charlie didn't know how it happened, whether he scooted back too far or Vince reached out first, but Vince's arm slipped around him. With a muscle memory Charlie didn't think he'd ever lose, he shifted to fit his body against Vince's. Their fingers interlocked, and he clutched Vince's hand against his chest.

Perfection.

He swallowed thickly and froze, wishing to hang on to the moment a little longer before someone realized what a bad idea this was and let go.

"Good afternoon," Vince whispered, his voice gravelly with sleep.

That rasp was all it took. Suddenly Charlie was awake, alert, and ready to make all kinds of mistakes. They'd had sex almost every afternoon after waking up, and as if it had been programmed, his body was ready.

Every day. Vince had wanted him every day, and each time he'd felt blessed.

He turned slowly to face his ex. He hadn't been this nervous since the first time they woke up together. Just like then, he had no idea what would happen next. Unlike then, last night wasn't a memory to cherish.

Vince was smiling, his hair flopping in front of one eye.

Why had this man ever wanted him? Vince was so damnably handsome it awed him, made him sigh like a lovesick poet of overwrought verse. It wasn't fair. Those blue eyes could fasten on him, and it didn't matter what Vince requested next, Charlie's answer was yes.

It was why he'd left the way he did. If he'd stayed for a rational conversation, he'd have let Vince walk all over him.

Even now, without thinking about it, he had his hand in Vince's hair, brushing the stray curl back. "Your hair is longer."

Vince tugged on Charlie's shaggy hair. "Your hair is longer too. Need someone to cut it later?"

"Yes." His response was too breathless.

"Cutting it yourself is that bad, huh?"

No, he just wanted Vince's hands in his hair again. "Am I taking advantage of you?"

"You rescued me from unspeakable evil last night. I'll cut your hair today. We'll call it even. Sound good?"

Charlie grinned at the joke. Did anyone know that he and Vince were in the same room, smiling like children with a secret? A knot of fear formed in his stomach, but he ignored it. Vince had come to him. After last night, Vince deserved whatever he wanted.

Vince snagged Charlie and pulled them together.

It might be a bad idea, but he couldn't find the strength to care. He'd been so angry—and that wasn't entirely gone—but the disappointment had faded. It had only been a couple of months before the breakup that Charlie had started to believe they had a future, that somehow this vivacious, joyful, nineteen-year-old god had settled on him and it could work. Now he realized that was crazy. But at the time, just looking at Vince had spun his head and made him believe six, seven, eight, *a hundred* impossible things before breakfast.

Right now was like the beginning had been, enjoying the present for the sake of the present with no worries or hopes for a future that didn't exist.

He enjoyed cuddling with Vince very much. He nestled his face against Vince's neck, the side without the bite, and closed his eyes. Vince's hands ran down his back in a soothing rhythm, more comforting than sexual.

It reminded him of a time they'd lain in his bed and listened to a thunderstorm showering the metal roof. They'd been together for about a month, and it had been the first time they'd held each other without sex. Touching for the sake of touching.

"How can we still do this?" Vince asked. "It shouldn't feel normal."

Charlie shrugged. "It's like that with some people. Time can pass—decades—and I see them again and it's as if we never split up, just acquired new stories to tell." He felt his face heat up. "But those are just friends."

"Is Cash one of them?"

The jealousy was gone from his voice, but Charlie still hesitated when he answered, "Yes." Vince didn't react, just continued stroking his back, and for some reason, Charlie kept talking. "Cash and I shouldn't be friends. We're nothing alike." Vince and Cash were a lot alike, actually. Both of them were enthusiastic and adventurous, friendly and well loved.

On the other hand, Cash wasn't the kind of man you could stay up late working on a project with, swapping jokes and comparing ideas on angles and negative space. And there was nothing sweet about him, no hopeful grins or cajoling tones. Things Vince excelled at. No, Cash listened—which was his saving grace—but he made decisions quickly and marched forward, expecting everyone to follow. Vince wanted to hold hands and walk together.

God, Charlie missed that. He missed Vince.

Vince tickled him in the ribs, making him smile. "I think you appreciate people who push you to do new things. Cash and I both do that." Vince's voice rumbled lower. "Now that I know you weren't having an affair in Vegas, I think he's pretty cool."

"I don't know why you were worried. That man has never had a gay thought in his twelve-hundred-year life."

Vince chuckled. "His loss."

The laughter was catching. "I know, right?" Vince's hands stopped as he rolled over enough that they could see eye to eye. He looked so serious that Charlie frowned. "What?"

"That's the first time I've ever heard you be positive about it."

"About what?" Oh, he knew exactly what Vince was talking about. But it was easier to play dumb.

"About being gay. You never bring it up, and when you do it's like it's something unfortunate. But it's awesome, right? I wouldn't change if I could."

"I'm glad you feel that way." Charlie didn't know what else to say. He knew what Vince expected of him, and like always, he wanted to please him. But he couldn't share the open pride Vince exhibited. So he looked away. "I accepted it a long time ago. I don't fear divine judgment anymore, either. But whether I'd change given the option is a pointless question. I can't change. It makes no sense to ponder whether I would."

Vince was still for so long Charlie feared he'd offended him. But he couldn't be proud of something he had no control over. Vince's father, the man who'd introduced them at the woodshop, had kicked Vince out of the house when he came out. It was an atrocious thing to do, and Charlie had made sure the man was never welcome in the shop again. But if Charlie had breathed even a hint to his master, the man who'd raised him since he was six, Charlie wouldn't have been kicked out the house. He'd have been beaten to death, and the town he grew up in would've condoned it as righteous.

But instead of censuring his lack of enthusiasm, Vince grinned at him. "You'd never have dated me if you were straight, and that's an irreconcilable loss."

Charlie found his gaze again, his sense of humor returning. "It was worth all the years of bigotry and despair just for you." The way he said it sounded light, like a joke. But he meant it.

Vince's smile turned into a wicked curl that boded no good. "Damn right."

The subject needed to be changed before playful turned dangerous. "I wouldn't be a vampire if I were straight."

That did the job of distracting Vince. "Why not?" He propped his head on his hand, listening like it interested him.

"Ramón—you saw him last night at the Liberi prison—has a habit of seducing and turning gay men, then leaving before we wake up. He was traveling through Prayssus, my hometown, on the way to Agen, a more respectable-sized city, and there I was."

"You woke up with no idea you were a vampire? Talk about

a serious hit and run."

"It was confusing." Maybe he should tell Vince more. The past still stung, but at least now he could see the humor in his ridiculousness. "That was an understatement. I think you know what happened with my neighbors."

Vince nodded slowly, his expression going darker.

"After they left the hill they'd, uh, taken me to"—dragged, throwing literal shit and rotten food the whole way—"and I realized I wasn't in Hell, I took the noose off. The way I got out of that tree would make excellent Monty Python fodder. I survived as a petty thief for a while. Cash and Galswinth found me outside a pub one night feeding off a drunk so I could feel something other than painfully sober. We can't get drunk without blood, so feeding off a drunk is, eh, efficient."

"I'm sorry you had to go through that." His eyes widened handsomely, the expression made more delectable by how earnest he looked. "But I'm glad you're a vampire because otherwise you wouldn't be here with me right now." Vince kissed him, a sweet, tentative touch that made him want to groan for more.

But he couldn't. He backed up. "We're not getting back together." The reasons they'd broken up hadn't changed.

Vince's mouth formed a word that looked like "Why," but he didn't make more sound than "Wuh" before he changed it to a noise of frustration. "I know that. Did I ask for a commitment? No. It's a kiss. Not a commitment."

A kiss wasn't normally a commitment, but Charlie had lost himself last time. Hell, he'd planned to tie his life to Vince's while Vince was spending half his nights with other people's hands down his pants. He still spent his nights that way. But pride wouldn't let Charlie admit that humiliating pain, so he grasped for some other reason. "You had a bad night—you're injured. I won't take advantage of you."

80 ♦ ©8

That was it. Vince was damn fed up with Charlie assuming he was too young or too fragile or too inexperienced to know his own mind. He wanted Charlie. Passionately. Deeply. Completely. He always had. He still did. They'd been talking, just like old days, days when they were friends and nights when they were lovers. He wanted all of it back. He wanted a second chance.

But even just one night was better than never again.

"Don't grab my wrists. Everything else is fine enough." If he was touching Charlie, he could ignore all kinds of aches and injuries. To prove his point, he shoved, and Charlie fell onto his back. Vince followed, leaning over him. He shifted until his ass went from near Charlie's hand to firmly in his grasp. Like he knew would happen, Charlie's fingers closed down, taking a handful. "Funny thing," Vince said, "I've never worried about taking advantage of you."

Charlie's breath picked up. "Of me?"

Vince dropped his hips down until his erection pressed through the thin fabric of his pants and rubbed Charlie's growing one. He lifted away, and Charlie gasped. His ex might play it cool, but Charlie's carnal response proved the steadfast attraction was mutual.

He could work with that. Slowly, Vince lowered his hips again until they touched Charlie's and slid their sexes one against the other with a bare friction that had Charlie's fingers squeezing him in sync.

"You may be older and richer and stronger. But I'm young. And I'm hot. And you still want to fuck me." He leaned closer so he could whisper against Charlie's ear. "I never got my breakup sex. It's not too late to remedy that." He told himself it was just that, just one more night. But he couldn't stop the hope that if he could get one more night, he could get two. And then three. And then the forever he'd lost.

"Breakup sex?" Charlie's voice was breathless, his hips starting to move in the rhythm Vince had started.

"Yeah. Where you give somebody one last hurrah before sending them out the door. I was supposed to get that." He worked to keep his voice steady. "Instead, you ran off to Vegas with another man."

Charlie opened his eyes in surprise and sputtered, "I didn't have your breakup sex with Cash. We went over that."

Vince stopped moving and put one hand on either side of Charlie's head, boxing him in. "Who did you have it with?"

Charlie's eyelids fluttered, his mouth moving like he had something to say. Vince didn't know if he wanted to hear it. But instead of an answer, Charlie grabbed a fistful of his T-shirt. "Come here." And he yanked.

Vince collapsed on top of him. The kiss was brutal, five years of pent-up anger and desire struggling to connect. Their tongues collided. Charlie's fingers dug into the muscles of Vince's ass, melding their bodies together as he ground his hips. The onslaught of sensation was as overwhelming as it was perfect.

Vince broke the kiss to suck in air. "I've grown up." He slid his hand down the back of Charlie's pants. "No more fumbling virgin. You're going to like it better." The skin of Charlie's ass was soft as he brushed his fingers downward, making a steady, slow path toward all the goodness between his legs.

Charlie stroked his face and touched his forehead to Vince's, gentle gestures for the violence of their coupling. "It was always better with you."

Vince froze up, eyes wide as he assessed Charlie's tone. He sounded honest. *Then why did we break up?* No. No, no. Don't go there. Charlie couldn't resist him before, and he wasn't resisting now. If now was all Vince had, he would take it for all it was worth.

He circled the pucker of Charlie's asshole, and his ex tensed with a pleasured gasp as his hands grasped at the air. Vince changed to teasing strokes on the sensitive skin between ass and sac. Charlie's gasp turned to moans as his hand found Vince's shirt and clenched. Charlie's leg slid further over Vince's hip, giving him better access.

Later, things would change. But right now Charlie was his. Vince nuzzled Charlie's hair, lust and love filling him with sadness and warmth. *A fuck to remember me by.*

Soon he would be a memory to Charlie. But to Vince, Charlie would never be less than everything he'd wanted and lost.

Charlie shoved at his shirt. "Get this off."

"Okay." Vince managed to keep his voice casual. As he removed his hand from Charlie, he touched every bit of skin he could from ass to back. "But you gotta take yours off too."

Nodding obediently, Charlie pulled his black T-shirt off, revealing his wiry frame and pale nipples.

"Good man." Vince took his own shirt off and pulled them back together. The way they should be.

Footsteps pounded outside the hallway, but Vince ignored them. The world could run its own course without them. Right now he had to kiss Charlie.

☙✦❧

The door opened with a gust of air and no sound.

Charlie broke away, desire popping in a prick of fear. He needed to apologize to Cash, then hopefully take a ribbing and have it over with.

But it wasn't Cash in the doorway. Charlie held still, fear lodging in his throat like a log of maple as his skin went cold. "Alaric…"

The queen's eldest son took up most of the doorframe. His face twisted into disgust as his gaze flipped between the men on the bed.

Damn. He was in a bed. With a man. In front of Alaric. Panic iced through Charlie as he scrambled away from Vince until he fell out of bed.

Alaric was physically the strongest vampire in CoVIn. He was crafty and well educated. He was also a flat-out bigot. He'd been friendly enough until he found out Charlie was gay, and then, like a switch, he'd changed. Cash didn't tend to realize when his joking hurt, but Alaric was smart enough to figure out what cut the hardest—and make it sound like a joke. When no one else was around, it wasn't just words he wielded. The main reason Charlie avoided CoVIn was to ensure he never accidentally met Alaric alone.

And now Alaric knew about Vince. Charlie had to get him out of here. And if he could, find a way to take the blame so Vince didn't have to.

"What the fuck is going on here? Does Cash know you're defiling his home?" His words came out harsh and clipped, with the vestiges of a Gothic accent he'd never completely lost.

Vince didn't realize the danger, though. Instead of keeping quiet, he shot Alaric the bird. "Get out. I'm trying to have sex with my ex-boyfriend here." To Charlie's continued horror, Vince reached down for him, trying to pull him back onto the bed.

Warning Vince with a glance and shake of his head, Charlie shoved backward but got more tangled in sheets.

Alaric pointed at Vince. "You, remove yourself. If you can't refrain from unnatural acts, leave my friend's house."

Charlie nodded, voice contrite and hands up, placating. "It's my fault. I forced him to come in here. He'll go—we'll both go— downstairs to the kitchen where everyone is." Or anywhere else where other people were. It shamed him to pander to jackasses like this, but he needed to protect Vince from Alaric's casual violence.

Vince looked at him like he'd lost his mind. "No. We're not going downstairs. What is this about you making me come in here? You're the out one now?" Bare-chested and sure of himself, he turned to face Alaric as alarm closed up Charlie's throat. "Cash invited me to stay the week. You can turn your prejudiced ass around and find the twenty-first century. Seriously, you vampires are a pack of bossy-ass bitches."

Alaric stormed toward them, his blue eyes wide in cold rage. "Did you just call me a bitch, you little cocksucking ass nugget?"

Finally Charlie got the sheets off. He grabbed his shirt, yanked it on, and tossed Vince his own. "Vince, we need to go." If Alaric would let them at this point. The vampire's face was white with anger.

Vince, pissed off beyond rationality, ignored his shirt and didn't get up. No, he grinned at Alaric with a devastating smile that made Charlie's heart stop. "Cocksucking ass nugget. The ass nugget is new. D-plus for effort there. But cocksucker?" Vince scooted forward, toward the edge of the bed. "That's a pathetic insult. You know why? Because I do suck cock. I like it. I am a damn proud cocksucker. You should try it sometime. Might loosen up your tight ass."

"Vince…" Charlie inched toward them, wondering if he picked Vince up and ran if they'd get downstairs before Alaric caught them, because right now that was looking like the best option.

Before he could make a decision, Vince got in Alaric's face, wearing no shirt and those jeans hanging off his hip bones. He looked so stunningly gorgeous in his futile bravery it made Charlie's heart stutter. "You know why I think it'd help? Because closet queens make the best homophobes."

The queen's eldest fledgling stared in gape-mouthed shock at his audacity.

For one moment Charlie thought he'd get away with it. That the sheer iron balls it took to lambaste Alaric to his face would make it work.

Then Alaric grabbed Vince around the neck and slammed him backward into the bed frame. Vince shook with the force of the impact, his head snapping forward. "You calling me a faggot, you little queer?"

"No!" Charlie's fury gave him speed. He ran to them, looking for something he could do—because if it came to wresting Alaric off Vince, even fury wouldn't do him any good. He forced his tone to remain calm, even if he wanted to scream. "Alaric, stop. We'll leave."

But still Vince wasn't quiet. He shoved ineffectually at Alaric. "You bet your ass-loving dick I'm calling you a queen."

Alaric slammed him again, harder, hard enough to leave more bruises when Vince already had too many.

Charlie forced himself between them, trying to push Alaric back. "It's my fault. Let him go. I led him here."

Vincent just laughed, a maniacal sound meant to enrage Alaric even further. "He didn't lead me to jack. Men turn me on. Charlie's fuckably gorgeous. You think you're going to scare me? Do you know how many times I've almost died? Do you know how many bullies I've fought just like you? Fuck you."

Alaric's fangs dropped down, his eyes turning a watery amber in his anger. The vampire was out, a predator enraged, and Vince was the prey. Charlie cowered, wanting to flee and not knowing how to do it with Vince. "Please, Vince, apologize and let's go downstairs."

Alaric's backhand sent Charlie sprawling. His vision dimmed

as the pain of a dislocated jaw brought tears to his eyes.

"I don't owe anyone a fucking apology!" Vince howled.

Alaric tossed the man to the ground and leaped on him, an animal going for the throat.

"What in the hell?" came Cash's voice. He ran in, followed by Nikolai. They each grabbed a shoulder and ripped Alaric off Vince. Using vampire speed, they dragged him across the room and slammed him against a wall. Alaric's muscles strained to get back at Vince as he yelled something about not being a fucking queer, but even he wasn't a match for the combined strength of the other men.

"Alaric! Get a grip, man." Cash looked over his shoulder. "The hell did you say to him?"

Vince didn't get up. Charlie dropped next to him, careful not to touch him and bring on more of Alaric's wrath. There was no blood. Cash and Nikolai had gotten there in time. Charlie popped his own jaw back into place, hissing at the pain. In twenty-four hours there would be no evidence he'd been hit, everything healed back to normal. Just like every other time.

But why wasn't Vince getting up? His eyes were wide, terrified, and his breathing heavy, but Charlie couldn't see any new damage that would keep him down—no bleeding, no bruising.

"They were fornicating under your roof, disrespecting your house." Alaric's deep voice rumbled in accusation.

Embarrassment washed over Charlie. He'd hoped Vince could stay here until the Liberi threat was taken care of, but they might've just blown it. What had he been thinking, being intimate with Vince in Cash's home? He hadn't been thinking at all. That was the problem with Vince. Being around him short-circuited his brain.

Cash sounded pissed. "I've barely had breakfast, and fucking

Kolyan shows up with prophecies, and fucking Alaric decides who gets to bang under my roof. Just *everybody calm the fuck down.* Let's go to the kitchen, drink some blood, and get a fucking grip."

Charlie waited for his name to be added to the list of problems, but it wasn't. He caught Cash's gaze. The man shook his head in shared irritation, like Charlie was the only sane one in the room with him.

Charlie blinked in surprise. Cash was taking their side? Which meant he didn't mind Charlie and Vince sharing a bed in his house. The idea that Cash truly didn't care—that he wasn't just putting up with Charlie's orientation but had completely changed his mind from when they'd first met—astonished him. Emboldened, Charlie put a hand on Vince's shoulder, hoping to offer some comfort.

Emma poked her head in, her cheerful smile strained like she'd plastered it there on purpose. "What's going on? Did someone say there's a prophecy? Like a big-deal thing or a little thing? I ain't never heard a prophecy afore."

Even Alaric seemed to calm down at that question, his murderous gaze finally leaving Vince and Charlie, now connected through a tenuous point of physical contact, to contemplate Nikolai.

While everyone else focused that way, Charlie turned his attention to Vince. "Vince?" Vince curled over on his side, dry heaving. Was he crying? Worry lit through Charlie as he rubbed his back. "What did he do?"

Alaric and Nikolai exited, Emma between them with her arms linked through theirs. Charlie couldn't decide if she was declaring sides or getting Alaric out. Didn't matter. Charlie was, as always, almost alone among the vampires, his tie to Cash the only thing keeping him from being ostracized and left to the Liberi.

He didn't want it to be that way for Vince.

He pushed black curls back from Vince's face. The man was sweating, but his skin was chilled. "Vince?"

Cash hovered over them. "Is he injured?"

"He got slammed against the bed frame pretty hard."

Cash kicked Vince's foot. "Did you really call him a molly?"

"No," Charlie said. "He called him a closet queen. After flipping him off and telling him he should loosen up by, eh, *faisant une pipe.*"

Cash chuckled and squatted down next to him. "He told him to blow a dude? Shit. Your ex is a font of stupid. I tried hating him on your behalf, but he keeps making it hard." He focused on Vince. "You know the difference between brave and stupid?"

Vince slowly sat up, the horror fading from his eyes as he watched the doorway.

"Whether you win or not. You just got your shit kicked. Ergo, that was stupid. Even if I wish I'd seen the look on his face."

Vince's gaze flicked to Cash. "Alaric was the guy in the mask."

Cash's laughter shut down, his voice cold with disbelief. "The guy in the mask who was with the Liberi last night?" Alaric and Cash didn't seem as tight as they had been a hundred years ago, but Cash's loyalties ran deep, and he and Alaric had been brothers in arms for over a thousand years, saving each other's lives more times than Charlie had days in his life. Vince's accusation would not go over well.

Vince nodded, unaware of Cash's change of heart, as he ran a hand behind his head, checking for lumps.

Charlie wanted to believe him—clearly Vince believed it—but that couldn't be right. Alaric was an ass, but he was also the queen's eldest son and the highest-ranking, most well-respected vampire in CoVIn beside the queen herself. What motive would he have for working with Liberi? He had too much to lose.

"I'm positive it was him." Vince shivered. "His eyes when they change are that crazy amber. He wears the same cologne. His voice. I didn't recognize it at first, but it's the same accent. I've never heard one like it before."

Ice crept up Charlie's back. Galswinth was the only other descendant of Modron with a third-century Gothic accent, and even in a mask she would be decidedly a female.

Cash stood, face hard and any sympathy gone as he distanced himself. "On the phone you said Emma attacked you. Now Alaric? Was I there? How about Charlie? When I bring you to meet Modron, will she also have been there?"

Vince sat up, still rubbing his head. "Emma admits she was on their side, and I'm willing to give her the benefit of the doubt that she was magicked or something. But the masked man? He wasn't like the others. He was calm, like one of you. I'm not randomly accusing people."

He struggled to stand, and Charlie helped him. It felt odd holding hands in front of Cash, but he kept Vince's hand anyway. He wanted to hold on and keep him safe, but it kept getting harder to do both.

It would be easier if Vince would just step down every now and then instead of bull rushing into every conflict headfirst.

Cash brought himself to his full height, straight backed and intimidating with his gray-ice stare, even if Vince had a couple of inches on him. "You may not be the gold-digging gigolo I'd assumed, but that doesn't grant you my loyalty. So Alaric behaved like a raging dick after you called him a homosexual. In his day—and mine—you could call a man out and kill him for that. The law allowed it. There was a time I thought you were all damaged too. I'm sure that makes me evil in your twenty-first-century view where we're supposed to spring from the womb holding hands and teaching the world to sing, but reality is, Alaric isn't Liberi just because he hasn't jumped on your gay pride wagon. I will not allow you to accuse him in retribution."

Charlie opened his mouth to defend Vince. Whether or not Vince was right, the man believed what he was saying. But jumping in now while Cash was defensive and belligerent would do no good. Charlie shut his mouth. Later tonight, when everyone's blood pressure was down and Cash might actually listen, he'd try talking to him again.

Instead of waiting, Vince stepped toward Cash, pulling his hand from Charlie's. "That's not why I said that."

Cash got a finger in Vince's face. "Then you'd better damn well come up with some evidence, because if it's your word versus his, you lose." He looked up, expression stricken. "I have a meeting to attend. Show up if you want to hear about the end of the world or whatever Kolyan's blabbing about this time."

"Cash," Charlie managed to say through a thick throat.

"What?" The word came out sharp as a slap.

"I'm sorry about this."

Cash looked away, trying to get his temper under control.

"Why are you apologizing? We didn't do anything wrong," Vince snapped.

"Please," Charlie insisted. "Cool your heels for a minute."

Vince's eyes flashed angrily, but he didn't say anything more.

Cash's jaw was still tense as he turned to Charlie, but his voice was calm. "Are you okay?"

"I'm fine. He didn't do anything to me."

"So that bruise across your jaw is from, what, you running into a wall?"

Charlie reached for it. He'd forgotten. "It'll heal quickly. I'm not complaining."

"A viable policy." A shrug. "Or you could tell him where to stick his shit attitude. You've got a human over there willing to do it with you."

There was censure in his tone, and it stung. "Picking a fight with Alaric is, as you just pointed out, stupid."

"Likely, but that doesn't mean living in terror is brave." Having practically called Charlie a coward—the ultimate Viking insult—Cash left.

Charlie turned back to Vince, feeling like he'd lost even though everyone had come out alive. In the past, that had seemed like enough.

Vince didn't say anything or even look Charlie's way, just grabbed his shirt off the bed and headed for the door.

"Where are you going? To the prophecy meeting?"

"I'm with CoVIn now, and the end of the world sounds important, so yeah. I'm going. Aren't you?"

He'd like to, but… "No. Alaric will be there. As you might have noticed, antagonizing him is a dangerous idea."

"My life doesn't revolve around appeasing that asshole. Or anyone else. If he wants to feel antagonized by my presence, that's his problem."

"You said he was the guy in the mask. Why are you hanging out with him?"

Vince stopped and turned around, pulling that tight T-shirt over his abs as he did. "Oh, now you believe me? When it doesn't cost you anything? I noticed your utter silence when Cash was reading me the riot act." He opened the door and headed out. "I'm hanging out *near* Alaric. Not *with* him. I'm not letting him stop me from being where I want to be." He hesitated, then turned back, pleading with his eyes. "You know, bad things don't go away when you ignore them. You have to stop them."

Charlie laughed bitterly. "Are you suggesting we stop Alaric? He's fifteen hundred years old and the queen's first scion. *Cash* can't stop Alaric. You yelling at him is just going to get you hurt worse and not change a damn thing."

"Well, then, let's quit trying to do anything good in the world. No. I refuse to think that way." His jaw was set, a wiser determination in his eyes than the blind optimism of his younger days. It still meant he was rushing forward, where Charlie couldn't keep him safe.

Charlie reached for him, but Vince backed away, out of reach. "Please at least keep your head down around him. He'll make life hell."

"He already is making life hell. That's what bullies do." He paused for a minute, struggling with emotions. "You're right about one thing. Yelling at him won't do any good. But I don't have to be able to take him in a fight alone. As soon as I get evidence that Alaric is working against CoVIn, Cash will fight with me. Emma? She'll fight too. She might be more pissed about what happened to her than I am about what happened to me. And Javi and Rhi. We get enough people, and we can beat any monster."

The words wanted to burn bright, firing Charlie up. But the thought of Vince's head snapping back against the bed frame stopped him.

He was so fragile. It could've gone so much worse. And if Alaric found out Vince was trying to destroy his reputation? He'd cut out his heart and tie a ribbon around it for Tzitzi. This should not be Vince's fight. "How many times have you been hurt in the past day? How many more times do you have to nearly get yourself killed before you realize this world is dangerous? If something happened to you..." Charlie shook his head, not wanting to think about that. "This is why I didn't get you involved before."

Another hurt look, this one so disappointed it made Charlie's stomachache. "I know it's dangerous. But some things are more important than merely staying alive."

Charlie caught up with him and put a hand on his shoulder. "Vince—"

Vince jerked from his grip, his voice a growl. "Go hide in a closet. I'm missing the meeting."

He left.

Charlie gripped the doorsill instead of the person he wanted. Vince terrified him. And shamed him. He could barely remember what it felt like to be so bold.

The master woodworker he'd apprenticed under had put him under a physician's care more times than he cared to recall, each one for stepping outside the narrow box he'd dictated. But Charlie had been supposed to feel lucky. He'd been an orphan with two meals a day, a bed, and a job waiting for him when he came of age. All he had to do was keep his head down, follow orders, and pretend he was exactly what everyone expected.

The philosophy had kept him alive and not unhappy for nearly three hundred years. So why, watching Vince rush off into danger again, did he feel like the foolish one?

Chapter 10

When Vince entered the kitchen, Emma was still cooking. This time, though, it was the simple fare of French press coffee and pots of simmering water with blood packets warming in them. Alaric sat at the table, his back to the cooking area, as he laughed genially with the man who'd helped Cash restrain him. Everyone relaxed like a few minutes ago wasn't screaming and fists. Alaric seemed comfortable and at peace with everyone, with no hint of guilt.

Vince finally took a good look at him. He was almost as tall as Cash, with dark-blond hair and narrow blue eyes. His hair was cropped short in a style that was too modern to be what he'd died with, and his facial hair was just past a five o'clock shadow in a way that took a lot of grooming to be so perfectly disheveled. He wasn't as handsome as Cash—or anyone else at the table, for that matter—but he almost made up for it by trying a lot harder.

For a moment Vince let his mind go back to the confusion and terror of yesterday as he focused on the masked man. Was he certain the mask had hidden Alaric? He'd been drinking pulque and scared out of his mind—two things that clouded his memories. But that voice. And the cologne of tobacco and myrrh. He was certain. Almost certain, anyway.

He glanced at Cash, who sat at the end, smiling with his mouth and brooding with his eyes. Between him and Nikolai sat a petite brunette with hair that ran down past the bench. She held herself with prim rigidity. Nikolai laid a gentle hand on her shoulder, and she softened at the touch, leaning into him like they were close. That was Galswinth then, Nikolai's wife and the queen's eldest daughter.

Cash noticed him first, then the whole room turned to stare, their conversation halting.

Alaric stood, expression affable. "You came down, then." He held out a hand as if to shake. "No hard feelings from earlier." From his tone, Vince couldn't tell if it was an apology or if Alaric was publicly forgiving him for what he'd taken as an insult. Maybe both.

Asshole.

Despite Vince's bold words to Charlie, made easy through anger, the closer Vince had gotten to the gathering in this room, the more nervous he'd become. So nervous he'd considered walking out the door and grabbing a cab back home to face the Liberi threat on his own.

And then he'd wondered if that was exactly what Alaric wanted. As long as Vince was under Cash's roof, somebody with power was protecting him, and nobody, not Alaric or anyone else, could easily get away with offing him. But if he went home…

He tried not to stare at Alaric's hand like it was made of poison. The room watched in silent anticipation. Vince wanted to smack away the offer of friendship; he didn't believe it in the least. But despite his disappointment with Charlie's inaction, his ex wasn't entirely wrong. On occasion, restraint wasn't a bad thing, and now, with a room full of vampires waiting to see what he'd do, might be one of those occasions.

Gritting his teeth, he shook Alaric's hand. The shake was firm and short, without a challenge.

Alaric smiled a confoundingly earnest smile and turned to the table. "Vincent Pagano, this is Nikolai Vyhovsky."

Nikolai reached across the table to shake his hand. He was the shortest man in the room—at least while Charlie wasn't there—with the stocky build of a wrestler and skin ruddy from sunshine he'd likely seen centuries ago. His most distinguishing feature was his haircut, shaved on both sides and the back with only a strip at the very top, which he'd combed forward and to the side. The dark lock of hair was long enough to touch the left handlebar of his mustache in a style that was clearly from another culture and century. Despite the funny-looking do, with his intelligent eyes and black T-shirt over taut muscles, he looked like a badass.

"Galswinth, his wife." Alaric motioned at the woman.

She gazed at him without expression and nodded. Vince held out his hand to shake. After a lingering moment in which Vince thought she'd refuse, she smiled and took his large hand in both of her tiny ones. "A pleasure. Cassius has been telling us of your bravery. You will make a fine addition to CoVIn's human division, I am certain. Be welcome among us, Vincent Pagano."

A muscle in Alaric's jaw spasmed, as if his smile was suddenly hard to keep.

Which made Vince's smile that much easier to find. "Thank you. Call me Vince."

She matched his smile with her own. "Winnie."

He lifted his eyebrows. "Winnie. I like that. I'm going to grab some coffee. Can I get you anything?" He included the rest of the table with a gesture, determined that he would fit in. "Anyone else?"

With four orders for red-eyes—he had a guess what that meant—one with sugar, he turned to Emma, feeling triumphant. "Afternoon."

Emma popped him on the hip with a kitchen towel as the conversation behind them resumed. "We-he-hell, ain't somebody the flavor of the afternoon."

He shrugged like it wasn't a big deal. "Is there cream? Or

just…" He motioned at the blood packets.

"Yup. Cream's in the refrigerator. None of them use it, so I didn't bother setting it out. Mugs are to the left of the sink." She took two plates of fudge to the table. "This one don't have nuts, since somebody's a whiner about that sort of thing."

Vince busied himself with mugs and cream. A shriek made him pop his head up.

Rhi was crumpled in Cash's lap, like she'd tripped. Or been pushed.

Anger launched him forward, sending the cream to splash on the floor. "Hey!" Was somebody picking on Rhi now? He'd leave right now with her in tow and never look back.

Her eyes went wide, and she slid from Cash's lap, expression guilty as she took the seat beside him.

Emma's hand tugged gently on Vince's shoulder. "Stand down, Tarzan."

"Rhi, you okay?"

"Yeah, yeah. Everything's cool." She pushed her hair behind one ear. "How'd you sleep?"

Was that a bite mark near her collarbone? He took another step forward. *Shit.* Somebody had bitten her. That was it. They were out.

Emma stuck a damp cloth in his hand. "Cream's a-pooling, sugar. Might want to stop it if you want any."

He glanced down at the growing puddle of white on the slate floor.

Rhi hopped up. "I'll help." She tugged the cloth from his hands and swiped at the floor.

He dropped down beside her and righted the carton. "Are you okay? Did someone hurt you? Who did that?" he whispered. They could probably hear him anyway. The whole room had gone quiet again.

Emma dropped mugs on the table. "Red-eyes for everyone who ain't human. Sugar in yours, Nikolai."

As her continued prattle eased the tension, Rhi leaned closer to him, her hair a fine green curtain between them. "I'm fine. I wanted to know what it felt like, and Cash is pretty hot, so I asked him to."

He stared at her, shocked. "You *asked* him to bite you? It hurts."

She shrugged. "Didn't hurt me." Blushing a little, she pushed back the neckline of her tank top so he could better see where she'd been bitten. Unlike the slashes he'd endured, two tiny dots, each about the size of a donation needle, were bright red and already healing. "It's a little itchy now, though."

It bothered him, even if it wasn't his right to be bothered. Rhi wasn't food.

She leaned in closer, as her eyes sparkled with the good kind of bad. "Might be it didn't hurt because we were already horizontal when I asked. Don't be mad."

"Seriously?" He stopped mopping up the cream to stare at Cash. He thought the vampire had been flirting last night. He hadn't been flirting. He'd been hunting.

Rhi pulled him back around. "Don't stare. It's okay. Totally my decision."

Normally he and Rhi snarked together over their sex lives like they did every other part of life. But this was different. "He wasn't flirting yesterday, he was *hunting* you. Like you're food. That's not okay."

"What, like Emma hunted Javier? Seriously, how is it different from any other hookup?"

Vince paled, suddenly stricken. "You're not going to be a vampire too, are you? Don't make me the only human."

She stuck her tongue out. "What? No! I'd have to drink vampire blood. Yuck. And Cash says regular donors don't make good turning candidates. Javi was lucky that was their first date. If they'd been out more than a couple of times, he probably wouldn't have made it." She looked toward the door, the direction Javi was still sunsleeping, worry turning her features sour.

Vince wiped up the last of the cream and tossed their rags into the sink. "Are you going to be okay with Javier turning?"

Rhi joined him at the sink, holding the coffeepot. He grabbed another cup from the cabinet, and she poured. "It's not like I have a choice. I'll feel better after I see him. I hope he's okay with it." She shook her head. "But I don't think he's going to be."

Vince drowned her coffee in cream and added a touch to his own. "Did he know they existed?"

She held the coffee mug tightly in her hands, like she was warming them. "Do you mean did I break my promise to you not to tell him?"

Vince raised his eyebrows and gave her a knowing look.

She rolled her eyes. "He didn't believe me." She pushed away from the counter. "I guess he does now."

The coffee was good, and it soothed Vince's frazzled psyche. He changed the subject. "Amid the touchy-feely with a vampire, did Cash mention a potential apocalypse?"

She took a sip, eyes closing in bliss. "Apocalypse? I heard Nikolai had some important prophecy. I didn't know it was about the end of the world."

He took her arm, and they headed for the table. "I don't think it's that dire. They just made a joke," he said, as much to reassure himself as her. Vampires were real. Were-beasts of various fauna were real. Why not apocalypses? Did that even have a plural?

"Oh, it's dire," Nikolai said quietly. "And it's not a joke."

All conversation ceased, and everyone turned Nikolai's way.

"I thought we were waiting for Modron," Alaric said.

Winnie turned her tablet around to show a woman on Skype. "She's here."

Vince had no idea what to expect from a two-thousand-year-old vampire queen from Wales. A teenager in a loose, navy-and-white-striped tank top wasn't it. Her hair was a light, almost reddish brown and curly, and was currently pulled up into a simple ponytail. Her skin was unusually dark for her hair color, more olive toned like his, and her eyes were somewhere between green and brown. She was pretty. Not gorgeous, just pretty—a difference brought into more relief by how beautiful everyone else in the room was. Vince supposed that since vampires were chosen, not born, the human preference for physical beauty would come into play.

Her smile when she glanced around the table, nodding at each person in turn, was disarmingly guileless. Her eyes had not a single wrinkle and, stranger still, no darkness or haunted emotion behind them. She looked peaceful, bordering on serene. It was hard not to like her on first impression.

"Thank you, Galswinth," she said, voice lilting just a touch. "Nikolai? What have you seen? I apologize for the lack of small talk, but there are a million things happening over here. One might think a queen could use some help," she added pointedly.

Alaric was quick to respond, "I'll be right back, my queen."

Good. As far as Vince was concerned, he couldn't get his ass out of here fast enough.

Cash snorted. "You know I'd just get in the way. What am I going to do? Pick out drapes?"

Modron's eyes narrowed. "You could work on furnishing your quarters."

Cash's jaw clenched and relaxed. "I am. Here. Come visit."

"Kolyan and I will be there presently, milady," Galswinth added. "For now, I believe we'd best spend our precious time with his vision."

The swinging door to the kitchen opened, and Charlie entered. Vince's first instinct was to smile and motion for him to join Rhi and himself where they stood. But he squashed the impulse. Charlie didn't want any hint that they might have a relationship. Not that anyone in here didn't know. And not that they had a relationship.

He drank more coffee.

Charlie leaned back into the wall by the door, making himself as unobtrusive as possible, and Vince imagined him ready to flee at the first provocation. His gaze went to Vince, as if trying to get his attention. Vince turned back to the table. Who needed romantic entanglements when there was a potential apocalypse and a vampire queen on Skype?

Nikolai's resonant voice with its cultured Slavic accent quieted the table. "An apocalypse is not the end of the world. It derives from a Greek word meaning to uncover. It's a revelation and harbinger of the chaos that comes with change. In the past, apocalyptic events such as the exodus of the Jews from Egypt affected a tribe or a country. Larger ones, such as the European arrival in America, could legitimately be seen as an ending of the world, depending on your perspective. And now, an apocalyptic event is at hand."

Winnie chimed in. "We fear, however, with the spread of communications, any apocalyptic event will surround the globe. We no longer live in a world of containment."

"There will be war," Nikolai added. "A striving of civilization against chaos incited by the Event."

"What event?" the queen asked.

Nikolai lowered his eyes to the table. "I don't know yet."

Alaric chuckled and patted him on the back. "So, something will happen. It'll change the world, and somebody will fight somebody about something. But you have no idea who fights or what will start it? I'm so glad we had this meeting."

Vince didn't want to agree with Alaric about…anything. But he didn't make a terrible point.

"Chaos versus civilization," Cash said. "That's pretty clear. We're fighting the Liberi." He frowned. "We're not ready for all-out war with them. We don't have enough forces. Alaric, your opinion?"

"I agree." He dropped the laughter and sounded appropriately grim. "We are significantly outnumbered."

"What about humans?" Vince asked. "We're forces of civilization. Mostly."

All eyes turned to him as if shocked he had the audacity to speak. Cash was the first to look back to Modron, hiding a grin with a sip of coffee.

Alaric nodded as if considering it. "Thank you for your offer, but how well do you think humans would fare in a contest with vampires? They're safer kept out of this."

His tone was innocent, but Vince knew better. That was a threat. He squeezed Rhi's arm, seeking comfort for the unease Alaric's false amity gave him.

Shit, she didn't know what had happened. Later. He'd tell her later, after the meeting, when Alaric was out of here.

Cash continued, "We'll utilize our human allies as best we can without endangering them. I'll organize treaties with the weres. Winnie, I could use your help with the fae factions. Kolyan, what else do you have that we can give them? Alaric is right. That's not a lot to start with."

Nikolai nodded. "There will be signs. I felt the air sucked

from the room, and we suffocated, CoVIn crumbling to nothing. Next a plague massacred thousands, mortal and immortal alike. A fire set the city ablaze until shadows escaped their prison, walking free."

Vince raised his eyebrows. That was sounding pretty apocalyptic in the *end of the world* sense. Even the vampires were looking ill at ease over Nikolai's visions.

Nikolai continued with, "The child of moon and sun arrives."

"My spell?" Queen Modron interrupted, voice full of excitement. "It will work?"

Vince turned to Rhiannon. Apparently the prediction wasn't completely opaque.

Nikolai blinked, his misty eyes gaining focus as he turned to the screen. "It comes to fruition in the next few years. Whichever side shall claim him will have the weapon needed to win—how they use it, however, will still matter. The apocalypse begins in earnest with a bloodbath far from here. Ashe and Emblem are born. Dust falls. Strength of voice and strength of force shall then decide the fate of the world."

Vince leaned into Rhi. "It's like listening to the book of Isaiah."

"I never read the Bible," she whispered back.

"Me neither," Cash said, not bothering to whisper.

He was still flirting with her? It made Vince uneasy, but Rhi was good at taking care of herself. He would take her lead. "Isaiah is full of predictive metaphors that don't make sense except in retrospect."

"Then what good are they?" Cash asked, frowning.

On the screen, the queen asked, "Is there anything else?"

Nikolai shook his head. "This isn't a vague feeling of

foreboding, my queen. This is the most shattering foretelling I've ever encountered. I believe details will be revealed as it gets closer. But for now…"

She nodded. "We start with figuring out how not to suffocate."

Vince glanced at Emma. When she and Javi had woken up, the first thing they'd done was gasp for air—an unusual thing for a creature who didn't need to breathe. He turned to Cash, trying to see what he was thinking. He, too, had an eye on Emma and a worried look. He caught Vince's gaze and shook his head in a tiny movement, as if to say, *Don't talk about it in front of everyone.*

For all his furious bluster about loyalty, he might be considering what Vince had said. The realization was comforting.

Cash stood, his smile smooth. "Are we done? We have a fledgling waking up any minute now, and if I remember correctly, Winnie and Alaric promised to return downtown and help you."

"Without you, yes. I remember."

"I'll be in my office every day—mostly—when it opens. You'll be sick of me in no time and glad to send me off, I promise." He blew her a kiss.

She rolled her eyes, but her smile said she wasn't that bothered. "Alaric, Galswinth, Nikolai, I'll see my good children soon. Give our newest fledgling my goodwill and congratulations, Cassius. I look forward to meeting him." She hung up.

Cash turned to Nikolai. "You two haven't told her about your condo yet, have you?"

Winnie patted his arm. "We are happy to let you clear a jaunty path through the wilderness for the rest of us to follow safely behind, Cash."

He flipped fingers under his chin in a way that Vince thought his theater teacher had said meant "fuck you" in Shakespearean. "Good thing I'm handy with a machete," Cash added casually.

Alaric stood, his expression a confused smile. "Jaunty is one word for it. Why she puts up with half your shenanigans, Cash, I'll never understand."

Cash ruffled Rhi's hair on his way around the table. "It's my charm. Don't be so dour, *ganipi*. She'd forgive you too if you got your own place."

"Requiring forgiveness means you've made a mistake."

"And by 'made a mistake,' you mean 'done something awesome.'"

The door swung open, and Javier poked his head in, looking mighty confused. "Hello? Rhi!" He ran to his sister. She caught him in a giant hug. "Vince?" He grabbed Vince too, pulling him in. "You're not dead. Good."

Vince hugged back, happy to be included. "Better than I can say for you, you immortal asshole."

Javier started to speak but stopped when a cork popped, then a second, and a cheer went up. Emma and Cash poured two bottles of champagne—one white, one unnaturally pink—into tulip glasses. Someone stuck a pink one in Javi's hand. He turned to Emma. "So we were rescued."

His sire's smile was as wide as the plains of West Texas, and every molecule of it was fake. If Vince had to guess, he'd say Emma was terrified. "Yup. Let me introduce you around."

Vince squeezed Rhi's hand. Her expression was pinched, but at the touch she managed to smooth away the frown. They could talk about the end of the world later. Right now, Javi needed all the support he could get.

⋙✦⋘

A couple of hours later, the door swung shut behind Kolyan and Winnie, leaving the kitchen calm. Alaric had left an hour prior, not wanting to keep the queen waiting. The man was slick as slime. If the earlier debacle hadn't happened, Vince wouldn't have suspected him for any sort of treachery, despite the accent and the cologne or any other evidence. It was like he was two people—the sane, somewhat uptight but friendly guy he'd been in the kitchen, and the explosive, amoral monster.

When he'd left, Charlie had relaxed enough to cease blending in with the cabinetry. He'd still spent the entire party sitting at the counter drinking pink champagne and eating snickerdoodle cookies while sketching in his notebook, his mind somewhere else. The fact that Charlie would rather be sketching projects than attending a party wasn't abnormal. The fact that he'd come at all was. But why show up if he wasn't going to enjoy himself?

Emma poked Vince in the shoulder with drunken aim. The woman could pack down wine. Seven vampires and two humans had put away nine bottles, and only one of those wasn't pink. "Calling him Kolyan now, huh? When're you signing up for the Axes?"

Vince turned away from contemplating Charlie and gave her a smile. He liked Emma. "Not on your life." Turned out he liked all of them except Alaric. Nikolai had given him permission to use his nickname after "Thriller" played on the stereo. Winnie had made motions like she knew some of the dance, and two minutes later the song was on repeat while Vince went over the steps with Rhiannon and six vampires—including Alaric—following along behind him.

Charlie had actually looked up a couple of times and cracked a smile once—*once*—at vampires learning the "Thriller" dance.

Vince couldn't figure out what was going through his head, and it was driving him crazy. It hadn't been that long ago that he'd had his hand down Charlie's pants while the man demanded Vince take off his shirt. And now he had his nose stuck in a notebook, cool as winter in Siberia.

He pushed the thought away and replaced it with the memory of Cash howling along with Michael Jackson as he drained the rest of his glass. "That is a memory I will keep to my dying day and pull out when I need to smile."

"Aw," Emma started. "Don't you talk about dying, now. I don't need to think about that. You're too fun to die."

Javier sucked in a hard breath, bringing their attention his way. He'd heard the comment about death, and his eyes widened in devastation as he looked at his sister. Vince ached for him. Javi'd had several moments of understanding at the party. The one when he realized why the wine was pink and spit it out. Then took another glass and drank it. The one when the men challenged him to pick up the dining room table with everyone else sitting on it—and like Atlas he crawled underneath and heaved it up on his back while everyone cheered him on.

This moment, when Javi realized he was going to watch his little sister grow old and die, had none of the fun, only pain.

Emma sighed and leaned against Vince. "I didn't have much of anybody to miss. He still should have his whole life. I wouldn't have done it if I could've thought of another way to save him, but it happened so fast. Honestly, I didn't even think he'd make it across. He was just... he was just too good to give the Liberi a shot at him, and I don't say that about many folks."

Vince squeezed her shoulders. "Give him some time. Javi's a survivor. He'll thank you for it. Eventually." Although, if it had been Vince, he didn't know if he could forgive. It was too much to take without permission.

Which was exactly what had happened to Charlie, but from what he'd heard, Ramón wasn't trying to help like Emma had been. He looked back at his ex. Charlie's gaze met his. He smiled with half his mouth, an expression between hopeful and sad, before looking back at his notebook. Vince clenched his jaw and tried not to grind his teeth.

Rhi didn't notice any of the drama from where she was eating fudge and chatting with Cash as he dropped empty bottles into the recycling. "What spell did the queen cast?"

Vince hopped up and headed for them, ready for an easier distraction. An easy distraction like the end of the world? He shook his head. Broken relationships felt like the end of the world. The actual end of the world didn't feel like much at all. At least not now, when it hadn't happened yet. "I had the same question."

Cash acknowledged him with a smile. "There's an ancient prophecy that one day a vampire will be born who can walk in the sun without burning—hence the child of moon and sun. A few centuries ago the queen got tired of waiting and cast a spell trying to force it. So far nothing has happened, but she swears it's 'incubating.' I don't think we have to worry about that right now. Kolyan said it should be a few years."

Emma wiped down a counter, lips pursed in thought. "I'm more worried about suffocating. That'd be a mighty strange way to go for folks who don't have to breathe."

Vince collected glasses and took them to the sink to start washing. "You and Javi gasped for air when you came out of that spell or whatever it was."

She hesitated in her movement across the counter, then continued, wiping the same path she'd already taken. "Yeah, I remember that. Javier?"

"It was like coming up for air after being underwater too long." He took up a towel next to Vince and started drying. "Is somebody going to explain what's been going on? Clearly something big happened before I got down here, but nobody has told me what. If someone hadn't left a note by the bed explaining the basics of what happened last night, I'd be completely lost."

The retelling began, and to Vince's surprise, Charlie got up and started putting away the glasses Javi dried. He stretched up to reach the cabinet, showing the lean lines of his muscular frame. Lithe. That was a good way to describe Charlie. He looked good with his short-sleeved button-down hanging off his thin abs and clinging to the well-formed muscles of his back.

Charlie caught him looking. Immediately he came down off his toes and back to neutral, hiding the sensual lines of his stretched torso like they embarrassed him. Vince had always thought it was cute how easy it was to make him blush. Charlie had no idea how good-looking he was. But now it seemed like part of a larger problem. Charlie hid his body, hid his relationships, hid himself. He would always reject Vince in public. He would always work to be as un-vampiric as possible—which was likely the real reason Charlie had never bitten him, since Rhi had said it didn't have to hurt. Hell, even if by some miracle they did get back together, Charlie might always look for a reason to break things off between them under the false assumption that Vince was better off without him.

After centuries of living silently, how could Vince expect Charlie to change? "Canivet" was the word Cash had used, as in someone who can't be taught new tricks. Vince needed to accept the reality of who Charlie was. They wanted each other, sure, but Vince couldn't live as quiet and closeted a life as Charlie needed, and that was the crux of the problem between them.

The realization that they never would work was a weight inside his chest that just made him want Charlie more desperately. They couldn't keep seeing each other like this, or he might start making decisions he'd regret. This week, with them both under one roof, was going to suck.

Rhiannon peeked out one of the curtained windows, then drew it back to reveal the yard in twilight. "It's dark enough outside you should be okay walking from the car to Mom's place."

Javi's look of horror bordered on comical. "You want me to go to Mom's like this?"

"Like what, a vampire? That can't be helped. Tzitzi had you kidnapped at your apartment. You can't go there right now. You may be immortal, but don't be an idiot."

The glass in his hands broke as he squeezed it too hard, which was probably a lot easier to do than it had been last week. "Shit. Sorry."

Cash shrugged. "Break them all. I don't give a fuck." Within the space of a second he had the glass shards cleaned up. "Why don't you two stay here? Emma hasn't found an Austin residence yet, and I told her she could stay until she does. Vince and Charlie are staying. We could make a house party of it."

"Sorry I ain't got a place yet," Emma said to Javier. "I didn't know I was moving to Austin. I was just in town for the festivities when I, er..." She cleared her throat as if she'd said more than she meant to. "But usually fledglings move in with their sires while they're getting used to everything. We're here to help. I'll be a good sire. You'll see."

Javi carefully set down the new glass he was drying and backed away from fragile things. "You're moving to Austin because you turned me into a vampire? You don't have to do that."

She set the cloth down and put her hands on her hips. "Don't get your knickers in a twist. With Cash here now and CoVIn moving in? It's a good time to be an Austin vampire."

"I understand why you did what you did. You don't owe me anything. I'm not going to let you alter your life around me."

She snorted. "You ain't going to let me? I'd like to see you try and stop me."

As they faced off, Charlie took Javi's place, quietly drying dishes while Vince washed. He looked like he wanted to talk, and Vince wasn't so sure he wanted to do that anymore. At least not while the smell of Charlie's skin was this close to his memory.

The air was so strained Vince could taste his own disappointment. "Rhi, stay. It'll be fun." He washed the last glass and set it down with a decisive *thunk*. "I hear there's a pool. Want to go find it?"

She looked between him and his ex, eyebrows raised in surprise at his brusqueness. Vince didn't care. As far as Charlie was concerned, he was so confused and disappointed he didn't know what to think anymore.

"Uh, sure," she finally said. "Javi?"

He glanced at Emma, then at Cash. "I don't know. I have a lot to figure out."

"They can help. Come find the pool with us and stay the week. If you go home, then I'll feel obligated to go back to Mom. Be the best brother ever. Stay and give me a week in wonderland." She grabbed his arm and squeezed it, shooting him her best puppy dog eyes.

Javier sighed at her. "Seriously? You don't have to stay with… Fine. I'll stay. But I don't have a swimsuit."

Emma waved her hand, a lascivious grin lighting her face. "Oh, I'm sure we've got one somewhere. And if not, just go skinny-dipping. Nobody'll mind none." Her voice changed to a stage whisper, and she cupped her mouth with one hand, like she was telling a secret. "Rhi, if you can get Vince and your brother naked, I'd be much obliged. We could use more naked eye candy around here." She snapped a dishtowel at Cash. "You should join them."

Vince locked arms with Rhi and Javi, trying to propel them out of the kitchen and away from the strain between him and Charlie. "You're on your own with Javi and Cash, but for me,

LongHorns Lounge, Wednesday through Saturday. Bring your dollars. I'm taking this week off, but next week I'll reserve you a VIP table." He winked.

Emma slapped the counter. "I'll be there."

Charlie's fingers squeezed the dishrag with white-knuckled force. Good to know if they couldn't work things out, they could at least piss each other off.

Chapter 11

Charlie leaned against the counter in the kitchen, feeling a sense of déjà vu as he swigged a beer and listened to eighties pop blaring through Cash's open house party in the next room. The music was more consistent than usual. So far they'd only played songs from the last seventy-five years or so. But get enough old vampires drunk, and somebody insisted they dance to "Minuet in G." The question of whether it'd be Bach's or Beethoven's had led to fistfights.

He'd wanted to talk to Vince for a week, but it had been made abundantly clear that Vince didn't want to talk to him. At first Charlie had thought that, given a little time, Vince would cool down, so he'd given him space.

He wondered guiltily if that was what Vince had thought five years ago.

By day four Charlie had been ready to carry Vince off to somewhere private and make him listen. As kidnapping was immoral, he hadn't done it. If Vince didn't want to be alone with him, it wasn't okay to make him.

But Vince couldn't stop Charlie from attending Cash's party. Charlie usually didn't come to these. Social events with large crowds were not something he enjoyed. But here he was anyway, hanging out in the kitchen next to the party, trying to work up the courage to go out there and face Vince. He'd tried dressing nicer than his usual jeans and V-neck or short-sleeved button-down. Vince had been so impressed with Cash's clothing. It hadn't even dawned on Charlie that maybe he cared about that sort of thing.

Cash had once described his wardrobe as another shield; it gave him confidence when he put on a perfectly tailored suit or a vintage shirt and a pair of hand-stitched jeans. Donning silk and other finery, however, just made Charlie feel like a fraud. Short where Vince was tall. Roughly built where Vince was toned. Charlie's hair was shaggy and nondescript and the freckles... nobody in their mid-thirties should still have freckles. All these things were fine for the woodshop. Nobody there cared about looks. They cared about art, and Charlie could craft with the best of them. But he hadn't the faintest idea if his tie was the right width or his lapels the right shape, and he couldn't care less.

The door opened, and Cash came in, probably for one of his assignations. The man couldn't keep his pants on. This was Charlie's exit. He stood to announce and excuse himself, a smile on his face at a memory from earlier today.

He'd asked Cash for help with his attire. Cash, unsurprisingly, had responded with a too-obvious joke about how he thought gay men knew clothes. Maybe it was perverse, but Charlie had tried something new...

Before he had a chance to imagine all the ways it could backfire, he replied, "Then I guess you're gayer than I am."

Cash's eyebrows lifted in surprise. Charlie nervously waited, preparing to apologize if needed, but hoping he wouldn't have to. If he did have to apologize, he would tell Cash to cut out the jokes too. Either they could both harass each other, or neither could.

Tossing shirts one by one, Cash had frowned at the week's worth of outfits Charlie had brought. "Bring on the dick, then, because I'm throwing away everything in here. My shopper will be here for you in an hour, and you're buying whatever she tells you to. Then, when you have real options, I'll help you pick out what's most likely to get you laid."

So they would harass each other. A weight lifted from

Charlie's soul—he could live with that.

"Uh," Cash added, a rare hesitation to his voice before he proceeded with his usual brashness. "Women usually look for quality ass and shoulders. That's... universal." The last statement came with a bare hint of question.

Holding back a laugh *was* tough, but Charlie managed it. "Yes. That's universal."

Cash *gave* him a smirk. "You'll be just fine, then."

And thus, earlier this very day, the hottest, straightest vampire in vampire-dom had informed Charlie that he had a nice ass. Charlie took a step toward the kitchen door, ready to say, "Couldn't make it half an hour into the party, eh?"

But instead of a woman, Alaric followed Cash in.

Charlie froze as all his good feelings from a moment ago disappeared. The men hung in the entrance and didn't seem to notice him on the far side in the dark.

"Glad you could make it," Cash said, already drunk.

"Of course," Alaric said back, not drunk at all. "What's in the kitchen you wanted me to see?" He started further back.

Charlie tried to make himself smaller without moving. He'd perfected the art of disappearing, but in an empty space like this it was hard.

Luckily Cash pulled Alaric back. "Nothing. I just wanted to tell you." He slapped his friend on the chest once, like he had a hilarious joke. "The stripper kid said you were with the Liberi."

Charlie's heart stopped. Was Cash trying to get Vince killed? The time had about run its course for the Liberi to forget his scent. He should be safe going home—if Alaric didn't kill him.

Alaric's good mood evaporated as he stood straight. "What?"

"Yeah. Said there was a guy in a mask, and that he had your

accent. Which is pretty distinct, being dead for the past fifteen hundred years."

Alaric shoved the kitchen door, and it swung open. "I'm going to kill him."

"Whoa!" Cash grabbed his shirt and yanked him back. "Why?"

Alaric's rage built as he shifted from foot to foot, trying to contain it as he usually did for Cash. "He's making up lies." He turned back for the door.

"And you care what some *ergi* says because why?"

Charlie flinched. *Ergi* was an old Viking word that was used to mean coward or defeated one, but literally translated to the receiving partner in anal sex. It was a nasty homophobic slur Cash had once dropped without thinking, but he'd promised not to use it anymore. Apparently drunk Cash didn't feel the need to keep his promises.

At least Alaric stopped. "Why are you telling me this if you don't want me to call him out?"

"You're going to call out a human? Please. You might as well call out a puppy. Besides, he's been cutting my hair this week, and we finally settled on something. What do you think?"

"You've got to be kidding me. You want him alive to fix your hair?"

Cash leaned against a counter, fortunately one facing Charlie's direction, forcing Alaric to face away. "I'm simply saying, he already told me he thinks the masked guy is you, so if whoever that was at Tzitzi's party murdered my barber, it would be a waste of effort."

Charlie closed his eyes in relief as Cash's actions suddenly made sense. By taking Vince in for a week, Cash had made Vince a person who mattered. If he disappeared or died, vampires would look into it. If Alaric thought Vince was a loose end, he'd likely risk cutting it off anyway. If Vince's knowledge was tapped out, however, Alaric had nothing to gain by taking him out.

Alaric looked at the floor for a moment, struggling to get his emotions back in check. When he did, he looked back to Cash, back straight but posture relaxed. "You know me, Cassius. You know I love Modron. You know what's most important to me in life is for her children to be strong." He looked away and then back. "I lost my temper last week. I should not have attacked a guest in your home, regardless of the provocation. It's strange to me that you let them behave so under your roof." He paused.

"The only sentient whose sex life I give a shit about is mine. Everybody else can fuck whomever they want. In fact, I think we should all quit sticking our noses in other people's bedrooms and fuck whomever we want without it getting reported."

Alaric rocked forward and back on his heels. "Made the tabloids again, have you?"

Cash didn't answer, just shook his head like he was annoyed.

Charlie smothered a smile. The supernatural community had their own press and their own bloggers, all full of gossip. If anyone caught wind that Cash had been seen more than once with a green-haired human, it would've sent them buzzing... and green hair was about to be popular in the female vampire community.

Alaric nodded. "I'll try to let their deviances pass if it will maintain goodwill between us. I'd hate to think, however, that the accusation of a scared, angry man could break the trust we have built over lifetimes." He held his hand out. "Even if he gives impressive haircuts."

Charlie glared in disgust. That was smooth enough that Cash would buy it.

Sure enough, Cash clasped Alaric's forearm with a hearty shake, then pushed away from the counter. "Witch beer's in the cellar. Want one?"

"Still drinking your murderers?"

Cash grinned his Lucifer's smile. "They taste better."

"At those prices, they should. Yes, I'll take your peace offering. Thanks for the warning, friend." With a halfhearted salute that Cash jauntily returned, Alaric headed back into the party.

Cash straightened. He was still under the influence, but not to the extent he'd pretended. His movements were pensive as he headed into the wine cellar and returned almost immediately with three beers. Without looking, he tossed one Charlie's way. "I hope you understand my oath-break. I didn't do it casually."

It was the closest Cash would come to an apology for saying *ergi.*

Charlie slid from the counter and brought him a bottle opener. "I understand why you used the word. What concerns me is how much of target Vince is."

"Then instead of hiding in here, get your ass into the party and help keep an eye on him. He should be safe under my roof, but accidents happen."

The pricey bottles of brewed witch blood and beer opened with a hiss of fermentation. "I thought you'd dismissed Vince's claim."

"I have." Cash took a healthy gulp, then pressed the cold bottle to his temple. He'd been dancing, and heat radiated off him. "Mostly." Another sip. Cash turned to Charlie, the conflict apparent in his face. He and Alaric went way back, further than Emma or Charlie or even Nikolai. "Who am I to judge?" Cash muttered. "I lost track of my body count while I was still human."

Charlie wasn't entirely sure how that connected to the current situation, but it clearly meant something to Cash. The Viking came from a time when violence was commonplace. In the years Charlie had known him, though, he'd slowly become more careful, less casual with life. "You end fights, but you rarely start them. It's different." He took a sip of beer, hesitating, before he said, "Wanting Modron's children to be strong is not the same thing as supporting CoVIn. Have you thought about that?"

Cash grunted. "Thinking is for miserable people. I'm hosting a party. Let's go dance." He headed for the door, stride determined. "Make sure your ex doesn't disappear down any dark hallways. Can I count on you for that?"

"I can try." Charlie caught up with him before he reached the door. "But it won't be easy as he's avoiding me."

"Don't let him. If you care, you'll watch out for the little shit whether he wants you to or not. He doesn't understand what he's gotten himself into."

Charlie dropped his head and raised his bottle. At the clink of "cheers," he raised his chin. "Let's do this."

The strains of a minuet started up.

Cash hustled out the door. "No. No fucking Bach *or* Beethoven. I told him."

Charlie put his hand on the counter and took a very unnecessary breath to steady himself. He could be brave. For Vince.

ಕ⋄ಣ

The party overflowed from a ballroom-sized den with furniture pushed to the walls, out past open, floor-to-ceiling windows overlooking the pool, and continued in and out of the water. It was a gorgeous estate, and as usual, Cash had brought Charlie in to look it over for both aesthetics and structural integrity before purchasing. It was nice to be useful.

Now, the main space was reserved for dancing. A DJ argued with Cash—that was going to go poorly—and the floor was crowded with vampires and a lesser number of humans. As usual at Cash's fetes, drunken revelry was the vibration of the night.

The only blood-drinking visible came from very civilized cups. Not that there wasn't any drinky-panky going on in the house, but Cash kept a firm "get a room" policy that nobody would break. Alaric may be the oldest son, but Cash was the popular one. Getting cut from his guest list was a social disaster.

It was hilarious to Charlie that he always got an invitation to the most coveted scene in town.

Vince looked amazing tonight in a formfitting button-up with rolled-up sleeves and jeans that hugged him just right.

Merde, did they ever hug him right.

Vince pushed Rhiannon up to the DJ's station, said something to Cash, and just like that Rhiannon was installed. Instead of getting shy, she asked a couple of questions, then turned to the music. *Minuet in G* cut out, replaced by Led Zeppelin sampling Bach's *Bourrée in E Minor*, which transitioned to "Kashmir."

Any protests died as the whole room melted into excited screams.

Cash put his hands together in a gesture of thanks, then he and Vince headed back to the dance floor. They made a beeline for the heartbeat of the party, both of them with megawatt smiles naturally in place. Projector screens, through some magic of modern technology, streamed what looked like cell phone videos from the dance floor. It didn't take long for nearly every video to show the blond and brunet owning the floor. Vince had been a good dancer when Charlie had known him. Now? He was amazing.

It seemed like all vampires should dance well, as they were strong with incredible reflexes. But all the reflexes in the world didn't give a person rhythm. They didn't give a person the kind of grace that turned jerky movements into art. Vampires could spin faster and jump higher than Vince, but they couldn't step, pivot, and smile with the pulse of the music in ways both perfectly attuned and still surprising.

Less than an hour into meeting them, Vince had a room full of strangers—of vampires—cheering his name.

Cash joined him, his moves as full of athletic grace on the dance floor as they were on the battlefield. Vince grinned at his rival for King of the Floor and stilled with an intentional hesitation that made people cheer for him to continue. Charlie smiled at how happy he looked, how in command of himself and his environment just a week after being abducted. The week spent relaxing with Rhiannon, Cash, Javier, and Emma had done him good.

Cash was having a great time too, right up there with him. It made sense. They were both golden boys, beloved everywhere they went. Watching Vince be so successful, Charlie couldn't be sad at what they'd lost, only proud for his ex.

"Charlie!" A friendly voice came up behind him, and he turned. A dark-haired human who looked like he belonged on the California beach, not landlocked in Austin, gave him a wink and a french bastard—a blood and Armagnac.

"Trey! Hi." Charlie's cheeks felt hot. Was he blushing? Hopefully with the lights nobody could tell. "What are you doing here?"

Trey held up a bright-red wristband with a key attached. "Scarlet got hired for the occasion. A dozen of us are here."

The vampire-run club Scarlet was referred to as everything from Fine Dining to the Bespoke Brothel. Bottles of blood were a convenient necessity, but it was hard to go for long without the warm intimacy of biting someone. It satisfied the soul and made a vampire feel less estranged from the world. Scarlet hired attractive humans to provide blood, among other services, for vampires who weren't in the mood for a hunt. Unlike some blood brothels, Scarlet took care of their humans and paid them well, making them CoVIn's most popular destination for the hungry and lonely.

When Charlie had been with Vince, the lack of biting hadn't mattered much. The closeness they'd shared had more than made up for going without. But after the breakup, followed by months of nothing—no sex, no blood connection, no nothing—he'd gone where everyone else went, and Trey was the only person he saw. But he wasn't used to seeing the man anywhere else.

Trey stood a respectable distance away, his smile casual enough to fool anyone. "Soon as I realized you were here, I thought I'd give you first dibs on Scarlet's best."

Charlie snorted. Trey struck him as a genuinely nice person, but Scarlet's clients paid good money for illusions. Trusting anything the handsome man said was naïve at best. "How many first dibs came before me?"

"Cynic," Trey admonished. "You know, one of these days you're going to believe me when I tell you the truth."

The dance floor was getting more crowded, and Trey nodded toward the edges of the room where there was seating. With another glance at the screen and the end of Vince and Cash's dance-off, Charlie walked with him. Cash was keeping tabs on Vince.

"You treat me like I matter," Trey said, surprising him. "Most clients don't bother. Not that they're mean or anything. But you're an agreeable change of pace." He grinned. "If you took this key and told me what time to be behind door"—he checked the number on his wristband—"number six, I'd be happy with that."

"And each pairing doesn't turn into tomorrow's gossip column because…"

"Our host lived through the Victorian Era. He knows how to design secret assignations." His eyes turned surprisingly hopeful. "We're already paid for. With tip. I'll go with whoever asks, but I haven't seen you in a while and figured I'd try to pick my client instead of vice versa for once."

Charlie paused at the eagerness in his voice. It was weirdly sweet of Trey to have sought him out. "I can't tonight."

Trey pouted for a moment before his eyes lit up. "Got a date? Who? Whom? Fuck it, I was born in the eighties. You immortals and your grammar drive me batty. Who is it?" He scanned the floor. "You deserve a date. Is he nice? He'd better be nice, or I'll beat the crap out of him." He paused. "If he's human."

Trey looked so excited about the possibility of Charlie having a date that he hated to disappoint him with reality. "Er…"

"Cash Geirson will beat the crap out of him too, I bet. I hear you're, like, his best friend."

That just made Charlie laugh. "His best friend? We're friends, but let's not get carried away."

Emma, drunk as a blond skunk, came barreling off the dance floor, dragging her new fledgling with her. "Treeeeeeeey!" She slammed into him and turned until her ass ground against his crotch. Trey laughed and threw an arm around her midsection, locking her against him before she fell over. "I have a baby bat, Trey! Can you believe it? Javi, meet Trey Morreli. Trey, Javier…shit. Javi, what's your last name? Y'all, I'm the worst sire ever."

Javier pulled her away from Trey in a move that looked jealous. The two of them had spent the week fighting yet seeking each other out at every opportunity. One might think they enjoyed fighting. "Reyes. I forgot your last name too."

"Oh, double shit. Granger. Emmaline Anne Granger." She turned to Trey. "Long story. We've had a rotten week. But I'm going to fix it and be the *best sire ever*. Starting with getting him the *best date ever*. I was thinking Jenna. She's good with baby bats, yeah? We're hooking him up!"

Javier's eyes went wide. "I don't need a hookup."

She patted him on the cheek, leaning further in than would be possible if Javier didn't have ahold of her. "You pick whomever you want, sugar. I worked with these fine ladies and gents, and they're the best damn hos on the planet. After me." She held a hand up, and Trey gave her a high five. "Did I tell you I was a prostitute back a long time ago? I ain't no more 'cause I don't have to work no more. But when I heard they was starting Scarlet, I wanted to make sure my brothers and sisters got their fair shake."

Trey grinned, his dimple showing as he patted her on the cheek. "She is the best pint-sized, pointy-toothed advocate a professional could ask for."

Emma guffawed at that. "Pint-sized, pointy-toothed! I'm putting that on my business cards. If I ever get any."

Cash arrived, his hand grasping Vince by the elbow to forcibly tow him along. Vince stared at the connection like he wasn't sure what was happening, but when Cash decide to relocate you, there wasn't much you could do but move. "Emma! Why aren't you dancing? I got a hotshot over here who thinks he can own the room."

"Sweet cheeks, if you can't out dance him, I'm fucked."

Vince's gaze traveled up and down Charlie, taking him in with what appeared to be reluctant approval. Charlie tried not to fidget, then gave in and tugged on his shirtsleeves. He hated being stared at, but after a week of avoidance, it was nice to have Vince's attention.

Emma chattered beside them. "I'm getting Jenna for Javi."

"I don't want a prostitute!" Javi announced again.

She took a step toward him, arms crossed. "You got a problem with prostitutes?"

"No! I just don't want one tonight. Or ever, really. No offense intended—world's oldest profession—I just…" Javier dropped his face into his palm, and Charlie felt sympathy for him. Emma had the right idea—he needed to eat and Scarlet was a safe place to figure it out—but she was too pushy.

"You're gonna get cold, sweet pea, if you don't tap a vein."

"What?" Javier said, shooting her a look like a man awaiting more bad news.

Emma straightened up a little, but her voice came out more hesitant. "Yeah. You only eat bottled, your skin'll start to get cold till you're room temp. How you gonna be a doctor then?"

The horror on Javier's face made Charlie feel the need to step in. "It'll take a few months before you're cold enough for anyone to notice. Around six before you're room temperature." Nobody knew why a vampire's body temp dropped from bottled blood—and so far they hadn't found any other health complications from the newfangled convenience. But if you regularly interacted with humans, it was necessary to feed directly from a vein every so often. Getting cold again was usually his own impetus for making an appointment with Trey.

"It ain't healthy!" Emma declared. "I know you say it is, Charlie, but we can't know! I want to make sure my boy's taking care of himself. It's my job."

Javier glared at her like he'd say something biting, which—judging by the past week—would turn into another fight. Charlie cleared his throat, feeling the need to stick up for someone who seemed to be a fellow introvert. "Being new-turned's rough. Sometimes we need to move at our own pace, don't you think, Emma? It's only been a week." In his experience, Emma didn't take offense easily, so hopefully she wouldn't mind his intervention.

Javier shot him a look of surprised gratitude as Emma stood there with her mouth hanging open, as if unsure what to say anymore. Meanwhile the music changed to a slower number, and after a moment Charlie recognized the sultry guitar of "Crash Into Me" by Dave Matthews.

Cash pushed Javi, sending him stumbling into Emma. "Em, take your baby bat onto the floor."

"When do I quit being called a baby bat?" Javi groused. But when Emma held out a hand like a peace gesture, he took it. As she turned away to lead him to the floor, the look that poor boy shot her was so fully of longing Charlie had to hold back a wince.

Cash slapped Charlie on the shoulder with his usual gusto. "Look at you, standing up for the downtrodden. Also, tag." He spun Charlie to face Vince and walked off.

"That's…not going to work," Charlie said, but of course, Cash didn't listen.

Vince frowned at him, arms crossed. "You look nice. I'm surprised to see you here without your head in a notebook."

"Thanks. I think." Charlie looked from his ex to Trey, the only man he'd been intimate with since the breakup. Awkward. Trey was just a friend—not really even that, since he paid the man, for God's sake—but still, Charlie shuffled from one foot to the other, trying to find something to say that was appropriate for a party. Nothing was coming.

Vince looked toward the dance floor. "Well, I'm um…" He pivoted to go back.

Charlie caught his arm. "I've been trying to talk to you all week."

Vince held up a finger in warning.

Charlie let him go, but his throat nearly closed up with emotion as he said, "Please."

For a moment, Charlie thought Vince would walk away. Then he re-crossed his arms and cocked his head. "I'll talk to you. If you'll dance with me."

Charlie just stopped himself from cringing. He wasn't much of a dancer, but if that was what it took. "All right. When the song changes, I'll—"

"Not when the song changes. Now. 'Crash' is an oldie, but I like it."

On the dance floor, couples—heterosexual couples—held each other close as Dave Matthews sang about sex. Surely Vince was kidding. They couldn't dance to this in the middle of a big party. But Vince looked dead serious.

"This song?" Charlie shifted, trying to come up with an alternative offering. All he could think of was a distraction. "It's not that old."

Vince almost smiled. "You don't want to know how young I was when this came out."

Charlie almost smiled back. "No, I really don't." His good humor was short lived. He looked out onto the floor and tried to imagine what it would be like to be out there with his arms around Vince. Holding him again would be wonderful, feeling the heat of his body and smelling the subtle spice of his cologne. Vince would think the grumbled comments and widening gap around them was funny. Maybe Charlie should be that cavalier too, but he couldn't.

He was trying. Last week he'd come down to the meeting while Alaric was there, and he'd stayed until after Alaric had gone. He'd thought about what Vince had said and realized Vince had gone down there to tell Alaric, without words, that he wasn't ashamed. He shouldn't have to do that alone, so Charlie had sucked up his antipathy and followed. Granted, he'd brought a sketchbook to work in so he didn't have to participate. But he'd gone—something he never would've done before. And he was here again, at a party, wearing a shirt so fitted he'd never have considered it without Cash's encouragement. The way it tapered with his torso not only made him feel exposed, it itched.

Vince seemed to like it, though, if his roving gaze was any indication. If a tight, itchy shirt was why Vince was talking to him at all, he'd wear them more often. He could make changes. He would, if it brought them closer together. But Vince wanted too much too fast. "We can't slow dance. Please ask for something else."

Though Vince had never looked hopeful, he looked disappointed now. "We can. You won't. Not the same thing." He turned to leave.

"Vince..." Charlie didn't know if he should try to stop him or not.

"Vince?" Trey sputtered. Charlie had forgotten he was even there. "Holy shit. You're *the* Vince."

Vince stopped two steps away and turned to look Trey up and down.

Trey winced, realizing what he'd done. "Sorry."

A noise like a laugh, but with zero humor in it, came from Vince as a look of absolute disgust crossed his face. "Scarlet." He turned to Charlie, eyebrows lifted. "Good to know I'm easy to exchange." He flung himself back into the crowd.

"Exchange?" Charlie called after him.

Trey, looking deeply chagrinned, cleared his throat. "We do look a bit alike."

"I'm sorry, I gotta—"

Trey nodded an encouragement. "Go after him."

Charlie hustled to catch up. "Vince, wait!"

ಬ◆ಚಿ

Vince threaded his way through the gathering crowd, huffing back tears. The tall prostitute who knew who he was had dark hair and blue eyes. Vince would even bet the guy had Italian blood in him, based on coloring.

Three months or so for people to notice a difference in skin temp, huh? And by six months, it was completely obvious?

Vince had dated Charlie for nine.

When Emma had said that, he'd been confused. Had Charlie been biting people in alleys, like some horror movie vampire, or what? Because he couldn't picture that at all. But Charlie never got cold, which meant he'd bitten somebody. Emma bit Javi during sex. Cash bit Rhiannon during sex. From what he could tell, sex and biting was the chocolate and peanut butter of vampiredom.

And here was a prostitute who looked a helluva lot like Vince and knew exactly who he was. Vince shook his head, trying to clear the thought. Charlie had broken up with him because he was a stripper. Would he be hypocritical enough to visit a prostitute while they were together?

He had to have been biting somebody.

Vince needed to face facts. He'd thrown himself at Charlie every step of the way, asked for every touch, every new connection. With each rebuff, he'd told himself it was because Charlie was shy, but that was looking more and more like wishful thinking. Charlie liked him, sure; lusted after him, definitely. But Charlie had never allowed him to be a serious part of his life. Face facts. Charlie had never loved him.

It was one thing to know they wouldn't work out over differences. It was another entirely to not be loved.

To Vince's left the dance floor buzzed with energy, beckoning him to have a shot or five and get lost in it. Anything to not think. A waiter carrying a tray of shots overhead sauntered by. Vince flagged her down and swiped a clear glass from the "human" side of the tray. Pound and down, and he grabbed another for the road.

"Spat with your friend?" A short, curly-haired man stood a little too close.

A lot of vampires at the party did that. Different eras, different places, different personal spaces. It did no good to back up, either. They just followed you. He took the second shot. The little man watched the drink disappear, avarice in his eyes.

Oh, goodie. A man who wanted him drunk was always a find. *Not.* "Everything's fine."

"You know Travert, then? Personally?"

The last word took on a lewd note. Vince took a closer look at him, ready to tell him to fuck off.

But this time he recognized the guy. Charlie's crazy sire, from the Liberi jail cell, had gotten out. "Ramón?" The vampire wasn't even CoVIn. What was he doing here?

He bowed. "At your service. If Travert won't give you what you want, I will."

Vince wasn't sure if he meant sex or vampirism, but hell no either way. Charlie had really slept with this guy? Options in small-town Bourbon France had clearly been lacking. *No, don't contemplate all the people Charlie has slept with who aren't you.* "You escaped?"

Ramón tilted his head like he didn't understand the question. Emma and Javi had had memory problems when she'd been spelled or whatever they'd done.

Shit. Fear cooled his buzz as Vince looked around the room with new eyes, trying to play spot the Liberi. Not that he could tell the difference until someone did something crazy. He needed to find Cash.

He backed up. And slammed into Alaric. The vampire's

smile turned nasty as he jerked Vince aside, keeping a too-firm grip on his upper arm. "From Charlie to Ramón. I see you've found your people."

He didn't have time for Alaric. Without thinking, Vince shoved back, trying to move past him.

Alaric grabbed his hand and spun him, pulling up on his arm until he controlled Vince as deftly as a puppet. His too-strong cologne of tobacco and myrrh—the same overbearing musk he'd worn that night at Tooth and Nail—made Vince's eyes water.

"When's the little wood fairy going to be done with you so you can die in an alley?"

Alaric may have whispered, but Vince didn't bother with privacy. He was pissed and wanted the room to hear, Cash's policy of silence be damned. "Are you still planning to kill me? Hand my heart off to a crazy witch for her spell? When are you going to let your mama know you're kidnapping CoVIn members and making them kill for the Liberi?"

Conversation ceased around them as their altercation became the focus.

Alaric's grip tightened until Vince thought he'd bruise, but Vince didn't stop. "What did you do to Javi and Emma?"

"Nobody believes your lies," Alaric growled, letting him go with a shove.

Even the music seemed softer as every eye in the circled crowd watched with suspicion or fear. Alaric was the known one here. It seemed equal parts good and bad for what people believed him capable of. But it spelled only bad news for anyone stepping up to help.

Vince needed out. He needed to tell Cash what was going on. But after practically tailing him all night, now that Vince needed him, Cash was nowhere to be seen.

A throat cleared, and they both jerked around to see Charlie stepping from the crowd. His face was stark white, but his gaze was steady. Vince held his breath, unsure what would happen. Charlie played it safe. He didn't stand up. This was completely out of character. And yet his rich, low voice carried through the crowd with only a hint of a waver. "I believe him."

Vince's heart picked up its pace, a flutter of hope battling the rage inside.

Alaric laughed. "The queer stripper you met, when, last week? I'm Queen Modron's first son. This brings your loyalty into question as well as your good sense."

Charlie took another step out of the crowd and into the ring, still out of reach but close enough for Vince to see the bead of sweat coming down his forehead. He'd never looked so terrified. "Vince and I met when he was nine; his father and I worked at the same woodshop. I watched him grow up and have good reason to believe him to be an honest man."

It wasn't a full declaration of what they had—not by a long shot—but it was the first time ever that Charlie had claimed him in public. Despite Alaric, giddy joy made Vince want to smile. Honestly, he didn't know whether to be thrilled at progress or depressed at how much he feasted on crumbs.

Alaric's eyes narrowed, and any thoughts Vince had for his own welfare turned to worry for Charlie's. Then a sly smile turned Alaric's face demonic. "When did he become aware that you are a vampire?"

Charlie froze.

"You expect us to believe that you've known this man for over a decade, and well enough to believe his aspersions over my truth, and yet he didn't know about you? No, clearly he does. But that's fine because you registered him as soon as he found out, as per CoVIn law, right?"

Oh. Shit.

Cash flung himself into the circle, jacket tails flying. "Alaric. Guests. We talked."

Alaric stayed maddeningly calm. "I have a room full of people who saw this man lunge for me. I'm keeping it rather cool here, considering that—all out of respect for our friendship, Geirson." He stepped back a touch, like he was the reasonable one.

Cash sent Vince a warning look to stay silent and docile.

Vince jerked away and out of reach, but he squashed the desire to mouth off. He would be brave, not stupid. So he stood between Cash and Charlie, arms crossed to try to control his furious shaking.

The queen stepped into the ring, bodies parting before her with efficient respect. She wasn't tall, maybe five foot three, and she'd cut up the dance floor with the frivolous energy of a teenager. But now she was all queen, stately and firm. "What's this?"

Alaric threw a hand out like he was in a melodrama. "This human, who isn't registered, by the way, is casting some serious accusations against me."

Vince stiffened. "I'm getting registered. It's being fixed."

Alaric smiled magnanimously, chilling Vince further. "Of course you are. And you should. I'll even forgive you for your accusation. You've been through an ordeal that would scramble the faculties of any human." He turned to the circle. "This man was attacked by the Liberi. Bitten. Strung up. Violated."

"Stop," Vince said between clenched teeth, hating the way he sounded victimized.

"He needs our protection. Despite what he said about me, I welcome him into our ranks."

Ire made Vince's muscles tense. Alaric had completely captured the crowd with his faux generosity. The queen had relaxed, smiling at her eldest son like he was a hero. Cash, however, stayed tense, as if waiting for the punch line.

And it came. "What concerns me, however," Alaric said, "is that one among us stands by his ravings and against our laws— Charles Travert." He said the name with the original French, making it sound formal and foreign.

Charlie's eyes closed slowly, then opened, head down like a man facing execution.

"Travert has been in Austin the entire time we've worked to open our headquarters here. Has he helped? No. He has broken our laws for years by keeping hidden the existence of a human who knew of us. Why would he do that? We could've protected Vince from the tragedy of this week. And now Charles takes the word of this confused human—his lover—against me, the queen's eldest son."

People pointed, and chatter buzzed loud. Someone behind Vince whispered, "I always thought he was bent."

Followed by, "But he's friends with Cash Geirson."

Vince gaped in realization that Charlie had kept his orientation a relative secret for centuries. How had he done that?

And Alaric had just outed him. Frustrated as Charlie's closeted existence could make Vince, it was Charlie's—and only Charlie's—decision when and who to tell. Anger boiled up again, needing an outlet. "Stop."

Alaric ignored him. "What I'm compelled to wonder is, did he put that idea in Vince's head to cause dissension? Who is the real traitor here? The queen's eldest supporter or the... man"— he said it like there was question—"who has turned his back on us for years?"

Vince lunged forward. Cash latched onto his arm, holding him back. "I recognized your voice from when you were that Aztec priestess's bitch last week, taking orders from a psycho.

Charlie had nothing to do with this."

Alaric balled his fists, eyes flashing dark, but he didn't flip to that other crazy version of himself, the one that would show the room who he really was.

The queen looked from Alaric to Cash, not Charlie. "Cassius?"

Cash's jaw clenched, but his shoulders stayed intentionally relaxed. "I'm thinking this is a party, not a trial, and this misunderstanding can get cleared up at a different time."

She smiled indulgently. "M'dear, for a warrior, you certainly are a pacifist when it comes to your friends. Charles Travert, your trial to debate the status of your CoVIn membership will be tomorrow."

"What?" Cash exclaimed, startled.

Charlie muttered something to his saints and nodded. "Yes, my queen."

Vince backed up in line with Charlie. "If you're kicking him out, I'm not staying."

Cash laughed through a muttered, "Son of a bitch," then added, louder, "Don't listen to him. Head trauma." He turned and shot Vince a shut-the-fuck-up look.

Before Vince could tell him where to stick it, Charlie put a hand up, voice soft. "Don't make it easy for anyone to kill you with no repercussions."

"But—"

"No. Take the protection. You being vulnerable to attack won't help me."

Vince turned back to face Queen Modron. He didn't understand the magnitude of being excommunicated, but even Cash looked worried. It was bad. "We need more time for an investigation to see if Alaric is the masked man."

The queen eyed him up and down. "This human is a bold one, isn't he?" She touched Alaric's shoulder in a show of support. "You can't prove what isn't true."

The confidence in Alaric's smile made Vince want to puke.

Until the queen added, "But if you surprise me, we'll change who's on trial. You have a week. Gentlemen, can we share the evening without a fight?"

The speakers squealed in electronic agony. Everyone hunched in pain at the sonic attack. "No," came over the microphone. "We most definitely cannot." At the DJ station Rhiannon was gone. In her place was Tzitzi.

Chapter 12

Tzitzi, in full Aztec regalia—how the fuck had she gotten in here looking like that?—smiled at the crowd. "I see you, Vince."

Vince froze. Charlie's hand inserted into his, and he took it, squeezing as hard as he could. At the moment he couldn't care less what Charlie had or hadn't done with anyone else. Fear overrode anger.

"You've been hard to find. Usually I wouldn't bother, but you've already been dedicated to Our Lord the Flayed One, and he'd like his offering."

"Somebody get her," Cash yelled. He shoved Alaric's shoulder, and together they ran toward the platform, fighting the crowd to get there.

Tzitzi yelled in some bizarre language—Aztec, Vince would guess—and beat on her chest. Each pummel of her fist made small bursts of blood on her white dress, like she pricked herself with every beat.

Around her, vampires defended her front and flank. Rhiannon had been slammed into a wall.

The witch's last stab punctured a shriveled black thing she wore around her neck. Blood spewed from it, spattering the first row of vampires and draining down her dress.

The crowd went crazy. Screams punctuated the room as the screens showed vampires biting each other without finesse, raking fangs across arms and necks in red abandon. Not everyone had changed—not even most of them—but enough to create a maelstrom of activity.

The queen stomped her foot and chanted in another language Vince had never heard. A few notes in, she grabbed a crazed vampire by the hair and swung him down. Her song-chant came faster and louder. Expression blank, she spread her palm over the struggling vampire's face, sang something with too many vowels, and a green current spread from her fingers. The man screamed in pain, then went silent. The song continued as she reached for another vampire.

At least she was still on their side.

"Fuck me…" Vince murmured, terrified.

Charlie took his elbow. "Let's go. I'm getting you out of here."

Vince nodded, wanting nothing more than to not be here. "Please."

An arm latched around Charlie's neck, hauling him backward. Ramón had come for him.

Emma had said she'd changed when her sire bit her. "No!" Vince cried, body-slamming Ramón and knocking the smaller man away.

"Ramón?" Charlie yelled over the noise. "What are you doing here?" He lunged between them. "Vince, get back."

"Don't let him bite you. That's how they changed Emma."

"Vince?" Ramón asked, interest piqued. "The stripper? Two birds. One stone. Marvelous." He swiped at Charlie. Charlie tried to back up, but a scuffle in the crowd shoved him forward instead.

Ramón reared back to strike with his fangs.

Vince punched him in the forehead. Ramón's neck snapped back, and his teeth failed to pierce Charlie's skin.

The vampire tossed Charlie sideways and grabbed Vince by the wrist.

His grip clamped down with unbreakable force, and he dragged Vince into the crowd. Vince dug his heels in, struggled, grabbed people as they passed, but Ramón sprinted forward, knocking through everyone so fast the room became a blur.

Charlie yelled his name, but Vince couldn't see him through the crowd.

They made it through the party, down a hall, and into a billiard room where four men played, oblivious to the chaos in the main room. "What's going on?" one asked, way too calm for the situation.

"Stop him!" Vince yelled.

Ramón drew a freaking gun from his jacket and shot three times. Darts stuck to one man's neck and another's shoulder, and the two men went down. The third dodged. The fourth leaped for Ramón.

Vince was tossed onto the pool table. Balls scattered as he slid across the felt on his side, blocking his face with an arm.

Ramón landed ass first on the ground but took the man with him. His gun went flying and skittered across the wood floor to rest under a piano bench. Vince rolled across the table and off the other side, heading for it.

"You're one of mine," Ramón announced triumphantly. Was he smelling the guy? He bit down. The man choked. His eyes rolled back in his head as he convulsed.

The last man standing kicked out.

Ramón dodged, rolled, and hopped up. An ax glinted on the wall—of course Cash decorated with weaponry—and Charlie's sire grabbed it. "You're not mine," he told the man, then swung. The ax connected with his neck, severing muscle and spine. Just as blood started to spew, the man exploded. Instead of liquid, dust sprayed over the carpet.

Vince stood, gun trained on Ramón as the man on the floor

continued to seize.

"You know how to shoot that thing?" the vampire asked.

"Pull the trigger," Vince growled. Aiming was a different question. His dad had taught him to box, not shoot. His hands shook as Ramón approached, the picture of confidence. His fangs dropped, and his eyes turned watery amber.

Vince pulled the trigger.

The dart stuck into the wall behind Ramón.

"Shit."

Ramón leaped forward and pinned Vince to the wall. His hands crushed Vince's, ripping the gun from his fingers. "Maybe I'll see what everyone's so interested in."

The horror of last week came rushing back, and Vince quailed, tears pricking his eyes. In a swell of mindless panic, his mouth went on auto, begging Ramón to stop. If the man touched him with his fangs, he was done. Dead. No way he'd come back from that dark.

"Get away from him, you bastard!" Charlie screamed as he shot through the open door.

Ramón turned from Vince, and the pressure eased.

Charlie tackled Ramón, and they both went down under the assault. Ramón turned his fangs to Charlie instead.

Blood spurted from a bite on Charlie's neck.

"Mine!" Ramón yelled triumphantly. He rose and smiled, fangs dripping with blood.

Charlie flopped onto the floor. He shivered as his arms flailed, and he yelled more French.

"Charlie!" Vince dropped to the floor beside him and tried to stem the blood. But Charlie writhed, curling in on himself and away from Vince's touch.

"Allez-vous en. Allez-vous en."

"I don't speak French."

Charlie panted. "Go. Away." His vocalization turned French again, or maybe it was just noise.

Vince backed up.

"You're going to need some protection, boy. He's going to wake up wanting you in a nasty way," Ramón taunted. "Why don't you come easy with me." The words dripped innuendo.

Vince grimaced. "You are disgusting. Go fuck yourself." He stood tall, scared but determined. "You know what you just did?"

"Finished off your boyfriend."

"The only way I know to get him back is to kill you. So guess what I have to do?" And he would, too. He didn't know how. But determination burned away the fear, leaving rage. Vince would kill this son of a bitch and bring Charlie back.

Ramón laughed. "Good luck with that."

Vince dropped to a boxer's stance, pushing away how ridiculous it was to think he could take on a vampire.

Ramón approached him slowly, his grin like a cat taunting its prey. Vince needed a miracle, and they both knew it.

Behind Ramón in a rush of air, Cash dashed in and stopped beside the pool table. He assessed the situation, picked up a pool ball, and pitched it at Ramón, nailing him in the temple. Ramón turned, and Cash fast-balled another one, this time straight to the nads. Ramón backed up, hands cupping the family jewels. Vince swiped a kick, and Ramón went down.

Cash tossed his special stake. Vince caught it and slammed it into Ramón's back.

Bone cracked and blood gushed from a hole, but the man didn't dust.

"Aim," Cash suggested. "Fuck." A scuffle started as the first vampire Ramón had turned woke up and punched Cash in the knee.

Vince yanked out the stake. Ramón rolled over and reached for Vince's middle. Instinct said to flee, but Vince straddled the vampire, stake raised.

Charlie got up. His gaze found Vince, and his nostrils flared, as if taking in the scent of the room. The look of covetous need Charlie lavished on him sent a cold thrill through Vince that was as sexual as it was terrifying.

"More fuck," Cash added, curses pouring from him like a happy sailor as he dove for Charlie. Charlie, Cash, and the third vampire slammed to the ground and wrestled for dominance.

Ramón reached for Vince's neck, his crazed eyes full of pain and hate. Vince ignored it, focusing his aim on the heart. Both hands on the stake, he drove it home with all the force he could muster. Bone cracked. Tissue split. The cavity of Ramón's chest sucked at the stake like meat.

"*Diable tapette*," Ramón whispered. Then he exploded, the stake in his chest exploding with him.

Vince dropped through his dissipating form and landed on his ass.

Charlie and the other spelled man gasped.

Cash hopped up to watch them. "Thanks. It's harder to fight two vamps who want to kill you when you can't kill them back."

"Is Charlie okay?" Vince moved toward them, but Cash held him back.

"We'll find out soon. Don't get in range yet."

"How're Rhi and Javi? And Emma?"

"Fine, fine, and fine. Things were already winding down when I noticed you two were gone." He looked at Vince's hands. "Where's my stake?"

Vince looked at the dust on the ground. "I take it I was

supposed to pull it out before he went ashy?"

Cash closed his eyes slowly. "Yes."

Charlie's breathing grew easier.

Vince watched him and waited. "I can make you a new one."

The first man sat up, dazed. "What happened?"

Cash helped him up. "You attacked me."

The man looked horrified. "I did?"

Cash waved his hand like it wasn't a big deal and turned back to Vince. "I accept the offer of a new stake. We can discuss specifications after the party."

"Sure." Vince tentatively reached a hand out for Charlie. His ex was still breathing like a human. Vince didn't usually notice its absence, but now that Charlie was inhaling and exhaling with the need of a man who'd just run miles, it was easy to see the difference. Charlie looked away, like he was ashamed, then back at Vince's hand. Just as Vince was about to step away, he took it. Vince tugged, and Charlie popped up, the space and silence between them awkward as hell.

"Geirson. Wow. Thank you," the other man gushed. "I'm so sorry I—"

"Cash," Cash announced, forcibly detangling himself from the man-hug the guy had foisted on him. "It's the twenty-first century. People use first names now."

"Oh-oh-oh-okay. Cash. Wow. That's…wow. Thank you Ge—Cash. Wow." He turned to Vince and Charlie. "I got saved by Cash Geirson."

Cash patted him on the head in the most condescending manner, but the vampire beamed like a rock star had touched him.

"Actually," Cash said, "Vince here saved you. He took out Ramón Triquell. You should thank him."

The vampire did a double take at Vince. "But he's a human."

"Yes, he is." Cash looked at him expectantly.

The man's adoring gaze didn't leave Cash as he said, "Thank you, Vince."

"Excellent. Now be a champ, get the darts out of your associates, and take them to the main room for an examination." He turned away, dismissing the man. "We have things mostly under control there. As soon as Modron got close to the platform, Tzitzi ran to the window, turned into an eagle and flew away. Coward."

Vince put his hands atop his head. "She can turn into an eagle? That's impossible. Conservation of mass and…"

"Shapeshifting is a common spell. Most witches can turn into at least one animal." Cash waved a hand like conservation of mass was not a thing. But magic was. "After her exit, the bespelled CoVIn vampires were easy enough to round up. This will be the most talked-about party of the year. Possibly decade." He grinned and clapped his hands once. "Excellent."

Cash's groupie reluctantly exited with one man over each shoulder like sacks of potatoes.

Cash threw an arm around Vince. "Good job tonight. First kill?"

"Kill?" Oh, god, he'd killed somebody. With a stake. "Yes. My first." It didn't feel like murder. It was a vampire.

Like Charlie was. If somebody killed Charlie, it would be murder. Or Emma, Javi, or Cash.

He'd had to stake Ramón to save Charlie. No question, he'd do it again, so there was no sense in feeling guilty. Even if he did.

"Congratulations. Drinks on me. Okay, tonight they already were. Next time we're out." Cash clapped his shoulder. "Now, as evidenced by tonight's debacle, I need a human ward. Pick a room—not mine—and it's yours. I'll have your things moved

184 • Jax Garren

over tomorrow."

The offer—more like an order—took Vince by surprise.
"Move in. Here? Are you telling me I'm moving in or asking if
I'm willing to?" He glanced at Charlie to see his reaction, but his
carefully blank face as he leaned against the pool table gave away
nothing.

"You can barber my hair for rent. That took you, what, five
minutes today? You'll have access to a pool, a billiard room, a
movie theater, and maid service, including laundry."

Even if Cash kicked him out after a month, it would be an
epic month. However... "That still wasn't phrased in the form of
a question." And frankly, Vince didn't want a place anyone could
kick him out of ever again. He blew out a breath, reluctant to turn
the offer-order down, but there was no way he could rely on a
capricious vampire prince who was still working out his bigotry
for a home. "It's a generous offer, but I like having my own
space."

Cash looked from Vince to Charlie then back and dropped
his arm. "If you feel more comfortable, we can sign a contract,
like a rental. We can start with a year and see if we hate each other,
but I like community, and this week has been good. I haven't put
a time limit on Emma's stay, which means she'll probably be here
for years. Whether Javier knows it or not, that means he'll be here
a lot. If I approve somebody, you'd need to invite them inside so
they can cross the threshold. Otherwise, the house is as much
yours as it is mine. Almost."

And still the dude talked like this was a sure thing. And still
Vince wanted to say yes anyway. He wasn't a fan of living alone,
either, and Emma was fun, and he was in a fucking billiard room.
Who had a billiard room? Cash's house was the shit. "What about
Alaric? He can't get into my current place, but he can come in
here." Although Alaric could get to Vince as soon as he stepped

out his front door.

Cash frowned. "Alaric fought on team CoVIn tonight."

"Because he's in public and just got called out."

"Modron is officially interested in your case. The highest authorities are now looking into it."

"Does that mean Alaric is investigating his own case?"

"Of course." Cash put his hands behind his back. "But once you live here, everything starts from scratch. You'll have to invite even me back in the first time I leave, and I signed the deed. We'll wait until a verdict for Alaric. But if he's cleared, he's invited in."

Invite Cash into his own house? That was a lot of trust. But wait. "I didn't have to invite Charlie in after I moved in with him."

"Yeah, you did," Cash said.

"No, I didn't."

"You did invite me in," Charlie said, speaking up for the first time. "I left to go grocery shopping, as I had no food in the house. I spent the entire time I was out debating how best to get back inside, then when I got home, my arms full of groceries, the first words out of your mouth were, 'Come in, come in!' You'd done all the laundry and scrubbed the bathrooms as a surprise to prove you'd be a good housemate and were anxious for me to see it."

Vince almost smiled at the memory. He had invited him in, hadn't he? "I'd also gone through all your cabinets and was trying to figure out how you lived with no television, no Tylenol, and no dishes other than coffee cups."

Charlie took a few steps toward him. "I had no idea why you didn't move back out the first week."

Had Charlie been seeing the prostitute back then? The question sent Vince right back to the cloud of anger he'd been in before all the chaos started. Vince turned away. "I had nowhere else to go."

Charlie froze like he felt the ice in Vince's words.

That wasn't totally true. There had been other places he could've bunked, at least temporarily. But he'd stayed because Charlie had been kind and cute and the only adult Vince could talk to who was gay—or at least who he knew was gay. He'd been so pumped at the opportunity to spend more time with a man he could talk to who understood him.

Charlie, the man Vince had relied on as a bedrock of honesty, stability, and kindness, had lied to him so thoroughly it was crushing.

Cash rolled a ball along the pool table, knocking things together impatiently. "Movers."

Vince put a hand on a hip. "Still not phrased as a question."

Cash frowned as he rolled the eight ball, sending three separate balls into baskets. "You're kidding me."

"Remind me never to bet you in pool. And no, I'm not kidding. You will eventually stop ordering me around, and we'll get along better."

"Do you know how many sentients would jump bonfires for half a chance to be in your position?"

"Plenty, I'm sure. You could order them to move here. But you haven't because you want me."

Cash rolled two balls at once, clearing the table in a complicated fiasco of cracking and banking. "Fine. Will you move in? Please?" He smirked like he was really proud of himself.

He should say no. But instead he said, "I'll think about it."

Cash barked a laugh and poked him in the forehead. "Don't think too long, or I'll give the position away to someone more annoyingly appreciative."

Rhiannon came into the room and sighed in relief. "Thank God. Answer your damn texts, man."

Vince pulled his phone out, checked, and whistled. "How many messages is this?"

"I thought you'd been kidnapped again!"

Vince held out an arm. "Are you okay?"

She snuggled under it for a hug and started texting. "Javi and Emma are searching for you too. I'm fine. Little panicked at the beginning there, when a dreadlocked girl took over my spot, but she was more interested in the microphone than in me. We have a plan, Javi and Emma and I. You think you're ready to go back to work?"

"Do you need me to take another night off?"

"No, I need you to go to work."

That didn't sound good. "What sort of plan is this?"

"To catch Tzitzi." She glanced at Cash. "We're assuming that's on the agenda? I overheard Alaric and Nikolai discussing plans to raid Tooth and Nail."

Cash shook his head slowly. "They haven't told me that. But it would make sense."

"Well, assuming Benedict Alaric is in on that plan, it's not going to work." Rhiannon believed Vince without question, even if she hadn't seen Alaric's nasty side up close and personal. Her constant faith was a bright spot in the grim evening.

"It's not going to work because they're no longer there," Cash said. "The jaguars cleared it after one of their own was sacrificed. They didn't get Tzitzi because the place was already deserted. What's your plan?"

Rhiannon squeezed harder, and Vince already knew he wasn't going to like this plan. "She made it clear tonight that she thinks she owes Vince to the god she mentioned, Xipe Totec."

The taste in Vince's mouth turned bitter. "That's the name of the god she called Our Lord the Flayed One?"

Rhi shivered. "Yeah, he's, uh, not my favorite god. He's known for..." She glanced at Vince.

"Flaying people?" Vince filled in.

"What he's known for isn't important. What's important is that she's already consecrated Vince to him. My guess is through blessed pulque—that white alcohol you said she made you drink. Which means she needs Vince specifically to fulfill her obligation."

Vince raised a hand. "Wait, she wouldn't be after me if I hadn't drunk the freaking pulque? That stuff was disgusting."

Cash ignored him. "This makes him perfect bait."

"Bait?" Vince asked. Purposefully putting himself in Tzitzi's path was the last thing he wanted to do.

"No," Charlie insisted. "Vince is not bait. We're not risking him like that."

Rhiannon's arm around him tightened. "I don't like it either, but he's going to be targeted as soon as he leaves this compound. I'd rather have a plan in place with Cash and as many other vampires as possible ready to drop down from the rafters than have him out there alone. He's not safe until we catch her. So let's catch her fast. That means..."

Vince licked his lips. Rhiannon had a point. "That means giving her a chance to get something she wants, and the only thing we know for a fact that she wants is me." He squeezed Rhi back, taking strength from the connection. Cool as Cash's place was— the infinity edge pool overlooking Lady Bird Lake was epic—that didn't mean he wanted to be confined here forever. The faster Tzitzi was caught, the sooner he'd be safe and the sooner he could get on with his life, be it in a cheap-ass apartment or luxury estate. "I'll do it."

Charlie stepped forward, more determination on his face than Vince had ever seen there. "No. We can figure out another way to find her that doesn't involve dangling Vince. 'Our Lord the Flayed One' is not a ceremonial title. I saw what she was doing to her sacrificial victims. Vince stays here until we catch her."

Breathe in. "How long will that be, Charlie? We don't even know where she is."

"As long as it takes."

Breathe out. "So I sit on my ass behind closed doors waiting for other people to make my life safe? She's stealing the awen of every CoVIn vampire she can get ahold of. There's a bigger plan here than just sacrificing me, and the sooner she's stopped, the safer everyone is." He lifted his chin and stared right at Charlie. "Besides, I've never been the kind of person who trades my freedom for security. I'm in. What's the plan?"

Chapter 13

Charlie drank his beer and stared at the condensation on the table, listening for any sign of trouble over the noise of some boy band blaring over the sound system. A man in too-small tighty-whities shook his backside in Emma's face as she stuffed bills into his waistband. Every now and then, he flipped his long hair, whacking Charlie with it.

He despised this place. When he died and went to hell for his crimes, he was coming back here, living out eternity in a crowded club packed with drunk women stuffing dollar bills down men's drawers to the sounds of pop music played through tinny speakers and by the light of purple-and-pink spots hitting a disco ball. He would spend every moment of it dreading Vince's entrance, knowing what he'd have to watch when Vince got onstage, and yet unable to leave because his fear of Vince in danger was stronger than the sickness this place inspired.

To top it off, the dancers, every one of them, had managed to jostle his seat, attack him with their hair, or worse, make him the butt of a joke, rubbing their hands over his head, grinding against his side, or otherwise turning him into the hilarious man-on-man action of their number. It was like Vince had said, "The redhead in the front is my ex. He hates attention. Have fun!"

He'd bet his antique plane collection that was *exactly* what had happened.

Cash added more blood to Charlie's beer from a flask he carried. He'd been keeping watch in the foyer until a moment ago, which meant Rhi had texted him that Vince's number was about to start. Rhi, as an employee, was the only one allowed in the dressing room, so she was stationed there. Javi had her usual place at the back of the club in the sound booth. Nikolai, who refused to come in, was patrolling the back door. The rest of them—Galswinth, Emma, and Charlie—were inside the club itself. Somebody had eyes on Vince at all times, and somebody had eyes on every entrance to the club. It was as good as they could get, but still, Charlie couldn't chase away the fear churning in his stomach that something would go horribly wrong.

"LongHorns is a terrible name for a club," Cash commented, drinking straight from his flask. "Or am I just not gay enough?"

Galswinth snickered. "I think the name is humorous. Surely they weren't intending it to be taken seriously?"

"Nah. It's dorkilicious," Emma answered, spanking the man in front of her as he headed off. She was having a grand old time making every dancer's night with her generosity. If she had a type, Charlie had yet to figure it out. She gave equally to black, white, tall, short, long-haired, crew cut, punk, and boy-next-door. The dancers had figured that out too, and everyone made the financially astute decision of visiting her at least once. It also gave them the opportunity to make Charlie's life hell.

"Yes, I do believe the name is referring to penises," Galswinth said over the noise, eyes tracking the mostly naked man. Nikolai hadn't been thrilled about her coming inside, but she'd kissed him on the cheek, whispered something in his ear, and he'd told her to have fun.

They were sweet together, the kind of trusting, friendly relationship Charlie and Vince had once shared, and it made Charlie both happy for them and excessively jealous.

Cash patted her on the hand. "'Dork' doesn't meant 'penis' anymore, my sweet Winnie. You should get around humans more often. Maybe do more than eat."

Galswinth smirked. "Yes, you do so much more with humans. Like fornicate. Blood and sex. I see how you are so much more versed in them than I."

Emma leaned in. "May I call you Winnie? I like that. So much cuter than Galswinth."

"You may."

"You are way cooler than I thought you'd be. Here, take some ones. You don't seem to have brought none."

"I didn't realize it was the protocol."

The music ended. Instead of bowing, the dancer came back to their table. Charlie braced for whatever was coming. But the dancer just took Emma's hand, and Charlie blew out a relieved breath. He was going to kiss it. Fine.

And he did kiss it, bending over so his derriere was shoved in Charlie's face. Charlie froze with a sweaty ass right next to his ear.

"If you slapped it," Cash offered, "everyone would think that was hilarious."

Charlie shot him a dirty look. "I don't care what everyone thinks is hilarious."

Cash stood and did it himself, swatting the man on the backside with a stinging smack Charlie could hear. The dancer jumped forward in surprise as Cash turned to the audience and blew them a kiss.

The crowd went crazy, cheering him as much as the dancer. Rubbing his ass, the dancer bowed again. With a good-natured grin he headed backstage.

"He'll feel that tomorrow," Cash said, sitting down. "You're welcome. Have they all been at you?"

"It's fine," Charlie muttered.

"Oh yeah," Emma said.

"Every one of them," Galswinth added.

"Has anyone seen the witch?" Charlie asked. If he was going to endure this for a night, they'd damn well better catch the witch.

Emma and Winnie—he was starting to think of her that way too—looked at him in confusion for a moment.

"The witch! The whole reason we're here? Has anyone even been looking for her, or are we wasting our time?"

Emma put her hand to her chest, affronted. "I have totally been looking. Besides, I'm teaching Winnie the valuable life skill of stuffing dollars down men's pants. This is absolutely not a waste of time. Want some ones? You can pay me back later. My sources claim you homosexuals are more generous with the tips than we girls are. You have a reputation to uphold."

Vince had said the same thing. He'd also said he'd quit taking those higher-paying male clients while they were together because, to him, that was cheating. He *had* changed his behavior because they were in a relationship. Yes, it wasn't enough to make Charlie comfortable, but it was at least a sign Vince was willing to compromise. Could they still find a compromise?

Not if Vince wouldn't speak to him, no. And something new was bothering Vince, something more than what had happened last week with Alaric. Ever since the party, Vince had been making cracks about doppelgangers and hypocrites. The only thing Charlie could imagine it might be about was Trey, but it would be ludicrous of Vince to be pissed off that Charlie had started hiring Trey over a year after they'd broken up when Vince had been receiving money for, not outright prostitution, sure, but still for sexual services rendered *while they were still together*.

Emma, misreading his thoughtfulness as consideration, shoved a fistful of bills at him. He jerked away from them. "No. No, thank you. This is not my scene. I'm not here to—I just want to catch Tzitzi and get out." He grimaced. "They clearly know who I am."

"Right," she said, grinning. "And the best way to get back at Vince for that is to enjoy yourself. Come on, these guys are hot. You gotta like that."

Of course he did. He was surrounded by amazing specimens of manhood shaking their assets. He'd be dead if it didn't turn him on. There was zero connection to his brain or his heart or anything other than base lust, the desire that had made him an outcast for three hundred years. Without love to give the feeling meaning, it was simply a splinter, jagged and buried deep, that he couldn't remove.

At least he'd always thought of it that way before. But Vince didn't. The world was changing, and quickly. Becoming better.

Could he change with it?

The thought made him ache with longing and yet afraid to move, like swinging by a noose after the mob had gone. He'd almost stayed there, terrified to leave, sure he was dead and would fall into Hell, covered in urine and cooling pitch, as soon as he took the noose off. But he'd landed on the ground, cleaned himself off, the burns had healed eventually, and he'd started a new life.

Galswinth peered at him from the other side of Emma. "Alaric didn't lie? You truly do prefer men?" Her tone was the politically neutral one that said she was horrified yet too polite to act like it.

He looked at his beer and made himself speak. "I don't prefer men. That implies I have some interest in women but given my druthers, I'd take a man. It isn't like that." He couldn't look up, so he started peeling the label off his bottle, slowly revealing the glass beneath. "Watch Cash, the way he sits completely unaffected as the men dance. He doesn't see them as attractive, even when they're naked, even when they're moving in ways designed to make people want them. That's how I feel around women. A woman could parade about like this"—he waved at the stage—"and I wouldn't feel anything." The label was gone, so he picked at the shreds, scraping the bottle clean with his thumbnail. "I can't help it. I tried to change. I have been intimate with women. I was unmoved every time." He rubbed the paper between his palms until it made a tiny ball. "That's why now they call it an orientation, not a preference. It's a direction you're programmed to go, not a choice."

He didn't look up, but he could feel everyone's eyes on him, particularly Galswinth's. After a moment she said, "I hadn't thought of it that way. I'm sorry you were programmed incorrectly. That would be a burden." Her tone was sympathetic, even if the words were harsh.

Vince would probably start an irate lecture at this point, but Charlie felt relieved at how much progress that statement made from a fixed point drilled into her since birth. She was thinking— changing, even—and that gave him hope.

Another pause and she added, "A friend of Cash's is a friend of mine. You may call me Winnie as well. I'm not sure Kolyan will feel the same way, but I will see what I can do."

He looked at her in surprise. She caught his gaze and gave him a nervous half smile as if she wasn't quite sure how to deal with him but was willing to try. He nodded. "Thank you."

The other half of her mouth lifted, finishing the smile into something genuine and beautiful as she nodded back. "You're welcome. Thank you, as well, for teaching me with patience. I know how annoying it can be to feel you must explain yourself."

"You're welcome." The first inkling of a different life took hold of his imagination. If Cash could change his mind—granted, that had taken a couple centuries—and if Galswinth could start to change her mind with a few words and Cash's support, a day might arrive when Charlie could introduce his boyfriend—his husband—to others, and nobody would bat an eye.

Vince saw that future. He believed in it. Maybe Charlie should quit dangling in the past and get out of the noose one more time.

He leaned across the table, taking a risk. "I appreciate your sympathy, Winnie, but my only burden, as you called it, is made by other people. I don't want pity. I simply want people to not care. It would mean everything if my friends cared about the quality of the people I see and not… what exists at the juncture of their thighs."

Cash snickered like a teenager, and Charlie looked at the floor. "I apologize if I speak too frankly."

"I'm far too old to be embarrassed by frank speech, Charles." Galswinth's grin turned just a little devilish, though her back straightened primly. "Yet far too young to be uncaring what lies between a man's thighs. There are reasons I did not return Alaric's sentiments all those centuries ago, you know."

Charlie's jaw loosened. "What?" Most of CoVIn knew Alaric had had the queen turn Galswinth, his human betrothed, in the thought that they'd marry and continue together as immortals. Rumors abounded about why she'd spurned him after turning.

The inadequacy of his manhood was not the rumor he expected to be confirmed by the woman herself.

Cash spit his blood and beer out in a burst of laughter. "Winnie!" He swiped at the liquid, sopping up the incriminating red.

Emma gasped in fake horror as she helped him. "Law's sakes, Winnie, you scandalized Cash. I didn't know that was possible."

Winnie raised her chin haughtily and smiled like the vampire who'd eaten the princess.

The queen's eldest daughter had always intimidated Charlie, but he'd never hung out with her in a place designed for irreverence. Maybe LongHorns Lounge wasn't the deepest pit of Hell after all.

The lights dimmed for the last performance before intermission. Vince's number.

It still might be the second deepest pit. The crushing disappointment Charlie had felt the last time he had been here was still too close. Jealousy had turned on his inner violence in ways he hadn't known existed. He'd itched to hurt the other patrons or to leap onto the stage and drag Vince off. Not to save him, but to use him in the worst ways he could think of. Hell, part of him had wanted to bite him on the stage in front of everyone. To claim him like an animal. He'd run away halfway through Vince's number when he couldn't take it anymore.

He hated that he had that in him. Even the memory of it made him ill. He glanced around the room at all the excited patrons, his frustration already building, and shifted in his seat.

A driving pop beat started, and Vince sauntered out in construction worker garb, looking damned gorgeous in low-slung jeans and a tank top that showed off his stellar blacksmith's arms. Charlie's stomach flipped in apprehension. The little *connard* knew that costume would be right up Charlie's alley. After Vince had sent all his friends to harass him, what did he have planned? And why did the thought that he had plans make Charlie's heart beat with anticipation?

What would it take to get Vince back?

The first catcalls rang out. Vince winked that direction, and Charlie slouched down in his seat.

What would it take to get Vince back and have him quit his job? A boyfriend didn't let other people put their hands down his pants. Charlie could make some changes; he wanted to, even. But that was not negotiable.

Vince spun, every bit as graceful as he'd been at the party, but there was a sexual energy to it, his knees bent and hips thrusting as he played with a prop hammer, twirling it or wagging it between his legs like an enormous member. His smile stayed honest and bright; he was enjoying himself. The orange vest came off to enormous applause. Charlie twitched at the noise of dozens of women cheering him on. This wasn't *so* bad, watching him strip. He was so perfectly formed, through God and hard work, that it would be sacrilege to hide that glorious chest from the world. Like if the Venus de Milo were in a private gallery.

The pants came off, ripped from the Velcro at the sides, and the crowd went nuts. *Now* it was bad. The red scrap of underwear barely contained him. No, it wasn't bad—it was obscene. And everyone loved it. Charlie licked his lips as the need to cover up his ex made him clutch the table in fear he'd go do something about it.

Emma leaned over, laughing as she cheered. "Please tell me that ain't a sock."

"No comment."

"Shi-i-it." She leaned over to Winnie. "Charlie says his ex, unlike yours, is not faking that rocket."

"Good… lord."

"I said, 'No comment,'" Charlie gritted out.

"Your tone is telling."

Vince hopped off the stage, heading straight for their table. Charlie braced for whatever was coming. He'd had his hair destroyed, his chair humped, a derriere in his face, and a man lying across his lap to drink beer Emma poured down his throat. Hopefully plain beer. Those other men, though, didn't know his triggers. Vince knew exactly how to rile him up or shut him down with an innocuous-seeming touch. That was the problem with ex-lovers. They knew exactly which buttons to push.

Vince started with Emma, who hopped up and danced with him, grinding pelvis to pelvis as she stuck bills in right above his ass, much to Charlie's irritation. But Vince laughed, carefree and happy. Charlie would *not* grab Emma and yank her away. She was his friend.

Emma pointed to Winnie, who held a stack of bills in her hand with an expression that said she was unsure what to do with them.

Vince turned his megawatt grin to the former princess and bodywaved next to her. In invitation, he hooked his thumb under the strap of his underwear right next to his hip, around halfway between his ass and his cock—about as innocent a location as you could get, given the situation.

Winnie looked from Emma to Vince, then shot Cash a glare.

Nikolai's war buddy smirked. "I won't tell him."

Winnie pulled the band with one finger, touching him as little as possible as she secured the bill. Then she patted the dollar on his hip with a pleased smile.

Vince pointed down and yelled, "Give Winnie a hand! First dollar ever!"

The crowd chanted her name as Vince rubbed her head, then... went to the next table.

The next table? He'd completely ignored Charlie. The first man to ignore him all evening was Vince? Disappointed anger made his head light and his body heavy.

Vince was supposed to do something horrifying and very public. Something where Charlie could touch him again.

Instead, Vince was one table over, giving some *salope* a lap dance. Cash's hand pushed Charlie back into his seat. He'd gotten up?

Vince continued to work the crowd like a champion dollar-earner. He was kissed, groped, and ground against. He took dollars from cleavage with his teeth. He picked a delighted woman up, her legs wrapped around him, and he dry humped her. Repeatedly. He did it all with a charming smile and then went backstage again.

Charlie was going to be sick.

No, he wasn't sick, he was furious, burning up inside and out and ready to scream. He stood again, this time with a purpose.

Chapter 14

"I gotta go." Charlie could feel everyone's gaze on him as he abruptly left the table. He didn't care. It felt worse than he'd imagined. So many people staring at Vince. Touching him. Fantasizing about him. And the twit soaked up all that attention from everyone, oblivious or uncaring of all the dark and primitive thoughts devouring him right now from every corner of the room.

Charlie pushed past a guard without effort and found the dressing room by smell. He entered, the idiot guard right behind calling for him to halt.

Vince was there, his backside still bare as he leaned over to grab a shirt. Bantering between the dancers stopped as Charlie entered.

"Charlie?" Rhi asked. "Is it... ?"

He ignored her and everyone else and stalked toward Vince.

"Oh," she said and sat back down.

Vince popped up and eyed him, his smile knowing as he oh-so-innocently asked, "What's wrong?" He motioned toward the idiot guard chasing him. "It's cool. I got this."

"Nobody's allowed back here," came the grunt behind Charlie.

Charlie grabbed Vince by the shoulder and hauled him toward a different door. "We're leaving."

"Ooookay. I'm in trouble, guys!" Vince joked. "Hands off my stash!"

Laughter eased the tension behind them but couldn't touch the thrum of pain and anger Charlie carried. The door crashed shut, and they were in a stairwell going down to the back exit.

"If anybody skims off my dollars, I'm going to be pissed. I worked hard for that."

Using vampire speed, Charlie yanked a bill out of his wallet and slapped it against Vince's bare chest. If paying was what it took, fine. He shoved Vince backward into the stairwell railing, pinning him with his body, and kissed him. If it was wrong, he didn't care. It hurt too much to breathe the lonely air. All those people out there had Vince, and they didn't love him. Charlie loved him. He was trying not to cry, he loved him so much.

Vince's hands shoved against his shoulders, pushing him backward.

Not mine, not mine. Everyone's but mine. He pulled back a hairsbreadth, still pressing as much of himself against Vince as he could, trying to shield the man's body from everybody's eyes. All those gazes having their way with him, and they didn't love him. They just wanted to have him. They'd never even consider dying to have a life with him.

"I take it you liked my dance, huh?" What Emma would call a shit-eating grin lit Vince's face, and it pissed him off further.

"Hated it," Charlie growled. He wrapped an arm around Vince's hips, pulling him as tightly to him as possible. His other hand touched Vince's face, his handsome face, and stilled him for another kiss.

Vince yanked the bill from between them. "I don't take money from you. Holy shit, this is a hundred."

"I've got more." Charlie slid his hand down Vince's ass, cupping the firm muscles. God, he was even more perfect than before, from the rock-hard roundness to the dented hollow in the center. Vince's squirming—thus far a half-assed attempt at getting away—became more like a rub-against. He was hard, harder than he'd ever looked dancing. Because Vince didn't give a fig about those woman outside, but his body still wanted Charlie's. It wasn't enough. But it was better than nothing. "I want you every way possible. I want to bite you. I want to be inside you. I want my mouth where my hand is."

"You've lost your mind," Vince whispered. But his hand slid up Charlie's hip and under his shirt, sending tingles racing through him. "And I told you, I don't take money from you." He stuck the bill back into Charlie's hand.

Charlie clenched it. Tears pricked at his eyes until one fell. "But you will from all of them?"

"Yes, you stupid boy. I can take their money because I never loved any of them."

He sucked in a breath of sharp, bitter air. Had Vince loved him? They'd never said it. "I loved you too." He still did.

Vince hesitated. "Did you?"

"Yes. I should have told you that."

Vince kissed him lightly on the forehead. "When I kiss you, it's free." He kissed his nose, a soft touch of lips that made Charlie want to die in his arms. "When I kiss you, it's because I want to." His mouth hovered in front of Charlie's. "And right now I want to."

That was all the encouragement Charlie needed. He kissed Vince again. This time Vince rose to the occasion, kissing him back with desperation.

Fear made Charlie retreat. "Fangs. Watch it." He'd never kissed Vince with his fangs out. Too dangerous. But he seemed to have lost control over them.

Vince kissed him again greedily, his tongue running over the surfaces of his elongated teeth, more curious than careful. "Damn."

204 ◆ JAX GARREN

The need to nick him and take was almost as overwhelming as the drive to pound into him. To mark him. Charlie pulled away before he did either.

"I love how even lust-crazed, you're taking care of me," Vince muttered. He stroked down Charlie's chest to the raging erection. "Want me to take care of you?"

Charlie spun him around, pushing his torso over the railing. "This isn't about me." But it was, wasn't it? About his need for the human.

Vince shook his derriere, taunting, like he had in the dance with all those people.

Darkness clouded Charlie's vision. He reached around and past the flimsy excuse for underwear and grabbed Vince hard, stroking him with a tight fist.

Vince exhaled a sound between a moan and a sigh as his cock jerked against Charlie's hand.

"Mine more than theirs." He couldn't say Vince was his. Not anymore. Maybe he never could, even back then. But for the moment, he could own him more completely than anyone else.

"All—"

He slapped a hand over Vince's mouth. He didn't want a false promise or hasty words spoken in lust. "Don't lie to me."

Vince bit him. Tiny, dull teeth worrying his skin. It was laughable. And nuts. Charlie dropped to his knees and pressed the flat of his fangs against Vince's backside. Muscles under skin, God, it felt so good. The man actually laughed, like he thought it was fun or a joke to have sharp points grazing his skin, so Charlie bit him, right there where everyone had been staring.

"Oh, God," Vince gasped, hips pistoning harder, as if he liked it.

Blood marred the perfection of Vince's ass, sullying it more than the supposed immorality of their act. Love was love—

Charlie believed that despite what the world told him. Sex was never wrong with Vince. But blood had nothing to do with love. Feeding was taking; it didn't matter if the person was okay with it. It was always unequal. Always taking advantage.

But he didn't have Vince anymore. This wasn't about equality. He was just taking—taking his blood and his body, as much as Vince would allow. He again pressed the flats of his teeth to Vince's ass, making the blood flow faster as he lapped it up, craving the salty taste and scent, the thick rush of feeding. It was so much better with him than a stranger.

Above him, Vince vocalized gutturally, urging him on with sounds more than words.

Still it wasn't enough. Charlie swirled his tongue one more time, then took his mouth further down until it covered the pucker of Vince's asshole. Some dim voice in the back of his mind told him he'd crossed a line and gone way over the edge. That he'd regret this fiercely.

He didn't give a damn. Regret was for later. Vince was now.

☙✦❧

The electric touch of Charlie's black kiss sent Vince sprawling over the railing. So yeah, he'd amped it up out there out of spite. But this…Charlie was annoyingly beyond reproach anywhere outside the bedroom, and here he was with his face between Vince's spread legs, a mere unlocked door between them and a dozen people. They should stop.

Stop the sizzling perfection of this? Fuck no.

Charlie's grip on his cock was rough, near painful. His mouth soft and teasing. Shivers ran through Vince's insides. Afraid he'd fall from the onslaught of sensation, he gripped the hard metal of the railing, warmed by his body heat. Sounds came from him that didn't make sense except in the language of a good fuck. The lost to reality kind.

With one hand he let go of his handhold and reached back, needing to touch Charlie, to be active instead of a mere recipient. His fingers brushed Charlie's hair, but Charlie intercepted his hand. Instead of slapping it away as Vince feared, Charlie twined their fingers together. Vince squeezed fiercely, warming at the connection. They were holding hands, palm-to-palm, like lovers instead of…whatever they were, whatever frenzy this was.

Emotion lit and grew with the ecstasy of touch until he was panting, crying, losing the battle to make this last. "I'm…I'm going to…"

Charlie bolted up, throwing Vince off balance. "Not yet."

Vince lurched left, but Charlie caught him and turned him face to face. Without a word Vince knew what Charlie wanted, and he wanted to give it. He wrenched at Charlie's pants, popping the button, and jerked down the zipper as he dropped to his knees. They didn't have lube. He had to get him wet for this to work.

Charlie keened at the touch of Vince's mouth, driving Vince's own arousal higher.

"Fast," Charlie grunted.

Concerned the new Charlie would yank him up and have his way, ready or not, Vince complied. This was going to hurt, and he craved the pain.

A moment later Charlie scooped under his knees and pressed him against the railing. The metal lines dug into his back, caging him between the drop and Charlie. Charlie's eyes shined dangerous green, like bloodstone in the rain. His teeth, elongated canines and shorter but still pointed incisors, held a splash of red. His blood.

This was the real Charlie, dark and frightening and holding absolutely nothing back. He was glorious, as beautiful and pitiless as a god.

Vince's heart raced in lust and fear and wonder. Charlie pushed into him, moaning as Vince gasped. His circuits were screwed, taking pain and pleasure as the same thing. It hurt. It hurt so good.

Charlie leaned in until that dangerous mouth was right at Vince's ear. "To hell with them all. You're mine. Mine right now. Mine."

Vince threw his arms around his ex, holding him. "Always been yours," he whispered, the words as true now as when they'd been lovers and as they had been since the beginning.

A feral growl, and pain at his neck. Charlie had bitten him again? On the neck?

Fear leaped, again sending his signals haywire. Charlie could kill him, and it would be easy. Drain him, snap him in half, probably fuck him to death. And he'd die happy. He dug his feet into Charlie's ass, urging him on as his body clenched around Charlie's dick. He was going to come all over Charlie's shirt, and Charlie was going to have a fit when he came back to reality.

Charlie's bite turned into a kiss against the broken skin. "I love you. I still do. I never stopped. I love you so much."

Vince's heart clenched at the whispered words.

How dare he say that now and not back it up with action that mattered? Fucking in a hallway was not a relationship. "Then keep me, you asshole." He wanted to be cool, like it didn't matter, like tomorrow would be as bright without Charlie as with him. But his body betrayed him, clutching tighter to his lover, taking every hurt both physical and emotional and transmuting them into ecstasy.

A pull at his neck as Charlie sucked again. One hand gripped Vince's cock, stroking a more gentle rhythm than the possession of body and blood. Love. Anger. Ownership. Independence. Power. The emotions between them were too tangled, but sex was easy. And complicated everything.

At this moment nothing mattered. His thoughts blanked as his body arched into Charlie's with the first shiver of orgasm. He took the moment to just be and let the world shrink to the pleasure of Charlie possessing him.

"Mine," Charlie said again when Vince released into his fingers. "God. Mine." Another thrust and Charlie did the same, pumping seed into him. Charlie muttered in French, then collapsed against him, holding him upright with the pressure of his body. He pulled out.

"Ow…" Vince muttered as he sank down.

Charlie caught him, tense against Vince's boneless wooziness. "Are you all right? I didn't. Oh. Damn. I hurt… Oh…"

Vince laughed, and it sounded drunk. "I got jizz on your shirt."

"Fuck." Charlie paled and tried to close up his pants and hold Vince up at the same time. "Are you okay? How much did I hurt you? Fuck."

"You cussed in English. Twice." He tried to find his footing, but his legs wobbled. "I'm gonna hurt tomorrow. But it's okay. Damn, that was hot."

Charlie's fingers traveled gently across Vince's neck, feeling the wound. His fangs were still out, his eyes still glassy. Instead of intent, though, he looked terrified. "It's not deep. Not on anything vital. What did…?" He backed up, eyes wide in shock.

As Charlie retreated, Vince grabbed the railing for support, trying desperately to stay upright. No falling in front of his lover.

Charlie sucked the blood off his fingers, as if it was an automatic action, then stared at them like he'd just realized what he'd done. "*Merde.*"

Of course it was automatic. Charlie was a vampire. Vince

could see that now. His ex had always been so shy—so reserved and so human. Not like this. Vince would have to reanalyze...everything. But it was good to know. Good to see reality.

Charlie, however, was not coping with reality, expression saying he was horrified at himself.

Vince managed to hold up a pacifying hand. "S'okay. I'll be okay." Charlie just needed to take him home. He could make his excuses to the group. They'd seen how much makeup it took to cover what was left of last week's attack. They would let him miss the last dance. Charlie owed him a cuddle after this one. A naked cuddle under the covers with a horror movie—Charlie hated those; Vince loved them—and a bottle of wine. He wasn't kidding when he said it would hurt in the morning. His whole body ached like he'd worked it to the limit and then kept going.

But hot damn, he'd do it again. The rush was incredible. The fact that Charlie was even capable of aggression like that was a shock.

The fact that one dance from Vince was all it took to bring it out? Now that was an epiphany. A powerful one. He smiled. He was going to own Charlie for the rest of his life.

With more muttering in French, Charlie backed up farther, eyes darting around the space like a cornered animal.

Where did they go from here? Vince tried to be casual. "I don't speak French, babe."

"I apologize," Charlie said stiffly. "I didn't mean..." Then the damnable man disappeared, running down the stairs and out the door at a speed Vince's eyes couldn't follow.

"Charlie?" Surely he was coming right back. Vince pressed a hand to his neck. It came away smeared with red. Not a lot, but enough to tell he was still bleeding. Was the bite on his ass still bleeding? "Charlie?" he called down, starting to crash from the adrenaline. Charlie needed to get his butt back up here and help him figure out what to do next.

But Charlie was gone, from god to ghost in the space of an orgasm.

Chapter 15

Cash was outside, a righteous smirk on his face. *Oh. God.* Charlie walked out the door slowly so that Cash didn't think he was running away. Running away from Cash usually ended with your face on the pavement. "Where's Nikolai?" The door slammed behind him, and Charlie sank back against it, his whole body shaking like an addict in withdrawal. He felt numb, spent in a way that he couldn't ever remember feeling.

He was horrified at himself. He could've killed Vince.

And yet he still he wanted more.

"Kolyan's at the front entrance," Cash said, his words barely making it through. "When I figured out where you'd be, I switched places with him. I assumed, in case you came running out that door—oh, look, you did!—you'd rather me be here than him."

He swallowed. That was true. "Vince is on the staircase. Someone should go…"

What had he just done? It was like he'd lost his mind. He'd killed people on accident, back when he was a new vampire trying to figure out how everything worked with no sire to guide him. He didn't bite people often nowadays, but when he did he was calm and fully in control of himself. Even then, he didn't bite them on the damn neck. You could nick a large vein or a muscle or, God forbid, puncture the person's throat.

He could've killed Vince. He hadn't. He'd landed the bite fine—that was the one thing he'd checked before getting away from dangerous temptation. But what had he been thinking to even try?

Cash looked him up and down, brows raised, likely taking in his dishevelment and discerning the situation accurately.

Charlie wiped his mouth. Did he still have blood on his lips?

He looked back at the door. Vince was up the stairs. He wanted to run back up, scoop him into his arms, and take him home. Charlie was supposed to take care of the man; it was what he wanted to do. Yet he'd just risked Vince's life in a mad rush of feeling. Charlie didn't need Tzitzi's spell to lose his sanity. He just needed Vince.

"Rhi'll be with him in a moment. We've been texting. You stalked out of the audience so intently we figured a fifty-fifty chance of live porn and wanted to give you space. But now she'll show."

Vince wasn't alone. Good. Charlie slid down to the pavement, where there was less danger of his legs giving out, but he kept his hand on the door. He longed to be up there with Vince yet feared what he might do in the future. Wanting to mark a lover once, maybe twice, was normal vampire instinct. But the thought of Vince dancing again made Charlie want to mark every spot those other hands had touched, leaving him the rightful owner of every piece of Vince's skin. That attitude wasn't sane and it wasn't safe.

"Although," Cash added, "if you are interested in getting back together, you should probably go back. If this is a hit and run, then hey, more power to you. But Vince is going to be my human ward as soon as the fucker says yes—and he's going to say yes—so I may have to kick your ass if you do it again. Pick somebody who won't be confused by a drive-by. Or somebody I don't give a shit about. Either one is fine."

"That wasn't a 'hit and run' as you call it. You know me better than that." But was it? He'd, eh, *hit* and then *run*—even if he hadn't meant it that way. He hadn't had any intention, any thought at all. Just need.

Cash sat down next to him on the stoop, expression pinched in confusion. "Honestly? The workings of your mind are a mystery to me. Me? If I want something, I go get it. You? If you want something… you go build a table. I have no idea where you're coming from half the time. I'm just saying, if you want him, you should go get him before he thinks you don't."

"There's more to it than that." Charlie hung his head. There was no way he'd explain to Cash that he couldn't bite Vince without worrying he'd kill him. It was tantamount to admitting he had sexual dysfunction. What was Cash going to do? Give him lessons? No. That was a sire's job. It was too intimate for friends. So all he said was, "I could've hurt him."

Cash straightened and looked back at the door. "Did you?"

"No. Not badly."

"No broken bones? Excessive bleeding? Internal hemorrhaging?

"No!"

"'Cause we've all been there. But the sooner we get him—"

"I wouldn't be here chatting with you if Vince was bleeding out up there. I'd be up there trying to save him and calling for help."

Cash stretched out, propping one loafered foot on top of the other. "You just mean things got a little rough. Did he say no?"

"Of course not. I wouldn't keep going if…"

"Then everything's fine." He pulled his flask out and took a swallow, then passed it off.

Charlie took a sip and smacked his tongue in distaste. Compared to Vince, he might as well be drinking turpentine.

His expression made Cash laugh. "You insult the good stuff,

man." His laughter faded. "Nothing's as good as *rosso amore*." Red love, vampire slang for the taste of a lover. Charlie had so rarely been in love, he didn't have much of a comparison, but Cash and everyone else claimed that love made blood taste different. It seemed like a romantic impossibility. After today, Charlie believed him.

"Why am I relationship counseling you? I've had four chances at my woman, and I can't get her. If I'm your relationship counselor, you're fucked."

Charlie bumped his shoulder. "It's harder when she changes with each lifetime." Cash had been chasing the same woman since he was a human, but each time she reincarnated, she died young. Last time he'd tried to save her, he'd been burned to a near cinder, giving Charlie the job of nursing him back to health.

Cash took another, larger swig. "It'd be easier if she remembered me. Or anything."

"I don't know. I've heard it makes you crazy having all those perspectives in your head, like multiple personalities. And what if in one life you were something bad, like…" His gloom cleared in a flash of inspiration. "Like an Aztec priest."

A snort of laughter. "That would make you pretty fucking crazy." Cash didn't get it.

"You read the report on Tzitzi, didn't you?"

Cash stashed the flask back in his jacket. "Yeah. Real name Ashley Paulson from Dallas. Psychotic episodes growing up. Institutionalized three times. Got into witchcraft in middle school. At sixteen she made soup with ketamine, fed it to her parents, then cut out their hearts. After that she disappeared."

"Did you read the other report that said a hundred years ago there was another witch named Tzitzimitl who worshiped Aztec deities and ran experiments on vampires and were-creatures?"

Cash frowned. "She was beheaded by Templar and her body

burned. She's dead."

"Right. The report suggested our Tzitzi may be a copycat. But what if she's not copying?"

Cash stood, excitement making him move as he finally understood. "What if she's reincarnated and somehow managed to remember it? That would explain how she's got such a powerful spell arsenal at her age—and how she got the fucking Liberi to follow her, a human. Her memories are older."

"Lifetimes of knowledge." Charlie stood. "I need to tell Vince."

ಐ◆ಖ

Vince huddled against the railing, knees to his chest as he tried to catch his breath. He needed to stand up, get back into the dressing room, and get ready for the final number. But his legs felt numb and his head light, whether from blood loss or emotional whiplash, he wasn't entirely sure. And his ass hurt where the bite met cold cement. That was going to sting for a while.

What had just happened?

Footsteps sounded in front of him. "Charlie!" He looked up, hopeful.

Rhi stood before him with a robe and too much sympathy.

"Dammit." He sagged back down.

She dropped beside him and tucked the robe around his shoulders. "I'd sarcastically say, 'Nice to see you too,' but I know I'm a poor substitute at the moment." Her arm wrapped around him, warm and protective. "That motherfucker."

Needing the contact, he lay his head on top of hers. "It's not like I didn't encourage him."

"Don't you take this on yourself. I know he's damaged by centuries of crap, but it's not your job to cure him."

He tsked a breath out. "I could say the same about your mother. Still planning to go back home after the dedication tomorrow?" CoVIn was officially opening the doors to their headquarters tomorrow at midnight with a ceremony on the top floor of the skyscraper that housed them. Technically, humans weren't supposed to attend, but according to Cash, no one would question it if they arrived with him and Winnie. Nepotism at its best.

Rhi stiffened. "That's different. She's family. You don't give up on family."

"I used to think Charlie was family. It's not always about blood, you know." He settled the robe more tightly around his body, sadness cloaking him along with the thick cotton. "I don't know why I still care so much. I think he might have been cheating on me, back when we were together. Then he came at me all hot and bothered, like he needed me." He closed his eyes, and the memory of Charlie with a fire in his eyes and no hesitation in his manner made him shudder. He opened them again, cold reality crashing back. "After one kiss I'm like, 'Do me in a stairwell!' What the fuck is wrong with me?"

Rhiannon's head had shot up. "Cheating on you? What makes you think that?" She squeezed his hand. "There're a lot of things you could say about Charlie that I'd agree with. Like he's an unforgiving, closeted stick-in-the-mud... except, we now realize, when your dancing makes him go crazy... but I don't see him cheating on you."

Vince leaned forward, relieved to share yesterday's gut punch with someone. "I know, right? I wouldn't think that either. But he never got cold, the whole time we were together. Which means—"

Her eyes widened. "He was biting someone."

"Yup."

She frowned. "But it doesn't mean he was having sex with them. I mean, yeah, they seem to like that." She puffed in irritation. "I think Javi's going to kill Emma. She keeps trying to get him to Scarlet so one of the blood whores can teach him how to bite a person without killing them."

Vince touched the cut on his neck. The blood had dried to a sticky slash, but it still stung. "They have to learn that?"

"If you were going to stick two ice picks into my neck and not kill me, where would you put them? And you have to aim with your mouth."

Well, when she put it that way... "I figured they just knew, like instinct or something. I mean, they're vampires."

"Nope. Cash explained this to me. The Liberi are real vampires, and they'll bite your neck because they don't give a shit if they kill you or not. CoVIn, on the other hand, has done extensive research to figure out where you can bite people without killing them, and they use sex because it's the least painful way for donors. And because *sex*, yes, please. But they have to keep their heads enough to not kill us while they're halfway to happy town, which has got to be rough." She leaned forward, gossipy. "I think Javi, with his doctor knowledge of how badly everything could go if he pierced the wrong spot, is having performance issues." She swished her mouth thoughtfully. "I'll get Javi to ask Charlie what's the best way to find a willing donor without sex."

"No! Don't ask him to do that. What is this, middle school note passing?" She looked serious. He took her hands and shook, getting her attention back on him. "I need to man up and ask him how he stayed warm. Don't stealth question him through your brother."

"I wasn't. Javi would be relieved if there's a way to keep his body temperature normal without resorting to sex with strangers—you know he can't handle one night stands." She made a frustrated noise. "Look what happened with Emma; one night and now he's a belligerent mess because he's crushing so hard he can't see straight. Meanwhile she keeps trying to introduce him to prostitutes."

They had been a rank mess all week with Emma cracking inappropriate jokes and Javier, who was normally serious but friendly, tense and brooding. "I'm not sure who I feel worse for."

"Javi, obviously. He's my brother." Rhi lightly thumped him on the shoulder. "All that goes to say, I'll bet you my signed Bradley Cooper photo against your Zeppelin vinyl collection that Charlie has a solution."

Hope snuck back in. Thinking more rationally about it—which he was totally proud of himself for managing right now—Rhiannon was right. Hiring a prostitute behind his back did not sound like Charlie. Even if right now was a disaster, Vince didn't want that suspicion to stain the memory of what had been. He held out his hand. "You're on. But let me talk to him first, okay?"

"You've got twenty-four hours. Then I'm putting Javi out of his misery."

He leaned back against the railing. "I still don't like him biting somebody else when he wouldn't bite me." But it was a helluva lot better than leaving him to go visit his lookalike hooker from the party. Clearly Charlie and Trey had done it—they had that vibe—but if it had been after the breakup, well, then the fact that Charlie had picked someone who looked so much like him was sort of a compliment, right?

Rhi eyed his neck. "He seems to no longer have a problem biting you."

"You should see the one on my ass."

That got a laugh. "Seriously? At least you can hide that one. I don't know how you're going out in public with that deuce on your neck. Yes, I said 'deuce.' I'm learning vampire slang." Her hand tightened on his. "He still pulled a shitty fuck and run. Don't let him off the hook for that."

Vince set his jaw. No, he wasn't letting Charlie get by with that crap behavior. No more sex. No matter how much he wanted it.

Rhi pointed, shoulders tense. "Why is that mouse growing?"

Vince leaned forward so he could see better. A rodent next to the dressing room door trebled in size, elongating and raising up on its back legs.

"Out. Out!" He scrambled up, yanking Rhi with him. He stumbled. She caught him. Holding hands, they ran down the stairs.

The lock clicked in front of them just as they reached the back door. Rhi yanked and rattled the handle. Nothing. "Get us out!" she yelled.

Vince turned. At the top of the stairs, Tzitzi looked down on them. Once again she wore her flowing shirt that was stained with old blood and her hair pulled back in a white ribbon. A stone knife hung at her waist.

"Shit," Vince murmured.

Pounding from the other side of the door meant someone was trying to get in. He slid to the side, pulling Rhiannon with him out of the way.

Tzitzi moved down the stairs with the efficient grace of a snake. "Sister, you could learn a thing or two from me. Are you interested?"

Rhiannon backed into the wall. "In learning to be a human-sacrificing psycho-bitch? No. Thank you, but no."

Tzitzi snorted. "In learning to be a witch. You've got the gift." She smiled. "Use it." With a word in Aztec—he assumed—Tzitzi clapped her hands.

Rhiannon stiffened like a metal rod. With an inarticulate yell, she toppled, limbs unmoving from their frozen position.

"Rhi!" Vince caught her. Her breath came out in wheezing rasps, like she couldn't get enough air. "Let her go!"

Tzitzi kept coming. "Once you're dead. Witch's honor."

"Get in here!" he yelled at the door. The pounding turned into a single crash that reverberated the door.

"Magically locked doors don't open with force." As Tzitzi approached, he set Rhi on the ground, debating his next move.

Rhi grunted, breath barely hissing as tears shined in her unblinking eyes.

Another crash. "Fine, fine," he said, hands up. "Take me wherever." He'd find a way to leave breadcrumbs or something. Or maybe he'd get close enough to knock her out again. Would Rhi die if he did that? "Just let her breathe." He took a step toward Tzitzi.

Tzitzi's smile sent a chill down his back. "A willing sacrifice. We should've brought her down the first time."

He shuffled across the distance between them, gaze darting between Rhiannon, who was turning red, and Tzitzi, who looked bored. "I'm not a virgin sacrifice. I don't know if that changes anything, but we could stop here, no harm no foul."

"I hired a stripper. You think I give a rat's ass if you're a virgin?" She grabbed his wrist and pulled him against her.

He swallowed thickly, fear lodging tight in his throat. Her grip was fierce for her tiny hands. The bloodstained shirt smelled of lemons. "You laundered your human sacrifice shirt?"

She pulled his back against her chest, her voice as casual as if they were discussing dinner choices. "It itches if I don't."

The irony made him laugh with grim amusement. "Yeah, sucks to be uncomfortable while you're scraping someone's skin off. Let Rhi go."

An amused snort was followed by more words in that other language. Were they going to disappear? Or would he become a mouse with her? He had no idea what she was capable of. He focused on Rhi, going from red to blue on the floor. She had to be okay. "Don't forget Rhi."

"I won't." Tzitzi raised her stone blade. Obsidian caught the red light of the exit sign, gleaming luridly in the dim staircase.

He scrambled away from it, shoving farther back into Tzitzi as a terrible realization overtook him. "Wait, you're doing it now?"

She stumbled but didn't fall. "So sorry for the lack of ceremony, but I'm busy and you're a to-do." Her sarcasm turned sympathetic. "Take solace. Tomorrow you rise with the sun."

"No, wait!" He elbowed her in the jaw, fear making him flail.

She swung the knife.

The back door sprang open, and Charlie barreled through, slamming into them.

They fell to the floor, Vince in the middle and Charlie on top, yelling in more French. His face filled with bone-deep rage, he reached past Vince and got his hands around Tzitzi's neck.

"Rhi!" Vince yelled. "Somebody get Rhi!" He struggled sideways. Charlie lifted his torso, giving him space, but his hands stayed clamped around Tzitzi's neck.

Vince shoved himself out from between them. Cash kneeled next to Rhiannon, no passion on his face, only clinical efficiency as he ripped the front of her shirt, bit into her wrist, and used her blood to draw a pattern on her chest. A few words, and Rhiannon jerked up, sucking in air.

Relief made Vince's limbs go limp. He turned back to Charlie and Tzitzi, ready to help.

The ritual knife was embedded in Charlie's shoulder.

Charlie had put himself between Vince and the killing blow.

It didn't seem to slow Charlie down any. The knife jerked with every vigorous shake of Charlie's fists as he throttled the witch. Tzitzi's short, black nails clawed at Charlie's face, trying to shove him off.

Vince pulled her grasping hands off Charlie. Again he was surprised at the strength in her fingers. Her nails dug into his hands, more spastic than steady as her endurance wavered. "Why isn't she casting?"

"She can't speak," Cash said quietly, standing beside him and loading a dart gun. "Can't cast if you can't speak. The closer you get to a witch, the greater your chances of survival. The farther away, the more you're fucked. If you're in danger and you can't hide, run toward her as fast as you can. Charlie." He pointed the gun.

Charlie yanked her up to her knees, presenting her back to Cash.

Cash shot her. "Ketamine, bitch. What you used on your parents. I thought you'd appreciate that."

It only took moments for her unconscious body to collapse in Charlie's grip. He dropped her like she was on fire and kneeled above her, his fingers clenching and unclenching as he heaved in adrenaline-fueled breaths of rage.

In all the time they'd lived together, Vince had never seen Charlie breathe as often as he had this week. He'd never seemed so alive, even as the blood on his chin and the knife in his shoulder proved beyond doubt he was undead.

Cash was already on the phone. "Got her. Back stairwell." He sauntered around Charlie and casually yanked the knife out.

Charlie grunted in pain.

Vince caught his good shoulder, helping him steady himself.

"Are you okay?"

"Yes. You?"

"Thanks to you." He cleared his throat as he stood up and offered a hand down.

Charlie took it, his hand still trembling in hyped emotion with nowhere to go.

Vince could think of a few good uses for that, but he pushed the lusty thought aside. They needed to get some sleep, find some calm, and have a real talk before they went anywhere near that again.

Even if Charlie had just taken a knife in the back to save his life. If that didn't make up for running off earlier, he wasn't sure what would.

The door opened to the dressing room above. "Everything all right down there?"

Rhiannon ran up a few steps and called, "Yeah! We're good. Working on a theater project. New work."

"Right on. Break a leg." The door shut.

Rhi shook her head as she ran back down. "Pretty boy. Stupider than dirt. But pretty." She patted Vince's stomach on the way past him, and he could almost hear her saying, "You've got better places to be than here."

He looked from Charlie to Cash as the spent adrenaline rush of yet another close call left him drained. Life was too short to spend it doing something he didn't love.

Chapter 16

Emma stood with her arms crossed as she faced the cage in the holding cells deep in CoVIn's basement. A dangerous look filled her usually cheerful face, revealing a depth of loathing most people never had the misfortune to feel.

Charlie decided he liked being on her good side. At the moment it was just the two of them sharing a mutual hate for the psychotic woman in front of them. Vince, Javier, and Rhiannon were back at Cash's, eating and resting. Cash was dealing with security, and Nikolai and Winnie were with the queen, explaining what had happened.

Charlie liked Emma. She was funny and kind and said whatever was on her mind without censoring it, so he tried to make conversation. "I was only under her curse for a few seconds, and it was unpleasant. I can't imagine what it was like for you." He didn't really remember it at all, but it seemed like the right thing to say.

"Shit," she said. "Unpleasant? The little I remember was fan-fucking-tastic. I didn't care about nothing. I didn't care that I'd turned a one-night stand into a vampire. I didn't care if I killed somebody when I was eating. I didn't care that I'd made my money on my back. I have an idea to start a business, a legit one using my cooking skills, but I know I ain't got the learning for that. For a few afternoons I didn't wake up anxiously wanting to try anyway. Only thing I cared about was having a good damn time. It wasn't unpleasant. It was awesome." She kicked the cage. "She made me a real monster. Her name can't land on the DB fast enough, and I plan on being right here with the pistol Joe gave me, waiting for the announcement."

The freedom of a monster. The salty taste of Vince's blood, the hard muscles of Vince's legs wrapped around his waist, the feel of Vince's tight ass surrounding his cock. The complete freedom from any concern but pursuing that abandon as Vince had gripped him back, his breath hitching in anticipation, his skin warming in response.

Charlie took a suddenly quite-necessary breath as need heated his blood. That need was without magic, just the drives of lust and jealous fury that he'd allowed to take over. He tugged on the collar of another fitted button-down, hot and uncomfortable despite his rolled-up sleeves and the blasting AC.

How was Vince right now? Charlie couldn't get the image from his head of the blood on Vince's neck. What scared the pants off him was how much he liked the visual. How much he wanted to do the whole thing again, despite the risks.

Emma was right. It was fun to lose your mind. The hellacious part was getting it back again.

Cash's carefree laughter interrupted his dark thoughts, and the man himself entered the jail, cell phone pressed to his ear. "Hold on…" He flipped the phone sideways, took a picture of Tzitzi behind bars, then sent it before finishing his conversation. "Drinks are on you, Alaric." Emma got a high five. He raised his hand again, and Charlie gave it a halfhearted tap. Cash winked at him as he ended the call. "Tooth and Nail had been cleaned out, just like I said. They've moved on." He waved his hand, indicating the three of them. "That means we bagged a witch tonight when Alaric and his team got nada yesterday."

Charlie wanted to point out that if Alaric was working for Tzitzi, he wouldn't have "bagged a witch" even if she'd been there. Instead he smirked. "I believe Rhiannon is the one who deserves the drinks. It was her plan."

Cash nodded. "She does. But I backed it. And, hell, I shot the witch and saved Rhi. Thanks for distracting Tzitzi while I did that. What did Emma do? She stuffed dollars down guys' Jockeys. But do I get all picky about who did what? No. It's about teamwork, and Emma is a part of Team Win, with all the drink privileges thereof."

Emma nodded, a jovial smile replacing her earlier ire. "Best damn plan I ever been a part of."

"Mo's on her way down to see the prize."

Charlie stiffened. Unless Tzitzi fessed up, which he had little hope for, they still lacked proof that Alaric was working with the Liberi—proof he needed to find within six days so the queen didn't kick him out. Yes, the politics of CoVIn weren't fun, but the protection it offered was necessary. Worse, though, leaving CoVIn would mean the end of his friendship with Cash. Cash could get away with keeping his own residence against the queen's wishes or playing fast and loose with rules—like inviting Rhiannon as his date for tomorrow's vampire-only event. But if he tried to maintain ties with someone the queen had excommunicated, she'd shut that down. It looked too much like treason.

Cash seemed determined to make sure it didn't come to that. He slapped a heavy hand on Charlie's shoulder, restraining him. "Don't you dare slip out. Greet her here with me and your spoils of war. This is a great thing. Are you attending the dedication tomorrow? Your answer is yes."

Charlie dropped his head. He hadn't planned on attending tomorrow's opening of the new CoVIn headquarters. As far as he was concerned, the fact that the queen was moving to Austin and bringing the focus of the vampire world to his town was in no way worthy of celebration. But Cash was right, and playing politics instead of avoiding them was, in this case, the smartest, safest path. He nodded.

The heavy hand at his shoulder moved, and Cash clapped him on the back. "Good man. We can salvage this." Modron entered, and Cash strode toward her with a muttered, "Hopefully."

Charlie tried to smile pleasantly, but it probably looked like a grimace. Despite Cash's assurances, he had his doubts that the queen would ever look kindly on him. She'd been born the daughter of a chieftain. She admired power, birth, and social grace, things an orphaned artisan from rural France with a universally despised sire didn't have.

Sure enough, Modron looked him up and down coolly before turning to the cell. "This is the witch who is gathering Liberi into her own little army? She doesn't look like much."

Cash elbowed him. "Tell her your theory."

Her head cocked as she turned her piercing gaze to him.

Charlie's face heated. "She's been reincarnated multiple times."

"So are many people."

He cleared his throat. "And she remembers." That was enough, right?

Cash nudged him again, hard enough that he wanted to rub his arm, but he refrained.

"She has esoteric knowledge and skills built over several lifetimes, not just the eighteen years she's lived in this one. My guess is this is a plan she formed one or more lifetimes ago."

Modron crossed her arms, as if rejecting his idea. But her expression said she was considering it. "Why now?"

Charlie eyed Cash, hoping he'd take over. No such luck. The man seemed to think putting Charlie on point was the best way for him to ingratiate himself. Charlie hated being the spokesperson. Usually he wrote the words, and Cash said them. That was the smart way to do things, as it was the most likely to result in people following their ideas.

But if Cash was going to let the ideas they'd hashed out in the car ride go unsaid, he'd forge ahead and hope for the best. "I think this has to do with Nikolai Vyhovsky's predictions. He says there's a reckoning coming. She's gathered an army of Liberi, figured out how to corral them, and made them hers. She wants to be a player in the coming events." He glanced at the woman in the cage. Her fingers twitched. She was waking up. Anger swelled, sudden and choking. The woman had tortured Vince. She'd chained him up and made him bleed, drugging, threatening, and terrifying him. When the DB order came through, Charlie might be waiting here with Emma, hammer in hand.

"Tell her the other part," Cash prompted.

Jaw clenched, he tore his gaze from Tzitzi. Here came the tricky part of his musing, the part the queen really wasn't going to like. He licked his lips and reminded himself to use "us," like Cash had insisted, despite his feeling of disconnection from most of his fellow CoVIn members. "The Liberi's great weakness is their inability to plan and work as a team, but she has a spell to make them work together under her direction. She has another that turns us into Liberi. Put those together, and the vampires, all of us, can be her army for the apocalypse."

He held his breath, waiting for the queen's response. Unlike Nikolai, he couldn't see portents or receive confusing dreams with future visions. But he had an uncanny knack for guessing which way the wind blew, and this felt right. Terrifying. But right.

Modron's hands bunched into fists as she pivoted from him to kick the cage. "Is that it, you little *gwiddonod?*"

Tzitzi chuckled, her voice high and light like a demented

teenager, as she pushed herself up to sitting, knees sprawled wide and hands behind her in a relaxed pose. Charlie wondered how long she'd been playing at sleep. "Do you know how many of your men it took to take me down? Three. It was embarrassing."

Cash stepped to the bars, all trace of a smile gone as he took on his real job: security for Queen Modron. Only Alaric ranked higher than he did in the chain of military command. "You're a young woman. I'm sure you're used to being underestimated. I won't do you the insult." With both hands, he pointed to the corners of the room. "Wave." Three men and one woman, all armed with pistols, gave salutes toward the cage. "I have no doubt you can open the door and walk out. But can you do it faster than a bullet at forty feet? If you even start speaking a language other than English, they will assume it's a spell and shoot you. You've got two options. Stay here until we determine your threat status and have you executed—which will happen. Or surrender and negotiate a treaty."

The second would never happen, but by CoVIn law they had to offer it.

He stepped back, ceding the lead position to Modron.

Instead of tracking to the queen, Tzitzi's gaze turned to Charlie with a bitter glare.

Cold closed Charlie's throat. His theory was right. This slip of a woman planned to peel out the soul of every vampire she could find and enslave the mindless results. He really hated being right.

⋈✦⋈

A shiny anvil stood in the center of the shop next to a forge that was already stoked and ready to go. Hammers lined one wall in an abundance that put the community college Vince rented space at to shame. Next to the open garage door was a permanent oxyacetylene hookup, ready with a Cobra, his favorite torch style, already attached. Grinders, cutters, and an assortment of other tools completed a setup Vince had only dreamed about before. And the view out the garage door? Spectacular. Cash's house, where this gloriousness had appeared, backed up to a cliff, sheer rock jutting over the narrow meandering of Ladybird Lake. A breeze kept the air fresh, bringing scents of summer flowers and juniper bark.

The crazy part was, as completely as the metal shop had been outfitted, only half the space was being used, the half in the sunlight. Charlie could move into the shaded back area with his woodworking equipment and…

No, no. Best not to go there. Some of yesterday's anger had subsided with food and the best sort of bad dreams. And with the grateful memory of that knife in Charlie's shoulder.

Vince was still mad. But he wasn't raging. Last night's sex had been epic—so fucking epic—but they couldn't hook up again. The crash was not worth it.

Or so he kept telling himself. Truth was, if Charlie had come down the hall before dawn and begged even a little, Vince knew, to his shame, he would've lifted the covers. But at least he wouldn't be the one making overtures again. And that resolution he could stick with. Hopefully.

"Whoa…somebody wants you to move in." He looked up from contemplating his rekindled addiction to an aggravating redhead to find Rhiannon nosing around the space, fingers trailing across hammers and vises.

"Or he really wants a new stake."

"Yeah, if that were the case, he'd buy you a guest pass somewhere, not acquire a tricked out metal shop."

Vince nodded slowly. There was logic in that. Then again, Cash was clearly the kind of rich that made money no object. She came close, and he nudged her, teasing. "I'm surprised he didn't ask you, my friend the blood tramp."

She stuck out her tongue. He laughed and sorted through the raw steel bin to find the right piece, dragging his fingers over the cool metal to get a feel for each one. He thought he could make the wood segments of the design himself, but it'd turn out a lot better if Charlie did it.

Rhiannon sat on a counter. "I wouldn't move in even if he asked. Not that he would. We're getting to be friends. Don't want to ruin a good thing by pretending it's something else."

"Are you sure it's not?"

"Yeah. He's in love with another woman."

That was news. "And she's not here because…?" He waved his hand vaguely at the splendor around them.

"She's dead."

He looked up from the metal, surprised. "And he's not moving on because…?"

"He's waiting for her to come back. Apparently she does that every couple hundred years, hence Charlie figuring out Tzitzi is a reincarnate." She shrugged. "That makes this the perfect relationship as far as I'm concerned. I really do like him, but, well, for all he's clever, he's not that bright. And his lifelong ambition is to be a soldier. I just… even if I did ever decide to try the whole family thing, which I'm not interested in, but if I did, that wouldn't be what I wanted. But we're friends and he's fun and that's a nice change." She fidgeted. "You're okay with that, right?"

He snorted. "Like I'm one to judge. But yeah. I like Cash. He's awfully pretty. Have fun."

His fingers found the right piece of steel, and he pulled it out, examining the length and flexibility. He checked his notebook for the designs. He was going to make two, the first one quick but effective to replace what he'd accidentally destroyed. The other, though, would be a piece of art—better than the original—that would be functional as well as beautiful.

He really could use Charlie's help. The metal provided the strength and sharpness needed to do damage, but the wood was what actually did the job. Without wood piercing the heart, the vampire would be hurt but not killed.

The door from the house opened, and two women came out, one waving a tablet and the other with an expensive-looking dress bag over her shoulder.

"Damn…" Vince murmured. "Somebody got a dress."

Rhiannon turned to them, her expression irate. "I told you, I am *not* wearing a dress he paid for."

The woman with the dress bag pursed her lips and without a word held the bag up and unzipped it. Silvery blue fabric spilled out in a lightweight, silken waterfall. The stylist jerked it higher to keep the dress from hitting the floor. Not that it would've mattered; the shop floor was clean enough to eat off of.

He'd fix that.

"That's pretty sassy," Vince acknowledged. He would be the worst dressed person at the thing tonight, the only one who couldn't afford bespoke and silk. Whatever. He was going, and that was the important part. He dropped his button-down on the counter next to Rhi and headed for the hammers in a tank top and jeans. His hair was already back in his red welding cap, his leather boots reassuringly heavy as he trudged across the floor.

Rhi's lips twisted in lust at the dress. It probably cost more than a month's rent on the house she shared with her mom. Temptation made her swallow.

He saluted her with a hammer. "I won't think less of you." He coughed into his fist. "Whore."

She gave him the finger. "I have green hair. Green hair doesn't go with a fancy dress."

The stylist nodded. "I can work with that."

Vince shoved the steel rod into the fire, letting it heat. "Go for it, Rhi. The guy bought a metal shop on the hope I'd move in and be his human alarm system. As you yourself pointed out, that dress is chump change for Cash."

"What are you wearing?" she asked.

He turned the steel in the fire, digging it deeper into the coals. "My Savile Row best, baby."

"Hmm…"

He looked up to find her frown had turned to him. She looked back at the stylist with a crafty smile. "I'll wear it if you can get him a suit that's equally nice for tonight. Either Vince and I sparkle together, or I'm going in my Goodwill finest. Got it?"

Vince snapped his head up. "You don't have to do that."

She shrugged. "As you said, this is chump change to him. So he can afford two things."

The stylist looked from her to Vince. Vince pulled the iron from the fire and gave it a pound. Man, he wanted a new suit. Something cut for him that would make him look like he belonged. It wasn't the price tag. He couldn't care less how much something cost. But for once, he wanted to be like everyone else without fighting for it.

Although, if it *was* a pricey, gorgeous masterpiece of clothing, he wouldn't mind looking in the mirror once or twice or feeling the perfectly draped fabric against his skin. Who wouldn't?

A sharp exhale from the stylist. "I can do that."

Vince laughed. "With what? A team of elves? You can't fit me for a suit in a few hours."

She pursed her lips. "Not entirely custom, no, but you'd be astounded what a team of elves can do."

He blinked, not sure if she was kidding or if vampires employed real elves.

Rhiannon stuck her nose in the air. "Fine. I'll play dress-up." The disdain in her tone was too thick to be real. She so wanted that dress.

The woman with the tablet stepped up. "When you're done with that, I have the book."

Rhiannon hopped off the counter, far more fascinated with that than she'd been with the pretty. "Already? They translated it?" She reached for the tablet.

"What's that?" Vince asked between hammer strikes.

"The Book of Hind and Salmon."

More pounding. "That sounds really strange. What's it about? I'm guessing that's 'hind' as in 'deer' not as in 'behind'?"

"You've guessed correctly. The book is about awen."

Vince stuck the rod back into the fire and was accosted with a tape measure. He paused to let the stylist measure him. "The part of the soul the Liberi are missing?"

"Yeah…" Rhiannon swiped through a couple pages. "There was this heretical monk in the ninth century named Lucan who believed all faiths were splinters from God's truth, and he included many Pagan ideas in his writing. He was fond of the Druidic concept of soul and wrote a treatise on it. Queen Modron has a copy of the original. I now have a translated file."

The stylist looked up from the floor, where she was taking Vince's inseam with less alacrity than she'd taken his arm length. "Ma'am, I need you to try on the dress."

"Huh? Oh." Without putting the tablet down, Rhi pulled her shirt off and started shoving her jeans down.

"Is that all you need from me?" tablet-woman asked, clearly uncomfortable now that clothes were flying.

"Yeah. Thanks," Rhi murmured, not looking up from the book.

The stylist cracked a smile, happy now that she had her way with the dress. "Could you at least stand on a chair?" She pushed a footstool over, and Rhi hopped onto it.

Vince resumed his work as Rhiannon read and the stylist moved from measuring him to maneuvering the dress onto her. "What do you think?" the woman finally asked.

Vince glanced up, then did a double take. "Damn..." Rhiannon always dressed down in scruffy jeans and hoodies. She was skinny in a too-few-calories sort of way, with big eyes and a sharp jawline. Her mom stocked their house with junk, which Rhi refused to eat. According to her, she'd been overweight for most of her life and was happy to have the opposite problem. He worried about her. But to see Rhi in a dress fit for a Hollywood siren was something else, turning hungry-thin into svelte and making the harsh angles of her face maybe not pretty, but definitely striking. The blue tinge to the fabric turned her green hair fashionably exotic instead of out of place. With the right makeup and accessories, she could definitely pull it off. Beautiful and different, that was his best friend. He loved her for it.

Rhiannon blushed as she looked up from the tablet.

He smiled at her. "If I liked girl parts, we could be friends with benefits too."

She gave him a shy smile back. "Only in my wickedest dreams." She shook her head at the stylist. "Do you know how hard it was being eighteen and getting to know him? He's so pretty, and you can't have him."

"He'll be even prettier tonight, I promise," the woman muttered around a mouth full of pins as she marked the hemline.

"Yeah, well, your date tonight isn't exactly hard on the eyes," Vince teased.

"This is a true point." Rhi looked down at herself and ran a hand across her belly. "I still have no boobs."

"Get him to feed you lots of bacon-wrapped steak."

She rolled her eyes. Like she'd let that happen. "Okay. Do you have everything you need?" she asked the stylist.

After a few more pins in places Vince couldn't tell needed fixing, the woman nodded.

"Cool. I think I'm going to go read by the pool." Rhi shot Vince a sly grin. "Doesn't that just sound *fabulous*?"

Vince snorted and went back to hammering.

She undressed, trying to look nonchalant but taking pains to keep the pins from moving or the fabric from wrinkling. The stylist left with the dress, and Rhi put her clothes back on. "I think you should move in here so I can come over more often. Have you seen the sauna?"

"You can't come over to see Cash?"

"That would imply a relationship I don't have or want." She hesitated for a moment. "You okay in here alone? Need any help or company or anything?"

He wiped his brow, already perspiring from the forge. In some perverse way, the sweat of labor made him feel clean, like all the little poisons of his day, the mistakes he'd made and the anger he carried, escaped and evaporated with the honesty of hard work. "Nah, I'm good. You won't be able to concentrate with all the noise I make. Think you'll find an answer to what's happening in there?"

She frowned. "I don't know. But I have to tell you something. Remember last night when Tzitzi called me *sister*? I asked Cash about it. He said I'm a witch. Like Tzitzi." Her ears reddened. "He can—according to him—taste it in my blood. I think that's why he likes me."

Vince huffed. "I doubt that's the only reason he likes you. And if it is, then I've lost all respect for him. But what does that mean, that you taste like a witch? How does being Pagan make you taste different?"

"It's not that I'm Pagan. It's that I'm a *witch*. He says everyone can do spells. They're just formulas. You pick one and follow it—like mixing the ingredients for a cake—then call on some other power to kindle it—like how the oven turns the goopy mess you made, if you did it right, into moist and delicious Italian cream cake. For that second part, magical practitioners make a deal with a demon or call on a god they worship. That's what Cash did for me last night. He wrote a rune on my chest, recited an incantation for breaking magic, and called on Odin, a Viking god, to 'bake' his counterspell. Odin, who's apparently very real, heard him and thought, 'Sure, why not?' Hence me breathing again. But Odin could've said no just as easily."

She sounded weirded out about more than just her near-death experience yesterday. So far, he didn't get why. "So does that make Cash a witch too?" And gods were real? Maybe he should tag along with Charlie next time he went to Mass.

"No, that's what I'm saying. Cash followed a spell, and a god did the magic part for him. But he said there's something different in a true witch's brain. Some part of it is turned on or whatever, and we can kindle our own magic. It's easier and you can do bigger spells if you work with another power—like Tzitzi with Xipe Totec and whoever else she's calling on. But witches, unlike everybody else, can do magic without petitioning for help."

Vince clamped the iron into a vise and turned to look at her. "So… you have godlike powers? Can you use them to kick Tzitzi's ass? Because that would be awesome."

"It's not godlike. It's… He compared it to being psychic—like Nikolai—or telekinetic or something. And I still have to learn spells. It's not like I can go, 'Fireball!'"—she clapped her hands together, then held them apart like she had an invisible basketball—"and it appears."

238 • JAX GARREN

He started to twist the metal, slowly and carefully to keep the spiral even. "So you have to train."

"Yes. And this is the part I've been trying to tell you."

"Not the 'I have godlike powers' part?"

"Shut up. *Queen Modron* wants to train me. Her last apprentice died in a fight with a siren—apparently nobody wins against a siren—and she needs a new one. I am Queen Modron's replacement witch-in-training. Cash says Modron isn't very gifted, but she knows a lot because she's been around for forever. So I got to borrow the thousand-year-old book—well, I got to demand it be translated into English and it happened in three friggin' hours—because according to Modron, I'm her apprentice now."

Vince looked up from his work, eyes wide. "Remember two weeks ago, when you weren't apprenticed to a vampire witch queen and I wasn't forging weapons for a vampire warrior prince?"

Her tension broke into a laugh. "And neither of us were casually screwing immortals?"

He scowled at her. "That was a mistake on my part."

"Charlie made the mistake. Not you."

With two-foot-long iron tongs, he put the weapon back into the fire. "Amounts to the same thing. Congratulations on your apprenticeship. I think."

"Thanks. I think." She hugged the tablet to her chest. "I didn't mean what y'all did in the stairwell was a mistake. Him leaving afterward was. He's totally in love with you still. You know that, right?"

Rhiannon had never been a fan of Charlie, so it surprised him to hear her say that. "He has a funny way of showing it."

"He's repressed. You're so brave you deserve better than that. But you seem to think the problem is he doesn't care about you, when that's not it."

He turned the metal in the flame, wishing it would heat faster so he could pound more. "And you know this how?"

"Because he looks at you like you're the center of the universe."

He crossed his arms, as if he could stop the hopeful words from sinking in. "What does that even mean?"

She walked closer, checking the flame. "It means when he walks into a room, he seeks you out, even if he doesn't come stand by you. When something happens that's interesting or emotional, he turns to you, and your reaction affects his. In dangerous circumstances he steps closer to you. He may not be brave enough to take your hand when people can see it, but he can't help turning to you, like you're his missing sunshine. Despite his many flaws, the man loves you. If you don't love him back, that's one thing, but if he's what you really want, don't give up because you think he doesn't feel the same."

Did Charlie really look to him that much? Vince had never noticed it.

On the other hand, so what if she right? That hadn't stopped Charlie from running away last night. It hadn't stopped him from standing on the sidelines instead of dancing two days ago. It hadn't stopped him from going behind Vince's back to get his needs met five years ago. Back at nineteen, Vince would've said that Charlie's love was enough. But now...

She bumped hips with him and echoed his thoughts. "Love can only be as perfect as the person who feels it. Imperfect people send out love imperfectly. Doesn't stop it from being real." She sighed, her breath heaving out in a rush that dropped her shoulders. "Since nobody's perfect, we all have to decide where we draw the line on what's good enough."

She was talking about her mother. Rhiannon put up with too

much from that woman, but the older Vince got, the more he understood her inability to let go. If his own dad hadn't kicked him out, how much abuse would he have taken just to stay a part of his family? He liked to think he was strong for cutting those ties, but he hadn't cut them. In some ways, his situation was easier than what Rhi was going through, dangling on a thin cord of love from a mother who was broken.

The world was a screwed-up place full of people sinking under the weight of their pasts and the connections they still clung to. He supposed that meant love was always a compromise. But could he and Charlie ever find a compromise they could both live with?

The shop door opened again. *Think of the devil…*

Chapter 17

Rhiannon whistled softly as Charlie lingered in the shadows at the back of the shop. He couldn't come out into the sun where Vince was working without catching on fire, but there was still room for him to work in the empty half where the light didn't reach. He was dressed in work clothes: jeans stained with wood glue and finish and a T-shirt that had seen better days. His hair was uncut and covered with an ancient University of Texas baseball cap that shaded his face, helping him avoid the sun.

"Cash said you may want assistance on a project for him." He stood uncomfortably, his gaze studying the line of light.

Vince raised an eyebrow. Any project they'd done in the past had been the other way around, Charlie the master taking assistance from Vince or ordering pieces, like hinges and handles, that Vince would craft. He'd never been the one with the design, ordering pieces from Charlie, quite possibly the world's foremost master furniture maker.

Rhi shot him a questioning look, offering to stay and play referee. Or to yell at Charlie so Vince didn't have to. She'd probably prefer that one.

He shook his head. "Go read by the pool. If you can figure out how they're stealing souls, that's the most important thing that can happen right now."

She frowned but nodded an acquiescence before she turned to Charlie, bristling with barely contained anger. "Do better."

Charlie rocked back on his heels, meeting her hostility with a somber expression. He didn't bluster or pretend he didn't know what she was talking about, just nodded as if he took her vague demand to heart. "I'll try."

Rhi rubbed Vince's back in support and whispered, "You look super sexy, by the way, all sweaty biceps, working-class bad boy. Be careful." She smiled wryly. "Unless you want to end up banging your ex in a metal shop, but that disaster's on you."

She popped him on the ass, the side that still stung from Charlie's bite, as if he needed more of a reminder, and headed out into the bright afternoon sunshine.

Charlie's hearing, like all vampires', was extraordinarily keen. Despite her hushed tone, he'd probably heard everything.

Vince picked up his designs, unnerved. He was going to show his work to a master designer and ask for assistance. The master designer was his ex. Whom he'd fucked last night. And the guy had bolted.

And, hell, Vince was still in love with him anyway.

Life probably got more awkward than this, but at the moment he couldn't imagine how.

When he turned to Charlie, trying to screw his courage to the sticking place—whatever that meant—he found the man's gaze nowhere near his face or the papers in his hands, desire clear in his eyes.

Charlie's gaze jerked up to his, and a blush turned his ears red. "Sorry." He looked away, then back, his eye contact intentionally steady. "I'll be professional."

Vince hesitated, suddenly afraid. He'd never really understood how strong Charlie was, how fierce he could be, until last night. It turned him on and made him wary all at the same time. He was safe in the light where the vampire couldn't get to him. As soon as he stepped into the shadows, though, he would be at Charlie's mercy. Vince might be taller and bigger with more obvious muscles, but it was a lie. He couldn't physically stop

Charlie from anything the man set his mind to.

Charlie frowned as if he knew what Vince was thinking and shoved his hands into his pockets, feigning harmlessness in Eric Clapton's *Fresh Cream* T-shirt. It was an act Vince had bought for sixteen years.

Now the visual made him laugh. "Stop trying to look weak. I know you're not."

"I'm not going to hurt you." *Too late.* The thought must've shown on Vince's face, because Charlie hunched. "I can't apologize enough for last night."

Vince shifted his weight. "What part of last night?"

"All…" He jerked his hands out of his pockets, fists clenched. "I don't know. I didn't mean to hurt you. I never want to hurt… Did I?"

Watching him flee down the stairs had pretty much ripped his soul out and stomped on it with giant boots, but that wasn't what Charlie meant. Anger made Vince's voice tight. "I'm not a porcelain virgin anymore, Charlie. I can handle things getting a little rough."

Charlie's fists tightened further, like he wanted to punch someone, as his body stiffened.

Had he always been this jealous? He'd seemed so damnably calm the entire time they'd been together.

Then again, Vince had finally gotten into Charlie's pants by talking about maybe losing his cherry. Flirting hadn't done it. Working together hadn't done it. Living together hadn't done it. Parading around the house nearly naked hadn't done it. But the evening after Vince had asked Charlie for advice on picking a man for his first time, Charlie had offered himself. It had been exactly the reaction Vince had hoped for—albeit nearly twenty-four hours later—and he'd left his scrambled eggs cooling on the stove to straddle Charlie's lap.

Then nine months later Charlie had dumped him over his job. Vince had thought it was over the lie, but maybe the man was just that pissed other people saw him mostly naked. Yesterday Charlie had acted completely out of character over one dance.

When Vince had been younger, he'd assumed Charlie was too rational and wise for petty emotions. It was a weird and welcome revelation to see how imperfect Charlie really was. "You get jealous."

"Yeah," he muttered, not loosening up one bit as he gave Vince a look like he'd said something glaringly obvious. "When it comes to you."

Which meant if they were ever going to get back together, Vince had to quit his job.

And that thought came from where, the land of hope and sugarplums?

It didn't matter. For the first time in their relationship, Vince was pretty sure he held the moral high ground, and he wasn't above parading around on it. "If I cross over into the dark, are you going to jump me again? Because I have work to do, and I don't have time for your bullshit. You want to be pissed I've had other men, be pissed at yourself. That's entirely your fault for dumping me." He crossed his arms. "And you know what? I don't regret a single one. You've been alive for nearly three hundred years. I should be the jealous one. How many men have you had?" Hundreds, likely.

"Twelve."

Vince dropped his arms, shocked. "Tw-twelve? How is that possible?"

"Well, between you and Trey, I've been exceptionally active in the twenty-first century."

His jaw tightened. "Trey. Is that the prostitute from Cash's party?"

Charlie looked at the floor. "Yes."

"Is that where you got your blood while we were together?"

To Vince's relief, Charlie's gaze shot back up without one iota of guilt. "What? No. I didn't meet him until after we were apart." Then he looked away, evading. "I drank bottled. You saw me."

That wasn't a lie, but it wasn't the truth either. Vince tried to keep his voice under control as his anger built. "But your skin never got cold."

Charlie's face relaxed as if a question he'd been puzzling over had been answered. "You thought... Eating and sex don't have to be connected." His face pinched like he was ashamed of himself, but he looked Vince steadily in the eye. "Every couple months I'd bring fifty bucks and takeout down under the I-35 bridge at Airport Boulevard."

The area beneath the overpass was a popular spot for homeless people to congregate. "You paid homeless people to let you bite them?" Of all the worrisome things Vince had lain in bed contemplating, that hadn't occurred to him.

Charlie shrugged. "We'd both get dinner out of it. I had volunteers every time. I'd bite someone on the wrist and five minutes later be on with my night. There was nothing remotely exciting about it."

"And nobody's going to believe a homeless person talking about vampires."

"Yeah. But it would still be frowned upon if word got out, so if you wouldn't mind keeping it between us, I'd appreciate that."

"I won't say anything. But be prepared—Javier's going to ask you about it. I told Rhi I thought you'd been going to Scarlet while we were together, and she defended you." He looked down and chuckled. "And now I owe her three Led Zeppelin records."

Under the circumstances, he was good with that. "You've really only had sex with twelve people?"

"Fourteen. You asked how many men the first time."

"You've slept with women? I'm sorry." He'd probably had to prove he was a man or something three hundred years ago. Society made being gay challenging enough now; it would've been torture in Charlie's day and age. How much of Charlie's shyness was inherent to his personality, and how much had been forced onto him for survival? Sympathy softened his lingering resentment over last night. Charlie should've stayed. But Vince could forgive him.

Charlie had taken a knife for him.

"Do I even want to know your number? Have you doubled my lifetime count? Tripled? You've had five years, and you're"— he looked Vince up and down again and swallowed heavily like he couldn't remember the word "handsome." Then he said, "Perfect."

Surprise made Vince blurt out honesty. "I haven't kept track. Grindr makes it pretty simple. I mean, when I asked, I figured you wouldn't know the answer either, and, eh…"

Charlie had asked the question so casually, but of course as soon as Vince answered, his face darkened. "Of course, you have no idea. It's easy for you. I bet you weren't out of my house for a week before men were banging down your door. What's Grindr?"

He ignored the question. "If you didn't want to know the answer, you shouldn't have asked. For what it's worth, I didn't have sex for almost a year." He took a step toward the shadows. "I kept thinking you would return my calls. Yeah, it was less than a week before I got *offers*, but I didn't take a damn one because I was waiting for you to forgive me. I didn't want to mess up my second chance. I was so sure you'd give me a second chance."

Vince took a ragged breath. "Fuck." Another breath as

Charlie stood there silently, his face an unreadable blank. "It's for the better. I grew up without you. I really was a kid before. I didn't know it at the time. But I was. I didn't realize how much I depended on you. I can stand on my own now because you made me do it. As much as I hated you for it, it's been a good thing." He was babbling. It was all true, but he didn't need to spill his guts like this. It made him feel more naked than any dance ever had.

Charlie's voice was soft. "I'm sorry I ran away yesterday. That's the part I'm sorry for. I feel so much around you it scares me. I left you five years ago with a note because I knew if I said it in person, you'd convince me to stay and I'd hate myself." He stepped carefully toward the light until his toes touched the shadow's edge. "You have no idea how much you had me wrapped around your fingers. One touch and you could've taken me anywhere, gotten me to do anything. The only way I knew to fix it was to sever the connection and let it bleed out."

Vince's chest constricted. He took another step forward until he was just out of arm's reach. "Did it work?"

"I thought it did. And then I saw you again and realized I'd just gotten used to bleeding."

A thousand thoughts flitted through his mind, a thousand hopes and wishes. But the problem remained that Charlie freaked out and ran away. He'd done it five years ago and he'd done it last night. Vince would be an idiot to think it wouldn't happen again, just like Rhiannon was an idiot every time she let herself believe that *this* time her mom was going to stay clean. People didn't change. He cared about Charlie. He always would. But he couldn't trust him to be there when things got tough.

Charlie wiped his hands down his jeans and rolled back on his heels, like he sensed Vince was closing off. "Would you like my help on Cash's stake?"

Vince gripped the designs tighter, thrown off by the change of subject. It was good. They had nowhere to go with this conversation.

On the other hand, he was plenty nervous about handing his drawings over. He wasn't a bad artist, but the fifteen years he'd been working had nothing on Charlie's experience. His face heated as he looked critically at the pencil sketches, suddenly finding flaws where before he'd only been proud. "They haven't been reviewed by anyone with structural knowledge. They could use some refining." God, what if Charlie suggested they scrap it and start again? If there was a flaw in the construction, that would be embarrassing. But if Charlie simply didn't like the lines, then he was just taking over, playing papa again, and that was not okay.

Charlie hissed in pain, bringing Vince's eyes up. The vampire had stretched his hand into the sunlight, palm up as he asked for the plans with a gesture.

"What are you doing?" Vince shoved the work into Charlie's hand and shoved him backward, bringing both of them into the shadows.

Charlie squeezed and flexed his hand. It was pink, like a mild sunburn, but otherwise looked okay. "Trying to be less afraid." His hazel eyes turned thoughtful as he turned to the drawings. "I've spent a long time making choices out of fear. The people I care about deserve better than that from me." He shuffled the drawings, putting the decorative design on top. "*I* deserve better than that from me."

Vince wouldn't let himself believe in change until he saw it. Not even hope.

Damn, there was the hope. *Stupid.* For now he held his breath as Charlie concentrated on the sketches. The weapon design blended a stake and a knife with a steel point leading to a metal-and-wood twist. It looked nothing like Cash's original piece, which was more like a star of wood in a metal cage. But Vince had shown early, very rough sketches to Cash, and the vampire had been enthusiastic.

"This is good." Charlie pulled a pencil from his pocket and headed toward the cabinet by the shop sink. "Mind if I..."

This was where he changed everything. Vince deflated. "Sure." Charlie's ideas would be amazing. He did know everything there was to know about crafting.

Charlie leaned over the design. "I don't do a lot of bent lamination anymore, and this is a tight spiral. I could use your help building the cauls." His pencil flew as he made notes.

Bent lamination was a complicated process some woodworkers specialized in, and most didn't bother learning. Vince had never seen it done, as it required a steamer and specialized clamps—cauls—built to the needed shape. It made his design a lot harder than he'd realized. "You can't just carve it?"

"No. It's near impossible to do circles without a short-grained section. It'd make the wood weak. It's okay. I can do this without carving," he assured, then said more sheepishly, "But it may require more than one practice run. It's been a century or so since I've done the technique, and to get that spiral out of one piece won't be easy." He took the prototype design and hovered a pencil over it. "Mind if I cut the first trial off at intervals while I get the hang of it again? With some practice, I'll be able do the final in a single stretch." With simple strokes, Charlie added metal flourishes, making the project easier on himself and harder on Vince. Which was about as backward as possible.

"You haven't even seen my recent work. You have confidence I can do that?"

Charlie's pencil hovered again. "I've seen a lot of your recent work. You post it on the internet. You're absolutely capable of doing this."

"Oh." Charlie had kept up with his craftwork? That was cool. Vince had assumed Charlie had done his best to forget about him.

"I kept hoping you'd make enough money to quit your other job and…" Charlie flushed. "Do whatever you want with the breaks. I'm not trying to design it for you. I just put something in at intervals that would most benefit me."

Vince nodded. "Yeah. Okay. I can do that." He felt dizzy. Charlie's approval meant more to him than it should.

Charlie put the pencil down and turned to Vince without even a shadow of patronizing in his expression. "Of course you can. You're a talented artisan. How do you want to proceed?"

Vince had lead on the project, and Charlie was waiting for instructions. No argument, no need to convince, nothing but trust that Vince was capable enough to design and craft something that's function was a matter of life or death for a friend. A wash of emotion carried him forward, and he hugged Charlie.

Charlie stiffened in surprise. Vince started to back up.

Quickly, Charlie's arms clasped around him, strong and sure. With a sighing hum, the smaller man relaxed into Vince, fitting into the curve of his arms, his forehead pressed against Vince's jaw. The tension melted out of both of them as they pressed together, chest to chest.

"Forgive me," Charlie asked, his voice small.

"For what? Walking out last night? You took a dagger for me. We'll call it even." He tried to make his voice light.

Charlie's voice was anything but light. "For all the ways I'm not the man you deserve."

Vince tightened his hold, and Charlie snuggled closer, his cold nose against Vince's throat. "There's nothing to forgive.

You're the best and worst that's ever happened to me. And I brought the worst on myself when I lied to you."

"Can we…" Charlie's voice trailed off.

Vince stiffened, fear and hope rolled together. He didn't know what he wanted anymore. This moment, just holding each other, this was perfect. No complications. No interferences like money or other people's fear getting in the way. But they'd always been good when it was just the two of them. Reality outside that safety was what had killed them. "Can we what?"

"Can we let the past go? It can't be changed. I don't want to be angry at each other anymore."

Let what go? Just the bad, or all of it? Was he asking Vince to forget they'd been lovers?

"I miss you. I miss being friends," Charlie added.

That answered the question. Vince sighed in regret. It was for the better. They made really good friends. Really bad boyfriends. They each needed too much that the other couldn't give. He nodded, his stubbled cheek catching in Charlie's soft hair. "Yeah. I think that's a good idea." Which meant he should probably quit holding the man like a lover. Friends hugged, but not like this. It felt so good though, as Charlie's strength surrounded him, his scent of lumber and bay rum teasing his senses, bringing back memories he'd just promised to forget.

A totally different memory from his childhood surfaced, of his immigrant grandfather, who'd lived with them briefly before he'd died. Every night before Vince went to bed, his grandfather had blessed him. That was back when Vince was still religious, still had a family, still believed life was safe and people were reliable. Holding Charlie made him feel that way again.

And Charlie was, somehow, still devoutly Roman Catholic. Vince had gone once to Charlie's annual communion. Annual, because the Eucharist went down a vampire about as well as lye went down a human. But it was important to Charlie, so he continued to torture himself. He even made Mass at least once a month, making him a vampire with an unusually high tolerance for crosses. Vince, on the other hand, had a history of rejecting whatever rejected him. Catholicism still considered him aberrant, so he wasn't about to call himself a Catholic. But Vince's rage at God and an institution that wouldn't accept him didn't erase the joy of an honest man's blessing given in love.

In a rush of feeling, he put his thumb against Charlie's forehead and made the sign of the cross. Charlie shuddered. It wasn't a pained movement, at least Vince didn't think so, so Vince sealed it with a light kiss over the spot his fingers had touched.

Charlie looked up. "What was that for?"

Vince shrugged and stepped away, feeling silly but less gloomy than he had in a while. "Grandpa Gio used to do that to us kids every night. It didn't hurt, did it?"

"No."

"Good." He turned to the drawings. "We have a weapon to make."

Charlie turned as well, facing the same way. Maybe it was Vince's imagination, but it seemed to him that they stood a little closer together now, hands less clenched and smiles more natural. It wasn't going to be the same between them, but it was going to be okay.

Footsteps pounded the pavement as Rhiannon rushed in, hair wild and eyes sparkling in excited fear. "Guys! I think I know what she's doing."

Charlie pulled out his phone. "I'll get Cash. He'll want to hear this."

Rhi didn't wait. "The thing tonight? They need to cancel it."

"Why?" Vince asked.

"Because the spell works through fledglings, biting them to

recreate them as vampires like the first time, but now evil."

"Yeah." Vince said. "We verified that the other night when Charlie's sire turned him for a few seconds."

She glared at him like he was a complete moron. "So they're going to put the mother of all good vampires in front of as many of her children as can be gathered? All they have to do is get one vampire—her—and everyone is vulnerable."

Vince looked at Charlie. That did sound like a bad idea.

"Guys!" she yelled, agitated. "You're storing Tzitzi in the same building as the ceremony. Alaric is on their side. He's going to let her out, and they're going to turn Modron tonight. They lock the doors, and every vampire in that building—almost all of CoVIn—will have their awens yanked by morning."

Cash's voice came tinny through the speakerphone. "Hey, how's my stake going?"

"Get down here," Charlie said. "The reception's in danger."

Cash hung up, and Rhi frowned.

"He'll be here," Charlie assured her. "He hung up because he took me seriously." He held up a finger and counted.

By three Cash was among them, his pace too fast to see him arrive. He just appeared. "What's up?"

Vince blinked. Charlie looked amused at his discomfort. "You get used to it." He turned to Cash. "Tzitzi plans to turn the queen tonight during the ceremony, then Modron will turn all of you."

Rhiannon stepped back, flushing. "Or at least, I think. I mean, that's what I would do if I was an evil genius hellbent on taking over the world."

Cash looked at her. "During the ceremony?"

"Yeah, when you're all in the same room—eldest together in the front. Tzitzi curses Modron, Modron infects you, Winnie, and

Kolyan, who are up on stage with her, then you're an unstoppable force of evil that takes out CoVIn in five minutes. You need to stop the ceremony."

Cash ran a hand through his hair. "Can you, I don't know, make a counter curse?"

Charlie rolled his eyes. "They're not stopping the ceremony. You could bring hard proof that a nuclear bomb was going off, and they'd want their pomp and circumstance."

Cash smiled tightly. "You can knock it with your artisan-class philosophy, but pomp and circumstance is a necessary part of governing peasants."

"I rest my case," Charlie said.

Vince frowned. "Who constitutes a peasant in a society of ridiculously wealthy immortals? That would be... me and Rhiannon?"

"No. Anyone kept in line through ceremonies, rallies, and other public events. Class isn't about money." Cash slapped him on the back with gusto. "Speaking of money, as I seem to have purchased you a five-thousand-dollar suit, I called the moving company. Do you know how long it's been since I've had a blacksmith on my estate? All the other vampires will be jealous."

Charlie huffed. "And you desperately need more reasons for everyone to be jealous."

"Ubiquitous envy is a lifestyle that requires constant fostering."

Rhi stepped into the middle of the circle. "Ceremony. Everyone losing their souls. Vince and I eaten. Can we stay on task?"

"Or what, no nookie tonight?"

"Not if I'm dead, asshat. You get no nookie then. At least not from me." Rhi flipped him off.

He blew her a kiss off his middle finger. "Tzitzi is caged in the basement and surrounded. How is she going to perform this spell?"

"Alaric is going to let her out."

All humor left Cash's expression. "I'm unconvinced he's an issue."

Vince stood by Rhi, forming a unified front. "That'll be real comforting tonight when every one of you joins Tzitzi's army."

Charlie looked at the counter where their project notes lay, as if looking for guidance in graphite and graph paper, then surprised Vince by standing next to him. "Not considering it as a possibility is foolish, Cash. So take unnecessary precautions, if that's what you have to look at them as. But I think you doubt him more than you'll admit."

Cash stepped forward, getting in Charlie's face with a threatening glare. "Are you challenging my judgment?"

Charlie paled as his fists clenched and unclenched with nerves. Vince wanted to take his hand but knew that wouldn't be helpful. Charlie had to stand on his own, or Cash wouldn't take him seriously.

Charlie licked his lips but kept his chin up. "I'm pointing out that your loyalty may be blinding you."

Cash stood for a moment longer, scowling. When Charlie still didn't back off, Cash stepped back, his intimidating demeanor shifting to a thoughtful nod as his gaze flipped briefly to Vince. "Okay." All his anger was gone, like it'd been an act, when he looked back to Charlie. "If you're that sure."

On a surprised inhale, Charlie folded his arms. "That's a backward way of deciding whose side you're on. You do realize a man can be sure of himself and still wrong."

Cash snorted. "It doesn't matter if a coward's right; he'll run when the fight starts. How can I trust your words if I can't trust you to stand by them?" He turned to Vince. "Do you forge spines too?" He lunged, and Vince could do nothing as Cash yanked his arms behind his back.

"Hey!" The pressure stayed just this side of pain as he struggled to get away.

Instead of hurting him, Cash gave him a noogie. "You're an impressive little fairy. We're going to make good housemates."

Vince elbowed him in the gut, hard as he could, knowing he couldn't hurt Cash. The vampire laughed and let him go. Vince got a finger in his face. "You cannot call me a fairy. That's housemate rule number one." Because apparently taking the suit meant they were roommates now. Standing in the amazeballs forge, he was okay with that.

"Molly."

"No."

"Warmer bruder."

"What is that, German? I don't even know what that means. But *no*."

"Bugger me, Charlie, he's even pickier than you are."

Vince should be pissed, but for some reason he was amused. "Fuck you, asshole."

"In your dreams tonight, baby. Movers are picking up your shit within the hour. You live here now. Make it so in that curly head of yours." His eyes gleamed with mischief. "Smithy."

"No! You…" *Wait.* "Yeah, okay, you can call me that. Technically it's just 'smith.' The place is a smithy."

"Sir, yes sir." Cash's tone and salute were equally laced with sarcasm, but he smiled like he was pleased. Then his smile faded as he laced his fingers on his head thoughtfully. "Don't forget I swore fealty to the queen. When I come from, that meant something."

When he came from? Okay, Cash wasn't talking about the place, but the time period. "What does that mean, from a practical standpoint?" Vince asked.

"As she goes, I go."

"Like, if she died, you'd throw yourself on her burning bier or something?"

Cash shot him an offended look. "No. If she died, I'd already be dust because they had to kill me to get to her."

For the five billionth time that week, Vince tried to put himself in the mind of someone whose worldview was completely alien to his. The exercise had been good for him. He glanced at Charlie. Made him a little more understanding. He tried to phrase his argument in a way that would jive with Cash's outlook. "Would you consider being loyal to her ideas instead of to her?"

"Yeah," Rhiannon added. "If I died or became a Liberi— which is the same thing, in my mind—I wouldn't want Javi to die with me. I'd want him to take care of Mom. If Vince died, he'd want us to work on making CoVIn a friendlier place for LGBTQ vampires. We'd want the people who loved us to live on and carry forward what was important to us."

Cash's expression softened, and for a moment he looked so old despite his young face. "I understand what you're saying, but that's not how it works. I don't expect you to understand or agree. But you need to know."

"At least think about it," Vince said.

Cash nodded genially, eyes going from serious to joking just like that. "Think? Why would I do something crazy like that? I've got a phone call to make and a species to save." He pointed two fingers at Charlie and Vince. "Build me a weapon." He pointed to Rhiannon. "Figure out a spell to stop Tzitzi. Go, minions, go." With a wink for Rhiannon, he strode out.

Vince crossed his arms. "Do you get used to it, or does he

always kinda piss you off?"

"Eh, both?" Charlie said. "Although, I'm debating a new strategy of never doing what he says. In all this time, it's never dawned on me to try that." He frowned at the plans. "Unless it's a reasonable order and I'm in danger of losing my soul. So, this time I say we get to work." Pencil back out, he started a list of supplies.

"Would he really stay loyal to Queen Modron even if she lost her awen?" Rhiannon asked. "That's what he was warning us, right?"

Charlie tapped the pencil against the paper. "I don't know. A hundred or so years ago, I'd have said that's exactly what he would do. But he's not as antiquated in his thinking as he used to be. You two said the right things. Despite his protest, he'll think about it."

"Good."

Vince looked around the shop. "Since I guess I live here, will I really be able to keep him out of the house if he *changes* tonight?"

"Yes." Charlie's pencil scratched across the page in the silence. "Once your bed—or whatever you consider your bed—is here, he'll need an invitation to reenter the house. My guess is he won't leave the walls until he's ready for tonight. Neither will I. Then, after we see who's caught in Tzitzi's plan, you can invite him in to make decisions about who else is invited or, worst case scenario, keep this as a safe house."

"What if I decided not to invite him in, regardless? That's a lot of trust in somebody he's only known for a little over a week."

"He talked to me about it, and I told him you're a good choice. He likes you, but he's trusting me." Charlie finished his list, folded it, and headed for the door. "If you're here, Cash will watch out for you. It's the safest place you could possibly live. And you'll respect his space, consult with him on who gets in, and in general be easy to live with. I should know. He needs a human here, and he could do a lot worse than you."

It was a compliment. But it was also a pass-off. If Vince lived here, then he couldn't move back in with Charlie. Not that he'd been intending to.

Had he?

The pain of that realization said he indeed still hoped for that in some recess of his crazy heart. He should just ask. Make it simple. But the words wouldn't come out. Despite knowing it was for the best, he still wasn't ready to hear that Charlie was done with him for good.

Charlie headed for the door, calling for a messenger as he held out his list.

Rhi, sensing Vince's mood, hip-bumped him. "So if things go south, you and I get back here and hole up?"

"That sounds like the plan."

"I'm going to do more research." She looked out the shop door. "Is it just me, or does the sunshine not look so bright anymore?" Clutching the tablet, she headed back outside.

Vince stoked the forge and stuck another rod into the coals.

A moment later, Charlie was back. "How can I assist while I'm waiting for my tools?"

You can hold me and tell me that tomorrow everyone will be okay and you'll be mine again. "You can work the bellows. If you don't mind the labor."

"Not a bit. I'm at your disposal for the next hour or so. Use me as you wish."

Vince bit his tongue at the too-broad invitation and shoved on his gloves.

Chapter 18

Charlie panted and cursed as he ran up thirty-two flights of stairs to Starlight Club on the top floor of CoVIn, where the reception would be held. Cash was going to kill him—metaphorically—if he wasn't there on time. The queen might kill him literally. Or, more likely, just kick him out of CoVIn and let him die.

The stake in his pocket made his suit jacket hang unevenly, and it slapped heavily against his chest with each footfall. He'd sent Vince off with Cash and Rhiannon, making sure the man arrived in desirable company, while Charlie waited for the hide glue to dry on their prototype.

Final floor. At the stairwell door, he folded forward and leaned his elbows on his knees. Everyone would stare if he arrived gasping for breath. A vampire gasping in anything other than ecstasy was a sorry sight indeed. Vampires were cool. Controlled. Polished like fine wood.

Charlie wasn't polished. He'd grown up in sawdust with freckles and calloused skin, and he liked those things about himself. Maybe not the freckles.

Vince liked his freckles.

With a final deep breath for courage, not necessity, Charlie popped open the door and headed in. Vampires clustered about, standing under the slim chandeliers or around tables festooned with flowers. Like the rest of the building, Starlight Club's foyer was exquisite. But the space's *pièces de résistance* were the double doors leading into the club itself. It had taken Charlie a year to craft the intricately detailed marquetry of the Austin skyline on a starry night that stretched across both doors. A group in floor-length gowns studied his work, running their fingers across the design and gawking in what looked like admiration.

Pride filled his chest and made him smile. It was the largest, most elaborate design he'd ever contemplated, much less completed, and he felt good about the results.

What would Vince do if he saw people admiring his metalwork? He'd probably walk up and introduce himself under the assumption that people wanted to meet him. He'd be ready to answer questions, accept critical evaluation, and hand out business cards.

Charlie took a few steps toward the doors, not to go inside but with the notion that maybe he would try that. He didn't need to hustle for commissions anymore, but he wouldn't mind answering questions or listening to their critiques. New perspectives helped him keep his creative process from stagnating.

His gait slowed as he approached, wavering between nodding at the doormen to open the doors and pausing to talk. Pausing to talk meant he'd have to start the conversation, and that made him queasy. What if he made an ass of himself?

Well, then he would turn tail, go inside, and find Vince. But what if they had questions? Then Charlie would answer them, go inside, and find Vince. The two paths ended up in the same place, which meant it shouldn't matter.

One man checked his watch and stared at the ceiling like he was bored, but the other was engaged in a debate with two women over the types of wood used. That was his in. Muscles so tight he could barely move, he took a step toward the group and nervously cleared his throat. "The water is bird's-eye walnut. That's what gives it those tiny swirls. And, yes, the stars are tortoiseshell. It's the only part of the design that isn't wood."

All four of them, even the bored man, stared at him, making his stomach sink and his already shaking hands practically rattle with social anxiety. Time to go find Vince.

"You made this?" one of the women asked, stopping him as he pivoted.

"Yes." Did he stick out his hand to shake? Or no, that was too much. There were still a shocking number of vampires who, contrary to all sense, believed Ramón had passed on homosexuality to his fledglings like a communicable disease, making them contagious. Just in case these vampires were that kind of idiot, he'd introduce himself without a handshake. "I'm Charlie Travert."

The man recoiled. "Isn't he—"

"I'm standing right here," Charlie snapped, surprised at his own temerity. "That makes me a *you*, not a *he*."

"You're friends with Cash Geirson, aren't you?" the other woman asked in a thick Catalonian accent.

You mean the one who still isn't gay after several centuries of contact? "Yes."

She stuck out her hand. "Loli Gasca." The name rang a bell. She'd been one of Cash's longer-term flings. He shook her hand while the others looked on with varying degrees of discomfort. "It is good to meet you. I have one of your jewelry boxes. Your work is exquisite."

Charlie ignored the other three and focused on the nice person. In the past, he would've done the opposite, and that would've sent him running. But Vince always gave his attention to the friendliest people until everyone else came around. It worked. Vince was charming, so that helped, but focusing on the good was something Charlie could do too. "Thank you."

"Maybe I will see more of your work soon. I am moving to

Austin."

He stifled a sigh. Her and every other vampire on the planet. Things were going to get crazy around here.

God, he sounded like an old fart. "I hope we're treating you well," he said.

"It is wonderful!" she said with enthusiasm. "Now, tell me more about your marvelous work. How did you carve the teeny-tiny bats?"

He chuckled. "Very carefully." At her encouraging smile, he launched into a better explanation.

A few minutes later, with the lights blinking to signal everyone into their seats, Charlie headed inside. The other three vampires had drifted off, but the lively and intelligent conversation with Loli had been worth shutting down the voices inside that told him talking to other vampires would always end in failure. Focus on the positive people. Ignore everyone else. It was a good lesson, and he wanted to tell Vince. It was a silly accomplishment, maybe, but it was a big deal to him, and Vince would understand.

Chairs were arranged in circles around a central stage with a lit fire pit. Cash paced around the fire in his military formal, a smile locked on his face as he scanned the crowd for a disturbance. Seeing Charlie, he motioned forward with two fingers and then down, pointing to a seat on the front edge. Cash had saved him a spot? Probably so the queen would see him and know he'd shown up like a good CoVIn member. He balked at playing that game.

But Vince would be up there. Charlie hustled forward, ignoring everyone he passed in pursuit of Vince. Cash shot him a questioning glance. Charlie patted his pocket, pretending the weapon misaligning his coat was his only concern. Cash gave him a thumbs up.

He rounded the corner of the first row and found Vince standing at the end with Jacobson, a toady of a man who leaned too far into Vince's space for Charlie's comfort. Being hunters, vampires often had boundary issues.

Vince looked arresting. His black hair curled around his ears, highlighting his bright eyes. Even the fake smile he wore for Jacobson was charming, too alluring for his own good. Jacobson probably couldn't tell it wasn't real. Vince's olive complexion was striking against his subtly patterned black suit and winter-white silk shirt, intentionally left open at the throat. The cut was pristine, highlighting his broad shoulders and tapering to his waist. The lack of a tie gave him a relaxed air, but the fine fabric—and the confident way Vince wore it—kept it from appearing informal. It was the kind of suit that looked good enough to take off slowly, one teasing inch of fabric at a time.

He wanted to be the one—the only one—there when that suit came off. Just the thought made him hard. Today had been fantastic, just like old times, laughing, arguing, and sweating over a project. He had fun with Vince. Life was too long to wallow in monotony when Vince was everything life could be. He could let this opportunity pass, sure of its failure, or he could fight for it.

Right now Vince had no faith in Charlie's ability to stay the course. If he wanted Vince, he needed to prove every day, over and over again, that he was going to stand by him, no matter who else was in the room. No more running, no more hiding. He'd have to be out and unafraid. Or, at least, keep his fear from ruling him. But if Vince could be patient, he could make it happen. He could change.

He *would* change. That meant starting right now.

Another step put him close enough to distinguish their conversation from the dozens—hundreds?—of others surrounding them. Sure enough, Jacobson was trying to weasel his way into an introduction to Cash.

News traveled fast.

Somehow the man leaned even further in, his breath filling Vince's space. "After the reception would be nice."

Charlie stuck his hands between them. "Back up, Jacobson."

The man jerked back like Charlie had ebola. "Don't. Touch. Me."

There it was, the ignorant fear he faced every day. Instinct told him to back up. He ignored it and leaned in. "Then back off. He doesn't want you in his face."

Vince did a double take at him, then turned to Jacobson, a gleam of understanding in his eyes. "I'm gay too."

"What?" the man asked, like he didn't understand.

Vince took a step toward him, and Jacobson backed up. "Queer. Fag. Homo. Whatever they called us in your fucked-up century. It's infectious, too. Might want to go away before I breathe on you like you've been breathing on me."

Jacobson's lips curled in disgust as he toddled away in a huff. Charlie narrowed his eyes at his retreating form. It was one thing for people to be vile to him. It was another entirely to watch them do it to Vince.

"Disgust and loathing as a perk? Who knew?" Vince smiled at him, keeping an "appropriate" distance. "Thanks. Emma warned me about setting off the predatory instinct by playing hard to get, and I didn't know how to get rid of him."

Charlie wanted to take his hand. Or maybe just bump shoulders. Something friendly and caring, but he had no idea what. He'd never let Vince be affectionate in public, so he didn't know what Vince was comfortable with. Instead, his mouth opened and he blurted out, "I love you." *Well, there was always that.* He resisted the impulse to bury his face in his hand as his face heated up.

Vince's jaw dropped, and he gaped. "Did you get your soul sucked out?"

"What? No. Why would you think that?"

Vince's gaze darted around them as if he was checking to make sure the room still had people in it.

Charlie knew he'd done something wrong, bumbling around like a baby taking his first steps. It was what he felt like, trying to let go of the carefully guarded self that had preserved his life and sanity for all these years. But he couldn't keep that and have Vince.

The music started up, pompous and overwhelming. Rhiannon, lovely in a silvery-blue gown, took the seat next to Vince and waved before focusing forward. Anticipation hung thick in the room as the doors opened at the back for a procession. Most vampires only saw their queen on rare occasions like this. Outside of this week, Charlie himself hadn't seen her in fifty years. Yet here he was in the front row, like a member of the aristocracy. Him, an orphan cabinetmaker who should've died in obscurity with no family to mourn him.

It should be momentous. He didn't give a damn. His entire consciousness revolved around the next words of the man standing next to him.

Instead of words, though, Vince's expression turned defiant as his fingers intertwined with Charlie's in challenge.

A familiar panic swept through Charlie. They were in the front row. He turned, watching for a reaction, but nobody was looking at them. Down the aisle, Alaric and Winnie proceeded forward, leading the entourage. Ten more feet and they'd be at the front. Alaric would see, and then what?

Charlie frowned at his own idiocy. Was Alaric going to leap out of the parade and point them out? No. He would scowl and keep walking to his assigned place—likely the same thing he'd do if they weren't holding hands. So what was Charlie so afraid of?

Vince's body shifted away, slumping a little as his fingers slipped out of Charlie's. Just like at Cash's party with the dance, he'd made an offer he expected Charlie to refuse.

Charlie wouldn't fail this time. He squeezed his knuckles, trapping Vince's fingers before they were gone.

Vince eyed him with a hopeful wariness that made his insides clench.

Time to put his design on the table and get to work. He shoved his fingers between Vince's and squeezed. "I love you," he said again, softly because it was rude to raise his voice at a ceremony but loud enough for a human to hear.

Vince exhaled in a surprised rush of breath. He squeezed back as his body rocked in, pressing shoulders with him in a gesture both friendly and intimate. But his eyes were sad. "I believe you. I love you too. But that doesn't mean we'll work."

Charlie swallowed. Focus on the positive. If Vince loved him, there was hope. And Vince hadn't let go. "We can make it work. We're worth it." He clutched Vince's hand in a fierce grip. "I can change."

"People don't change." Despite his panic-tinged whisper, Vince's thumb moved slowly, making gentle circles on Charlie's wrist that sent frissons of heat from his hand to his groin. Vince wasn't scared of holding hands in public. He was scared of Charlie dropping his hand in public. The realization made him feel like an idiot.

If Charlie could convince Vince there was no reason to fear, surely he could get him back. "I guess it's a good thing I'm a vampire, then."

Vince shot him another startled glance. His thumb stopped circling, as if he hadn't meant to make the gesture more intimate. "What has gotten into you?"

Charlie frowned as he tried to figure out how to phrase it. "I realized you're worth growing up for. Or maybe 'growing a pair,' as you say."

☝✦☞

Vince breathed sharply through his nose, trying to hold back an emotional outburst. He was holding hands with Charlie. In public. And not just public, in front of all the vampires Charlie was terrified of.

They were in the front row, and Vince had received a personal invitation from the queen. He had a job smithing for someone who appreciated good crafting, and a home where he and his contributions were valued. It was everything Vince wanted—family, belonging, magic, and most importantly, Charlie—all wrapped up in beautiful packaging. So where was the catch? The shoe that dropped, the price that was too high, the boot that kicked him out so he was once again looking in the window at his family instead of eating at the table?

It was too much to hope for and too public a place for a meltdown. So he held Charlie's cold hand in his own trembling one and stared forward so he didn't do something crazy and break everything.

Alaric turned the corner and took Galswinth's hand as they marched up the stairs toward the stage where Cash, his shoulders back in military stiffness, stood behind a black cauldron big enough to fit a small human. Behind Galswinth and Alaric, Nikolai's bland smile turned to a grimace as he watched the connection between Alaric and his wife. There was a story there. Vince would have to ask Charlie later, when all these vampire ears couldn't hear them.

Cash had explained the ceremony to him and Rhi on the way here. The cauldron was a Welsh spiritual thing and had been an important part of the spell the Druids had used to transform

Modron. CoVIn used one in all of their important ceremonies as a reminder of the magic they came from.

The cathedral ceilings of Starlight were mostly glass, letting the light of the full moon in, and Vince could almost pretend they were outdoors on a rooftop.

A silver dagger with a jeweled hilt hung from Modron's belt. When she reached the low platform, she pulled it out, raising the dagger over her head as Alaric, Winnie, and Kolyan took places around the cauldron.

The music changed, drums beating faster as Modron sang in ancient Welsh. Her voice was rough and filled with energy. The pounding drumbeat, the smell of the woodsmoke and the spicy scent from the cauldron, the warmth of the fire and the chill of the room, made a dreamy concoction. Unlike Tzitzi's ritual, though, there was no hysteria, no bloodlust. Vince relaxed under the comforting weight of a ceremony performed unbroken for almost a thousand years.

Charlie whispered a translation in his ear, his low, resonant voice too sexy for Vince's own good. "By awen we sing, by blood we live, while earth shall stand and tide shall flow and breeze shall blow. Sing with me, my children, drink with me, my children, while earth shall stand and tide shall flow and breeze shall blow. By blood and by awen we sing together, we stand together against all who oppose us, while earth shall stand and tide shall flow and breeze shall blow."

As the final echo of words faded, Modron nicked her wrist with the dagger and dropped exactly three drops of blood into the cauldron to mix with the spiced mead that was supposed to be there. Although according to Cash, occasionally somebody got bored and put something more potent in. Vince had asked if Cash was the one who'd gotten bored. He'd given an offended, "Me?" and didn't answer.

Regardless of what ended up in the pot, at the close of the ceremony a chalice would be filled from it and all on the stage would drink. Then the audience would be invited to come forward and share from the common cup, like at the weekly Catholic Eucharist Vince had attended growing up. He had to admit there was a primal beauty in sharing a cup with community. Cash had told him he could share too, if he wanted. There wouldn't be enough blood in it to matter. And he'd warn him if there was something other than mead in there.

At first he hadn't been too keen on the idea—all those vampires clustered in a ritual reminded him too much of what had happened at Tooth and Nail. But maybe he would. And maybe he'd drag Charlie up and make him drink too.

Cash, Kolyan, Winnie, and Alaric sat, and Modron began the talky-talky portion of the event where everyone under the sun got thanked and the glory of CoVIn was praised to the skies.

Apparently some things were universal, even with vampires. So, as Vince had during church homilies almost every Sunday, he turned to his neighbor. Vampires had crazy good hearing. But that meant he could speak in barely a whisper of noise and Charlie would understand. It wasn't the place for hashing things out, so he asked something innocuous.

"What are they wearing?" Cash, Nikolai, and Alaric all had similar attire of black, fitted trousers tucked into boots and a sash, like Girl Scouts wore, made of undecorated red silk.

But their tunic overshirts, which Cash hadn't worn on the way there, were made of a scaled fabric Vince had never seen before that glinted midnight blue and slate gray. The material conformed to their chests and arms but hung loosely a few inches past their hips, and an attached hood of the same material was pushed back. Each man wore one glove of a similar midnight blue, but with smaller scaling, that ended in ornate claws. Cash wore his on the right—hadn't he said something about being a lefty?—and Nikolai and Alaric on the left. Galswinth and the queen wore dresses of similar material that clung to their skin with a shimmer somewhere between armor and silk.

Charlie leaned in, his breath warm and distracting against Vince's ear. "Their dress uniforms. Functional as well as handsome. We've yet to find anything that pierces that hide."

Hide? More like scales. He'd almost believe it was snakeskin, if there was a snake with scales that large and a hide big enough to cut a dress out of a single piece. "What's it made of?"

"The Axes claim it's dragon skin and that the gloves are tipped with pieces of dragon claws."

Any vestiges of boredom with the speech left in a wash of wonder. "Dragon skin? Like fire-breathing, flying dragons? They're real?"

Charlie squeezed his hand in warning to be quiet as Cash looked their way, a smugly amused smile on his face. Charlie's voice was almost unintelligibly quiet as he said, "The oldest anivets claim they existed once but went extinct in the Middle Ages. According to Cash, he, Alaric, Queen Modron, and Galswinth downed one. It took all four of them, and they barely survived. If the claim is true, anyway."

No Nikolai? But that was right, he was younger than the others by quite a bit. He'd advanced because of his prophetic skills and his marriage to the queen's eldest daughter. "Winnie fights?"

Charlie nodded. "Quite well, though she doesn't do it unless she has to. Cash taught her, much to Alaric's disgust." He shook his head mockingly, making a joke. "Vikings. Always doing uncouth things like handing women swords."

Vince shifted, wondering if dragons, despite everything he'd seen, were still too magical to believe in. "Do you think dragons were real?"

Charlie looked at the floor, then back at the stage. "The world has changed so much, even in the few centuries I've been around. The idea of multi-ton lizards winging the skies sounds too fantastical to me. But Cash remembers when we thought the world was flat and the sun revolved around it. There are more people in the US right now than there were on the whole planet when he was human. Dragons don't make sense now. But they did then."

Vince turned to face him, knowing there was desperation in his voice as he softly insisted, "I want to know all of these things."

Charlie's smell of wood and bay grew stronger as he leaned in, and his breath was warm against Vince's ear. "Can we talk later?"

His heart fluttered like a butterfly as all his hope came alive. Charlie wanted him in bed. He'd always known that. But Vince needed more, so much more to believe in the potential of them. "About what?" he whispered.

Charlie's gaze dipped from his eyes to his mouth and back. "What we need to make us work."

Vince nodded, unable to speak. It wasn't forever. It couldn't be. Charlie was immortal, and Vince couldn't be. Didn't *want* to be. But how long was long enough to make a relationship with Charlie worthwhile? Was the eventual pain worth the promise of today?

Despite how it had ended, he'd never once wished he'd never been with Charlie. He wouldn't regret it this time, either.

Would he?

"My whole life," Charlie whispered, "I've never met anyone like you. Please have patience with me while I learn to be what you need. I want to spend our lives together."

It was too good to be true. Something was going to ruin it.

A screech like ripping metal cut through the queen's speech. Cash leaped forward to guard her front.

Yup. Something was about to ruin everything.

Chapter 19

The crowd hunched at the painful noise, and Vince was glad his hearing wasn't vampire good. He clutched Charlie's hand and pulled Rhi against him, as if proximity could save them. The queen stopped talking and stood shoulder to shoulder with Cash, drawing her dagger once again, but like a weapon.

Tzitzi swaggered down the main aisle, hands red with blood and her ceremonial shirt freshly stained. "My gods, your speech, woman. I was going to wait until the passing of the cup, but I couldn't handle another second."

Charlie shoved Vince behind him, as if he could block Vince's body with his own smaller one. It wasn't going to work, but still Vince took comfort in the protective weight of Charlie's hand on his hip.

"I see keeping you alive was a mistake," Modron said. "By royal decree I place Ashley Paulson, known as Tzitzi, on the death blood list. The council may judge my actions later."

Vince leaned forward into Charlie, frustration battling his fear. "If it was that easy, why hasn't she already done it?"

"My guess? Cash wanted it, and she was feeling petty because he bought a house. But now Tzitzi's interfering with her speech. Bureaucratic monarchy. Worst of all worlds."

Vampires near Tzitzi hopped up, ready to defend CoVIn. Tzitzi twirled, yelling in Nahuatl—Rhiannon had corrected Vince last time he'd called the language "Aztec"—and flames rushed from her in a circle, sending the vampires back. She jumped, leaping higher than a human should, higher than the reaching hands of the vampires below.

And she didn't come down.

"She's flying," Rhiannon muttered, hand over her mouth.

"You witches can do that?" Vince asked.

"It's a power traditionally ascribed to them. Us. And she's up in the fucking air, so I'm going with yes."

Rats the size of large dogs with something strapped to their backs charged down the four aisles. Vampires reached for them, howling in pain as they touched whatever was tied to them.

Modron screamed in Welsh. Lightning poured from her fingers and struck the nearest rat. Cash pulled his ax from its sheath.

From the air, Tzitzi yelled more Nahuatl and blew kisses at anyone who moved. Each time one struck, a vampire screamed and lurched blindly.

"She's taking out their eyesight," Charlie told them, shoving Vince down. "Don't attract her attention. She may not realize you're here."

How were they going to stop this? Panic made him tremble. "She can blind people, too?"

"Witches. We're bad," Rhiannon said weakly. "Except me. I'm useless. Gods, I promise not to be useless in the future."

Six rats reached the stage and transformed as they leaped up, landing as naked humans.

Strapped to their backs were crosses. Each yanked theirs off as they transitioned. Half spun to ward off the crowd. The other half brandished them at the fighters on the stage.

Liberi poured into the room from the main doors, trapping everyone in.

Above them, Tzitzi chanted as the Liberi beat the walls and stomped in rhythm, some moving down the aisles past CoVIn members struggling with cross-wielding rats. Vampires screamed. The scent of burning flesh tinged the air.

On stage, Nikolai and Galswinth fought as Cash and Modron were forced back by rats calling on the name of God and brandishing chest-sized crosses. Modron struck again with lightning. The energy spooled around the cross and was sucked in.

"They're blessed," Charlie muttered. "They had them blessed." He turned to Vince. "I get excommunicated, but the church blesses crosses for those *espèces de bêtes*?"

Despite being fucked, Vince laughed. "I love it when you speak dirty in French. Should we do something? Tzitzi's busy chanting instead of blinding everyone. Which is probably not good news."

"I'm not ready," Rhiannon whispered, gripping his hand. "I can't get Modron's awen back if they get her."

Charlie caught Vince's eye, his expression wracked with guilt. "I'll be back."

"What are you doing?"

"Crosses. I can help."

Vince put a hand on either side of his face.

"Don't try to stop me, Vince."

"No, idiot. I'm not afraid of crosses either. I'm going with you. If Tzitzi turns the room, it won't matter if she's seen me or not. I'm going to die." He leaned forward to kiss him, something quick that hopefully no one would notice. But he needed the strength, even for the fleeting moment he'd get by surprising Charlie.

Their lips touched. Instead of leaping away, Charlie's arm went around him in a fierce hold. A real kiss in front of the whole room left Vince breathless.

"Don't die," Charlie ordered. He turned to Rhi. "Unbless the crosses."

"How?" she asked.

He growled. "I don't know. I've never desecrated anything. You're a Pagan witch. Figure it out."

Together they charged forward, Rhiannon yelling, "Just because I'm Pagan doesn't mean I desecrate things. Cretin."

Charlie slammed into two rats. Vince skid-kicked another.

Rhiannon grabbed the rat's cross as it fell. "But I'll figure something out."

Center stage, Cash and Modron continued backward, forced to retreat by the power of the blessed holy symbols. Behind them Alaric stood firm.

"Watch out!" Vince yelled.

Modron and Cash backed into him. Alaric clamped a hand onto the queen's shoulder.

"I got her," Alaric said. "Get the rat."

"Get her out of here," Cash yelled. With a howl of pain, he lunged forward blindly at the cross, striking without aim.

Alaric slid a foot under Cash, tripping him. His ax went flying, and he landed bodily on the cross. Smoke hissed upward as his face hit the wood, searing his flesh. He dropped to the ground, one eye blinded.

Modron spun, her fury focusing on Alaric. "It's true?"

Cash struggled to get up, but the rat bashed at him with the cross like a pike. He rolled, barely avoiding the stabs.

Rhiannon shoved a cross into Vince's hand. "Go beat a rat. I think I broke the blessing. It'll still be bright to the vampires, but not like those."

At the cauldron, Alaric gripped the queen's throat in a chokehold, blocking off her ability to speak—to cast. He didn't look triumphant, though. His voice pleaded with her. "We're too small and too weak to survive as we are."

She kicked at him as her hands scrabbled at his fingers, trying to release their hold.

He dunked her head into the steaming cauldron. "Too many rules. Too much guilt and confusion holding us back." Modron flailed but was no match for his strength. "I won't let you die because we're too weak minded to do what must be done. To become what we must to survive. This is freedom. This is power."

Vince couldn't take on Alaric, but Cash could. Vince charged at the rat on his housemate, cross held horizontal like a battering ram. The rat lurched sideways, away from Cash.

Cash scrambled to Alaric and pulled him off the queen. She didn't move, head still in the steaming cauldron.

The rat turned on Vince, dragging him down. The cross smashed between them, digging into Vince's ribs. Above him, yellow teeth dripped saliva that smelled of decayed meat. The rat snapped at him. Vince dodged, trying to push it off.

The rat's head wrenched around, its neck broken, and the putrid weight lifted. Charlie winced, affected but not blinded by the cross. Vince hopped up.

Behind Charlie, Cash had his forearm around Alaric's throat, fangs out and rage like Vince had never imagined the laughing party boy could feel burning in his eyes. Alaric's arms were in the air, like he surrendered.

That didn't made Vince feel one bit better.

At the cauldron, the queen rose slowly, eyes blinking awake. Her mead-soaked hair dripped on the dragon dress. Not a breath issued from her perfectly still torso. Above them, Tzitzi laughed. The room stilled, all eyes on the stage to see what would happen next.

Vince didn't need to see anything else. It was done. The

queen's awen was gone. She was Liberi. Which meant everyone was in danger. Vince had to get Charlie out of here before she started biting, passing the spell to her children through blood.

Cash stared at his queen, his mother, the one he was supposed to protect, horror on his face. He dropped Alaric to his knees, arms twisted behind. "What did you do?"

Alaric didn't fight. "I told you, Geirson. We need to be strong. The reckless compassion of the human world has made us weak. We're holding meetings and filling out paperwork. We have lost who we are."

"So you're selling us to a witch?" He slammed Alaric forward into the stage. Blood exploded from his nose, slid down his chin, and spattered across his forehead.

"Cassius…" the queen whispered, sending goose bumps down Vince's arm.

Cash looked at her across Alaric's bloody form. "Modron. Please…"

She smiled and offered a hand like nothing was wrong. But everything was wrong. If it were still her, she'd fight.

"Cash." Charlie tossed the stake. "You have to do it.

Cash caught it and stared at his friend, then down at the weapon.

The rats still held the circle, crosses high, as Tzitzi watched from above.

"My boy," Modron said. "I'm fine. Don't let them worry you."

But she wasn't. Cash had to see that. He tossed Alaric aside and strode to Modron, the indecision on his face clear.

Vince's stomach lurched in fear. "Shit." Cash wasn't confused. He knew exactly what had happened; that wasn't the problem.

Cash turned to them, expression utterly defeated. "Where she goes, I go. Run."

"No!" Charlie yelled. "Don't!"

Cash dropped the stake.

Modron leaped on him, biting deep into his throat. Blood sprayed as the crowd yelled in fear. The scent of iron mixed with incense as the room warmed and the rats dropped their crosses. Vampires swarmed forward, racing for the queen.

Tzitzi laughed, the sweet sound demented amid the carnage.

Vince backed up, pulling Charlie and Rhiannon with him against the flow.

The queen released her son. Cash dropped into an unmoving pile at her feet.

"Is he dead?" Vince whispered.

"I have no idea." Charlie's frozen muscles released into action. "Out. The two of you. Out."

"You too," Vince urged. "We can regroup. I'm not leaving you behind."

Rhiannon's eyes went wide. "What the fuck is that?"

The whites of the queen's eyes had turned red. Her hands lifted to the sky as she murmured in an ancient tongue. Cash's blood drained down her chin, coating her dragon-skin robe with scarlet.

Winnie crouched to pull Cash away. The queen reached down and gripped her hair.

Nikolai ran forward, screaming for his wife. Electricity came from the queen's fingers, flinging him back.

"Mother!" Winnie yelled as she was yanked to her feet.

"Your blood runs in me," the queen said, each syllable clear. "You are mine."

Red energy arced between them. Winnie shook like she was

having a fit, eyes rolling back in her head.

"We need to go," Vince said, tugging harder on Charlie and Rhi.

When Winnie's eyes opened, they were as red as the queen's.

"I'm with you," Rhiannon agreed, terror in her voice.

Charlie resisted, fear in his eyes. "She doesn't need to bite us."

"My blood runs in you!" the queen yelled, arms spread as her children reached for her. Cash was hoisted into the air.

"Go," Charlie ordered, shoving Vince away.

"I'm not leaving you!" They were together now. They'd just said so not half an hour ago.

Charlie took Vince's chin, forcing him to see his pale face and stricken expression. "Go before I turn and I'm the one who kills you."

"You are mine!" The queen's fists closed. More red energy scattered from her like lightning, slamming into the vampires nearest her and bouncing about the room in a hissing storm.

Charlie dropped to his ass and started to shake. "Get him out!" he yelled at Rhiannon.

Charlie was turning into one of them. Vince had to do something. But what? He stood rooted to the spot, trying to come up with some way to stop it. There had to be a way.

Kill Modron. Winnie stood in front of her like a guard, hoisting Cash's ax, as Modron surveyed her children with Cash's blood still staining her face.

Rhiannon shook him. "Vince! We have to go. You can't do anything here."

Charlie gasped in pain. His body wrenched in tortured jerks.

"We have to kill her." How did he get past Winnie?

Rhiannon slapped Vince. His head whipped around, the pain

clearing some of the fog.

"They're all turning now," she said. "We have like two minutes. We will solve this, but gods dammit, now is not our stand. If you somehow get past an ax-wielding vampire trained by a Viking warrior, the queen will electrify your ass. Cash was stupid. I need you to be brave, not stupid. This is not our hill to die on."

She was right, but it was hard. Charlie shuddered on the ground, eyes rolled back. Around the room the whole company seized, the vampires losing the connections to their souls through their connection to Modron.

It was a slaughter. And he couldn't do anything about it, not with Winnie—and, fuck, now Kolyan—standing guard in front of the queen, Tzitzi flying through the air, and a horde of were-rats and Liberi waiting to pounce.

Another tug from Rhiannon, and Vince stumbled forward until they were next to the fire. Rhiannon slammed the button Cash had pointed out for the nearest exit, and a trapdoor opened that gave musical acts easy stage access. Down a short flight of stairs, they ran for an elevator shaft.

A cry went up behind them as vampires woke from their stupor.

Rhiannon got out a key card and swiped it at the elevator panel.

"We weren't supposed to need this route," Vince said, his stomach already dropping at what would happen next. *Charlie is one of them.*

"I'm scared shitless," she said. "Four and then start braking, right?"

The doors opened. Cash had rigged them ropes with descenders, free fall being the only way out faster than a vampire could run.

Vince looked thirty-two stories down into blackness. "Oh, fuck." Fear made his hands slick and his muscles shake. He reached out for the descender. Rhiannon caught his eyes. "We got this," he reassured her, though he was pretty sure that was a lie. *Charlie...*

She nodded, not believing him but agreeing anyway. She snapped onto the cord. One hand on her cable, she reached for him. "What are we doing here, hanging with vampires and playing at witchcraft?"

Saving Charlie. And everyone else. He clasped her hand and filled his lungs to say something flippant, because God knew he couldn't say what he really felt. "Living in interesting times."

She squeezed his hand, the same hard fear in her eyes and forced lightness in her smile. "Probably dying in them too." Rhiannon closed her eyes as she swung into space. "Oh my goddess..."

Footsteps shuffled and pounded like rain down the steps. Vampires were coming.

Vince hoisted himself onto the rope. "Go, go, go!" He squeezed the descender and shot down the oiled rope. His breath left as fear turned to exhilaration. Rhiannon whimpered next to him. The girl didn't even like roller coasters.

"Brake," he commanded and slowly released the descender. She slowed her own descent beside him.

Above them, vampires hooted and yelled from a square of light.

His feet touched the top of the elevator on the second level of the garage.

Sucking in air, Rhiannon folded over.

Vince grabbed her key card, swiped the doors open, and took her arm. "Come on. We've got a head start, but not for long." He pulled a key ring from his pocket containing Cash's house keys and the fob to a bronze-black Aston Martin Vanquish. "We can fix that, though. Cash gave me his keys."

She blinked at the fob as they jogged forward. "I want to drive it."

"No way."

She followed. "I'm fucking him. I get the keys."

Vince opened the door with a grim smile and shook his head. "He gave the keys to me. It's a boy's club thing." Before she could protest again, he sunk into the soft leather that hugged him so sweetly.

Rhiannon hustled around to the passenger side. "You—"

"No. There's no such thing as too gay to be in the boy's club. I'm one hundred percent a man." He shut his door and opened hers. "Besides, Cash gave the keys to me. Shut up and get in the passenger seat, bitch."

Rhi shot him a glare as she slid inside. "Fine. But I'm driving it after we win." She buckled her seat belt as he turned the engine over and sighed at the purr. She put her hand on his.

He looked up, ready to meet her snark with his own.

Instead her eyes were dead serious. "Hey, despite your selfish hogging of the driver's side, I'm glad I'm in this with you."

He managed a smile that he hoped was reassuring. "We got this." He broke eye contact as he pulled the car out of its spot. "We have to. How close are you to figuring a magic-y thing out?" It was frustrating to rely on someone else for the important part. Charlie was in danger. His new friend Cash was in danger—if he wasn't dead. Vince needed to do something.

"I have an idea. I don't like it—at all. But it's the best I've got."

"I'm in. Let's do this."

She slumped back in the seat. "Wait until you hear the idea."

Chapter 20

"Vince, I'm not ready for this." Rhiannon's face looked almost as green as her hair. "Up until yesterday, my version of magic involved chanting at the moon for inner peace. It doesn't matter how much potential they think I have. I've had one lesson with Modron. *One.*"

The car shot out of the parking lot and into downtown. It was twelve-thirty on a weeknight, and traffic was light. Vince hit the gas hard, and they flew through the city toward the safety of Cash's hilltop compound of a house. "Hopefully, given the circumstances, it was focused on how to give vampires back their awen."

Rhiannon bobbed her head back and forth in a way that meant *sort of.* "Originally, she wasn't turned into a vampire and then given her awen back. She never lost it. Awen is inspiration. It's love, it's art. It's creativity and the appreciation of beauty. For most people, awen makes the challenges of living worth facing, and we cling to it. The original spell relied on her wanting to keep that passion."

Vince thought about the way Javier had described his vague memories of being a Liberi. "But once you've lost it, why would you want it back? You don't care about anything." He glanced at Rhiannon and winced. "Sorry about your brother." Javier and Emma had been toward the back of the room, which meant they were back to being Liberi. Javier was going to have more experience as a bad vampire than a good one at this point.

"I'm not thinking about that right now. I'll freak too much."

Rhiannon reached into the useless backseat of the car and grabbed her tablet and notes out of the messenger bag she'd left there. "But you're exactly right. It presents a harder challenge than the first spell did. The first spell was to make an ensouled vampire out of a human who still had a connection to her soul. This spell has to reforge that broken connection. We need something so compelling it makes a vampire willing to take the pain of living to have that connection back, even if the vampire can't remember what it feels like."

"So we have to find the great passion of every vampire in the world and handcraft a spell for each one? We might as well give up now and go into hiding." In hiding, they could develop a spell for Charlie and Javi. The futility of saving everyone crushed down on him.

"No, that's actually the good part. Vampires create new vampires through blood magic—generally regarded as the most powerful and dangerous type of magic. When a vampire is created, the fledgling's soul patterns itself after the sire's, which is why Liberi create Liberi, and Modron's children still have their awen. With me so far?"

"Mostly."

"Okay so bear with me on some magical theory for a moment. Hypothetically, once we have one vampire with a complete soul, I can—maybe—make a potion using his blood. There're some ideas about it in that book I had translated, though they didn't go quite this far. But Modron's first lesson was on potion craft, and it makes sense. I think."

"That's a lot of *maybe* and *I think*."

"Yeah, I know. But our other option is to kill Modron."

Vince nodded slowly. "Point taken." There was just no way two humans could pull that off, even if she didn't have an army of vampires and were-creatures and a lunatic witch standing between her and anything wanting to do her harm. "So, what does the potion do?"

"It'll let another vampire borrow that first vampire's awen for just a few seconds, long enough to give them a chance to choose for themselves what they want to be, CoVIn or Liberi. Once we get a second vampire back, we can add that vampire's blood to the spell, and the potion becomes stronger. The more vampires we get back, the more blood we can add to the spell, and with more blood comes more awen—more art and love and reasons to have a soul."

Vince nodded, not completely following, but he didn't need to understand all the mystical whatsit. He just needed to help make it happen. "What do you need from me?" She hesitated like she really didn't want to say the next part of her plan. "Rhi? Talk to me."

"It's getting that first one without killing ourselves that's the real trick. I'll throw every magical aid I can think of in. But it hinges on convincing someone without a soul to choose the pain of a conscience—of feeling shame and regret."

"Why would someone do that?"

"Not to sound like a Valentine's Day ad, but I'm thinking love."

"Like the connection Javi has to you? Could we base a spell on that?"

She flipped pages on her tablet, the backlight casting shadows on her frown. "Javi and I are tight. But the last time I wrote a poem about my brother was in the fourth grade, and it involved the word 'butthead.' We're like a fortress. We stand firm together. I think Javi would just turn me, and we'd be a fortress of evil." She grimaced. "Like Cash and Modron. He warned us, and I still can't believe he did that." She shifted uncomfortably in her seat. "Inspiration, if you break the word down, means *to breathe into*, which goes right along with Nikolai's vision of the CoVIn vampires suffocating. Javi and I don't do any heavy breathing together because ew, and that's illegal. Honestly, I think…" She stopped with a shake of her head.

"You think what?"

She seemed reluctant to continue, and Vince had a terrible suspicion of what she was thinking. A suspicion that made his skin cold and his palms sweat. "You think you could get Cash? You two like sharing air, and it would be nice to start with somebody who could fight."

She let out a frustrated breath. "Were you listening to anything I said? We're talking poetic inspiration, not sorta-friends-with-great-benefits."

He stared grimly out into Cash's neighborhood of towering homes behind imposing gates. "You want me to be bait again. This time for Charlie."

"I absolutely do not want that at all." She turned off the tablet, sending the interior of the car into darkness. "I just think it's our best bet."

He slowed as the gates to Cash's estate opened with weighty preponderance. She thought he could inspire Charlie. Fear made his blood pound in his ears. "Charlie has—*had* too much morality to ever choose to lose his soul. But he also spent our entire relationship hiding our love because he cared too fucking much what other people thought. Losing his awen would be heaven for him. He's free." He pulled in slowly and took the circular drive to the four-car garage. At least they were stuck hiding in a mansion. How long would it take for vampires to be crawling the grounds, waiting for them to leave? One of them would probably be Charlie. "I almost feel happy for him. It's high time he had a chance to let go and live a little."

Rhiannon was quiet for a moment as the garage door closed

behind them, trapping them in safety. "The doors to Starlight Club were extraordinary, don't you think?"

He frowned at the unexpected question. He'd loved the doors. They were quite possibly the finest thing Charlie had ever done, and to have them in such a prominent place made Vince so proud of him. Charlie deserved that. "I can't imagine anyone else making something that incredible." Vince could've studied it for hours and always found something new. Yeah, Charlie had the advantage of time over other woodworkers, but he'd used that time to hone his skills and develop his eye. He was a true artist, relishing the work and always striving to better himself. Vince loved that about him.

And then he understood why Rhi had brought it up. "He'll never create another piece of art." Charlie would never be truly happy without art.

Rhiannon shoved her things into her bag, head ducked as if she was conflicted that she'd made him realize that. He believed her when she said she didn't want him to do this… but didn't see an alternative.

Vince closed his eyes. Today Charlie had promised he would change. He'd held Vince's hand and professed his love and promised to be a new man who chose their relationship over fear. Vince had listened to every word, new air castles forming with each promise. Hope was a rotten thing that took you up the mountain, only to throw you back down. If you didn't hope, failure didn't hurt. If he did what Rhi was suggesting, however, being tossed down that mountain wasn't just an emotional black hole. Charlie would kill him.

Would Charlie really choose him over a life without fear or shame? Because that's what Charlie had just been given.

Vince opened his eyes. He didn't know. Fear of what he had to do mixed with certainty that, succeed or fail, Charlie's soul was worth the risk.

ಐ•ಚ

An hour later Vince paced Cash's bathroom and practiced the words Modron had sang at the ritual. Half an hour ago vampires had begun pounding on the front door. The incessant noise made a pulse that his heartbeat had tuned to. The air already felt charged with magic, ready to blow.

At least he'd seen Cash among their numbers. The Viking was Liberi, but he wasn't dead. If they got Charlie back—and that was a big if—they'd go for broke and make Cash the first target of the next spell.

Vince shivered. "Cash's bathroom is bigger than my living... than my *old* living room." He winced at the near slip. Considering this house his own was the only thing keeping every vampire in the city from crossing the threshold and killing them.

"I know, right? I think half my house would fit in here." Rhiannon put the last of nine votive candles on a painted circle around the tub.

Floor-to-ceiling windows looked out over the cliff and down to Ladybird Lake. A wood burning fireplace took up the wall between the bathroom and bedroom. On a pedestal in the center of the slate tile sat a round whirlpool bath that would fit four or more.

"I'm guessing the paint job is new," Vince said. In addition to the ten-foot circle, three green swirls, evenly spaced, emitted from the tub.

"It's a triskelion, a Celtic power symbol. Think Cash will kill me for painting his floor?"

"I think he'll forgive you if painting his floor helps get his soul back, and if we fail, forgiveness isn't the problem we need to worry about."

She looked up from where she kneeled, and her worried gaze found his. "Good point."

"Okay, you want me to get Charlie naked and into the bathtub. I'm understanding better why you didn't want to do this with Javier." Vince set down the bottle of mead and two goblets Rhiannon had sent him to the kitchen to find. He clutched the edge of the tub and watched it fill from copper taps. What was he doing? In his experience, unbreakable connections didn't exist when you *had* a soul. How could they come close to existing for someone who didn't?

She turned off the faucet and switched the whirlpool on, transforming the still water to a bubbling, steaming cacophony. "Cauldrons, in Welsh mythology, represent the space between the worlds, a place for transformation and rebirth—like a womb. But only the bravest heroes are given access to their magic."

Like usual, when things got too intense, he made a joke. "Heroes accessing wombs sounds very hetero."

"Everyone's got a feminine side. You're the witch midwife, helping Charlie be reborn."

She was trying to make him smile, but he couldn't. "If a midwife has an opposite, it's me, a stripper who's not sexually attracted to the women I dance for. I'm all arousal, no follow through. This is out of my depth." He sighed and looked at the floor. "The only consistent connection I have to Charlie is sex. So unless you want your ritual desecrated with fornicating men, I'm useless."

Her forehead wrinkled. "You think sex will interfere with a Pagan ritual? You clearly know nothing about Paganism." With a long match she ignited a fire in the fireplace. She wouldn't look at him as she went about finishing the pieces of their spell. "If you don't want to do this, that's fine. Maybe I'll figure something else out. Or maybe we'll be here drinking Cash's wine until this apocalypse thing happens." Her voice was strained and high as she continued, "But if you can't inspire feeling in someone who loves you while naked in a bubbling whirlpool-cauldron on the full moon, there is no hope. That's about all the magic you can throw at something." She tossed leaves on the fire, and the pungency of sage and lavender sifted through the room. "I know this is unreasonable. Our reasonable alternative is giving up and hiding." Finally she looked at him, her expression lost as she stared at him across the water. "I'm sorry I'm not better than this. If you just want to hide, I'll hide with you."

"Are you sure I can do this spell without you, even though I'm not a witch and can't do magic?"

"Love is magic, stronger than any witchcraft."

Vince gripped the rim of the tub and stared into its steaming contents, his emotions as hot and volatile as the water. He was trusting the judgment of somebody who was still trying to save her mother after a lifetime of neglect and methamphetamine abuse. At some point, your faith in someone went from being a strength to a failing. "Love isn't enough to make a relationship good, Rhi. Both parties have to be willing to work for it."

She headed for the cabinet where she'd left her tablet and swiped furiously. He wasn't sure if she was looking through her notes or the book of deer and fish or just flipping randomly to keep her fingers busy. "I've already kindled it. The tub holds the spell. If it's going to work, it'll work in there."

He frowned. She knew what he'd been referring to and was ignoring him. In the end, it didn't matter. Either he had faith that other people wouldn't let him down, or he walked away. No lie, he wanted to walk. Life had taught him to leave before he was evicted.

Rhi had the opposite problem. She stayed long past sanity, long after she should've run. Of course she'd want to prove that love could conquer anything. The only thing that was bothering her was it put him at risk. She'd be somewhere in the house, waiting for him to yell some code word so she could come in and get herself killed too.

The realization struck him with frightening clarity. If this had any hope of working, he, the one who had lost faith, needed to trust, and she, the one who clung, needed to go. Then Charlie the hermit needed to literally share his soul with the rest of the vampires.

They were fucked six ways to Sunday.

He thought of Charlie, red hair, friendly smile. The way he took care of people, even when they treated him like crap. The time and artistry he put into his work. The way it used to feel when they'd lie together just before dawn, Charlie's head on his chest, with his fingers tapping to the rhythm of Vince's heart. Charlie had never said he loved him back then. But he'd said it just a few hours ago.

Vince couldn't walk away from that.

He went around the tub and took Rhi's hands. "Are we ready?"

She nodded. "I think so. You've been practicing the chant?"

"Yeah. I've got it. And I say it… when it *feels like it will work*?"

"Yeah."

"That's really vague."

"You'll know."

He dropped his head.

Her hand cupped his jaw. "Hey."

He looked up into her serious face, her eyes wide and full of more hope than anyone with her background should have.

"You are deeper than you realize, Vince. Deep as the sea. Powerful as an earthquake. More magnetic than polar north." She squeezed his hand. "You have this."

He squeezed back. "Okay." He didn't have this. "I'll do it. But you have to promise me you'll go."

Her smile returned, quick but teasing. "No worries. I have no desire to be in the bathroom while you do whatever it is you two are going to do."

"No. Out of the house. We need somebody alive who knows what's happening and can try again." He handed her the keys to the Aston Martin. "You can drive Cash's car now."

Her momentary levity turned to panic. "You've got to be kidding me. You can't put this all on me!"

"You can't help me here. The only thing you can do is get killed."

"But—"

"No." This wasn't working. He shifted tactics. "You need to go home. Make sure your mother doesn't let Javier in."

She shifted from foot to foot so quickly she almost looked like she was vibrating. "I don't want to leave you." But she would because he'd made it about her mother. Rhi would risk her own life for him. She wouldn't risk her mother's. Her arms went around him, and she squeezed.

"Charlie and I will be at your place in an hour. Or…" He trailed off, not wanting to state the alternative.

He felt her nod against his shoulder. "I'm sorry." His neck was wet. She was crying?

"When I see the car head out, I'll turn my phone on and call him." He'd turned it off after the fifth call from evil-Charlie. His voicemail was probably full of things he didn't want to hear.

It should be therapeutic to be the one not returning phone calls. It wasn't.

She nodded and knocked tears off her face with a fist. "I'm

so sorry," she said again.

"Don't be sorry. Just get out of here and let me do this."

She hugged him again. "Charlie loves you and you love him. He'll pick you. You'll see. His soul will come back, and then you'll know that the two of you are the most beautiful thing in the world."

He squeezed her harder, let go, and she ran from the room. A long time ago he'd given up caring what was right or natural. He didn't believe the universe had a plan or, frankly, that it gave a shit what he did. But maybe that was wrong. If he could save Charlie's soul, maybe he could believe in his own. He pulled out his phone before he lost his nerve.

Chapter 21

Vince lit the third candle with a shaky hand, going around the circle in a clockwise manner. He wasn't sure if the direction mattered or not, but he knew he needed the candles lit, so here he was. Meanwhile, Charlie's phone rang, the sound echoing on the tile. Vince had set his own phone on speaker and called without looking at the voicemail or text. If he was still alive in half an hour, he'd delete the whole mess of it unseen and unheard.

Kinda like Charlie had done to his. Ironic that.

It picked up on candle four of nine. Laughter dug into him with its sharp violence. "Charlie Travert's phone. How's it going, baby?" Who was that? He had no idea.

"I need to speak to Charlie."

"I'll be your Charlie. I've got plans for us."

The voice changed as somebody else took over. "*We* have plans for you. Tzitzi is waiting."

Candle five. "If you hand Charlie the phone, I think you'll like the results."

"Oooh…" A chorus of male voices before someone added, "Sissy-boy wants his boyfriend."

He clenched his jaw at the slur. Candle six.

"What?" It was him.

Charlie sounded pissed, no kindness in his tone, no frustrated need. Just anger. Vince swallowed. His fingers shook so hard the match went out. He cursed as he lit another one. He was about to let a Liberi vampire come up here. Someone strong and fast and utterly insane. It was his last chance to change his mind.

The match burned almost to his fingers. He lit candle seven. "Charles Travert, born February nineteenth of 1736 in Prayssus, France, you, and only you, are invited in."

"Charlie!" somebody yelled, laughing as a chorus of howls went up like the man had scored a game-winning touchdown. Suddenly they were chanting his name.

Another voice—Alaric's—came next. "You lose, asshole. See you in two minutes."

Vince lit candle eight.

If Charlie threw him over his shoulder and ran out, it was over. He hung up the phone, unwilling to listen to more hate, and lit the last candle. Whatever happened next, it was done.

৪১ ✦ ৫৪

It was good to be a vampire. Charles followed his nose upstairs to claim his prize. He was supposed to bring the boy to Tzitzi so she could cut out his heart and peel his young skin from his muscles. She'd wear it like a suit in honor of her god.

She would look ridiculous, and what a waste of handsome male flesh.

Whatever. Charles would bring Vince back to her. Eventually. There were other handsome men in the world, but this one was different. This one had once made him unhappy.

The double doors to the bathroom opened with a satisfying whoosh, and Charles entered like a king. Not long ago, he'd been nothing. But in here, Vince was nothing, a human whose body was too weak to turn. In here, Charles ruled absolutely.

Vince sat on the floor within a circle of candles, head on his knees in front of the largest bathtub Charles had ever seen. The water steamed and bubbled enticingly and smelled of lavender and sage.

A smile curved his lips. The boy was trying to seduce him? What was he thinking in that little human head of his? An offering, maybe. Ingratiating himself with someone strong. That was smart. "If you're trying to win my favor, it's working."

Vince looked up. His face was pale and his eyes afraid.

Charles crouched down, getting to eye level across the ring of lit candles. "You should be afraid." He smiled, laughing inside at how funny it was that the man whose existence had tortured him for years was here at his mercy. And the boy had placed himself there like an idiot. "You know I don't care about you, right? Your entire value lies in that..." He breathed in so the scents of Vince's fear and the salty sweat of his skin could send ripples of desire through him. Oh, he was beyond the love of God and man, and for once in his life he didn't fucking care. "That gorgeous body. I want it bent in half. I want you screaming, and I don't give a damn if it's from pleasure or pain." He reached across the candles, the heat from one tiny flame warming his cold skin as he caressed Vince's thigh from knee to ass. "You are my pretty thing to play with. Keep me entertained, and I'll keep you alive." For a while. "Upset me or bore me, and I'll take you to Tzitzi." He leaned in closer. "Make me very angry, and I'll help her skin you."

Vince shivered. He understood. Good. Vincent Pagano was all his to enjoy. It was a good night. Charlie pinched down, squeezing firm muscle between his fingers.

Startled, Vince jerked back, out of his grasp.

"Not acceptable." Charles yanked Vince forward. The boy fell, face planting onto the painted tile. Charlie picked up the candle and poured wax down Vince's arm. The boy screamed. "You will not shy away from me. You are mine. You live and die because I say so."

ഇം✦ൽ

Vince's stomach lurched with a horrible truth. This wasn't going to work, and he was going to die. Probably here on the floor of the most luxurious bathroom he'd ever been in as soon as Charlie lost control and bled him out.

At least it was better surroundings than a hospital room. Or the basement of Tooth and Nail.

He looked up into Charlie's cold eyes and gasped for breath. The pain from his burned arm was rapidly fading, replaced with desperate pain inside. No sympathy came back to him from Charlie. No love. No sign that anything had ever existed between them that went deeper than flesh meeting flesh.

"Yes," Charlie whispered. "You get it. I don't have to play nice anymore. I own you."

Playing nice for access to the hot piece of ass, Vince's greatest fear about their relationship. He closed his eyes, his hand pinched in Charlie's waxy palm. Despite the touch, there was no connection. Just a threat.

He'd thought the blackest moment of his life was leaving Charlie's house when the love of his life wouldn't call him back. The anger and self-recrimination of that moment haunted his worst dreams. In Vince's nineteen-year-old mind, it had been clear Charlie didn't love him. If he had, he'd have given Vince another chance.

But staring into those dead eyes, he realized something. If Charlie hadn't loved him, he'd have stayed. If all he'd wanted was Vince's willing body, he wouldn't have given a shit what Vince did anywhere else.

Charlie's face was next to his, studying him intently. "What's running through that little human brain of yours?" His eyes were full of greed as his gaze ran over Vince's face and down his body. His stance held the bold certainty Vince had only seen Charlie exhibit once before, in the stairwell of the club.

His lover wouldn't run away this time; he would stay until he was satisfied. Every lingering hesitancy or fear that had plagued their relationship was gone from Charlie's eyes. *Why was that comforting?* A selfish beast of a man sat in front of him, a man who wanted without apology.

Vince had it wrong. He wasn't going to connect to this Charlie with a caring touch or a meeting of minds or the niceties of love. If he had any chance, it was connecting to the instincts Charlie had spent his life denying. Vince's mouth felt dry and his tongue thick as he said, "I think I want to dance for you."

Charlie's brow raised. "Oh, yeah?" He sat back as a slow smile played at the corners of his mouth. A smile that was all Charlie in his most unguarded moments.

"You're going to kill me, aren't you." It wasn't a question.

His smile didn't waver as he shrugged. "You're human. You perish easily."

"I have music. I've been working on a new number." Vince stood and turned to the table with the mead. He'd set his phone there with the intention of playing something sappy. Instead he went to his strip list and pulled up an unusually dark number he'd just added.

There was a growl in Charlie's voice as he said, "I'm the only one who's going to see it." Was that just a threat, or did a hint of jealousy thread through the sound? Charlie wouldn't be jealous if he didn't care in some way. Hope took the first few steps back up the damn mountain, but Vince didn't stop it. He might as well die with hope as without it.

The table had two goblets on it. He ignored them and took a swig right from the bottle. The slow strains of a twisted gospel song rumbled through Cash's speakers. Vince turned to the moonlit cliffside out the window behind him, his hips already swaying to the hypnotic rhythm. He downed another sip of mead and rolled his head, loosening his stiff shoulders.

He hadn't planned to dance. But if there was one thing outside the smithy that connected him to everything, it was music. Maybe, *maybe* he could use it to connect to Charlie.

And if not? He'd die in a bathtub making love to the soulless man who owned his soul.

He didn't want to die, but there was a peace in it. A self-sacrifice he chose instead of the two deaths that had been nearly forced onto him.

A last gulp of mead, and he passed the bottle. Charlie took it, his gaze transfixed as Vince ran his hands through his hair and down his chest, undulating to the music. One button. Charlie's fingers clenched in desire.

The heady rush of power put a smile on Vince's face. He untucked his still-buttoned shirt. Slipped his hands down his thighs. He didn't have to watch Charlie to know the man couldn't take his eyes away.

Vince removed his shoes and socks. There was nothing sexy about socks. They went outside the circle. Barefoot, he spun and grabbed the edge of their cauldron. The fire crackled, scenting the air with woodsmoke as he swayed slowly, bending over the edge to dip his hand in the water. He ran the water through his hair, a strange baptism, and turned back, water dripping from his curls. Charlie had stood up.

"You're still dressed?" Vince teased, his feet gliding easily across the tile in time to the chorus.

"So are you."

Vince flicked open another button on his shirt.

Charlie's eyes narrowed in impatience.

At a curl of Vince's fingers, Charlie kicked off his shoes and entered the circle, still carrying the bottle of mead. Vince grabbed his hips, pulling them together until they were grinding. Charlie had never been a dancer—pity that—but his hips kept rhythm with Vince's, making up for any faults in grace with eager desire.

Vince ran a hand over Charlie's cheek and through his hair, amazed how he looked the same as he had a few hours ago. Yet everything was different. Vince had always been forward about his desires, doing everything from flirting to flat-out asking for what he wanted. But at the same time, he'd never been gratuitously sexual about it with conservative Charlie. Not how he was at work, shaking his ass unabashedly and filling the air with the power of desire.

But that was the old them, two guys with all their insecurities trying to work out a peace. There was nothing peaceful about tonight. No hopes for tomorrow spoken. Chances were, this ship was crashing. There was no time for hesitation or restraint. Tonight was the only thing that mattered.

He unhooked the buttons down Charlie's shirt. His fingers just touched the last before the man pulled back.

"You still have your shirt on. This is about you."

Vince's gaze raised to Charlie's as hope kept crawling forward. "I thought everything was about you now."

Charlie stepped out of Vince's arms, breaking the rhythm of their movement and throwing Vince off balance. Vince grabbed the tub behind him to steady himself. Charlie grabbed Vince's lapels in both hands and yanked, ripping the buttons off Vince's new shirt.

"Hey! I like that shirt."

"I don't give a damn about your shirt." Charlie pushed, and Vince toppled back into the water, sending waves splashing out. His head went under. Hot liquid soaked through his clothes as he got his knees under him and came out sputtering.

Charlie was amused, and just that hint of his smile turned

Vince on. He grabbed Charlie by the T-shirt and yanked him in. Their lips slammed in a kiss. Charlie shoved his back against the tub wall, fingers and mouth demanding.

His lip was cut. Vince didn't care. He dug his fingers into the soaked folds of Charlie's clothing, reaching for skin.

He was a sinner. Not because he wanted Charlie but because, at this moment, he didn't give a damn about his soul. He'd take him however he could have him. His legs wrapped around Charlie's legs. Charlie ripped at Vince's soaked clothes until his shirt and undershirt were gone.

"I like chest hair," Charlie muttered, his fingers sliding against Vince's smooth chest.

What? Charlie had never mentioned that before. What else would he admit when he wasn't trying to be nice?

He shoved at Charlie's shirt. The man raised his hands in the air, and Vince pulled the sopping mess off and tossed it away to slap wetly on the ground. Charlie had chest hair, rough texture beneath his exploring fingers. He had a treasure trail too. Vince ran his fingers across hair he knew from memory was auburn.

Charlie kissed him again, their mouths clashing with the honey taste of mead and a trace of salty blood. The bubbles from the whirlpool tingled against Vince's skin, and the heat from Charlie eclipsed the steaming water. "God," he moaned. "Oh, God."

Charlie's sounds were more guttural, not even words. He peeled Vince's pants down, scraping the soft fabric across his straining dick and making him buck with sensation. Charlie's arm latched around his lower back, drawing his hips forward.

With a startling suddenness, Charlie broke the kiss and wrapped his lips around Vince's cock. Vince gripped the tub in ecstasy, trying not to slam into Charlie's throat.

Charlie held him down, his own head underwater.

"You gotta…" Breathe? No. Charlie didn't have to do that. He was a vampire. Vince relaxed his knees and threw his head back, letting Charlie have his way, both fearing the elongated teeth sliding on either side of his shaft and loving every moment.

Charlie's hands worked him from behind as the sensations built to a crescendo. This wasn't how he'd pictured it, insane Charlie pinning him in rapture while he gave whatever was asked.

His orgasm crashed through him, and Charlie took it. His head emerged from the water, eyes closed in rapture as he swallowed.

Vince's heart raced, and he tried to refocus his bliss-scattered thoughts. This wasn't over. Charlie stared at his neck. Vince registered it through a haze just before Charlie latched on with the vicious hunger of a starving animal. Fangs, so careful a moment ago, sliced painfully just above his collarbone, and Charlie pulled, drinking him down fast.

Too fast. It hurt, making his head light and his fingers cold. He struggled once, panicked. His motions ripped a bigger hole, a faster death, and he forced himself to freeze. Charlie had him pinned tight, predator to prey.

This is it. The knowledge struck Vince with a fearful clarity. Vince could go down fighting furiously or he could go down in quiet despair. Didn't matter, he was going into the darkness.

He didn't want anger or despair. He wrapped his legs around his lover's waist, his arms around his back so he could hold him until the end. To his surprise, Charlie slowed, just a mite, his fingers pulsing against his back like a cat kneading a beloved owner. Charlie may kill him, but what they'd had was real and so powerful some part of it had outlived Charlie's soul.

And if it was real…

Vince opened his eyes, hopeful despite the blood running down his chest. The spell.

"By awen we sing, by blood we live, while earth shall stand and tide shall flow and breeze shall blow." Charlie didn't stop his feast, letting him continue the chant. "Sing with me, my children, drink with me, my children, while earth shall stand and tide shall flow and breeze shall blow."

Nothing was happening. Vince's stomach quivered. It wasn't going to work. The water kept him warm, but he knew he was paling. Dizziness swam in and out as spots danced at the edges of his eyes. "By blood and by awen we sing together, we stand together against all who oppose us, while earth shall stand and tide shall flow and breeze shall blow."

Spell completed, not that it seemed to do anything, he heaved in a breath, hoping it wasn't his last. But if it was, he knew what he'd say with it. It was what he'd always wanted to say with his last breath to his immortal lover and best friend. "I love you, Charlie."

Charlie let him go. With a gasp, he thrust back against the tub, breaking Vince's hold. A speaker blew out with a pop and sizzle. The jets on the whirlpool sent fountains out onto the floor as the water heated uncomfortably.

The dimmed overhead lights flickered before all the electricity in the room shut off. The bubbles ended, the lights, the music, all gone. Behind them the fire still crackled, providing warmth and light. Charlie's erratic breathing sounded loud in the gloom.

"Ch-Charlie?" Vince muttered as love filled his chest but blackness encroached further across his vision. He tried to find the strength to touch Charlie, to wipe the blood off his chin. He wanted proof Charlie was back, but his hands weren't working right.

Charlie squeezed the edge of the tub until one side cracked, leaking a stream down the side. His breathing came back under control. The water barely reached Vince's waist now, and he was cold.

Charlie's gaze found him. His eyes softened with confusion. "Vince?" He reached forward and touched Vince lightly under the chin.

Vince sighed at the gentle touch and worked to keep his eyes open as long as he could. They'd done it. Charlie had chosen love over fear. Vince wanted to be around to enjoy it. He just had to hold on…somehow…

"You've been bitten." Horror widened Charlie's eyes. "No. No!" With that, the damned man ran away again, leaving Vince to die alone. Vince closed his eyes and let hot tears roll down his cheeks.

Chapter 22

Charlie sprinted to a bedside table and dug through it for the rubber tube and silver cannula almost every vampire kept near the bed. Needy confusion clouded his head as exhaustion threatened a…a headache? He hadn't had one of those since the last time he'd gone drinking with Cash.

Where was he? In Cash's house? Reasonable guess. He hadn't been in Cash's bedroom before, but Charlie was pretty sure he'd made the piecrust table next to the window sometime in the mid-1800s.

Nothing in this drawer. He looked across the bed, which was easily big enough for four.

He didn't want to think about that as he scrambled over it for the other nightstand. Had he made these too? Maybe so.

Unimportant. The equipment was here. He set it aside, turned down the sheets, and ran back to the bathroom.

How he'd gotten here was completely fuzzed out. But he'd woken in a tub with Vince. Vince was pale with blood loss. His blood was on Charlie's tongue. Everything else could wait.

Vince's eyes were closed, and his head lolled against the side of the tub. God, he looked bad. In his native language, Charlie prayed to the patron saint of diabetics, the one he'd always relied on in prayers for Vince. "Pauline, I need aid for the wounded…" The words felt like dust on his tongue. He had done this. His heart squeezed. Why would a saint listen? He was a naked vampire praying over his male lover whom he might've just tried to murder.

He checked Vince's pulse. Weak but still going. His skin outside the water was cold, but his eyes tracked Charlie's movements.

"You came back," Vince said gently, like that surprised him.

"I didn't leave." Charlie wasn't praying for himself. It was for Vince. That had to make a difference. He prayed for intercession as he grabbed a towel, scooped up Vince, and carried him to the bedroom.

"Oh. I thought you left." Vince shivered and tucked himself close. "You left last time."

He laid Vince down, dried him off as best he could, and pulled the blankets tight up to his chin. "I did leave at the club. I was wrong and an idiot. I'm not leaving this time."

"Are you praying for me again? You used to pray for me." Dark circles under his eyes looked like bruises.

Charlie took the tube and cannula and inserted it into his own wrist, starting the process of a transfusion. "I never stopped." Blood flowed from his arm to the clamped tube. "This is going to hurt. I apologize."

"Whoa!" Vince's eyes went wide as Charlie pierced his elbow with another silver needle. "I don't want to be a vampire!"

Charlie let the clamp off, sending his blood into Vince. "You won't, love." He brushed Vince's wet hair back. "For reasons I don't understand, you have to drink the blood to become one of us. This is just a transfusion to replace what you lost—what I took."

"Oh."

He brushed back Vince's hair again. The room was comfortably warm, the fireplace that separated the bathroom from the bedroom roaring. Who in Texas lit a fire in June? But then the whole house was kept like a meat locker. Trust a Norwegian to think sixty-four was an appropriate summer temperature. "You'll want to check your insulin extra carefully the next few days. Vampire blood can have side effects. But it's better than no blood."

"Will I be able to run as fast as you and pick up cars?"

"No. But you may heal a little more quickly if you get an injury." He swallowed. "Like the one I gave you."

Vince touched Charlie's jaw with a careful delicacy, like he was stroking glass. "You're *you*."

Charlie squinted, trying to remember what had happened. "I lost my awen. Everyone did." Vince smiled. His pallor was already improving. Good. "How did you bring it back?"

"We had sacred sex in a cauldron. There was a ritual. Rhiannon designed it based on that book she's reading. I'm kinda surprised it worked, to be honest."

Panic at what could have happened filled him. "You were alone with me when I was psychotic?" He clamped off the tubing. Too much blood might cause a rejection, and that would be dangerous. Not as dangerous, though, as *seducing a soulless vampire*.

"Ow!" Vince complained as Charlie pulled the cannula out of his arm.

"You give yourself shots every day. *That* did not hurt." And *that* sounded irritable.

"My needles are tiny. That thing's enormous." He shifted. "I'm cold. Get your ass under the covers. I just saved your soul at great personal risk to my life. I get cuddling."

Charlie huffed in frustration at the suicidal man he was in love with as he dropped the used tubing on the nightstand and slid under the covers. He'd clean up later. "What if I'd killed you? What if I'd taken you to Tzitzi? What if I'd tortured you into inviting everyone else into the house?" Vince was still cold as Charlie slid an arm around his midsection and pulled him close. It felt so good it was a relief, lying naked with him, skin against skin, his senses filled with Vince's clean scent. Life was better when he got to do this every day. Life was better with Vince in it. "Don't die and leave me here."

Vince snuggled against him, his hands tucked up between their chests. His skin was damp, his muscles relaxed, almost wilted, as he struggled to get as much of them touching as possible. "You're immortal. I'm going to die and leave you one day."

Charlie's muscles clenched involuntarily, pulling Vince closer to him as if he could stop the march of time. With some people he could. About fifty percent of them. "We could try it. Making you a vampire, I mean. If you really wanted to. The odds aren't in our favor, but... if it's what you want." The thought terrified him. If Vince didn't make it across, he didn't think he could keep living.

Vince was quiet for a moment. "You wouldn't mind that?"

"Mind what, making you a vampire? Of course not." *As long as we succeeded.*

"You'd never get rid of me then." Vince was trying to sound playful, but it came out strained.

Charlie stroked his back, feeling the taut muscles and supple skin that would stay that way forever if Vince was a vampire. He could make some joke about the world being a big place, but it would be a lie. If he tried turning Vince, it would be for one reason and one only. "I'd never spend another night without you, making me happier than I've ever been in my life."

Vince didn't answer for a moment as if he was actually considering it. If Charlie knew Vince would make it, there would be no question. But the risk was so high. Half the people who tried to turn didn't, and failure meant death.

"It's tempting," Vince finally said, "even with the bad odds. I have this stupid faith that if you tried to turn me, it would work.

Because it's us."

The hope that filled Charlie at Vince's words was unfounded. It was completely illogical and based on dreams, not facts. And yet, if Vince asked, Charlie would make a go of it, completely sure that Vince would wake up immortal.

And if he didn't, Charlie would tie himself to Cash's dock and wait for sunrise.

"Here's the thing," Vince continued softly. "Death motivates me. I think about it sometimes, and then I get brave. I try things, I risk things, I do things because I know I won't always have this life. I need to live it now or I'll waste it." Vince's eyes sparkled with the vivacious energy that made Charlie's heart beat. "I have to taste the new food. Meet the new person. Travel to the new place. I have to take care of myself. I have to make plans. I have to make love. I have to be the person I want to be *right fucking now*. Because I don't have a million tomorrows to procrastinate. I don't even know for sure if I have one tomorrow. Death is the reason I live. So, yeah, the notion of being immortal is tempting. But I have to pass. I've faced down death more times than most people my age, and yeah, I fear the unknown of the other side, but I've made my peace. My life means more because it will end."

Admiration welled in Charlie for the man he held. He'd spent three centuries living mostly to avoid death. And it made everything mean nothing. Vince had faced down death and chose to live, not in fear, but in defiance. "You are amazing, you know that? When I thought I was dying, when the town poured the pitch..." He flinched at a memory that still burned like boiling tar on his skin.

"Good God." Vince looked horrified.

He wasn't looking for sympathy, so he continued in a rush. "I didn't know I was immortal. New vampires always wake up at midnight on their first night. Ramón was gone when I woke up.

I thought I'd passed out from the grappa we were drinking. I had no idea…"

"Your sire was a serious fuckhole."

Charlie shuddered. "Thank you for killing him." It wasn't very Christian of him, but he meant it. Vince's arms tightened around him, and he felt safe. Strange that, how a weakened human made him feel so safe.

"I had some help," Vince admitted.

That made him grin. "I hear Cash was quite pleased to pass the stake to you, despite you disintegrating it."

Vince rolled his eyes. "Oh yes, the great insult of having a mere human kill him."

He looked really cute all insulted. Charlie touched his forehead to Vince's. "There's nothing 'mere' about you."

With a happy noise, Vince kissed him in thanks. "I didn't mean to interrupt. You tell me about your life so infrequently. I want to hear."

Charlie shifted uncomfortably. "You faced death and you came out with a philosophy for living. The only revelation I had is that a person can be so irrationally hateful, he'd torture a man today that he'd smiled at yesterday when he picked up a repaired table."

"Oh, babe." More sympathy, and it made Charlie more uncomfortable. Vince ran his thumb across Charlie's cheek. "He probably didn't hate you. Mob mentality can be freaky as shit the way it changes people."

"Can be? When is it not?"

"Mmm…like when you're at a club dancing, and everybody has their hands in the air, and the music is loud, and you don't care who's touching you. You just want to be there, in the moment, part of the movement, one with the world." He'd closed his eyes, his smile ecstatic as he relived some moment of blissful connection.

How amazing would it be to feel that way in a crowd instead of terrified? "I want to see the world through your eyes."

Those blue eyes opened, taking Charlie's breath away at their clarity and brilliance. Vince smiled at him. "Does this mean you'll spend every night with me, even if I'm human?"

"As many as you'll let me."

The smile turned coy. "So we're back to being boyfriends?"

Charlie grinned back, ecstatic. "I just tried to kill you, and you're going to take me back?"

Vince's eyes sparkled. "Yeah, I'm forgiving that way." He grabbed Charlie's hand and interlaced their fingers. "I'll even quit my job—just let me give them two weeks' notice, 'kay?"

Some of the joy fizzled. Charlie didn't like it, but Vince had saved his soul tonight. If this was what he asked for... "Yes. Okay. Two weeks. But no more secrets."

Vince poked him in the chest. "From you either. *And* you have to move in with me instead of me moving in with you."

Charlie blinked. "Here? To Cash's? Or to your apartment?"

"Here. Cash needs his on-site blacksmith so he can play medieval lord. More importantly, I can use the equipment to make my own stuff. I won't make much money at first. The living of a modern artist sucks. But my rent's free, and every vampire around seems to think Cash's shit smells like roses, so I should be able to make sales sight unseen because I'm his personal metalsmith. So I need to live here or keep my job that involves public nudity."

"We'll live here," Charlie said quickly. As long as Cash approved. Which, strangely, he thought Cash would.

"Good."

"You don't mind quitting?"

Vince struggled up until he could prop himself up on an elbow. "Look, I started dancing when I was eighteen. Before that I'd been working for eight dollars an hour, and I was killing myself trying to work and finish school."

Charlie's jaw clenched. "You didn't have to do that. I didn't expect you to pay rent."

"Yeah, but that would've made me totally dependent on you. I…" Vince sighed. "I really liked you. But I knew you thought of me as a kid. The only way I knew to overcome that was to pay for myself, like an adult. So there I was, barely holding it together, and then I got this offer from a friend of a friend. And suddenly instead of bagging groceries for a pittance, I was working fewer hours making a thousand dollars a week doing something fun. Suddenly I could buy clothes. I could save up for classes. I had time for friends. I didn't stress about rent or groceries. There was no reason not to do it… other than I knew you would disapprove. But we weren't dating, and I wasn't sure we ever would. I mean, I used to walk around your house in a towel and you barely looked twice at me."

"Looking away seemed more prudent than gawking. You were really young." He frowned. "You're still pretty young. Just counting my human years, we're eleven years apart."

The incorrigible man shrugged. "Sounds good to me. We'll have more time together before… you know."

"Earlier you were waxing eloquent about death, and now you can't say the word?"

Vince looked down toward their feet, heartbreakingly sad but resolved. "Before I'm too old and you find somebody else."

Charlie pulled him close, pressing their bodies together. Vince's gaze darted to his in surprise, and Charlie kissed him. Vince's hand cupped his jaw as he kissed back softly.

"Not going to happen," Charlie assured him. "You're it for

me. I don't want anyone else ever again."

Smile sad, Vince traced the contours of his face with the pad of his index finger. "You can't mean that. You're going to outlive me, and I don't want you to turn into a hermit."

"I'm not." It was a grim topic, but Charlie had thought it through before. Last time they'd been together, he'd even broached it with Cash. If he and Vince were going to make a life together, they were going to do it right. "I said a minute ago that I want to see the world through your eyes. I'm sorry I can't grow old with you. But that doesn't mean we can't live and die together."

Vince stiffened. "No. No, you're not killing yourself over me. Cash told me about the bell thing, and that's crazy."

Cash had told him? What exactly had Cash said? No matter. Vince could know. They'd agreed to no more secrets. "It's not suicide—I don't see it that way, anyway. I was born human. The fact that I've lived as long as I have is unnatural. A fluke."

"Charlie," Vince moaned.

He put his hand on Vince's chest, feeling the steady rhythm of his heartbeat. "Or maybe it's a miracle."

"One you shouldn't give up."

"No. A miracle because it let me find you." He slid his hand up Vince's chest to run his fingers through his curls, love filling his heart and making him feel whole. "You give me hope. You make life mean something. I can continue on into infinity and keep doing the same things by rote, no real story to tell. Or I can live, like you said, knowing the end is in sight. We can be together and both of us know this isn't an affair, it's a lifetime. I can finally sell my work under my own name because I'll have a normal lifespan." He looked at Vince's neck, then away. He'd ripped into him pretty good. But even as a Liberi, he'd picked a safe spot to bite. He needed to talk to Vince about that—about maybe biting him. He wanted it, badly. "Maybe I'll even take a few risks, knowing opportunities won't come rolling back in an infinite wave."

"That's a lot to give up."

"Yes." He couldn't deny that. Death scared him, mostly because he'd always assumed he'd go straight to Hell. But that meant Vince would too. Hell was suddenly looking up.

Or more likely, that wasn't the way it worked.

He kissed Vince again, and the warmth and love he got back burned away the fear. "It's a lot more to gain."

Vince choked back tears as his touch turned greedy, caressing him like he couldn't get enough.

And yet Charlie worried. "Is that all right with you? I don't mean to pressure you. You don't have to stay with me because—"

"Yes, you stupid man. It's perfect. I love you. I always have, and I always will." Vince leaned in to kiss him.

Charlie stopped him with a finger to his mouth. "You know I love you too, right? I have for a long time, and I will for the rest of my life. We'll make this work. You didn't run away from me tonight, even when you should have. I'll never run away again. I'll never deny what you mean to me to anyone." He shuddered at the next promise, but he made it anyway. "And I'll dance with you when you ask."

Vince whooped in joy and kissed him, making that final promise almost worth it. "I'll go easy on you at first. Promise. We're going to have so much fun!"

Charlie kissed him back, amazed that someone so full of life and joy could love him back. But he wasn't going to protest, just do his best to be a good boyfriend and keep his promises.

A knock on the door interrupted them. "Vince? Everybody alive and awen'd? I'm sorry. I can't wait any longer. I'm freaking out."

"Rhi?" Vince asked. "What are you doing here? I thought you left. The car—"

The door burst open, and Rhiannon took three quick steps in before halting. "I gave it to the maid and told her to grab my mom and leave town—Cash really will kill me. Are you okay? You look okay. A little pale. Is he okay?"

Charlie flushed and pulled away from Vince. They were naked in bed together. Where were his clothes? On the floor in the bathroom? Embarrassed, he sank down further under the sheets.

"I'm fine. It worked. You're a witchy genius," Vince assured her, unaffected by her presence. "Charlie, what are you doing?"

Rhiannon squealed and launched herself at the bed. Charlie froze as the girl landed between them, one arm around his shoulders and the other around Vince. She kissed her friend. "Holy crap, you're amazing!" She turned to Charlie. "You too." Her lips patted his cheek in a quick kiss before she scrambled to the bottom of Cash's enormous bed, where she could stretch out without lying on top of them. She grabbed one of Vince's feet and squeezed. "Trey and five other people are already holing up here. Word is spreading for human associates of CoVIn to hide or come here."

More people. Charlie wasn't sure what to do next. He couldn't leave the bed without flashing Rhiannon. But he wanted pants.

"Get back here," Vince grumbled, pulling him back. "You're not running away anymore, remember? How are you going to dance with me around strangers if you can't stay here with Rhi in the room?"

Embarrassment made him flush. "This isn't about us. It's about my lack of trousers." Maybe it was a little bit about being naked in bed with a man while somebody else was in the room. That was not something he thought he'd agreed to.

Rhiannon laughed, her obvious relief making her giddy, and headed into the bathroom. "You know, clothes are made of cloth, which is also what sheets and comforters are made of. I promise I can't see anything." She returned with his slacks. "These are soaking wet. Are you sure you want them?"

He eyed the wad of black, sopping fabric. No, he didn't want to put those on. "You aren't uncomfortable?" he asked stiffly.

She rolled her eyes in answer. "I work at a strip club. Naked men are not new to me. I think you should put your arm back around my best friend. He earned it, so get cute and cuddly." She tossed the slacks back into the bathroom and hopped back onto the end of the bed. "And we have less fun things to talk about, so you might want the moral support." She grabbed Vince's foot again, shaking it this time. "I get his foot. You get the rest of him."

Vince patted her on the knee with it. "You can always have my foot."

"Thanks. Although it will be less convenient to grab in most situations."

Vince had leaned back against Charlie's chest, his hand under the covers on Charlie's thigh. It felt too intimate for anybody else to see, but Rhiannon didn't seem to mind in the least. Vince's hold on him felt more like security than lust, like he needed the touch, and that made Charlie hesitate.

If Vince needed him and nobody minded... *Merde.* If Vince needed him, then that was reason enough. They were a team now, for the rest of his no-longer-immortal life. Vince's needs had to come before anyone else's wants.

It was still hard. He tried not to be so terribly stiff as he leaned against the padded headboard and put his arm around Vince's back. The grateful look Vince sent him wasn't enough to make him relax, but it was enough to make it worth the discomfort.

Rhiannon clapped her hands and blew out a long breath. "All right, kittens, it's time for Save CoVIn: Part Two." She turned to Charlie. "To sum up, before the reception Queen Modron went through Awen 101 with me—how it works, what the original spell looked like, and extra credit reading, which I've been doing diligently."

Charlie pulled Vince closer. "We can't put him in charge of turning anyone else, even if it doesn't involve nude bathing. It's too risky."

Rhiannon looked him right in the eyes, her gaze unnervingly steady. "I'm glad you feel that way because this time you're in charge."

He blinked in surprise. "Me?"

"Yup. Judging by your voice, I'm guessing you can sing?"

"Sing? Right now?" He'd been told he had a pleasant singing voice, but he wasn't a performer.

"No," Rhiannon said, her harried smile returning. "In front of everyone we need re-ensouled."

His throat closed up. "Why do I have to sing?"

Rhiannon sat up, legs crossed. "Okay, so while Vince was up here curing you, I was working on details for the next spell."

A faint banging rang through the house, like someone was knocking. Vince frowned. "They're starting again. Somebody's getting tired of waiting for you to come out."

Charlie waved a hand dismissively. "They can break down the door and stand stymied in the entryway. What's your plan?"

Rhiannon shook her head. "I don't have a plan. I have a spell. Totally different. I'm going to make a potion. Then we need a gathering of the vampires we want to fix. The ritual we do will give the vampires access to your awen for long enough that they can choose to get their own back."

"Access to my awen?" She wanted to let other vampires see his soul? The idea made him cringe. "Would they see inside my thoughts? My memories? What does that mean?"

"They shouldn't see thoughts or memories—I don't think. They'll experience the world through your inspiration, giving them a chance to see what they're missing without a complete soul. If they want it back, they can use your awen to find their own for as long as the song continues. You're a great candidate for this, actually, because you're a working artist. My guess is a lot of vampires will end up with a deeper appreciation for woodworking."

Charlie glanced at Vince, his main inspiration for living. Would they see his love too? His shoulders tightened. That wasn't something he could share with anyone.

"It's beautiful," Rhi said softly. "Seeing through your awen will help them understand."

She was even more of an optimist than Vince. "Or make them reject everything without considering what else they stand to gain."

Even Vince looked uncomfortable, ducking his head. It was refreshing to find they were on the same side for once. "I believe everyone *should* accept us as equals," Vince said softly, "but I'm not blind enough to think they already do. But once the spell has started to work, we can gather blood from everyone who rejoins us, giving the crowd more inspiration—more variety, more things to love. If we have you, Cash, Javier, Winnie, and Emma, everyone left is going to be less likely to focus on that one thing and will see how Cash loves to dance and Javi is a walking *Doctor Who* wiki and Emma is passionate about cooking. So we focus on Cash first—he'd be a giant physical asset and your friendship will help. Am I right, Rhi?"

She nodded. "That's the plan." She reached over and shook Charlie's foot, like she was including him in the circle. "I admit I haven't always been your biggest supporter when it comes to dating Vince. Not that my opinion matters, but this week, when I started to see *you* and not just some surly misanthrope happy to hide my best friend in his shadowy closet, I changed my mind. You have a kind heart, and you create incredible things. I think we're going to be friends… if you let us. This is the same thing. Let them see you. You'll be surprised."

Charlie realized he'd scrambled backward into the headboard when Vince tugged him back down with a soothing, "Babe, it's okay."

No. It wasn't. Rhiannon's suggestion made him feel like an animal caught in headlights, wanting to run and not sure which way to go. "That's not the way it works. People always find reasons to condemn you. This will just give them more."

Vince squeezed him. "That's true. But not everyone will. Don't focus on the asshats. Focus on the people who get you. They're the ones who matter."

Charlie squeezed himself as close to Vince as he could. Focus on the nice people, like Loli yesterday at the reception. But three others had walked away, and this wasn't about making friends. This was about saving CoVIn. "One out of four isn't great odds for your spell."

Rhiannon's face pinched. "I don't know how you came up with that statistic, but one out of four is better than zero out of four, and that one can add blood to the pot and start drawing in more. Are you going to do this? Because otherwise, we're screwed."

He didn't have much of a choice. He could abandon them. Or he could let Rhi do this horrible thing and face the

322 • JAX GARREN

consequences with them. "I promised Vince I'd stand by him. I don't like this. But I'll do it."

Vince kissed his cheek. In automatic reaction, he stiffened, then remembered that Rhiannon, if anything, thought it was cute. He leaned his head against Vince's, taking strength from his strength.

Rhiannon nodded briskly. "Good. The ritual starts with you singing the spell over a cauldron. You drop three drops of blood in, which finishes the brew—like Modron did at the ceremony earlier. Then we have to, somehow, pierce Cash—or somebody—with a potion-dipped knife or arrow or whatever to give them access to your awen."

Charlie wrinkled his forehead. "You expect Cash to stand still while I sing a song and we stab him with potion water? He wouldn't do that *with* a soul."

She shook her head, her own brow furrowing. "As I said before, I have a spell, not a plan. That's the difference between the two." She slid off the bed. "Dude, I just read a shit-ton of esoteric gobbledygook out of very old books and put the finer details into a spell based on a magical system I'm barely familiar with. You two can figure out how to implement it. I'm going to go gather supplies and start brewing and maybe, if there's time, take a nap."

At the door she stopped. "Charlie, I'm really glad you got your awen back. And both of you? I'm glad you're cute. Don't stop being cute just because the world has stupid people in it. It has not-stupid people in it too, and we need happy couples like you guys to give us hope."

Chapter 23

Vince stared into the refrigerator, trying to decide between another half-pound of brisket or making himself some eggs. Maybe it was the vampire blood. After eating the bushels of food Charlie had brought up to him, he'd drifted to sleep, woken up several hours later with Charlie dead to the world, and now he felt great, all things considered. Except he was ravenous.

Rhiannon slept in a pool of sunshine on the kitchen's window seat. A cold tea sat on the ground next to her, and her tablet was pressed to her slight chest. While he'd been lazing about with Charlie, eating and discussing potential plans, she'd spent the night trying to perfect a spell that would save all of them.

The bell at the gate rang, and he frowned. Vampires shouldn't be out yet; it was too early. But hired rats would.

Rats probably wouldn't ring the bell. His unfilled stomach growled a complaint, but he ignored it and headed for the video-com. A stretch Hummer purred at the gate. Of course, whoever was visiting Cash did it in a limo-Hummer. "Hello?"

Whoever was out there couldn't see him, but they could hear him. The driver leaned into the panel. "Marcos Hernandez of Familia de Tejas is here to speak with Vincent Pagano and Rhiannon Flynn. Geirson called yesterday and explained the situation. We understand it's gone poorly since then, and we're here to offer our aid against the witch who murdered one of our own. Have we an invitation to enter?"

Hope and relief washed through him at the unexpected

offer. He, Rhi, and Charlie weren't alone. "Yes. Oh, God, yes, please come in. You're invited. I invite you. Whatever I need to say."

The driver chuckled. "That will do."

Relieved beyond measure, Vince opened the gates and watched as car after car passed inside, bringing them an army.

80 ✦ CB

Charlie stared up into the dastardly tall blackness of the elevator shaft at CoVIn HQ. According to the jaguars, the Liberi and the CoVIn fallen had moved in, taking over CoVIn's space the very night they were supposed to christen it as their own.

He, Vince, Rhiannon, and a dozen jaguars were climbing up the service ladder. Two more jaguars waited for them in the building. They'd snuck in while the vampires were sleeping to keep watch. So far, the building had stayed quiet while Tzitzi performed what the jaguars referred to as "a ghastly ritual" in Starlight. All Charlie knew was he didn't want to be on the cleanup crew for that. "I can't believe you slid down an elevator shaft from the top floor."

Vince kept moving, his pace fast for a human. Maybe Charlie had given him a little too much blood. Normally he'd worry about the long-term effects, but if it gave Vince an edge today, that wouldn't be a terrible thing. Vampire blood was like opium. One use rarely hurt anyone.

"It would've been fun if I wasn't running for my life and terrified you were permanently evil. Maybe I'll take you on a rappelling date."

Charlie's fingers slipped on the next rung before he grabbed securely. They'd never talked about dates in front of other people before. But he'd promised never to publicly deny Vince. That meant he had to answer like it wasn't a tremendous thing to discuss their plans in public, just like any other couple might.

What would he say if they were alone? He kept his eyes on Vince, just above him, and the comforting sight gave him strength. "As long as you're up for night rappelling." There. He'd casually responded like it was no big deal. It felt pretty good too.

"Good point." Vince turned his head so he could smile down at him, expression full of pride and love. "Bungee jumping then."

Charlie caught the smile and gave it back, proud of himself and happy that Vince understood what it meant to him to have this conversation in front of everyone. "You are going to be the death of me."

Vince's smile softened. "Not for a long while, babe." And he kept going up the ladder.

Tied together, in life and death. It was a good thing—the best.

Rhiannon grumbled, "I wish I could fly. This would be so much easier if I could fly like that stupid other witch."

Above them a jaguar chuckled. "Just be glad we're only going up two floors."

"I wasn't talking about the ladder. I was talking about the fact that we're going to be fighting in a thirty-story atrium, and the only one with use of the whole space is not on our side. If I could fly, we could have a flying witch battle, like in the movies. But no. I'm stuck on the damn ground while Tzitzi gets to fly. One day I'm going to fly too. I vow this now."

The top jaguar stopped at the second level and forced the doors open with his hands. "Clear," he called down before hefting himself out and helping everyone else into the atrium. It was after dusk on the first night the building was open. The place should have been hopping, yet CoVIn was eerily silent.

The building was gorgeous, designed for aesthetics, not utility. An atrium soared from floors two to thirty-two, just below

Starlight Club. The first three floors of the atrium had no railings and made a mall. Storefronts lined the walkways with gaudy displays. Old saloon doors led into a general store, clear walls filled with falling water led to a bar, a storefront made of real geodes led to a jeweler, and on they went, ringing the space. Glass elevator shafts, not the ones Vince and Rhiannon had come down yesterday, took up the center of the room, ready to whisk vampires up to offices for those who did CoVIn's work and condos for those important enough to live near the queen but not important enough to get out of living near the queen.

Charlie shouldn't love this building. It represented a society who'd never accepted him. And yet it was his. He was CoVIn, born into it and pledged as a member. The failure of this place to be alive and vibrant was his failure. To turn it around and make it a place where his fellow members could live, work, and play together would be his success. After tonight, he wouldn't let anyone make him feel like a second-class citizen. Tonight, he and Vince and Rhi were going to save them all. Or they were going to die trying.

The jaguars made a loose circle in the atrium with Rhiannon at the center, her tiny cauldron over a Bunsen burner looking less than mighty. She poured her potion from a flask and two jaguars with guns knelt beside her ready to dump bullets in when the spell was ready and fish them out to shoot. Usually bullets didn't work against vampires, but they weren't trying to kill anyone—just get the potion into their blood.

Charlie stepped into the atrium and looked up. Somewhere behind all those doors were hundreds of vampires and one crazy witch. Hundreds against their little band. The thought gave him vertigo. Or maybe that was just because he had to sing. His throat closed up in fear.

Why did *he* have to sing?

Rhiannon nodded at him to start. He closed his eyes and forced out the first few shaky notes. His voice caught and he stopped.

Blessed Virgin, he was singing the same song the queen sang at every gathering in front of everyone. He'd known that coming up, but actually doing it sent ice through him, stopping his voice and freezing him in place with fright.

Vince squeezed his hand. "You got this."

He shook his head.

"Babe. You got this. Someone's going to spot us. We need you singing."

Charlie tried to nod, but he could barely move.

"Vince!" Rhiannon called. "Get him going! We have to start."

"Shut up! He has stage fright. Happens to the best of us."

Charlie shook his head. "Never happens to you," he whispered.

"Take my strength." Vince kissed him, slowly and sweetly.

Charlie sighed into it and took the strength offered in love. With Vince he could push back the tide of fear.

A catcall sounded from above them. They'd been found. It was time to start. But Vince held on for a moment longer, as if determined not to let anyone else dictate when he did what.

"Saint Cecilia be with you," Vince finally whispered.

Saint Cecilia, patron of musicians, believed in the importance of music in church. He was singing in a Pagan ceremony with his lover to aid vampires. This was about as far from a Catholic Mass as it got.

But he was still Catholic. He believed in love and forgiveness, tradition and redemption. Tonight he was trying his best to do the right thing and save people. Surely a God of goodness would listen. He squeezed Vince's hand. "Saint Cecilia, bless this endeavor."

Another catcall, as vampires came out to the balconies above them. The sound was his call to action. Five stories or lower, and they could jump. Above that, they risked hurting themselves. So far, nobody was low enough to make the leap. They needed to start the spell now. Charlie began again, singing softly but not missing a note. He could do this.

At the cauldron he offered his wrist. Rhiannon nicked it with a muttered, "Louder." Three drops of blood went into the potion.

"He's doing well," Vince chastised her, standing up for him even if it wasn't really true.

He could sing louder, though, so he did, then louder again, letting his voice echo in the cavernous space, filling the room with his voice as Rhiannon would fill it with his soul.

May they not fail because of him.

Rhiannon sighed in relief. "Much better."

She dipped her chalice into the cauldron and handed it to Charlie. He took a quick sip between stanzas so he didn't miss a beat and handed the cup back.

She poured the remainder back in and nodded at the jaguars, leading to a dozen tiny splashes and clinks as bullets dropped into the potion. Now came the part where they had to pray the spell worked before someone got killed.

"Charlieeeeee!" came screaming from the sixth story. Cash leaned over the railing. "What're you doing with the kitty-cats? Did you bring us treats?" He turned to Rhiannon and made kissing noises. "Already had that one." Despite being too high, he launched himself over the railing, flipped in the air, and landed in a crouch. After a moment, he straightened up, the epitome of a badass. "But she tastes good. I'll take her again."

He strode forward. Terrified jaguars fumbled for bullets as

the futility of what they were doing kicked Charlie in the gut. They were going to stop a force like Cash with a song and a few drops of liquid? No way in heaven or hell. But Charlie kept singing anyway.

Cash continued blithely forward, slamming jaguars aside with ease until he reached Rhi. He dipped his finger in the pot and licked it. "Mm. Mead."

Finally one jag got his magazine in the gun and spun it to Cash, his hands shaking unsteadily. Charlie didn't blame him. Cash's ability to kick ass against incredible odds was legendary. With no conscience to hold him back he would be practically unstoppable.

"Is that supposed to do something? Against me?" He grabbed Rhiannon around the neck, pulling her back to his front with a smile. "And here I'd thought you might be a real threat."

"Shoot him!" she yelled.

The jaguar stabbed the gun against Cash's arm and a giant bang reverberated throughout the building. Cash jolted to the side with the impact, his fangs dropping and eyes turning the glazed gray of stormy seas—but he didn't take the gasping breaths of someone who'd earned their awen back. With a growl, he grabbed the hot gun from the guy's hand and smacked him across the face with it, sending the jag sprawling. "That hurt a bit." He turned the gun around and aimed it for the jaguar's head. "But it'll hurt you more."

Vince launched at them. "Let her go!"

Cash backhanded him. Charlie's heart stopped as Vince spun and dropped onto the wood floor. Vince's breath knocked out on impact, but he pushed himself back up.

He wasn't seriously injured. Yet.

Which just meant Cash was playing with his food. They were going to lose before they'd even begun when Cash took all of them out. Charlie's voice faltered. They were dead.

ಬ♦ೞ

"Come on, spell," Vince muttered, stabbing a machete into the potion. Rhiannon had worried a gun would burn too much potion off the bullet for it to work, but it had been worth trying. Unfortunately, it looked like her fear was right.

Cash shot him a nasty look. "You should've invited me in. Watching everyone else bang on the entrance would've amused me enough to keep you alive. For a while, anyway. But if you won't invite me in, there's still a way to get my house back." He pulled their prototype stake from his pocket. "Did you know that stabbing a human through the heart with this works too?"

Yes, Vince was well aware. He stared at the stake in apprehension. If he moved, would Cash strike?

If he didn't move, was he making it too easy?

Charlie punched Cash, vampire fast. The balconies erupted in hooting, like they were watching a prizefight.

Cash's head popped back, but he held his ground as he let Rhi go. Rubbing his chin in surprise, he turned to Charlie. "Why are you with them?" He looked from Charlie to Vince, then back again. "Awwww. You want this pretty *ergi* more than you want everyone else?" He turned the stake toward Charlie. "What can you expect from someone broken from birth?" He raised the weapon to strike.

Vince lunged with the overlarge knife, aiming for the heart. Cash launched backward, but through some miracle, Vince actually hit him—not a good stab, but enough to draw blood between his ribs.

"Sing," Rhiannon ordered.

Charlie started singing, looking for all the word like he'd already given up.

Cash turned back to Vince, taking a knee. "You know... stabbing me only works... if it's wood." He tried to get up but slipped back to his knee. "What's wrong with me?"

Charlie sang louder as Rhiannon scribbled sigils on the floor. Cash collapsed face-first into the carpet.

Vince clutched the machete, waiting to see what Cash would do next. His hands were slick with nervous sweat. From the balconies, hundreds of vampires taunted them, booing and screaming as Cash writhed. "What are the sigils for?"

Rhiannon cringed. "Sorry. It's amateur night at the death match. I, uh, forgot them."

He squeezed her shoulder in support. "It's all good. We got this." As long as Cash woke up on their side.

Still on the floor, the vampire rocked back and forth and ranted in some other language. Old Norse maybe. What was he seeing? Would it be enough to make him choose his soul when he'd given it up voluntarily for his queen? Cash gasped, sucking in air like a man near drowned, fingers scrabbling against the carpet as he struggled.

The fit ended, decision made. Cash lurched up to sitting, panted like he'd run a race, and darted his gaze around the circle, eyes wide and—for once—fearful. "What the unholy fuck is going on?"

Vince laughed with a deranged level of relief, hope edging out despair. "Give three drops of blood to the cauldron, dip your weapon in it, and join the fight. Sorry I stabbed you. Welcome back." He looked up at the hundreds surrounding them. "We pretty desperately need you."

Chapter 24

Without hesitation Cash wiped blood from his chest and flicked it into the cauldron, then turned to face the crowd. "What's my modus operandi?" With an irritated noise, he adjusted Vince's grip on the machete. "How do you make weapons if you don't know how to use them? Remind me to give you lessons. Your form is unacceptable for anyone in my household."

Vince tried to hold the machete as instructed but didn't understand how the awkward grip made fighting easier. Whatever. Cash was back. He didn't know why Cash had chosen them this time when just yesterday he'd let the queen take him. But it didn't matter. "Draw blood on everyone who attacks us, but try not to kill them."

"Such limits you make. You will explain this later. Why is Charlie singing?" He started humming completely out of tune with Charlie. "I like it. Sing louder, Charles. Be our battle bard!" He turned to Vince, a bloodthirsty gleam in his eyes. "Try not to die, human. I like you."

The first wave of vampires rushed out of the stairwell.

Rhiannon shouted in Welsh.

Cash screamed a war cry as the jaguars howled and shot guns or charged into the fray like extras in a fantasy movie.

"Seriously?" Vince asked, completely lost. "This is so not my scene." A vampire made it past the front lines. Forsaking Cash's advice, Vince gripped the machete backward in his fist, point side out. He didn't have to kill anyone; he just had to land metal on skin.

Instead of slashing, he punched, like his father had taught him. A scrape, small but welling blood, appeared across the vampire's arm.

The vampire grabbed Vince's throat and squeezed with a vise grip.

Vince punched him in the stomach. The vampire began to shake, his grip loosening.

He went down.

"I got him! Did anybody see that? I got him!" Vince yelled to no one in particular, then quoted *Star Wars,* "'Great, kid. Don't get cocky.'"

Above them, more vampires appeared. Where was Modron?

More frightening, where was... On the very top floor, white robes stained with red appeared.

"Tzitzi..."

She jumped from the balcony, transformed into a black bird, and dove for them.

Vince backed up until he was side-by-side with Rhi. "Have you learned the spell to turn yourself into a bird yet?"

"No." She looked up. "Oh, shit."

"Incoming!" Vince yelled. The vampires ducked as a raven the size of a vulture soared over their heads.

Cash swung for it—and missed. "Can I kill the bird?"

"Kill the bird!" Rhiannon yelled.

The Tzitzi-bird came back for them, aiming her beak at Rhiannon.

Vince swung his machete like a bat. A whoosh of air. Feathers slid against his blade—

—and the bird flew past, unharmed.

The first downed vampires were getting up. Cash swung at

one. A jaguar stayed his hand. "No, no. Only new ones."

"See what I said about him not being too bright?" Rhiannon said.

The bird wheeled about for another run. Vince readied his machete-bat. "To be fair, he just woke up from losing part of his soul. I can see how that would be confusing."

"Is defending inanity a boy's club thing too?"

"Totally."

Instead of flying at them, the raven dipped into the crowd and vanished.

Vince dropped down to look for her near people's feet. "She's gone."

"Good," Rhi said.

"No, not good. Gone, like I can't see her. Not gone, like out of the fight."

"Bad."

A mouse ran between them. "Shit." He hammered at it with the hilt, whack-a-mole style, and missed four times when it dodged between feet or around the cauldron.

The mouse stretched up, shifting forms.

Vince swung, striking Tzitzi on the shoulder.

She yelled as she fell over.

Vince reared back to hit her again.

She grabbed for Rhiannon's ankles. Both witches disappeared.

"Rhi!"

"Vince?" she yelled back, sounding as though she was still right beside him.

"Come and get us," Tzitzi whispered.

"Vince!" Rhiannon shrilled.

He leaped toward the sound and slammed into invisible people. They crashed down in a heap of narrow bones and Tzitzi's wet, sticky shirt that Vince didn't want to think about. Vince grabbed a handful of dreadlocks. "I got her!"

Tzitzi rolled toward him, using her invisible momentum to slam him onto his back. He punched. She flew backward. A thunk of bone on metal, and she came back into view against the cauldron.

The cauldron skittered forward and tipped over, spilling bloody potion onto the floor to be trampled by warring vampires.

Rhiannon screamed as her shirt caught fire on the Bunsen burner. She rolled on the ground to beat it out.

Tzitzi lay in the spell-muck, eyes full of frustrated hatred. "You," she growled at Vince. "You need to die. The gods do not smile on me with an owed sacrifice."

He scrambled up into boxing stance, ready to knock her out.

She swiped a hand through the air and yelled in Nahuatl.

Pain carved into his belly like claws, sending him to his knees gasping for air. Tzitzi lunged on top of him.

Behind her, Charlie yelled his name and came running. Vince reached for him. And everything went black.

☙✦❧

"Vince?" Charlie stopped singing—the crowd had taken it up; that'd have to be enough—and scrambled for him. But the air was empty. Tzitzi had fallen on him, and they'd vanished. "Where is he?"

Rhiannon leaned against the spilled cauldron, tears making her face wet. The shoulder of her shirt was a blackened hole, revealing severe burns beneath. She'd live, but that would leave scars.

He ran to her. "Where's Vince?"

"You're not singing." Her eyes weren't focusing well.

He snapped his fingers in front of her. "Where is Vince? Where did Tzitzi take him?"

Her unfocused gaze found him, then went to the space where Vince had been. "I don't know. He was just…" She pushed herself up, suddenly full of frenzied energy, and Charlie helped her stand. Around them the fight still raged, the opponents almost equally matched, but Rhiannon ignored it, her expression panicked as she looked around for Vince. "Tzitzi thinks she owes Vince to her god. She took him as a sacrifice."

Dread made him swallow hard. "Where?"

"I don't know. Didn't the jaguars say she'd made a ritual space?"

He nodded. "Starlight. Are you coming?"

She wiped her nose with her hand and nodded. "To the elevator."

"Too slow." He crouched. "Can you hold on?"

"I think so." She climbed onto his back and held tight with one arm. "Go."

He grabbed a dark-haired vampire who was just waking. "Tell Cash Geirson to meet us in Starlight. Bring reinforcements."

The confused vampire focused on him long enough to nod as she gasped in air. Charlie pulled the familiar woman—a friend of Galswinth's, Elvira maybe?—to standing and pointed. As soon as she was on her way, Charlie used his speed to zip through the fight and leaped for the first balcony. Feet on the second floor, he jumped for the next one, fear driving his speed faster and his distance farther than he'd ever pushed himself. They had to get to Vince in time.

೫೦ ✦ ೪

Vince blinked at the brightness of the bonfire in the middle of Starlight. They'd materialized here, as in *teleported*. The room steamed with heat from the fire and smelled of smoke, body odor, and carnage. Vaguely human shapes were piled around the stage, unmoving, and blood ran down the steps. Bile rising, he turned away in horrified revulsion before he saw more details of the slaughter.

Tzitzi let him go and fell back on her ass with an exhausted breath. Her skin looked tight and sallow, as if that bit of magic had cost her.

Legs trembling, he blocked out the atrocities in the room and pushed himself to standing, the machete still locked in his grip. He had to finish her off while she was weak.

Alaric appeared between them, moved there from elsewhere vampire fast. Vince backed up involuntarily, needing as much distance between them as he could get.

"What are you doing?" Alaric asked, his voice tired. He sounded normal, like he hadn't changed with everyone else. Vince wondered if that had to do with the necklace of tiny, clicking bones he wore over his dragon-skin armor.

Vince opened his mouth to answer, but Tzitzi spoke first. "We owe him to Xipe Totec. Things are going to shit down there, and it's because we've lost His blessing."

Alaric glared down at her in acrimony. "*We* owe your god nothing. You are in charge of magic."

"And *you* are in charge of fighting. But I don't see you down there leading our forces," she snapped back. "A few animals, two humans, and one vampire are defeating us." Standing, she drew her dagger from her belt. "Once we get His blessing back, the tide will turn."

Vince backed up until his ass hit the steps and his hands landed in stickiness. *Blood.* He jerked away, but the hot blood stuck to him, coating his palms in someone else's messy death.

"I am here," Alaric raged, "because *this* was not the plan." He threw his hand out, pointing to center stage.

Modron's body lay still among the dead. A blue aura surrounded her with the energy and hum of electricity. Vince couldn't tell if she was alive inside it or not. No, she had to be alive, because otherwise everyone would've changed back already. Should Vince try to kill her? Or was it going well enough downstairs that he could focus on getting the fuck out of crazy town with his heart intact?

"You wanted her awen gone. This *is* the plan." Tzitzi strode toward Vince, steps determined and firelight gleaming off her black dagger. He backed up the steps, ignoring the gore as he slid and bumped through it onto the stage.

Alaric grabbed her shoulder, spinning until they both faced the stage. "Modron should be a complete vampire, powerful in her ruthless grace. She is a queen, not your prize to freeze and store. I'll fight when she goes with me."

Tzitzi shoved him, but of course he didn't move. Instead he tightened his grip, a dangerous light in his blue eyes. Tzitzi hummed in anger. "They're going to kill her. I told you, we're keeping her safe."

"She's kept herself safe for two thousand years. She doesn't need your self-serving protection. Release her."

While Vince appreciated them fighting instead of sacrificing him, releasing soulless Modron to fight for Team Evil was not going to improve the situation. He still had the machete. He shifted his grip, the warmed metal pressing into his fingers as he held on tight. He could run for the stage exit. Or he could try and behead Modron and end this whole thing. He'd be lucky to get one of those in before Alaric caught him with his super-speed. Accomplishing both was out of the question.

As they bickered, he backed up, each step feeling loud and clumsy, until the queen was within reach. Whatever the blue aura was gave him pause. Was it keeping her asleep? Or was it protecting her somehow? There was no way for him to know. All he did know was that if Modron woke up, the fight downstairs got a lot harder. And if he ran for the exit, Alaric would catch him before the stage door finished opening. Decision made.

Quickly as he could, Vince slammed the machete toward Modron's neck. The blue energy coated his hands, setting his nerves on fire. Like an elastic band it bent, then sprung, tossing him away with a snap of power. He screamed as he landed on his back. His hands throbbed with painful energy.

Alaric jogged up the steps, eyes on the queen. "Ah, Vincent Pagano. Geirson's flavor of the month. You think you could break through that spell when I couldn't?" But by the way his gaze took her in, he hadn't been sure. Still he continued, feigning confidence. "One of these days you're going to get through your head what it means to be a human among immortals."

Tzitzi followed at a slower pace, as if she was still tired. "One of these seconds, you mean. Hold him while I finish this. Then we can discuss your queen."

Next to Vince, a dead woman's empty eyes stared at the glass ceiling. Her long hair was matted with blood. Her chest, just beneath the ribs, had been sliced open, her insides red and meaty where Tzitzi had reached in for the heart. That was about to be him. Animal terror shot him to his feet, and he sprinted for the main doors.

"*Our* queen," Alaric insisted. "She was born before your first life."

"Fine. Our queen. Get him."

Strong fingers latched into Vince's as the hated scents of tobacco and myrrh overtook the putrid air of the room. Wild energy filled him, and he lashed out with hands and feet in a frenzy of motion as Alaric dragged him back. Hair yanked from his scalp, sending fresh pain through him. Alaric grabbed him under the arm, still dragging him toward the stage.

The main doors opened. Electric light from the foyer outlined Charlie, Rhiannon on his back, like angels of salvation.

"Charlie!" Hope made Vince redouble his effort. If he could get to Charlie, he would be saved. He got his feet under him and charged. His arm wrenched as Alaric didn't let go. A popping pain jerked his left shoulder. Pain didn't matter. Getting to Charlie did. He lunged again, howling in animal determination. Charlie would keep him safe.

∞ ✦ ☙

Charlie's breath hitched in and out in gasps from thirty-some-odd floors of climbing with a human on his back. Starlight was hell on earth, hot as the tropics and smelling of blood, fire, and human waste. The orderly chairs of the night before were scattered and broken as if a ransacking mob had run through. At least a dozen bodies slumped on the circular stage or the steps leading up to it. The central fire crackled and raged, shooting sparks and lighting the room in twisting light and shadow. And Vince was in the middle of it, being dragged by his arm toward the sacrificial wreckage as he flailed and screamed.

Fury pounded through Charlie and sent him charging down the floor. Rhiannon latched on tighter, yelling for him to stop.

Alaric spun and released his clutching hold. Vince slid across the floor toward the stage.

Charlie lowered his head and rammed into Alaric, shoulder to the solar plexus. Alaric staggered back from the impact.

Rhiannon dropped to the ground and crawled toward Vince.

Alaric swung in a roundhouse toward Charlie's temple, trading speed for power.

Charlie ducked and jabbed low, planting his fist into the flesh over Alaric's liver. To his shock, Alaric grunted and backed away, clutching his side. Charlie bounced on the balls of his feet, ready as he could be for Alaric to come back fast and hard.

But Alaric didn't furiously rush in. Though clearly in pain, he smiled. "Not as incompetent as I assumed. Cassius can't seem to stop himself from teaching everyone how to fight."

Charlie glanced to the side, where Vince and Rhiannon huddled on the stage steps, whispering. Where was Tzitzi? Not an immediate threat. Didn't matter. "Vince taught me that hit." The liver, the organ that cleans blood, was one that still mattered to a vampire. He hoped it hurt, not because it gave him any advantage, but because Alaric deserved the pain. The need for vengeance shot reason out the door, and Charlie clenched his fists, ready for a fight he couldn't win.

Alaric straightened. He wasn't tall for the modern era, but he still loomed large over Charlie. "You know you're going to lose, right?"

That didn't matter anymore. Alaric had tormented him for centuries, and now he was tormenting Vince. Charlie shook his fists, trying to loosen them from the clench of anger and fear that had kept him hidden his whole life. "I don't care if I lose. I'm done taking your insults."

Alaric dropped down to a fighting stance. "Then I respect your death more than I ever respected your life."

Not a single phrase in French had the simple, guttural hatred he needed. "Fuck you, you two-faced son of bitch."

The smile left Alaric's face. In a blur of motion, he struck.

ಬ◆ಚ

Rhiannon's arms held Vince pressed tight against her thin body as she rocked him and repeated over and over, "It's all right. It's all right. You're all right. I'm here."

He listened to her words, holding them in his mind like a life raft, and slowly, painstakingly, pulled himself back together.

Where was Charlie? Fighting Alaric? Fear for someone else cleared the lingering madness, giving him a new focus. "It's not all right," he told Rhi.

She squeezed him once more before letting go. "Yeah, but it's a lie you needed to hear. Been there." She stood, and Vince gazed up at her for a moment, wondering when exactly she'd needed to hear that and knowing he'd probably want to kill somebody over it. She'd never talked much about growing up in countless households. Only the funny stories—same as all the ex-soldiers he knew who'd been to war.

Now was not the time. He had to get Alaric off Charlie.

"What happened to her?"

"Tzitzi?" He hopped up. Dizziness made him waver, then he steadied himself.

"No." Rhi pointed at the queen.

Tzitzi came up from the other side of the stage, blood running down her chin. Her eyes were full of madness as she spread her arms wide and began to speak. Her words slurred, like her tongue wasn't working.

"Did Tzitzi eat somebody?" he asked.

Rhiannon grabbed his hand fiercely. "She slit her tongue. The Aztecs used to do that as an act of auto-sacrifice. She's doing something big."

Slit her tongue? Heart sacrifice? *Flaying people?* The grisly violations of human decency made him want to go back to the crazy place in his head. "What sort of severely fucked-up religion is this?"

Rhi's voice was high and fluttery as she said, "Aztec culture had its good points too. Artists. Astronomers. Architects. We really need to stop her."

They needed to stop *Alaric*. Charlie's face was crunched in. Blood spattered his shirt and poured from his nose. With a sweeping kick, Alaric brought Charlie to the ground.

There was too much to stop, and they didn't have the power to stop any of it. What did he do?

The queen. Alaric was already pissed over Tzitzi's treatment of the queen. Vince grabbed Rhi's arm and pulled her close to whisper, "Announce that Modron is dead. That the blue thing holds her dead body together." He shoved her toward Modron, trusting Rhi would lie like a champ and praying Alaric would react the way Vince thought.

Hold on Charlie... Vince bull-rushed Tzitzi. His hurt shoulder screamed in agony as they went down. She kept chanting. He punched her in the mouth to stop the flow of words and whatever evil they would do. She howled and spat at him. Hot drops of bloody spittle spattered his face. The faint pounding of drums sounded in the distance.

Before Vince could wonder where they came from, Rhiannon yelled, "You killed her! Modron is dead!" The conviction in her voice made everyone turn.

On the ground, Charlie panted. One eye had swollen shut.

Alaric's foot stopped inches from his face. "What?" Leaving Charlie behind he ran up the steps. "She's not dead. She's protected." But sure enough, he turned to Tzitzi, all the anger and doubt of their argument in his gaze.

Rhiannon stood up to him, eye contact perfectly steady. "No. She's dead. This spell is holding her body together so it doesn't burst into ash. Modron was a powerful witch. She couldn't be trapped by magic like this if she was alive. Tzitzi needs her dead to control her."

Vince could kiss her for the compelling improv performance and for her trust in going with his plan. But the drums grew louder, beating a complicated rhythm of power.

"Not true," Tzitzi garbled, barely intelligible around her mangled tongue.

"Where are the drums coming from?" Vince asked. "Am I the only one who hears that?"

Tzitzi laughed, stretching out on the ground in ecstatic insanity. "Xipe comes!" She pointed to Vince. "Since I've failed, he'll cut your heart out for me."

"My gods," Rhiannon uttered. "She has lost her fucking mind."

"What?" Alaric exclaimed. "You called your psychotic god here?" His fists clenched in anger, and he took a step toward Tzitzi. "This is not even close to what we agreed. You are an oath-breaker."

Vince scrambled away from her, toward Charlie, now on the steps with Rhi.

The doors to Starlight opened, and Cash came running in with other vampires charging behind. "Great Loki, this is worse than a cesspit." He pointed his stake at Alaric. "You."

Vince pointed at Tzitzi. "We may have an Aztec god on the way."

More vampires poured into Starlight, filling it. Fighting broke out anew as mostly weaponless fighters pounded on each other, echoing the drums in the smack of fist and crack of bone. Cash ran through it up to the stage.

"Why are they fighting?" Vince asked.

Cash laughed as though the situation wasn't dire. "They're fucking lemmings. I came, and everyone followed. CoVIn. Liberi. Undecided. Jaguar. It's a zoo. Did you say a god is joining us? Because I've never killed one of those." He glanced around. "Who are all the dead people? You know what? I don't care. Everyone I give a shit about got all their bits?"

"Javi! Javier!" Rhiannon yelled.

Javier flitted through the crowd to the stage, face pale and expression stricken. Rhi threw her arms around his neck, and he hugged her tightly. "Is my life going to be like this all the time? Because just stake me."

Cash surveyed the fight, then looked over to where Alaric yanked Tzitzi up from the floor and shook her. "No, this is special." His expression turned grim. "Excuse me. I've got an old friend to stake." He started toward Alaric.

The drums reached a crescendo, their cacophony pounding over the clash of the fight. The floor shook like an impossible earthquake.

Cash stumbled backward. "What the…?"

The glass ceiling cracked. Shards of glass shot into the room. Charlie's weight landed on Vince, blocking him from the assault with his body. Howls of pain replaced the clash of fighting.

Charlie lifted himself away. A gaunt man stood center stage, firelight dancing over him. A fanciful red headdress added several feet to his height, with green plumes fanning up like a Mohawk. Two red stripes ran down his face from forehead to chin over each eye. A golden nose plug pierced his septum. He was naked except for a feathered loincloth, a profusion of stiff, scarlet ribbons, and more green feathers, which stuck out behind him like wings.

Something was wrong with his yellowed skin. It didn't move right over his muscles. The man raised his arms, and the emptied flesh of an extra hand hung down from each wrist. Vince looked at the floor. The desiccated skin of an extra foot flapped loosely over each sandaled foot.

His skin didn't move right because it wasn't his. He was wearing a human skin.

"Xipe Totec," Rhiannon whispered. "Lord of the Flayed.

I'm going to be sick."

Cash sat heavily, his face extra white. "Definitely special. I don't know Aztec shit. Tell me there's some reasonable explanation for him sporting a skin suit."

Rhiannon, keeper of all weird knowledge, answered, "It represents the sloughing off of winter and rebirth of spring. Like a snake sheds its skin."

Vince tried to breathe. "So that's *his* skin." That was disgusting, but better than the alternative.

"Um, no. He flayed himself to make plants grow and provide food for people. So now people are expected to offer skin suits in recompense. They made a festival of it every March."

Vince shivered. "A festival of skinning people?"

Cash's expression turned dark. "Perfectly reasonable logic. If you're a god."

The bitterness in his voice gave Vince's brain something to focus on other than the flapping hand-skin. He was done being shocked. They needed a way out. Panicking over every new atrocity wasn't going to accomplish anything.

Alaric raised his voice from across the stage. "Cassius."

Cash stood, his fist clenched around his stake. "What?"

Xipe Totec turned his head from one to the other, his skin rustling freakishly as he moved. His eyes held no expression, his solemnity unnatural. It made Vince feel like an ant, running in hurried but predictable patterns under the eye of something ancient and alien.

Alaric ignored the god at center stage, as if he could make his—its?—presence irrelevant by pretending it wasn't there. "I suggest a temporary truce before we all kill each other." He sounded defeated, like the supposed death of his queen had taken the fight from him. "I will leave and take the Liberi. You stay here with any CoVIn members who are still eligible."

Hisses from the crowd belied the notion that he could carry through with his half of the deal.

"Our lord is here. We do not need to compromise." Tzitzi shrugged away from Alaric and ran to prostrate herself before Xipe Totec. "I bring you war, my lord. And your sacrifice." She rose and motioned at Vince.

Charlie shoved Vince behind him. "No."

The god shifted, and his attention landed on Vince with the force of a hammer strike, nailing him to the spot. Xipe's eyes were almost entirely white, the pupils mere pinpricks of black. The god inhaled deeply, as if the scent of the air told him something, and his whole body seemed to grow, filling the skin suit until it fit him.

Vince swallowed and tried to clear his thoughts. What did a god, with its fathomless gaze, see as it studied him?

The god smiled, the second lips lifting to reveal his own brown lips and white teeth.

The heat of the forge, the feel of a hammer, the smell of coal fires, and the weariness of pounding metal for hours on end layered over Vince's reality like a dream state, pulled from his memory to his consciousness in a shared thought. But instead of iron, he worked gold.

Xipe was a goldsmith. Vince didn't know how he knew that, but their shared love of the craft echoed between them like a communion. Xipe expected an offering from him, but it didn't have to be his heart or his skin.

Relief mixed with awe as he found common ground with something ancient. Vince nodded, accepting the commission. He'd keep his heart, and in exchange he'd make Xipe new ear gauges out of gold and quetzal feathers, like the magnificent green plumes in his headdress.

He hadn't known those were quetzal feathers. But Xipe didn't need to speak for Vince to understand. He just knew what the god wanted him to know. Knew the shape Xipe wanted him to make, the colors of the feathers he needed to acquire, the weight of the gold it would take to make them.

Acquiring that much gold and rare feathers would empty Vince's bank account, and goldwork wasn't his specialty, but he'd damn well figure it out. He'd hand over the jewelry, and he'd never have to hear from Xipe Totec again, the promised tribute paid in sweat instead of blood. Vince would totally take that trade.

In front of him, Cash leaned on his sword, feigning casual with a grace Vince didn't think he could match in these circumstances, even if he had a thousand years to practice it. "Neither your partner nor your vampire companions of choice seem eager to go along with your plan, Alaric."

Alaric shot a disdainful gaze over the crowd and its uneasy peace in the presence of Xipe Totec. "They'll be under our control once the binding spell is complete. We need a sacrifice, and then we can be gone."

"This isn't enough?" Cash looked around him, incredulous, as he waved his hand at the carnage. "I saw a sacrifice or two back in my day, but this is… extra special."

Tzitzi answered, "This is a temple dedication, not a spell. If you want the Liberi to follow us, we need a new binding, as you've destroyed our first one."

Charlie's grip on Vince's arm tightened.

Vince waved his hands and announced, "Xipe Totec doesn't want my heart. He wants me to make him jewelry. Feathered earrings. He just told me."

Charlie and Rhiannon looked at Vince, mouths agape like he'd lost his mind.

He ground his teeth. "In my head where nobody else could hear. It happened! Xipe's a goldsmith. We had a moment." Or he was going nuts.

But if gods were real, why couldn't they speak in his head? No, he'd had divine communication and was going to make earrings for a god. *Fuck me, my life is different.*

Rhi rubbed his shoulder, her eyes filled with awe. "He is a goldsmith. Holy shit, a god talked in your head. Let's live through this so you can tell me about it."

Alaric looked from Vince to Tzitzi, eyes ablaze in the fury of defeat. But his rage wasn't directed at Vince. It was directed at her. "I don't care who the sacrifice is. It just needs to happen to complete the spell." He strode to the center stage and grabbed Tzitzi by the throat. "And you killed my queen." He chanted, and the phantom drums grew maddeningly loud.

Cash grabbed Vince's shoulder. "Modron is dead?"

Vince shook his head ever so slightly, eyes never leaving the drama at center stage. "They were fighting, and we figured they'd fight more instead of killing us if he thought..."

His grip relaxed. "Sneaky. I like your style, Pagano."

Vince wasn't sure if that was a compliment or not. But he didn't have time to ponder it. Tzitzi's eyes bulged as she gasped for air. Xipe licked his lips.

Tzitzi swung her dagger. Alaric ducked it and grabbed her hand. He took the dagger and ended the chant.

"Do we stop them?" Vince asked. "He's going to kill her." He tensed to do something. Yeah, she was crazy. But she was a person being murdered with an obsidian dagger right in front of him.

Charlie put a hand on his shoulder, holding him back. "Be a little old fashioned on this one. Sometimes violence is the answer."

Alaric slammed the knife below her ribs and slashed. He released her throat. She screamed in fury, but it was too late. Alaric punched into the hole, and out came her heart, pulsing faintly with each dying pump. With a twist of his wrist, Alaric snapped the vessels holding it and dropped her lifeless body to the ground.

He turned to the god, her heart fisted in his gore-coated hand. "This is payment for the spell. There is nothing between us after this."

Xipe Totec nodded, his gaze riveted to Tzitzi's heart.

Alaric tossed it to him. The god caught it in one hand and snapped the fingers of his other.

With a sound like the flapping of wings, Tzitzi's skin unzipped from her body and was gone.

Xipe smiled, his skin less yellowed, one dreadlock hanging in front of his headdress, and he vanished.

The drums silenced.

In the center of the stage, Alaric dropped to his knees, his eyes downcast. "It wasn't supposed to end like this."

Cash stood, weapon ready. "What does the spell do?"

Alaric sat back on his heels but didn't look at Cash. "They'll obey any direct orders I give. Since I'm their leader, they'll likely have some emotion through me that they wouldn't otherwise feel. Otherwise, nothing has changed."

Winnie came forward through the silent crowd, Nikolai at her side and CoVIn members trailing after them. "Then take them, get out, and know that after you cross the threshold, you'll be Liberi in our eyes."

The pain in Alaric's gaze reached a new height as he looked her up and down. There was definitely a story there. Something that hurt him so badly Vince almost felt sorry for him.

Almost.

But Alaric didn't say a word, just set his jaw and stood. He looked over the stage toward Modron. And stopped. "She's still there." He turned to Rhiannon. "You were wrong."

Cash put a hand on Vince and another on Rhiannon, pushing them behind him. Vince got the message. Don't admit they'd played him.

Instead of raging, Alaric bent down and scooped Modron up, holding her with covetous intent. "She's mine. She's Liberi too. Ban me. But you ban her as well." He dashed forward with a call. The Liberi followed, out of Starlight and into the foyer and stairwell.

Winnie and Cash shared a look of understanding and determination. They were going after Modron.

Charlie put a hand on Cash, holding him back. "What would we do with her? She lost her awen."

Cash knocked his hand off. "I don't know. Start singing."

"The spell is over. It doesn't work like—"

"Sing!" Cash got in his face. "Be one of us. Try something, dammit. Don't stand there and tell me it can't be done."

Charlie backed up. "Sure, yeah, fine." He started the song again, his low voice carrying through the crowd.

A voice picked it up, then another as Cash and Winnie led CoVIn out. Between the solemn chant and Modron lying so still, it reminded Vince of a funeral procession. Not knowing what else to do—and wanting out of this room as soon as possible—Vince joined in. He grabbed Charlie's hand. After an instant's hesitation, Charlie squeezed back.

୫୦✦ଓଃ

The elevator doors opened to the ground floor. The parade had taken the stairs, but Charlie was with humans, and thirty-two floors were too many for them. He, Javier, Rhiannon, and Vince had taken the elevator. The atrium was quiet except for the air conditioner and the faint echoes of the song, sung throughout the stairwell. The spilled potion stained the floor, still sticky and wet with mead and blood and whatever else Rhiannon had put in it.

Rhiannon turned off the Bunsen burner and righted the cauldron. "We should be happy the Bunsen burner didn't set the whole place ablaze." She started humming the tune as she dropped her spell accoutrements into the cauldron, packing up.

Charlie had never been the queen's biggest fan. She wasn't cruel, but she was calculating, capricious, and played favorites. And he hadn't been kidding when he'd said a bureaucratic monarchy was the worst of all worlds. And yet, to have her gone made their community feel broken on the day they were supposed to celebrate unity.

He sang with Rhiannon, softly at first, but growing louder as the footsteps progressed forward.

Vince touched his back. "What are you thinking, babe? You have thinking-face."

How did he explain that part of him wanted Modron back—despite not liking her very much—in a way that Vince would understand?

The stair doors opened, sending song to fill the atrium, and vampires came out in a pack. Alaric carried Modron close to his chest.

Charlie squeezed Vince's hand one more time. "I have to do this."

"Wait!"

He strode to Alaric and halted in front of him.

Alaric shot him a look of promised pain. "Out of my way."

Charlie's swollen eye throbbed at the sound of his voice, but he stood his ground. He'd stood up to Alaric upstairs, and he wasn't backing down ever again. "She never got to choose. Everyone else did. Even you."

Vampires crowded around them as tension rose again between the two divisions.

"The spell is over," Alaric growled. "There are no choices left to make."

Modron stirred in his arms, eyes closed and fists clutching at nothing.

Alaric hushed her. "We'll be on our way." He tried to brush past Charlie.

What was Alaric going to do? He didn't have a hand free. Charlie punched him on the jaw. It wouldn't hurt him much, but it would get his attention.

Alaric's head snapped back. "You little—" He released Modron, hands coming up to fight.

Charlie caught her.

Alaric swung.

Cash caught his hand. "Go!"

Modron in his arms, Charlie dashed back to Rhiannon, unsure what she could do but knowing with that vague sense of certainty he sometimes got that it wasn't over yet. "Do something."

Wide-eyed, she used her ritual dagger to slash a quick line in Modron's palm, smacked her hand in drying potion on the floor, and pressed her palm to Modron's now bloody palm. "Come back to me. Be my mentor."

The queen sighed, her hands twitching again.

Winnie saw what they were doing, ran her fingers through the spell, and drew a cross on Modron's forehead. "Come back to me, mother. Teach me more about how to be strong."

Nikolai came next, leaving fingerprints on her bare feet. "Come back to me. Give me purpose."

In a wave of emotion, Charlie and the queen were

surrounded. CoVIn crowded him, everyone placing their spell-touched hands on her body as they gave reasons for her return. Charlie hated crowds, and they pressed in on every side, smothering him.

Vince's hands—he knew they were Vince's, though he couldn't see the man behind him—settled on his waist. "You got this, my brave man."

Brave. When was the last time anyone had called him that? To hear the word from Vince's mouth made pride straighten his spine and steady his nerve. "Will it work?" Charlie asked as more voices begged her return, painting her body with their fingers and the air with their pleas.

Vince held him tighter, and Charlie didn't mind. They were the heartbeat no one noticed in the body of the crowd, vital but not the focus. Everyone had eyes and hands only for Modron, coming slowly awake in his arms.

"You came back to me," Vince said simply.

"I came back because I love you." Charlie could never repay him for the risk he'd taken.

"I love you too." Vince looked at the crowd. "And she loves them." He nodded at her. "Why do you want her back enough to stand up to Alaric for her?"

It wasn't Modron, exactly; it was what she represented. Charlie ran his thumb through a thick patch of potion on her shoulder and smeared it. "Come back to us. I just realized I belong."

Vince stroked the spot next to Charlie's messy finger paint, blending his streak with Charlie's. "Come back to us. I found a family with your children." He put his hand back on Charlie's waist, and they watched and waited as everyone paid their respects.

Cash pushed his way in and pressed his potion-sticky hand

to Modron's heart. "Come back to me, Mo. I need you to keep me good."

She grabbed his hand and took a breath, lungs filling to capacity as she inhaled. Her eyes flew open, hazel and clear, as she panted. "Cassius?"

The crowd pressed tighter, calling for the queen with voices, hands, and sighs.

She looked up at Charlie, surprise on her face as she realized who held her.

Charlie flushed—he had royalty in his arms—and set her down. "Your Highness."

"No!" came Alaric's furious cry from across the foyer.

"Part," Modron ordered. Like the Biblical sea, her subjects moved to each side until a path was formed between her and her eldest son.

Alaric's stance was wide and straight, his face pale in anger. "Modron—"

She waved her hand with a muttered word of Welsh. Lightning arced from her palms to his abdomen. Alaric bent in half, then dropped to his knees. The lightning stopped, and Modron strode forward, Cash and Winnie at her back. "Your trial is concluded. Charles Travert will stay. You, my once-son, have relinquished your death blood."

Vince squeezed Charlie around the waist, and he sank back into him, relieved beyond measure to hear the words.

As Modron raised her hands for a new strike, five vampires—Liberi, Charlie assumed—stepped in front of Alaric.

Tensions rose as the temporary truce weakened. If Alaric died, the fight started anew.

Cash stayed Modron's hand. "My queen, we don't know where we stand. Alaric has agreed to take the Liberi with him. If we don't want an ash-fest in the foyer, I suggest we wait for a better opportunity."

Modron's rigid stance said exactly what she thought of that. But she nodded her head. "Is that your official opinion as the general of CoVIn's forces?"

Cash stiffened. That had been Alaric's job.

The mantle of responsibility didn't sit lightly, if Cash's pained expression was anything to go by. Charlie's sympathy went out to him. Cash liked to be with the crowd, leading by popular consent, not by authority. He turned in a circle, eyeing the gathering. At the moment, with everyone poised for action but no one in motion, it was impossible to tell who was with whom. What the numbers were. Which side had the few weapons scattered among them. There was no way of calculating odds for how the fight would end.

Marcos, the leader of the jaguars, stepped forward, hands up. "The witch who killed our family member is dead. If you vampires choose to fight, we have no stake in this."

Cash nodded once in acceptance and turned back to Alaric, eyes full of resentment. He didn't like what he was about to say. "Yes. That's my official opinion. Our home has seen enough violence for one night."

"Coward," Alaric muttered.

Cash crossed his arms but otherwise didn't react.

"Go," Modron spat. "Show yourself here again, and I'll ram a stake through you myself."

Alaric's bravado failed, face pinched in anguish. Without a word he pivoted, military straight, and walked away. The crowd separated into sides as the current Liberi followed, new lines drawn between friend and foe after Rhiannon's spell. It was going to be a hard recovery as some former allies had switched sides. But, to Charlie's surprise, some vampires he was sure had been

Liberi remained behind. Not many, but a few.

Cash noticed it too. He studied Rhiannon, his arms tight and eyes thoughtful. She might not know what she was doing yet, but she had the power not only to bring Modron's children back but to reconnect souls to vampires who'd never had their awen. CoVIn had a powerful new ally, and it was now Cash's job to use her.

As Modron and Cash quietly conversed and the last of the Liberi left, Charlie whispered to Vince, "Look out for Rhiannon. She just proved herself an invaluable asset."

Vince squeezed him, and the public contact felt strange and scary and absolutely wonderful. "That's good, right?"

"Not if she'd rather be a person than a tool." He leaned forward as Emma stepped up, Javier and Rhiannon just behind. Vince let him go with a knowing look, but he didn't complain.

They'd figure out lines eventually. The important thing was they were working together on them.

Cash shook Marcos's hand and jogged toward them too, his job over when the queen's staff of nonmilitary advisers surrounded her to discuss the fallout. Nikolai and Winnie came with him, solemn and dazed, as if the weight of all that had happened was just sinking in. They gathered like friends seeking comfort from each others' presence—the queen's general, her daughter, her psychic, and her witch in a circle with Charlie, Vince, Javi, and Emma. In the past, Charlie would've ducked back and assumed himself unwelcome. He didn't feel that way anymore. Despite the dangers of the last day, he smiled. They'd won. It didn't matter if everyone in CoVIn liked him. He had friends and he belonged.

"Who wants fudge?" Emma asked. "I feel an epic baking marathon coming on."

"As long as it doesn't have nuts," Cash said, the new

general's tone every bit as petulant as it had been last week. He started toward the elevators to the parking garage and everyone followed, like they always did with Cash.

Emma rolled her eyes. "Goddammit, Cash, just try them. You'll like them."

Vince smirked and hit the button for the garage floor. "Like green eggs and ham?"

Winnie wrinkled her nose. "What do green eggs and ham have to do with nuts?"

"Dr. Seuss?" Vince asked. "Please tell me you guys know who he is."

"No idea," Cash said, followed by a chorus of "no" from the anivets.

Vince sighed melodramatically. "I'll buy you all copies. So far, I'm teaching vampires about appropriate strip club behavior and children's literature. I'm not sure what that says about me."

Chapter 25

Two weeks later, Charlie sat between Cash and Modron at a VIP table in the place he'd renamed LongHell. Watching the vampire queen stuff dollars into G-strings was a sight he would never get out of his head. But once Winnie and Emma had showed her the protocol, the queen had...gotten with the program. Enthusiastically.

He supposed she was still a sixteen-year-old at heart. Or libido.

Cash leaned across him to talk to her. "How have you never been to a strip club? You're two thousand years old."

She leaned in, and Charlie found two of the most powerful vampires of his acquaintance practically in his lap. "In the past, these establishments catered to male patrons. I find it refreshing to see such equality in modern society."

The vampire queen was pro strip clubs. Okay then.

CoVIn's headquarters had been cleaned up and rededicated quickly while everyone was still in town. Modron was less than thrilled that she no longer fully carried the awen of CoVIn, and Charlie, Rhi, and Vince had sworn not to explain the details of the spell to anyone. Upsetting the power structure with an apocalypse on the horizon didn't seem in anyone's best interest.

Charlie had a secret of state. It was bizarre.

Cash had taken his new leadership position surprisingly seriously. Instead of the unilateral decision-making Alaric favored, he was interviewing soldiers from around the world to create what he called his *birdh*, a retinue of advisors patterned after his Viking days. Vince had been commissioned to forge "swords of unparalleled quality"—extra special stabby things, as Vince referred to them—for the chosen team.

Vince had almost completed his jewelry for Xipe Totec. Two days after the uprising, he and Charlie had borrowed a CoVIn jet, flown to Guatemala for a short vacation to study Mesoamerican art, and returned with gorgeous green feathers and two fistfuls of gold. It had been their first vacation together, three precious days of laughter, adventure, and beauty. Charlie was already looking forward to their next trip in the fall, two weeks in France to see Paris, the countryside, and to show Vince the town he'd grown up in. It would be his first visit to Prayssus since he'd left, but the ghosts that had once haunted him no longer held power. Not if Vince was with him, anyway.

The lights changed for Vince's performance. Charlie tamped down a surge of jealous emotion. It was Vince's last night. Everyone in the room, except Cash, might want him, but only one of them had a ring in his pocket. Charlie jiggled it nervously. He should've planned a romantic proposal, but he hadn't. There had been nothing flowery about the decision. Today was Vince's last day. Charlie was no longer sharing, and he wanted a ring on that man's finger as fast as he could slide one on.

He thought Vince would say yes.

Hoped.

"For his final performance at LongHorns, ladies, give a big round of applause to Vince!"

The spotlight hit Vince's naked derriere. The man already had his clothes off? Cheers erupted around the room as he...what had Vince called it?...twerked, making his tight glutes bounce. Charlie looked away, trying not to stare. He could see Vince do this whenever he asked. Everybody else? Jealousy sizzled in his blood, but he rolled his neck, crossed his arms, and kept it in check. Everybody else could watch and wish.

Vince turned to the audience, and that devilish smile lit up the room. His gaze immediately went to Charlie, and he winked. The women around them screamed louder, like he had winked at them. Charlie wanted to shoot them the evil eye. But he didn't. They were just having fun.

His emotional upheaval was not going to be contained so easily once Vince got out into the audience. Charlie didn't know how he was going to sit still while everyone pawed his future fiancé, even if it was the last time. He'd only come because Rhiannon had said it would mean a lot to Vince for him to see his last show. Vince was a good dancer and proud of it. So Charlie had agreed to come, albeit grumbling the whole way. The kiss Vince had given him in thanks, however, had curled his toes and made him forget why he wanted to say no.

Then he'd arrived, watched the first few acts, and remembered—vividly—why he hated this place. At least this time no one had attacked him with their hair.

Vince came to the front of the stage where a hat had been placed and bent to swipe it. Women reached for him, waving dollar bills. He shook a finger at them. "Not tonight, ladies. This dance is on me."

The words were to them, but he looked at Charlie as he said them. Charlie's gut eased.

Vince wasn't going to make him watch other people touch him. Charlie's shoulders relaxed too. It was one thing for other people to see him, to appreciate what an exquisite form he cut. It was another for people to touch him. He didn't love this, but he could handle it.

Vince danced with the hat, jauntily setting it on his head, then rolling it down one arm with dapper grace. He picked up a pair of slacks. There should be no way to make shoving a pair of pants on elegant or sensual, yet somehow Vince did it, hopping and sliding the fabric over his thighs. Charlie bit his lip then released it self-consciously. It was hard not to be sad whenever Vince put his clothes back on. The room agreed with him in a cheer that was more like a groan.

Irrepressible, Vince turned back to the room and grinned. Another shake of his finger told them they were all naughty, and Charlie had to agree. Himself included.

Then Vince really started to dance. He wasn't formally trained, but his athletic grace shone through in street and club moves taken to new levels. The crowd went crazy with appreciation, including Emma and Modron.

Vince pulled on a tank top, then eventually a button-down. By the time the music was over, he was wearing a suit, looking cool and coordinated as if he didn't just throw it on in front of a crowd without a mirror. And still he emanated every bit as much sexual energy as he had in his underwear. The room screamed for him, more than one person yelling, "Take it back off!"

Never again. Only for Charlie, the way it should be. Charlie couldn't help a smug grin.

Vince approached the apron, his bare feet the only sign that he hadn't just walked in from the office. He raised his hands, as if to quiet everyone, but the cheering got louder until the crowd was chanting his name.

Charlie hadn't realized how popular he was. The patrons seemed to know him, or a significant percentage of them anyway. Vince wasn't just giving up an income, he was giving up a family of sorts.

"Awwwww, you're gonna make me cry." Vince faked wiping a tear as the crowd settled down. "I want to thank everyone for being here tonight and for making my six years at LongHorns such a pleasure."

"We'll miss you, Vince!" someone yelled.

"I'll miss you, too, Delia," he said with a blown kiss. "But to calm the nine million rumors I've heard, let's see...I'm not dying of cancer, AIDS, or anything else. I haven't joined the military. Seriously, people, me? Following orders? What were you thinking?" Laughter followed. "I'm also not moving to L.A. or New York to pursue a career in anything. Thank you for your faith in me, but no. What I'm doing is much better. I am in love."

"With who? Is she here?"

"Introduce us!"

Vince's gaze flicked toward Charlie automatically, then passed over him. "He's shy, so I'm not going to call him out."

Charlie waited for the gasp, but it didn't come. A few whispers, but they quickly dissolved as the mindset of the room adjusted just like that. "If Vince's lucky man is here, stand up!" somebody yelled. "We want to see if you're worthy."

The room started laughing as beneath the table, Emma knocked knees with him.

Vince waved his hands. "Ladies, sorry, not going to happen. Like I said, he's—"

Charlie awkwardly pushed himself up to standing. "Completely unworthy." As soon as he was up, the disconnect between action and emotion that had allowed him to move crashed back. His body stiffened in embarrassment, and his mouth went dry.

On stage, Vince's jaw dropped in shock. "Ladies, the amazing and completely worthy love of my life, Charlie."

The shock in Vince's expression turned to joy, and suddenly Charlie knew he wasn't asking Vince to marry him after the show. God, this was going to kill him. He pressed the ring box against his skin. It was also going to be worth it.

꽁 ✦ ꚉ

Vince realized his mouth was still open and closed it with some effort. Charlie had claimed him in public. Not when emotions were high or danger was imminent or there were only a couple of friends around, but in a group setting full of strangers. Joy made his grin wide. Charlie was so getting laid tonight.

But surprises never ceased as stiffly, deeply uncomfortably, his boyfriend walked the short distance from his table to the stage and up the stairs. Cash punched him in the arm as he passed, cheering him on in his own violent way. What was going on?

Charlie stood facing him, their sides to the audience. His green eyes were luminous, and his freckles stood out in a face that was ghostly white. It panicked the man to be on the same stage that Vince had owned a few times a week. And yet they were both here. "Hey, babe. Everything okay?"

"Uh…" Charlie muttered, reaching for Vince's hands. Vince took them, twining their fingers together. Claiming, touching, getting on stage…something huge was happening, and after all the huge of the last few weeks, Vince wasn't sure what to think about that.

Then Charlie dropped down to one knee in what looked a helluva lot like a proposal pose.

"Charlie?" Vince tried to keep his voice light as a lump formed in his throat. He didn't want to hope. God, he didn't want to. Charlie had once told him, a long time ago, that he didn't see the point in men getting married. He called it a piece of paper that meant they were doing the same thing they were already doing without it. Vince had figured he'd work on that one of these days, but he was trying to move slowly for Charlie's sake. He didn't want to push too much too fast like he had in the past. But it was so hard not to. His heart raced as his fingers held on tight and he waited for what Charlie would say.

"Vince." Charlie's voice came out rough, and he cleared his throat. "Vince." It was steadier this time. "You came into my life a long time ago, and I didn't realize what I had. I didn't realize you'd come to breathe life into my death, to find my soul and bring it back. You did this, as you do everything, without being asked. You remain generous and hopeful and full of goodwill for a world I tend to see as unforgiving. But your forgiveness is all I really need." He shifted uncomfortably.

This was really happening. Charlie was proposing. Vince squeezed his fingers as his eyes burned with tears.

Charlie licked his lips nervously. "I know a ceremony isn't necessary for us to spend our lives together." He cleared his throat again as Vince remembered that Charlie had already made a bigger promise than marriage—to not just live together but die together. Vince dropped to his knees so he could look Charlie in the eye. Charlie's gaze locked onto his, and his nervous quiver steadied. "But we deserve one."

Vince nodded. "We do. We really, really do. Ask the question, dammit."

Charlie smiled, expression shy and voice gentle. "Vincent Pagano, will you marry me?"

Vince scooted across the floor to press up against his fiancé. "Yes!"

The room echoed with applause and catcalls as they kissed.

"Why is everyone applauding?" Charlie whispered.

"Because love won. People like that. Put my ring on!" He held up his hand. Charlie slid a metal band onto his finger, and Vince stood, pulling Charlie up with him. "Hey, everybody, meet my fiancé, Charlie!" More cheering. "I quit, so I'm going to go sit over there with my future husband and watch the last number." He took Charlie's hand and led him back to the table.

Charlie was blushing, but he smiled as they sat. "I hope it's okay with you. Modron and Rhiannon agreed to do the ceremony together."

If Modron did the ceremony, none of the vampires could deny their marriage was real. *Smart.* "That is perfect." He nodded at Modron. "Thank you."

She scooted down, making room as she waved long fingernails his way. "My pleasure." The vampire queen wore press-ons?

"If you're there, a lot of folks will be there," Vince mused aloud. A huge wedding at Starlight, with tuxes and hundreds of people. It would be awesome. Charlie would hate it.

Sure enough, he groaned. "It's going to be a zoo. Everyone will be there from everywhere."

Cash reached a hand over. "Congratulations. I'm throwing the after party."

"Thanks! You mean reception?" Vince asked.

Cash shot him a dirty look. "You want a string quartet or a party?"

Vince grinned. He wanted a party. But this sounded huge. He turned to Charlie. "Are you sure you're okay with this? I mean, I like a big deal, but you…" *Don't. At all.*

Charlie squeezed his hand under the table, then started to pull away. Vince let him go. But before their fingers slipped apart, Charlie stopped. And put their linked hands on top of the table. "I'm terrified."

"We don't have to…" But he really wanted a big party and couldn't keep the eager hope out of his voice.

"No, it'll be good for the community—and for us—if—"

"If this is a big deal blessed by the queen. Damn, Charlie. You're a social advocate! Who knew?"

Charlie rolled his eyes, but he looked pleased. "Go gay

vampire rights." He shook their hands, and his expression turned serious. "The important thing is, after the hullabaloo is over, you'll be my..." He laughed a little, like he couldn't believe the next thing he was going to say. "You'll be my husband. And that makes you mine for the rest of my life. Guard my soul well, Vince. It's yours."

"With my life."

Emma banged softly on the table. "Kiss, kiss, kiss, kiss!"

Charlie glanced around the table, looking for disapproval. Cash pointed to his mouth like he was gagging, but it was a joke. Charlie shoved him on the shoulder. "Then don't look."

"I love you," Vince told him, heart full of joy for the life they were going to build.

"Love you too." Charlie leaned in for a very public kiss.

೮‣೧

Acknowledgements

Nothing I do would be possible without my amazing husband Scott, who puts up with a wife who lives in other worlds about as often as she does the real one. I don't know how I lucked out so much to get you in my life. Also, thank you for answering all my woodworking questions! Charlie would have no idea what he was doing without you.

A huge thanks to beta reader Jenna Gabiola. Your patience with me and your amazingly quick turnaround were a lifesaver.

Thanks to the team who put this together: editors Rhonda Merwarth, Heather Long, and Abby Webber, and cover goddess Daqri. You ladies are awesome professionals to work with!

Though I doubt any of you will see this, thanks to the blacksmiths of Angel Sword for inspiring Vince's profession. I love watching you guys work at Faire. And thanks to Tom Gingras, my first welding instructor. Your class was as inspiring as it was fun and educational. I hope to get back to the shop soon!

Thanks to the lovely Goldie Candela, whose burlesque number "Gold Digger" inspired Vince's final dance.

Finally, thanks to ARWA and to the Digital Darlings. You folks give me the drive to keep writing, the faith that I'm not alone, and the passion to do my best, even on the hard days. Love you guys!

Books by Jax Garren

Austin Immortals
Immortal Longing
Immortal Redeemed (novella)
Immortal Rage

Romancing the Fae
Her Christmas Elf

Godstones
Found Magic
Death Magic
Owl's Cry (novella)

Tales of the Underlight
How Beauty Met the Beast
How Beauty Saved the Beast
How Beauty Loved the Beast

The Never After, a multi-author series
Never, She Lands: A Grown-up Tale of Peter Pan

About the Author

Jax Garren is the author of romantic urban fantasy that brings ancient myths into a modern setting, including gods and rock stars in the Godstones, vampires and witchcraft in the Austin Immortals, and fairy tales re-imagined in the Tales of the Underlight.

A die-hard Ravenclaw and former English and theater teacher, Jax can spend as much time researching obscure historical details for her books as actually writing them. When not falling down a research rabbit hole, Jax dreams about traveling anywhere cold (which Texas, her home, is not) and loves to play foodie with her husband. They live with two amazing tween/teens she's proud to call her daughters and three cats who didn't get enough treats last night. Just ask them.

www.ingramcontent.com/pod-product-compliance
Lightning Source LLC
Chambersburg PA
CBHW051320250626
47155CB00007B/2389